Edwina Currie is a fo[...]r fourteen years was the [...]t for Derbyshire South. S[...] caster and bestselling n[...]

'The irrepressible Edwina Currie is back' *Express*

'Move over Bridget Jones – your newly liberated mother has hit town' *Daily Mail*

'It is impossible to dislike . . . Currie does have some pertinent and often moving things to say about a woman whose life was invested in looking after others' *Glasgow Herald*

'You could see *Chasing Men* as a handbook for the newly single. But it is cleverer than that: in the era of makeover mania – house makeovers, garden makeovers, fashion makeovers – Currie has written a life makeover for the middle-aged frump' *Sunday Independent (Ireland)*

Also by Edwina Currie

FICTION

A Parliamentary Affair
A Woman's Place
She's Leaving Home
The Ambassador

NON-FICTION

Life Lines: Politics and Health 1986–88
What Women Want
Three Line Quips

EDWINA CURRIE

Chasing Men

WARNER BOOKS

A *Warner* Book

First published in Great Britain in 2000
by Little, Brown and Company
This edition published in 2001 by Warner Books

Copyright © 2000, Edwina Currie

The moral right of the author has been asserted.

The author gratefully acknowledges permission to quote from the following: 'A
Change Would Do You Good' Words and music by Sheryl Crow, Brian Macleod and
Jeffrey Trott © 1995 Old Crow Music, Weenie Stand Music, Warner Tamerlane
Publishing Corp and Rambling Blah Music, USA. Warner/Chappell Music Ltd,
London, W6 8BS (70%). Reproduced by permission of IMP Ltd. 'You're the Top'
Words and music by Cole Porter © 1934 Harms Inc., USA. Warner/Chappell Music
Ltd, London, W6 8BS. Reproduced by permission of IMP Ltd. 'A Wonderful Guy'
Words by Oscar Hammerstein II and music by Richard Rogers © 1949 Williamson
Music International, USA. Reproduced by permission of EMI Music Publishing Ltd,
London, WC2H 0EA. 'Hey There' Words and music by Richard Adler and Jerry Ross
© 1987 Richard Adler Music and J & J Ross Co., USA. Warner/Chappell Music Ltd,
London, W6 8BS. Reproduced by permission of IMP Ltd.

*All characters in this publication are fictitious and any resemblance to real
persons, living or dead, is purely coincidental.*

A CIP catalogue record for this book
is available from the British Library.

ISBN 0 7515 3103 0

Typeset in Berkeley by M Rules
Printed and bound in Great Britain by
Clays Ltd, St Ives plc

Warner Books
A Division of
Little, Brown and Company (UK)
Brettenham House
Lancaster Place
London WC2E 7EN

www.littlebrown.co.uk

With warmest thanks to

Gillian, Diana, Rowena, Rob, Liz, Julian, Fronnie,
Christiana, Alan, Sheila, Jonathan, Marion, Valerie, Victor,
Trevor, David, Sharman, Deb, Susie, David, John, Carole,
Terry, Georgina, Matthew, Clare, Jane and many others

for your help and wise advice.

CHAPTER ONE

Sod the New Curtains

Hetty pulled her collar closer. The wind whistled down Aviary Road, leaves swirling damply in its wake. Above her head the wooden for-sale sign swung and creaked; it reminded her of a gibbet. The thin estate agent shuffled his feet and thrust bony hands deeper into his overcoat pockets. He sniffed. ''Fraid that's the best there is. For a hundred and eighty thou' you won't get anything smarter, not south of the river.'

'It's a staggering sum. For that I could buy a grade-two cottage with timbered walls and open fireplaces in Dorset.'

'This isn't Dorset. I have three more clients booked to see it this afternoon. Aviary Road is *quite* desirable. Now I'm sorry, Mrs Clarkson, shall I cancel them, or what?'

He didn't sound sorry. Weeks of fruitless searching had confirmed his pessimism. The bijou apartment she had hoped for, overlooking a park, in immaculate condition with secure parking, a snooty concierge and a private swimming-pool, was not available to her except in her dreams. Even if she blew every penny of the divorce settlement, took on a hefty mortgage and left herself with no savings whatever.

'I'll take it,' she said weakly, and immediately regretted the decision.

'Glad to hear it.' He pulled out his mobile phone, prodded it like a piece of dodgy meat and issued brief instructions. 'That's settled. Come into the office this afternoon and you can initial the papers.' He chuckled, as if at a private joke. 'Hope you like the neighbours. Some of them are a little – ah, odd, I hear. But, then, what can you expect, at that price?'

It was a question of choice. Or, rather, of precious little choice. Several weeks later, keys in hand, Hetty stood in the grimy shrubbery that passed for a front garden and examined her purchase with more care.

The block was an undistinguished brick edifice about thirty years old, one of several built in the oversized grounds of a Victorian mansion long since demolished. Hers, the one called The Swallows, contained six flats; others nearby were larger, each named after birds. Here and there, mature trees were a reminder of what had previously flourished, though their leafless state added to the air of desolation and neglect. Or perhaps not neglect exactly. There was no litter; the paths to the front porch and around the back to the bins were tidy and unbroken. Someone had pruned the rose bushes and cut back a buddleia. A large ginger cat peered at her curiously from under drooping bushes then waddled off, tail held high. With a bit of luck, in spring she might see green from every angle of the flat.

As she fumbled with the security lock Hetty caught sight of herself in a window. She straightened up automatically, as if somebody else might be watching. The woman who stared back at her was neither slim nor tall. No longer married, but not a spinster, dried out or shrivelled up. Still ripe. Not exactly pretty, but not plain either; brown hair tinged with grey, hazel eyes, a clear skin without wrinkles, a ready smile, mostly. Not young, not old. Nondescript? She sighed, and pulled a rueful face at her reflection. 'Not sure who I am,' Hetty murmured to herself. 'Perhaps it's time I found out.'

The hallway was dingy. The jute floor covering was stained, though upstairs, on what she must now call her landing, it was cleaner and less scuffed. She tried the key in her front-door lock. It was stiff, but worked: a good omen.

Inside, a pile of glossy circulars slithered like snakes away from her feet. Hetty riffled through them. Leaflets for home-delivery pizzas were stacked on the kitchen window-ledge alongside a flowery 'Good Luck In Your New Home' card from her mother, postmarked Amsterdam. Off on another Saga coach holiday, probably. No letter with it. Hetty's mother was not given to organised effusions of maternal emotion.

The flat's alarm was off. Trying to remember the estate agent's instructions, Hetty played with it experimentally, panicked briefly when it started to howl, then sensed a personal victory when she managed to switch it off and on correctly. Stephen would have laughed indulgently at her efforts and taken the key from her hand. Now she would have to do everything herself. A shiver ran down her spine.

The lights worked. One bulb was missing. The bathroom had cheap pale green tiles. It required a thorough scrub but was a fair size, with a modern shower. The kitchen needed a roller-blind. Hetty began to make a list. It would be days before she could move in, maybe longer. She must resist the temptation to splurge, to redecorate in a hurry or buy expensive new curtains. No Stephen to pick up the bills.

'So, sod the new curtains,' Hetty said aloud, with a shrug. They would have to wait until she found a job.

'Hello? Anyone there?' The voice was unmistakably an East-Ender's. A short woman in a flowered dress peered round the door. A faded cotton apron was swathed across a bulky torso; she smelt faintly of fried onions. Her hair, frizzy and almost white, was bundled up in a headscarf tied as a turban. In her arms was the fat ginger cat Hetty had seen in the garden. Its orange eyes examined her coolly.

'Yes. *I'm* here.'

'Oooh! Are you going to buy it? It's been empty ages.'

'I might,' Hetty answered cautiously. So the estate agent had been economical with the truth when he implied he had lots of customers. That explained why he was so keen to tie up the deal. Then, 'Well, yes, I have. I've just signed for it. It's mine, as from today.'

'Oooh!' the woman said again, her eyes round but red-veined, like ox-eye marbles. Her front teeth were prominent and square, a bit battered, and brought to mind nothing so much as a stout old mule. Yet there was something of the gypsy about her. The cat struggled to escape and was restrained. 'Needs a bit of money spending on it. But it'll be nice to have somebody living here again – you're the flat over mine. You're not a noisy person, are you?'

'No, I don't think so. Are you?'

'Me? Nah. I live with Thomas here. The cat. Only rented, mind, can't afford to buy. I don't have many visitors. Only me gentleman friend.' The woman simpered. 'That's Jack and he's very quiet. My name's Doris Archibald, but most people call me Mrs A. I like my place. It's not bad round here, honest.'

Hetty realised that her own expression might be home-counties haughty or suspicious, probably both. Was this one of the odd neighbours? She extended her hand and smiled warily. 'I'm Hetty Clarkson. Or I was. I might take my maiden name again – I'm not sure yet.'

'Bad idea, that. Nobody'll be able to find you in the phone book if you change your name. That's why some folks do it.' Mrs A ventured further into the room. The cat wriggled; ginger hairs detached themselves and floated to the floor. 'Carpet's okay. Kitchen's quite respectable. I can help with unpacking, if you like. Were you married long?'

Hetty hesitated. Was caution advised? Was it necessary? The woman seemed harmless enough. She took the plunge. 'Over twenty years. Is it that obvious?'

'Course. You're not the first, you won't be the last. These flats are full of 'em. Lots of marriages break up, these days. Singles come and go here all the while. At least you had him tied up proper. My niece Lindy had two kids by a chap and never saw an altar. So when he takes up with a younger lass and shows her the door, her and the kids got nothing. Did you do all right? Must've done, to buy this place. Got family, have you?'

Hetty stepped back. 'What is this, Mrs A? The Inquisition?'

The cat hissed and threatened to escape. The prospect of cat hairs everywhere to add to her woes made Hetty feel weary.

Mrs A appeared chastened. 'Sorry. You look done in. Cup of tea?'

It would be best, now, to move as quickly as possible. The journey from Dorset was too far, the trains too uncertain; the furtive glances from Stephen too powerful a reminder of what she had to leave behind. He stood on the landing by the guest room she had occupied for the last few months, his big shoulders blocking the light. Behind him, in the main bedroom, could be glimpsed the carved four-poster bed they had found in Winchester. His, now, not hers. She carried on packing clothes, mementoes and photographs into suitcases and boxes, and tried to ignore him.

'Will you still be here at the weekend?'

She took a decision. 'No. I'll take a few things tomorrow. Hire a van. Then that should be the last you see of me.'

'Hetty . . .' He extended his hand, then let it drop. 'Thank you for being so . . . understanding. You could have been bitter – made it awful. It has helped. We did have some good times together, didn't we? And there's the children. We can stay friends. I hope you'll be – okay.'

She bit her lip. I will be okay, she thought, but no thanks to you, Stephen, she should have retorted. He turned, discomforted by her silence, and trudged down the stairs. It might have been easier to have a row, a shouting match; behaving as civilised people, as both instinctively did, left so much unsaid.

His habits need no longer detain her. His preferences, his little quirks. What had been going on in his mind? How could she have missed it? He was not a bad man, far from it. She pinched herself, once, hard. It had happened: her husband had fallen in love with another woman. She had lost him, even as she had congratulated herself on her wonderfully stable marriage. This was not a nightmare from which she might wake up, dazed and breathless, thankful to return to complacent normality. This was the reality.

He hoped they might stay friends, and no doubt they'd

meet at family events: Peter's graduation, Sally's engagement – if any man of hers ever got round to it. Their daughter worked for Britannia Airlines in Luton and fell in love with pilots. But Stephen wouldn't be there as her husband, or as *her* closest friend. Somebody else would be on his arm.

Friends – real ones, human beings – would be at a premium from here on. A sob rose in her throat and was forced away. It would feel dreadful and disorientating to be alone, not be part of a couple. Most social activities were designed for pairs. Their acquaintances were mostly couples: from work – Stephen's work – from the village, from the summer fête and church events she had actively supported. In all their activities, indeed, the Clarksons had been a visible and successful part of coupledom. They had tended to shun singles who didn't seem to fit in. Nothing whatever from her previous life could be taken for granted. Precious little could be taken with her, except regrets. None of it prepared her for what was to come.

But help was needed right now. She snapped the locks on the first suitcase, lugged it to the top of the stairs, then tipped it flat and kicked it down to the bottom like a sled on a hillside. The second one went down more slowly, banging against the banisters, but did not burst open. Solidly made, both were too heavy for her to lift more than a few yards – chosen by Stephen, they were made for a man to carry. She followed them down to the hallway. Stephen had disappeared into the garden.

Her hand shook a little as she reached for the phone. She kept her voice steady and light.

'Sally? Glad I've caught you. Yes, it's Mum. Listen, darling, I shall need another pair of hands. Mostly lugging boxes in and out of a van and up and down stairs. No, I don't think I should ask your father to pitch in. Or his pals from the golf club – I don't need any of them averting their eyes. Tomorrow morning? Thanks, that'll be lovely. Wear jeans, darling. 'Bye.'

CHAPTER TWO

Getting to Know You

Sally stood, hand on hip, and pushed a lock of fair hair out of her eye. A streak of dirt marked her Tommy Hilfiger sweater and she scrabbled at it crossly with a wetted thumb. 'That should do it, Mum. Pity there's no lift. You didn't bring much, did you?'

'No. Clean break.'

Sally rubbed her arms. 'It's cold in here. And I could do with a drink.'

'I haven't figured out the central heating yet. I'll ask one of the neighbours. Sorry, I didn't think to bring any booze. Tea?'

Sally shook her head and glanced at her watch. Hetty was becoming more adept at reading body language. I have about ten minutes more from my daughter, she thought, then she will have other priorities. The young woman would not take kindly, for instance, to anyone suggesting supper tonight.

'Mum, I think I should say it. This is a crazy idea.'

'What is?'

'Oh, leaving Dad, and coming to live here on your own.'

'I didn't have much option. Your father had made it clear that if I made him choose between his new love and myself, it wouldn't be me. He does love her, you know.'

'That's rot. Dad loves you, always has. He's just not very good at saying it.'

'On the contrary. He was very good indeed at *saying* it. Best in the world. He drew the line, sadly, at keeping the rules that go with *meaning* it.'

Sally brooded. 'But I'm sure he didn't want you to go. He as good as told me. That girl isn't important to him, not important the way you are. *Were.*'

Hetty tried to stop herself sounding sad, but became brusque instead. 'You're kidding yourself, Sally. Whatever we had, it wasn't there any more. I wish it had been. Splitting up is a horrible business. Though maybe in a way it was my fault too.'

Sally flopped down in the armchair. In her handbag she found a cigarette, lit it with a silver lighter and glanced round for an ashtray. Finding none, she had to cup her hand under the cigarette as she smoked it. Hetty smiled to herself but resisted the temptation to fetch a saucer. The new flat, she suddenly resolved, her flat, would be smoke-free.

'I'm still in shock, Mum. You had so much going for you. Our home was super – it was great, knowing you were always there. Most of my friends thought you had the perfect home, the perfect marriage. They were envious. *I* was envious, come to that.'

Hetty shrugged and did not answer. Inside, something began to burn, as it had the day she had caught her husband enfolded in the embrace of their neighbour's wife. Younger, lissom, attractive. The two had clung resolutely together, arm in arm, blushing, as they faced her. Her instinct in the year since had been to suppress her anger, to behave as calmly and cogently as possible. Now, it dawned on Hetty, rage could be useful, as armour, to counteract her own muddled feelings of guilt and shame, and as a defence. Especially from those who, like Sally, saw themselves as fully qualified to tell her what to do.

'You and Dad always seemed to get on. I don't think you should have left, honest. Surely you could have worked something out?'

'Don't, Sally. I don't know why it went wrong. Perhaps because I bored him. He didn't bore me, but there you are. Maybe I took too much as read. What I'm absolutely not going to do is dwell on the past. It's done, finished. Time to move on.' Hetty spread her hands to indicate the flat.

Sally rose, irresolute, as if there were a lot more to say. She pulled on her London Fog jacket, made a great play of tying her muffler and finding her leather gloves. 'I must go. You have my number. Ring me in a day or two, won't you?' She pecked Hetty on the cheek and let herself out.

Hetty wafted away the fumes of cigarette smoke and stood silent. Then she picked up her keys. 'Took too much for granted, Sally,' she said to the closed door. 'Didn't realise it. But I do now.'

'There, that'll do it. You'll need to get that boiler serviced. Nobody's had it on for ages. Now, while your place is warming up, how about –?'

'A cuppa?' Hetty found herself smiling. 'Thanks, I'd love one.' She locked the flat and followed the woman's solid body downstairs, grateful for the invitation.

Mrs A's tea was strong and sweet. Her flat was small and dark, on the ground floor, in the corner facing another block. But it was warm, blessedly so, with a coal-effect gas-fire in the living room. Thomas, the cat, was curled up on a cushion; his fluffed-up fur made him look enormous. Cat hairs gave every surface of the furniture a faint sheen, but Hetty resisted the urge to brush her chair with her hand. The smell of cabbage and fried fish lingered from the kitchen. Hetty suddenly felt hungry. Her own crockery was still crated; that was the set she had liberated from the house – the second best service – and she had not thought to bring anything to eat.

'Where do we shop around here, Mrs A? Is there a late-night grocer's? And what about cafés, or restaurants – any decent ones?'

'Wouldn't know about that. My gentleman takes me to the West End when he's in funds. The garage has a mini-supermarket – fine for most of what you want, nothing fancy. That's open till eleven at night.'

'That's better than Dorset. We had one village shop that closed at five thirty, and half-day Wednesdays. Then they wondered why everyone hared off to Tesco's in their cars.' Hetty snorted. 'My freezer was stuffed with food. Heavens, I used to spend whole days baking.'

'You like cooking?'

Hetty pondered. 'No, I don't,' she answered slowly, in surprise. 'Hot drudgery. I did it because, well, it was expected of me. I was a great hostess.'

'Bet you were. No need now. Near here there's Tesco's, Safeway, Sainsbury's, Asda, the lot. Ready meals. You got a microwave? Then you won't starve. Pensioners' bus goes to Sainsbury's Tuesdays and Fridays. How old are you?'

'Heavens, do I look like a pensioner?'

Mrs A shrugged. 'Can't tell, can you? That Joan Collins, she's older than me. Mutton dressed as lamb, but gorgeous with it.'

'I'm – er – forty-seven. Nearly forty-eight. And I don't have a car. So it'll have to be the little shop at the garage.'

It was a lie. Her last birthday had been her fiftieth, and not celebrated. Stephen had passed that mark two years before. Maybe that explained the changes in him: a mid-life crisis, a desire to postpone middle age. An attempt to recapture his carefree lost youth. Perhaps, it suddenly dawned on her, Stephen had *wanted* her out, needed pastures new himself. One thing was for sure: he would not be alone. Solitude was not his line.

'Are you divorced, Mrs A?' Helen was startled at her own question. What had happened to her natural reticence – to feeling ashamed?

'Me? Nah, I'm a widder.'

'Oh. I'm sorry.'

'What for? Not your fault. Anyway, me and Thomas here suit each other. He's no trouble, and I can say whatever nonsense comes into my head with no fear he'll answer back. We gets on fine, don't we, Thomas?'

The cat yawned. A few more hairs worked loose and floated gently to the floor, as if the moulting animal were determined to leave its mark.

Hetty remembered the estate agent's comments. 'One more thing, Mrs A. What about the neighbours?'

The old woman chuckled. 'You'll meet 'em soon enough. You can be sociable or not, as you like. Next to me are the McDonalds and their kiddies. Down from Scotland, keeps themselves to themselves. Upstairs there's two nice people living together, artistic types. You've got three girls renting number four next to you – right larks they get up to. They drink too much, if you ask me. I like a tipple meself, but not enough to pass out on the stairs. If you find one, just bang on their door and they'll take her in. Top-floor flat belongs to a foreign couple, out of the country mostly. That's the one over yours, so it'll be quiet for you. Bin-men come on Thursdays and the post office is by the newsagent's. Anything else?'

'No, thank you.' Hetty laughed. 'God, I'm ravenous. Must go and get some dinner. D'you think they sell single-person packs at the garage?'

'Oh, yes. I should put on a bit of lipstick before you go. It's quite a pick-up joint for singles.' Doris prodded Hetty's knee with a stout finger, as if testing the plumpness of a chicken. 'Or so I'm told.'

'Pick-up joint, huh,' Hetty muttered, as she struggled back to the flat laden with plastic bags. The only men in the store, apart from motorists paying for petrol, had been the elderly Bangladeshi manager and a pimply boy lingering near the lighter fuel. The sole good-looking man, a tall figure in an Aran jumper, had left immediately she entered. 'Anyway, I'm not interested. Why does everybody think I should be chasing men? Been there, done that. Got the scar tissue to prove it.'

The answerphone light was blinking. Another infinitesimal shard of progress. Cards announcing her change of address and phone number had been sent off the day she had signed for the flat. The light felt like a confirmation that she existed in her new form. The Swallows, a swallow. Not yet a summer, but she had spread her wings.

'Mum? Sally. You all right? I'm sorry I left in such a hurry.

I'm worried about you, there on your own. I spoke to Granny. We should have a council of war so you can decide what you want to do. Maybe while Erik's on his next tour of overseas duty. He seems to get sent abroad a lot at the moment. Men – we have to put up with them the way they are, don't we?'

Her daughter's voice wittered on until after ninety seconds the tape cut off suddenly, bleeped and went on to the next message. Hetty smiled grimly. Sally was currently in a relationship with a man about whom she was very cagey. At the same age, Hetty had been engaged and flat-hunting with the love of her life. At least, Hetty consoled herself, she'd had years of happiness. And the kids. It was a lot to be thankful for.

'Hetty? Do hope I've got the right number, darling. It's Clarissa. Dreadfully sorry to hear what happened – I can't believe it, not you, thought your marriage was a rock. Are you up for lunch? I can be a shoulder to cry on anytime. How about a week on Tuesday? It's on me. Lots of love. Call me.'

Hetty fetched her diary, though it was hardly necessary. Apart from a final visit to her solicitor and the need to wait in for the central-heating man, blank pages stretched ahead for months. Lunch, Tuesday? Certainly.

'Hetty? Brother Larry here. Hope you're okay moving in – sorry, like to help but we're a bit pushed at work right now. Hey, listen, soon as you're settled, Davinia and I would like you round. Supper, you know. Nothing elaborate. We'll invite a few friends for you to meet. Can't have you moping on your own, can we?'

Larry, her only sibling, was three years older than Hetty. Larry and Davinia were not married. Publicly, boastfully, they lived together in a high, narrow house in Fulham with their two little boys and a sullen nanny on the top floor.

Davinia was an advertising executive with an impressive client list, Larry did something lucrative with computers. Their favourite restaurant was the River Café, but they were not important enough to get a table on demand. Davinia was thirty-five, and was Larry's third long-term partner. All his women had looked alike: big, robust blondes, whose starting age had crept up only slightly. This, however, was the first liaison to have produced children. The boys were aggressive and materialistic, miniature versions of their father. The prospect of being comforted by her brother and sister-in-law over quails' eggs and ratatouille did not fill Hetty with delight. She made a note.

'*Hi, Hetty. Rosa here. Rosa Weston. Thanks for the message. Commiserations – sorry to hear your news. Never mind, some fabulous bloke will come crashing through the jungle to carry you away. Anyway, that's my theory, though I'm still waiting. As for a job, well, budgets are tight. If you can accept peanuts, we could use another researcher. Fancy working in television again? Gimme a ring . . .*'

'*Hi, Mum. It's Peter. Hope you're all right. Listen, my student loan hasn't arrived – it's two weeks late. Can you let me have some money?*'

Hetty reached for the remote control and switched off the set. Her back ached from heaving boxes, two fingernails were broken, the plaster over a cut was dirty. A Bird's Eye frozen lasagne had filled a gap, but the remains congealed in their polystyrene box were a dismal reminder of her lowered status. She must not let her standards slip. If it meant learning how to cook for one – for the first time ever – she would have to do it. There must be cookery books about it. Or maybe a TV series.

On the other hand, it had not been a bad few days. Everything was in place, the new light-bulb inserted, the heating making the flat habitable, though a dank smell came from one corner where a radiator leaked. Photographs in frames sat on a half-full bookcase: the children, her mother, not Stephen. A bunch of tulips curved gracefully over the edges of a vase like a glowing pink fountain. A few minor treasures sat on the mantelpiece: a Lladro figurine, a collection of old perfume phials, their coloured glass ghostly in the light. Her bed was freshly made, her nightie wrapped around Peter's childhood fluffy hot-water bottle to cheer her up. She was desperately tired.

And her diary was no longer empty. Clarissa was a friend from schooldays, married to Robin. It came to Hetty that she did not know Robin well and had seen him through Clarissa's eyes as easy-going and readily exploited. Her new position gave her another perspective. What were they really like? Would she get on with them as a couple now she was no longer a couple herself? Or would Clarissa, on her own, be part of the rescue party?

The call from Peter was par for the course, and a cheque – a small one – was in the post to him. The brightest spark, the response that had made Hetty's eyes light up, had come from Rosa. They had worked together years before, at the BBC, as underpaid young secretaries and researchers. Rosa had been one of the Shepherd's Bush quartet, the most ambitious, the most sophisticated. Her own mother had originally come from Barbados and Rosa would joke that in certain politically correct circles her colour was a distinct advantage. They'd kept in touch, via Christmas cards; Rosa was on the Clarkson list for parties and birthday events, while invitations had occasionally arrived to launches of her television series. She worked for an independent company, these days. It had been natural to ask her advice, among others, about employment. It looked as if Rosa, more than anyone else, might come up with the goods.

The new-home card had been moved to the small table. It was sweet of her mother to send it; amazing, given her busy social round, that she had remembered. The elegant widow of an army colonel, the old lady seldom sat still long. 'I hardly know her, either,' Hetty mused. 'My own daughter hardly knows me. What a family we are. Or have been.'

She found a piece of notepaper and an envelope. 'Mum – Thank you for the card, much appreciated. When you get back from your travels, would you like to come round? Or, better still, shall we meet – go to a movie – whatever you'd like? I have a bit more time now.' She stopped: it sounded too much like a plea. 'I'm coping fine, so don't feel concerned about me. But it'd be fun. I'd make it fun. Lots of love.'

Hetty paused, pen in hand. Then she added, 'PS Sally thinks we should have a proper discussion, to help me decide what to do next. Would you come? You might talk more sense than any of us.'

It still felt weird, sleeping alone: no one else's breathing by her ear, no heels and ankles in the wrong place, no sleepy gurgles from another's alimentary canal. Nobody pinching most of the duvet on a cold night. No cold feet. Hetty smiled despite herself, then snuffled. She cuddled the hot-water bottle.

And allowed herself a few tears.

To her surprise the weepy feelings did not persist. Underneath, below the layers of bewilderment and despair, beneath the anger and the hot shame, beneath the fear of the unknown, somewhere deep inside, something new stirred, like a dormant volcano. *Excitement*.

She rolled over, flat on her back. The hot-water bottle clutched over her heart made her pulse race. The ceiling above her was blank, smooth and empty. Like a sheet of paper in a typewriter, waiting for her to begin tapping.

'I can write on there anything I want,' Hetty whispered. 'I can do what I want, go or stay, as I please. Don't have to satisfy anybody else. How extraordinary! I am free of all obligations, other than to myself. I am *me*.'

The thought made her hug the unprotesting hot-water bottle so hard she feared it might burst. In another moment she was asleep.

CHAPTER THREE

Council of War

Hetty drank deeply. The second glass of supermarket wine would probably give her a headache, but so would the promised council of war. Sally was slumped on the sofa. By her side were a notebook turned to a blank page, an unopened packet of cigarettes and a half-eaten bowl of cashew nuts. In the best armchair sat Hetty's mother, stylish and composed as ever, her silvery hair beautifully coiffed, charm bracelet jingling, a stuffed olive between finger and thumb. She was dressed in a grey trouser suit, legs crossed at the ankle. Size twelve, Hetty guessed. She sucked in her stomach.

'Are you quite sure, darling, that this is the right place for you?' Her mother's tone was oleaginous, her roaming eyes disapproving. The white chrysanthemums she had brought were too large for their vase and looked wintry.

Hetty shrugged. 'It was all I could afford, unless I wanted

to start borrowing heavily, and for that I'd need steady employment.'

'Perhaps, dear, you shouldn't have allowed Stephen to keep the house. You put yourself at a serious disadvantage.'

'Did I? If I'd made a fuss, I'd have been stuck with bad feeling, six bedrooms and a lot of neighbours taking sides for and against. No thanks.'

'Have they set the wedding day yet?' This from Sally, who would expect to be invited. The girl was not famous for her tact.

'No. They can't get a licence till the decree absolute comes through. To be frank, I suspect they may hold off for a bit. See if it works. Your father has his practical side.'

Sally snorted. 'But what will you do for money? You haven't earned a living in years – Dad's settlement won't last for ever.'

Hetty had not revealed that, after the first few months, no further maintenance payments were in the offing. It had seemed to her wrong to expect Stephen to pay for two households from one income when she was perfectly capable of looking after herself. It might also have undermined his new relationship; revenge was not on her mind. She decided against telling them about Rosa's call, since nothing might come of it. 'I shall get a job. I've made a few enquiries, and we'll see.'

'I can't quite grasp,' her mother said – a slight deafness meant that she occasionally missed snippets of conversation, though wild dogs from hell would not have drawn the admission from her lips – 'why you *didn't* want to be left with the house. You could have sold it. Bought something better than this.'

'I doubt it. This flat cost as much as a fair-sized country

property. The Swallows is not exactly a dosser's joint.' Hetty prayed silently that that was true. 'It's done now. This is my new address. I think I could be quite content here. It's no worse than anywhere else.'

A silence fell, during which Hetty and Sally both drained their glasses. Hetty fetched a second bottle and opened a packet of Ritz crackers. She was not up to cooking a meal for them, and nor yet was the kitchen.

'Why London, though?' Sally again. Hetty noticed that a few scrawls had appeared on the notebook. A single unlit cigarette had emerged from the packet, as if begging permission to be smoked.

'Why not?'

'Well, you and Dad lived the rural idyll for yonks. A quiet life, but one that loads of people would give their eye-teeth for. Suddenly you throw it over to bury yourself in this urban wasteland. I don't get it.'

'Because . . .' Hetty hesitated, '. . . this is a contrast. That was a very conservative life. I was occupied, even though I didn't have paid work. But when I look back, perhaps it wasn't quite enough. Or was heading that way. I think underneath I was a bit restless.'

These remarks drew blank looks from both women.

Hetty groaned inwardly. This might be an exercise in misunderstanding. Was she so hopeless at making herself clear? Or was it that her ideas were still muddled? Maybe she was expressing views neither her daughter nor her mother could credit. She tried again.

'If I had stayed, much of what I'd busied myself with would have vanished into thin air. Divorced women in a traditional setting have a tricky time. Everyone's scared of them – even I used to be. They're seen either as unfortunate or as a threat. I'd have had to give up the parochial church council for a start, and sit by myself in church. Then I'd have been pursued by slippy local men who saw me as fair game with black looks from their wives, and had to put up with nosy-parkers on my meals-on-wheels round giving me their opinions. Or pity. That's a recipe for terminal decline. Not ready for that.'

Sally frowned. 'So how will you pass the time? You're not going to be one of those dotty women who goes shoplifting for fun, are you? I can't come and bail you out.'

'Don't talk rubbish. I'm not about to start breaking the law. More likely to find the local library and start reading Proust.'

More blank looks. 'I shouldn't, dear,' her mother said. 'It sounds dangerous.'

Sally refused to be deflected. 'Come on, how many years is it since you've lived on your own? Or have you ever?'

Hetty considered. 'No, you're right. I never have. At college I was in the hall of residence. Then in the early days at Television Centre I shared digs in Shepherd's Bush with three other girls. We lived on Ski yoghurt and Vesta dried meals, and had a whale of a time. I met your father and fell head over heels. We started off with a tiny pad in Ladbroke Grove. Proper little love-nest. We were happy. In those days.'

'See? You can't possibly live by yourself. You'll be so lonely. You'll never get used to it. It's awful.' Sally lunged for the cigarette and disappeared into the kitchen to find an ashtray. She emerged with the cigarette lit, a saucer in her hand and gloomy defiance on her face. 'Don't tell me I can't, please, Mum. It's hard enough trying to sort you out. Doing it in a smoke-free zone is beyond me.' She returned to the sofa.

'You aren't going to take up smoking, are you?' Hetty's mother sat up sharply. 'It's dreadfully bad for the skin. Especially for older women.'

Hetty and Sally exchanged glances, then both smiled. It was the first time any of them had smiled. Hetty relaxed a little and munched a cracker. 'About as likely as Proust, Mother. That's not an issue,' she answered, and was careful to make her voice soothing.

'Staying single,' Sally prompted. 'Is that definitely the game plan?'

'I don't know. But why not?'

'You *can't* manage on your own. Nobody could, in your circumstances.'

'Your grandmother does. Has for years,' Hetty answered, with a nod in the older woman's direction.

'That's different,' her mother retorted. 'We learned self-reliance in the war. Never short of a date then.' Her eyes became dreamy. 'Anyway, at my age there are so few men left. The rest are too decrepit for words. The ones who want a wife don't deserve one. Or else they're after a housemaid, cook and nurse in one.' She glared. 'I've washed enough dirty socks in my time, and wiped bottoms. I'm not about to start again.'

Hetty and Sally giggled, and took refuge in their wine. 'I feel much the same,' Hetty responded at last, 'though for the moment being alone is simply the result of being the innocent party in a divorce. It was devastating, but I don't intend to get bitter if I can avoid it. On the other hand, I'm not about to pick up any old bloke on the rebound.'

'Maybe that's exactly what you should do.' Sally brightened. 'Find somebody else quickly, while you still can.'

Hetty brooded. Most of the crackers had gone. She

tipped up the packet; salty crumbs cascaded on to the carpet. 'Damn,' she said, then shrugged. 'But is that all there is? Hunting down a replacement for my erring ex? Isn't there more to look forward to than that? Here I am, in the midst of the world's greatest metropolis, *compos mentis*, more or less solvent and fancy-free. Lord, I sound like one of those contact ads in the *Daily Telegraph*.' She struggled. 'Up till this month I've lived with, and for, other people. My entire life, Sally, has revolved round other people – your father, Peter, you. Perhaps it's time to find out what *I* want, how *I'd* like to spend my time. Who with. With nobody, maybe.'

Sally dragged on the cigarette. 'You'll suffer from depression. Do you know what SAD means? Single and desperate. I'm seriously worried about you.'

'I'll manage – you'll see. I'll have to. And it might save me giving in to the pressure, and inviting you to come and live with me,' Hetty added wryly.

Sally looked aghast. 'I don't think that would be wise. Erik, for example. It'd put him off.'

'Yes, I can see that,' Hetty drawled. 'And maybe, if I follow your advice and go chasing men, it'd cramp my style, too. There are advantages in living alone.'

'You don't mean it,' Sally chided. 'You're probably still in love with Dad. Aren't you?'

Hetty sighed. 'Maybe. We were together half our lifetimes. We had a lot of good years – in fact, I assumed it would simply go on for ever. My mistake.'

Sally leaned back, eyes closed. It is so obvious, Hetty thought, that she longs for what I had. Happy marriage is still the ideal. How astonishing that they had never had this conversation before, these three women; it was as if they had never communicated anything of import till now. It had taken heartbreak to bring them together.

Hetty's head ached. She rose and put the empty wine bottle on the mantelpiece. There she played with the perfume phials, rearranging them, lifting each up to catch the light. 'Loads of options, now,' she observed. She prodded the wine bottle. 'This is one, since I no longer have to be ultra-respectable. Or I could get fat – comfort eating can be *very* nice. Or become SAD, a depressive, and make a career of crying for help.' She began to move an ornament with each sentence. 'That's three. I could, however, be sensible – get a job, find a new church and a local charity to potter about in. According to you two, I could chase men or be chased by them. That's seven – or is it eight?'

'You could go back to the country on your own and make a go of it there.' said Sally.

'A recipe for genteel poverty. This is where the work is.'

'*You could go back to Dad.*' Sally again.

Hetty's chin came up. 'That's ten. Enough.'

She put the gew-gaws back in their original places, then laughed. 'In a year or so we'll see what I've done. Whether I've survived or not. Along with my ten green bottles.'

'Chasing men isn't the problem,' the old lady said loudly. Her speech had become slower and grander: she, too, had drunk more than her normal quantity on an empty stomach. 'It's spotting the defects from the distance, so you can be choosy. Then, if they're any good, catching them and holding on to them.'

'All advice gratefully received, but I'm not sure that's on the agenda. Yet.'

'You've been hurt. I can see that.' Sally spoke quietly. 'I'm impressed that you're putting on a brave front. But there are lots of ways you could meet new men, and make friends. Not just those *Telegraph* ads. Even if you didn't want to . . . you know. Take it any further.'

Hetty was drinking her fourth glass of wine. Her tongue was loosened and she giggled again. 'Oh, Lord, Sally, sex with strangers. Are you about to warn me to carry condoms?'

Sally gaped. The old lady swivelled round in her chair and stared. '*If* you go chasing men, dear, do choose clean ones,' she said.

'Yes, Mother,' Hetty answered, and hiccuped slightly.

Sally stubbed out her cigarette and immediately lit another. 'We haven't decided anything and it's getting late. What are you going to do?'

Hetty remembered the pizza leaflet and made a decision. 'Enough talk for one night. I am going to phone out for a Meat Feast with garlic bread,' she announced. 'With chocolate chip ice cream to follow. Would anybody like to join me?'

CHAPTER FOUR

The Odd Couple

Hetty was beginning to find her bearings. The children from the downstairs flat, whom she took to be the McDonalds', had scurried past her one morning. A boy and a girl, aged about five or six, though not twins, in the uniform of the nearby primary school. Mrs McDonald, a dumpy woman in her mid-forties, had bobbed quickly behind them with an anxious look, carrier-bag on her arm. There had been no time to exchange pleasantries, and Mrs McDonald did not appear to want to. You can be sociable or not as you wish, Mrs A had said; apparently, the McDonalds did not wish.

Mrs A would greet her cheerily; indeed, made it her business to greet everyone who came near the block, often by leaning out of the window. It must be her method, Hetty reckoned, of coping with life alone, though 'alone' was hardly an apt description. Some of those the woman hailed would accept her offer of a cup of tea, as Hetty had. The postman did every Saturday, the milkman on pay-days, though he confided in a whisper to Hetty that that meant The Swallows had to be at the end of his round.

The newsagent did not deliver. 'I'm here from five a.m.,' he whined. 'Enough.' To spite him, Hetty bought a copy of the *Big Issue* from a scruffy man who crouched on an orange-box nearby, and whom she had seen roundly cursed by the shopkeeper.

The *Big Issue* seller had looked her over in a fashion that made Hetty distinctly uneasy. She hoped he would not start following her home. He was dirty, his oiled jacket greasy with caked food, his fingers brown from cigarettes. One lip had an ulcer. Whatever he had been before fate brought him to this, he was not a pretty sight.

She was musing thus in the little supermarket, and thinking that she should not make snap judgements: perhaps the man had had bad luck and his current state was not his fault. Maybe selling the magazine was his first small step back to·civilisation. She joined the queue absentmindedly.

Suddenly another image came into her view. And made her stare openly.

This man was impossibly handsome, with a shock of tousled golden hair, blue eyed. Over six foot. Probably around thirteen and a half stone. Breathtaking. He was in the queue ahead of her. Hetty rebuked herself. She might not be in the business of chasing men, but it was undeniable that she had begun to notice them, both good and bad. Unfortunately, her taste and preferences had been formed years before, when she was a twentysomething on the lookout. This sort of man, so tall, his lean body hinting at some athleticism – did he play squash? cricket? – was exactly the type that had once made her catch her breath in wonder. At a guess, however, he was of an age to be her son.

'Hi,' he said, his voice deep. His jaw was prominent, the nose Roman, the chin dimpled. Above the green round-necked sweater his Adam's apple moved gently up and down, as if saluting her independently.

Hetty was startled. It was one thing to daydream, surreptitiously spying the man's basket to see whether he was buying for two. It was another to have the vision open its mouth and speak to her.

'Hi,' he said again, and grinned. 'Aren't you the new resident at The Swallows?'

'Oh!' Hetty found her voice. 'You mean the flats on Aviary Road? I've just moved in, yes.' She was about to add, 'Flat three,' then remembered to be circumspect with strangers. He may look an angel, but you couldn't tell. 'I've bought it. Why?'

'Because that's where I live. Upstairs from you.' Then he must know her number. Of course: it had been on the for-sale sign.

'Really?' He must be one of the artistic types Mrs A had mentioned. No doubt about it, as the azure eyes gazed down at her. If the rest of the neighbours were as 'odd' as this, her days at The Swallows could be . . . enjoyable. If frustrating. She was not about to go in for baby-snatching. Maybe he had an older brother.

'My name's Christian,' he told her, as his basket was taken from him by the cashier. 'It's not bad round here, don't you think?'

Hetty nodded as her own meagre groceries were charged. She gave her name and began to tell him her circumstances, then trailed off. If she were to start afresh, as she meant to –

as she must – then offering a sob-story as the opening to every conversation would have to stop. Dorset, the Aga and the four-poster bed were gone. It was foolish to dwell on them. Or to seek sympathy. She squared her shoulders.

What would Mrs A have done? The old woman seemed to make a success of singledom.

'Are you going back there now?' Hetty asked. 'Would you like a cup of tea?' Mentally she checked: the crockery had been unpacked and washed. There was milk in the fridge, two kinds of tea in the cupboard, and plenty of biscuits. She smiled encouragingly.

'I'd love one, Mrs Clarkson.' He smiled back.

Hetty felt her heart skip a beat. Her new life had started.

The answerphone was blinking as she opened the door. Christian indicated his bags with an easy politeness. 'I'll go and dispose of these then come back.'

'Hello, Hetty, dear. This is Mum. Back from my latest jaunt. Scotland this time – chilly! Are you in tonight? I'll come round and we can have supper. Forgive me neglecting you. I'll bring my photos. Edinburgh was wonderful . . .'

'Damn!' Hetty's first reaction was the realisation that, while entertaining a neighbour to tea was well within her capacity, cooking for her mother in an unfamiliar kitchen still was not. The freezer section of her modest fridge contained only ice cubes and a piece of frozen salmon. There was no time to shop again. In any case, she did not feel like cooking. A tinge of resentment surfaced, quickly suppressed. Her own attitudes had shifted alarmingly already: in her previous incarnation, refusing to serve a four-course dinner on demand would have been unthinkable.

'Christian,' she said, as the boy tapped at the open door

then strolled in, 'if you wanted to take a girlfriend out to eat, somewhere in walking distance, nice but not too expensive, where would you go?'

The eyebrows shot up. 'Well,' he said uncertainly, 'you could try Chez Bruce. Just by the station. Quite fair food and *ambience*.'

'My mum is a much-travelled lady. D'you think she'd like it?'

Christian visibly relaxed. 'Rather. I take mine there sometimes and she loves it.'

'That's settled, then.' Hetty felt inordinately relieved. Tea was duly made, Earl Grey, and served quite respectably in a teapot, with almond biscuits on a doily on a plate. 'Tell me about yourself,' Hetty invited. 'What do you do?'

'I'm an actor. With the Old Vic company. We go into rehearsals next week for the Pinter revival.' His chest swelled with pride. 'That's why I'm home at the moment, but once we get cracking it's a fourteen-hour day. Exhausting.' He rolled his exquisite eyes and puffed out his cheeks.

'And do you live here alone?' Hetty could not recall what else Mrs A had said, but this was a tactful way to find out more.

'No, with my partner. We've been together five years.'

'Ah.' Hetty was cross with herself for feeling disappointed. She was not about to fall in love, and certainly not with someone who could not recall Abba first time round, but it did no harm to admire beauty and to take vicarious pleasure in it. Friends were to be garnered where they could be found. She and Stephen had enjoyed going to the theatre, but despite her early BBC experience, no current actors or theatricals were among their acquaintance. This was something new, and to be savoured.

'Is your partner an actress too?'

'Actor, not actress. They hate being called actresses. That's what women were called in the days when stage-door johnnies were also part of the scene.'

'Sorry,' Hetty simpered. 'Aren't they still? Don't men still hang about the stage door waiting for their favourites?'

Christian chuckled in a knowing way. 'They do, Mrs Clarkson, but they're just as likely to be waiting for the male lead.'

'Oh!'

He put his head to one side. 'Is that a problem, Mrs Clarkson?'

'Call me Hetty.' She thought for a moment. 'Well, I have to admit, I don't know any . . . homosexuals. I did, years ago – must have, I suppose. And there were a couple of teachers living together in a cottage in the village. But one didn't mix with them.'

'Why not?'

'I'd have thought that would be obvious. One worries about people like that being teachers, for a start. Apart from anything else, I have a teenage son. And my husband had views on the matter. We wouldn't have wanted anybody's feelings to be hurt. It was a *small* village.'

'You don't think maybe their feelings were hurt at being left out?'

'No, why should they have been? They had their own circle. I imagine.' Hetty halted, uncertain. 'Where's this conversation going, Christian? Are you a campaigner, or something? I know there are lots of gays in your profession – is that it?'

'Thank you for the tea,' the boy said, and stood up, though with no indication of hurry.

Hetty rose hastily. 'Have I upset you? I'm sorry. I thought–'

'No, Hetty, you didn't think. I'm an actor, and my partner is not. He's a senior producer, quite well known.'

'He? But you said she–'

'I said nothing of the sort. We're gay, Mrs Clarkson. Both of us. And your son would have been perfectly safe in our company. Now I must go.'

It was an incident she did not feel she could share with her mother, or with Sally. But living in such close proximity – she could not avoid seeing Christian on the stairs, and realised that the older, greyer man who had nodded at her vaguely on the front path was probably his partner – she would have to find a way to make amends. The discussion, her stupidity and unthinking rudeness, made her go hot every time the words came back into her mind. She felt tortured by them for the rest of the day.

Eventually she wrote a note, the first on her new notepaper. 'Christian, I am sorry if I was rude. I didn't know, but that's no excuse. Hope you'll forgive me. I'd like to meet your partner, if that's okay with you both – sorry, I don't know his name. What would you like – a glass of wine, maybe? Hetty.' Then she scribbled underneath, 'Don't call this evening. I don't think my mum would understand. Anyway we'll be out – I booked a table at Chez Bruce as you suggested.' That, she suddenly saw, was both redundant and compounded the rudeness. She tore up the note and started again, using only the first three sentences. Then she bit the end of the biro and thought hard. At last she gave a little whoop of delight and wrote underneath, 'When your play is on, I'd love to come and see it. Would that be possible?

Could you let me have more details?' And added, 'Love, Hetty.'

A strange kind of love. If Christian and his partner ignored the note, she would have been rebuffed, and have deserved it. And would know better next time. But they were 'luvvies', weren't they? Lots of people in London were. If she were to avoid the loneliness that Sally obviously regarded as her lot, then it was up to her to make an effort. That included learning to speak other languages, however foreign they seemed.

Anyway, she meant it. It'd be fun to go to the theatre, to a preview or maybe at the start of the run when everyone was still keen, and to be able to say to the person in the next seat, 'I know that young man. Isn't he great?' It would be participating instead of standing on the sidelines. And there would be no dashing away to catch the last train. If she were invited for drinks afterwards she could go . . .

That was gazing too far ahead. For the moment, she had been taught a sharp lesson.

Hetty's mother, despite her seventy-three years, could still cut quite a dash. In the restaurant, in her navy suit, Peggy Morris looked ten years younger than her age. Hetty felt dowdy beside her: under the influence of comfort eating (the easy sin – those darned biscuits), her own waist was spreading and her size had crept up to a fourteen.

'Wonderful. How did you find this place?' Peggy was tucking into Bruce's calamari in Chardonnay with gusto. Without waiting for the answer, she continued, 'I must say, it's an improvement on that ghastly steak house in that village of yours. At my age one gets picky. I'm not sure I can cope with Saga coach cuisine much longer. Too many chips.'

Hetty paused, a french-fried potato and a slice of pep-
pered steak speared on her fork. Her mother had always
been a strong personality. Had she spent more time in
Hetty's vicinity, with Stephen nearby, there would have been
little left of Hetty Clarkson. Now was not the moment to
kowtow to her. Hetty raised the fork defiantly and ate.
'Thank you for your ideas on the night of the council of
war,' she ventured. 'I was grateful. You hadn't said much
about my divorce.'

The old lady chuckled and poured another glass of
Moselle. 'Frankly, what did you see in him?'

'Stephen? That's easy. I loved him.'

'Honestly – and you never suspected?'

'I adored him – blindly, yes. He was a fine-looking man,
he could be totally kind, was charming, generous. He was
intelligent, successful and well thought-of. I still think I
chose well. And, remember, I was a free agent – I could do
what I wanted with my day. That's not so common.'

'But he was unfaithful.'

Hetty sighed. 'I see it now, though I was completely naïve
then. Her husband guessed, but I didn't. Perhaps my ignorance was no bad thing – it kept my home intact as long as
was necessary for the children.'

'Huh!' Peggy sniffed. 'Your marriage trivialised you.
Turned you into a doll.'

'What?'

'Something else you weren't aware of. Made you brain-
less, darling. You're better off without him. You have a brain,
now you're going to have to use it.' The empty plate was
pushed away with an air of regret. 'Do you no harm to have
to stand on your own two feet. You might even enjoy it.'

'But what do you mean "trivialised" me? I couldn't have

competed with Stephen. He was so able. And I wouldn't have wanted to try. I played it low-key in company – you can't have two prima donnas in a family. One has to take a back seat, support the other. I'm a bit shy, really. Right now there are moments when I'm bloody terrified.' Hetty drained her glass – anything not to meet her mother's candid gaze. The alcohol was making her maudlin. 'I've none of the social skills I'm going to need. I'm trained and experienced as a wife. There are no etiquette books written for women like me.'

'So I'm right. He helped make you what you are. Correct?'

'Correct.' Hetty's voice was low. 'Don't push, Mother. You could say my confidence is a bit low at present. For all my bravado, I'm not sure how I'll manage on my own.'

The plates were cleared, menus re-presented. The two women dallied over the choice of dessert as Hetty struggled to understand her own emotions. A woman's role: that was how she had seen it, and had taken an inordinate pride in her fulfilment of it.

'It wasn't that easy, keeping a big house running, and being a stay-at-home wife,' she continued. 'I did the lot, as was expected of me: I was a school governor, I stage-managed the village pantomime, I helped out whenever anyone asked. A vanishing breed, they called me.'

'And now you can see why.'

'Too darned right.' The Death by Chocolate arrived, a darkly gooey contrast to her mother's sorbet. 'I entertained Stephen's business colleagues and their tedious wives – whole weekends of it. Endlessly cooking and weeding and clearing up and laundry, even though we had help in the house. No wonder the kids are so helpless. They think toothpaste grows in the tube and loo rolls reproduce by magic. I don't think either of them can boil an egg.'

'Don't put yourself down too much, Hetty. Your stamina always used to amaze me. Though I did wonder. You're not stupid, dear, and never have been.'

Hetty pouted. 'Many women, frantically juggling home, family, garden, and a career on top, would have been quite jealous. Many children suffered far worse. I made my bed and was content to lie on it.'

'A bed – or a doormat?' An elegant eyebrow was raised.

Hetty nodded sadly. 'Overdid it. And had no fall-back. What happens when the kids have gone? When the husband gets restless? Sometimes I did feel a little under-appreciated, but then I'd tell myself that that was women's lot through the ages too.'

'Not any more.'

'No. But what is my lot? The world is full of couples, or people wanting to be couples. I'm single. I really don't want either the loneliness, or the indignity of trying to start again.' The luscious dessert was nearly finished. With an effort, Hetty refrained from eating the crumbs.

'But there are loads of people like you!' her mother cried. 'Single women, and men! Didn't I read somewhere that we have the highest divorce rate in Europe?'

'Probably in your Saga magazine,' Hetty responded grimly. 'And it'd be higher if more people got married in the first place. That's no help. Sad divorced men aren't my cup of tea. Remarriage seems to me, right now, a thoroughly bad idea.'

'I wasn't suggesting that,' her mother retorted.

'But do you see? Most single girls are doing just that – looking for a bloke, desperately seeking a husband, home, mortgage, children, the lot. What about those of us who are not into that game? Not least because we're beyond it.

Beyond having more kids, I mean, and probably too old to get another twenty-five-year mortgage. But not past having ambitions and hopes. Not too old to want to have *fun*.' She paused, breathless, and startled at her own temerity.

'The men have it easier. They can't manage by themselves at all, poor dears.' Peggy chuckled deeply, as if at some long-forgotten memory not to be shared. 'You're right, darling. A man of fifty can start again – might be quite a catch, if he's kept himself in trim. New family – why not? Proves something about him.'

'What, exactly?'

'That he can still get it up, aim it at the right place and fire live ammunition at will.'

'Mother, you're disgusting. There must have been extra alcohol in that sorbet.' Hetty laughed, despite herself.

Her mother smiled wickedly. 'You should start listing your advantages,' she continued. 'You're not about to get pregnant. You don't want to tie a man down. You can be mature and fascinating at the same time – remember Cleopatra or Katherine Hepburn or Marlene Dietrich. They had no trouble attracting men well into old age. And neither have I.'

'This is my mother?' Hetty asked the air in wonder. 'This is solidarity? Suppose, however, that I might like to fill my life in other ways. Forget men, and find other things to fill that brain you so admire.'

'Fine. But don't forget the men,' her mother admonished. 'I can only tell you my recipe,' she offered. 'When your father was alive, we went all over the world with his postings, and I had a marvellous time. If he'd strayed one tiny inch I'd have cut his balls off, and he knew it. When he died, I grieved – not just for him but for myself. Then I did three things.'

Hetty raised her eyes. 'And those were?'

'Counted my money: sufficient. Renewed my passport. And had a face-lift.'

'You didn't!'

'I did.'

'You never told me!'

'Don't have to tell you everything, dear, and I don't expect you to confide in me either, unless you want to. But one more point. Some of this you should keep to yourself. I'm not sure Sally is quite ready for this kind of conversation, and of course Peter, darling grandson though he is, never will be. This is a woman's world, quite different from a man's. A singles world – a universe apart from couples and your old life. And believe me, darling, it can be fabulous. Wait and see.'

The stylish old lady picked up the empty bottle. 'Another?'

They went back to the flat for coffee. On the mat was a small white envelope. Inside, a photocard of Christian, professionally done, looking his moody best, the shadows across his face bringing out the jutting jaw and cleft chin. 'Love to see you at the theatre. Come to the first night. Two tickets await you at the box office. Knock one evening before then. Take us as you find us. Love, C.'

Later, her dinner companion sent home in a taxi, her head pounding from too much wine, Hetty lay in bed and let her mind rove. Her mother might have judged Stephen accurately, but Hetty remained sure that he had been splendid to begin with. She had not made a mistake in marrying him or in wanting to be married. She was not about to write off her entire previous existence, or abandon all her old values.

Now it was her turn. No compromises. No going back. New languages. Getting to know strangers. Odd couples. Getting to know people who had been strangers, like her mother. Telling white lies – about her age. Keeping secrets. *Her mother had had a face-lift? Ye gods! Was that the future?*

Two days later, a Sunday morning.

Hetty had slept fitfully, though the hot-water bottle had been relegated to the cupboard under the sink and a glass of wine had replaced cocoa before going to bed. She had jollied up the flat with a bunch of lilies, then realised they looked like funeral flowers and bought a scarlet cyclamen instead. She had explored the common, trudged across its windy wastes, discovered a whole shopping centre on the far side complete with a bus stop. A pot of apricot emulsion had brightened the kitchen. W.H. Smith's had a bewildering plethora of cookbooks. The ubiquitous Delia Smith must be psychic: *One Is Fun* was relentlessly spot on. Or maybe, Hetty reflected, her situation was all too commonplace in the modern world, and Delia knew it.

And she had started to live sloppily, in a sweater and jeans, with no makeup, no nail varnish, her hair a mess. That would not do. As she yawned into the bathroom mirror, dressing-gown askew, one more item was added to a growing list: find a hairdresser and smarten up. Preferably before seeing Rosa next week. Maybe Christian could recommend one? It was the sort of thing a gay man might know. Would he take umbrage if asked? What was patronising and what wasn't? She would call on them tonight – Sunday might be a free day for theatricals.

There was a noise outside the door. It sounded as if somebody had dropped a heavy bag. Hetty cocked her head and listened. Another noise: as if the bag was being rolled about. Then a long drawn-out wail, low and heartfelt. And a dull bang, something being thrown against the wall.

This could not be ignored. Hetty rose, tied her dressing-gown decorously, tiptoed down her narrow hallway and peered through the peephole. She could see nothing. Cautiously she opened the door a few inches, only to have it crash inwards with the weight of the heavy thing leaning against it.

'Oh!' Hetty jumped backwards, as the *thing* opened its mouth and sent forth a jet of yellow vomit on to the mat, just missing Hetty's slippers. A dribble slid over a black T-shirt and jeans stretched over plump thighs.

'Yurk!' said the thing, and retched. On the far side of the lobby an empty vodka bottle rolled tipsily where it had been thrown. 'Yurk! Oh, God. I want to die . . .'

Hetty ran to fetch an old towel and tried first to clean up the thing – a fat girl, flushed and gabbling – then the floor. The job was hopeless: no sooner had one slimy mess been wiped away than another stream surged forth. Hetty squatted on her haunches, a hand on the girl's shoulder. Last time something like this had occurred had been at Sally's twenty-first when some of her pals had hit the Amaretto.

'Hello, I'm Hetty,' she said, uncertainly. 'Who are you? What's the matter? Can you stand up?'

'M Annabel. Live *there*.' She gestured drunkenly at the opposite flat. 'And I'm too fat. He said so. I wanna *die* . . .'

'No, you don't. Come on, Annabel, can you get up? Then at least I can get you into the bathroom and you can be sick in the –'

'No-o-o!' the girl howled, as she struggled to her feet. 'He doesn't love me. He said so. He loves Flo!'

A small brown bottle fell from her inert fingers. Hetty picked it up then glanced sharply at the girl. 'Aspirin? You haven't taken the whole lot, have you? And the vodka? God in heaven. Wait! I'll call an ambulance.'

Ten minutes later an anxious Hetty, her dressing-gown stained and smelly, saw off the paramedics with their red-blanketed charge, but declined the offer to travel with her to hospital. An unshaven man from the flat opposite had volunteered instead. His sheepish manner suggested that he knew the cause of Annabel's anguish; the girl clung to his hand pathetically.

There was so much gunge to clean up. It was everywhere – in the hall, the bathroom, the lobby. To paraphrase Lady Macbeth, who would have thought the young woman had so much sick in her? One thing every mother knew, Hetty reflected gloomily, was what bodily fluids looked like. On the other hand, it had probably saved the girl's life.

She threw her dressing-gown, nightie, the towels and bathmat into the washing-machine with a double measure of bleach and set it to wash at the highest temperature. While the machine whirred, she treated herself to a shower and realised she was shaking.

A cry for help. But to what avail? *No man is worth that.* Especially if his evaluation of the girl stretched to her girth and nothing else. As if only her appearance mattered, and not her soul or her – brain.

Annabel. One of the girls living in flat four. Odd neighbours, indeed.

Whatever next?

CHAPTER FIVE

First Steps

Hetty pushed a stray lock of hair from her eyes and handed over the Harrods, Nicole Farhi and Harvey Nichols bags with relief. Her fingers were raw from carrying them.

'I am *exhausted*. Heavens, Clarissa, how often do you do this?'

They were in a narrow stone-flagged lobby. A circular marble staircase curled behind and above. Opera music – *Tosca*? – floated down, with the sound of tinkling glasses and a murmur of well-bred voices. 'Is this new? I don't recall Stephen ever mentioning it.'

'Darling!' Clarissa feigned surprise. The charm bracelet jingled. 'Christopher's is *the* place. It was in *Harper's and Queen*.'

'It used to be the National Liberal Club,' said the receptionist. She was a thin, angular girl with a fashionably wild haircut. She jerked her head skywards. 'Lots of intrigues. Government disasters and that. Years ago, of course.'

'And men only, I'll bet,' Clarissa added. 'Wasn't it a brothel once, too? Lucky devils.'

The airy upstairs room was sparsely furnished: minimalist was in, Hetty noticed. A polished plank floor, pale drapes, colour-washed stone walls, simple ironwork tables with white linen. The flowery fabrics and Laura Ashley style left behind in Dorset suddenly seemed impossibly twee. She tugged down the new jacket and wished the trousers did not chafe so. Perhaps size sixteen would have been wiser.

They were seated by the oriole window. Hetty could see the colonnaded Lyceum Theatre opposite, the activity at its stage door – it must be a matinée day – and caught the bustle of taxis and a fruit-stall in the street below. She wriggled her shoulders. 'Thanks, Clarissa. You're a pal. I love my new suit.'

The menus arrived. Hetty was about to order lamb in red wine with roast potatoes, then checked herself. Her mother had set an example. 'The seafood,' she said, 'and a salad.'

'And to drink, madam?' Like the receptionist, the waiter was young and skinny with a gelled hairdo that had taken much art to appear as if he had just got out of bed.

'It's on me, remember. Let's celebrate.' Clarissa smiled sweetly at the youth. 'Two glasses of champagne, please.'

'What are we celebrating?'

'Oh, I dunno. Your divorce? Did you screw him for a lot of money? Will you get the house?'

'Lord, no. I got enough to buy the flat, and to tide me over. Stephen still has a hefty mortgage, and we have to think of Peter – it's his home too. Anyway, I didn't want it.'

'But it's worth a packet! You mean, you walked away?'

Hetty shrugged.

'You're crazy. You should have nailed his ears to the wall. I would have.'

The seafood was beautifully served in a shallow soup dish with a knife, fork and spoon. A fleshy prawn, a black mussel shell, chunks of translucent monkfish poked like miniature atolls from a lagoon of garlicky sauce. Hetty glanced at other diners and saw it was permitted – encouraged – to eat the sauce with the spoon. And, if she wished, to wipe up the dregs with a piece of walnut bread.

She took two swallows of champagne. 'I am, however, beginning to feel I have something to celebrate. Getting over the hurdle of the divorce is one. My mother believes I was put upon for too long.'

Clarissa was twiddling with a green salad. Her mouth full of frisé lettuce – not the easiest vegetable to eat daintily. Only a nod was forthcoming.

'And now I find myself living on my own. It does feel weird. My daughter says I'll go bonkers and end up in a psychiatric hospital.' Hetty paused long enough to prise open a mussel. 'This is truly delicious, Clarissa – thanks a million.'

'Terribly fattening,' Clarissa said. 'All that cream in the sauce. Murder for the hips.'

'Don't be depressing. I've enough on my plate without that.'

'She's got a point, though, your Sally.' Clarissa pushed away the remaining rocket. 'You mustn't stay at home and mope. If you like, we could do this once a fortnight or so. Have lunch, then go to a movie or a show. Go shopping – Ikea, say, for anything you needed for your flat, or further afield, like Lakeside in Essex. Even take the Eurostar to Paris – that's great. We'll go dutch after today, unless it's a birthday treat. Some of my other friends would join us. A riotous girls' day out!'

Hetty pondered. 'Is that what you do with your time?'

'Mostly,' Clarissa replied. 'I can't go too far. Robin likes me home in the evening, even though the children are away at school. He says that's the way to keep a marriage strong – sorry. You stayed at home, and it didn't work for you.'

'Umm . . . How is Robin?'

'As per usual. He'll be head of chambers next year, so lots of black-tie dinners when I'll be on show too. The darling's given me a clothes allowance. Aren't I a lucky girl?'

He trivialised you. Turned you into a doll.

'Does that completely fulfil you, Clarissa? Is that all you need from life?' Hetty was startled to hear her own words. 'Seems a bit . . . frivolous to me.'

'Well!' Clarissa sounded annoyed. 'I'd rather be in my shoes than *yours*, dear. Shall we take a peek at the puds? Not that I want one. But *you* might.'

Abashed, Hetty considered the patisserie, then shook her head and ordered a filter coffee. Black.

Clarissa leaned across the table. 'We've been friends for years, so let's be blunt. You're the wrong side of fifty, you're . . . well, sliding into middle age would have been an apt description several years ago. What are your qualifications? Your earning power must be limited. What're you going to do? Work in a shop? After decades as mistress in your own home, would you take so easily to being a minion and being told what to do? No. That's not the answer.'

'And what is?'

'Stick with me, baby. I'll smarten you up, then we'll sort you out – I know a few decent older chaps who are in the market for a kind-hearted lady. We'll have you organised in no time.'

Hetty's eyes widened. 'You think I should be chasing men, do you? But what for?'

Edwina Currie

'Because it's the best for you! Because we should let them do the hard slog, the frightful stuff like working for a living. Let them be the wage slaves. They think they're exploiting us, but it's the other way round.' She touched her Rolex watch, a slim ladies' model, like a talisman. 'Darling, most divorced men are helpless. Infants. They're desperate to get hitched again – formally or informally. And you're exactly what they're looking for. You might have to lie about your age, though.'

'I'm already doing that,' Hetty muttered into her coffee.

'Good. Then you're on the right track.'

'But would it not,' Hetty chose her words with care – she had few enough shoulders to lean on, without alienating any – 'give you more satisfaction, if the money you spent was your own? That you'd earned?'

'No,' said Clarissa, and called for the bill. 'Apart from anything else, I simply wouldn't get anywhere near the amount I tend to splurge. Come on, Het, be reasonable. How many women do you know who earn more than men?'

Christian and his unnamed partner had been out on the Sunday evening when Hetty had knocked. She had left a warm note of thanks for the tickets under the door. Determined not to give up, she watched for a light in their flat. It was on as she returned home, laden, after her day with Clarissa. The purchases stored on hangers, she brushed her hair, applied lipstick, decided against perfume and climbed the stairs.

At the last moment, hand poised to knock, she recalled that in part she was trying to make amends. Quickly she ran back downstairs, grabbed her purse and hurried to the off-licence.

'Hello!' The vision stood at the door, his face breaking

into a slow grin. 'Come on in.' He called behind him, 'Markus, she's here – our new neighbour. Hetty.'

How gracefully that was done, Hetty thought. The way I used to introduce people at Stephen's business parties – so no one should feel awkward. Markus and Christian. Do they use the same surname, I wonder. Is that the fashion among gay couples or not?

Hetty was ushered into the tiny hall, the mirror image of her own. On the walls were framed theatrical bills and prints. Michael Redgrave and John Gielgud brooded in black-and-white photographs. In the main room stood the grey-haired man she had seen on the path. His skin was grainy and loose under the chin; he was much older than Christian – perhaps the same vintage as herself.

Markus accepted the wine and examined its label. 'Jacob's Creek Shiraz Cabernet,' he commented approvingly. 'You like Ozzie wines?'

Hetty was nonplussed. 'I don't know,' she confessed. 'My husband used to choose the wines. I just asked at Oddbin's what would be suitable for –' She stopped.

Christian laid a gentle hand on her shoulder. He was so *tall*. 'For a couple of poofters, hey, Hetty?'

She was scarlet.

'Come on, you're forgiven.' Christian led her into the living room where Markus was already pulling the cork of her gift.

The older man had a more serious expression on his face as he poured the wine. 'Perhaps I understand better than you do, Christian. When Hetty and I were young, it was illegal to be gay. Nobody would admit it. They'd be sentenced to ten years. Even Wolfenden regarded it as an illness. Our family doctor offered psychiatric treatment.'

'That's why he needs someone mad like me,' Christian
teased. 'He still hasn't properly come out.' He kissed Markus
full on the mouth. Hetty blinked. Markus brushed him off
and motioned courteously to Hetty to sit down.

The furniture was minimalist: tan leather, with a Persian
silk carpet in shades of lilac and gold. A few books, large and
glossy. Ovoid glass tables, a fig tree in a rough ceramic pot.
Ikea? Hetty wondered, then understood. *Not* Ikea. Carefully,
she asked, 'D'you mean it's a secret that you – ah – live
together? Would you rather I didn't mention it at the theatre?'

'He hasn't told his mother yet,' Christian butted in, in
the same teasing tone. 'She still thinks he's playing the field.'

'It's not a secret – exactly. But I prefer not to be the centre
of attention for that. I am entitled to my privacy, like anyone
else. My work, that's more important to me, and the most
important thing *about* me.'

'We argue about it, as you can see,' Christian continued.
'I reckon if he said it it'd make it easier for lots of other
men. The more the merrier. He's a public figure, on the Arts
Council. He was in the honours list last year, CBE. He has a
duty.'

'I'm a producer, not a professional homosexual,' said
Markus irritably, 'and I find it much harder than you do,
Christian, to talk about it. I'm not an exhibitionist.'

Christian laughed.

Hetty suspected that the glass in his hand was not the first
that evening. She decided to take sides. 'I can see Markus's
point of view, Christian. You're too young to remember. But
anyone caught had to go and live abroad, and careers were
wrecked. Particularly politicians. It was seen as – dirty. Nice
people didn't. Only . . . entertainers, I suppose, and writers.'

'More than that. They got married,' Markus said, bitterly.

'I nearly did, once. We thought you could overcome the urge if you fell in love with a beautiful girl. Well, I was in love but I couldn't go through with it. She married somebody else soon after and was terribly unhappy. But I couldn't tell her.' He brooded, and mentioned a well-known name. 'Still can't, but she must have guessed by now.'

There was a silence while Christian poured out the remainder of the wine. That didn't last long, Hetty thought. And this is my second go at alcohol today. 'Thanks, but no more for me. If I carry on like this, my daughter will be proved right. She says I can't possibly manage on my own and that I'll go bonkers. Funny how any – ah, *unconventional* behaviour has our friends and family calling for the psychiatrist, isn't it? Maybe I'll go under without meaning to. Getting sozzled might be one way.'

'I'd have gone bonkers alone,' Christian said suddenly. 'I was a raving drunk when Markus met me. Plus the cocaine. Ever tried it?'

'No!'

'He pointed out that if I carried on I'd ruin my looks and end up in the gutter before I was thirty. I was so confused about being gay. He rescued me. I adore him.' He cast a mocking, loving glance in Markus's direction, but the older man kept his head down.

'Talking of drinkers,' Hetty said brightly, 'can you tell me anything about our other neighbours? The ones who live in number four – that's below you, isn't it?'

'The Bridget Joneses?' Markus hooted. 'Ah, you were involved in that commotion. I hear you were quite the heroine.'

'She's okay. They let her out later that day. What did you call them?'

'The Bridget Joneses. The three BJs, when we're being cruel. Don't you know *Bridget Jones's Diary*?'

'I've heard of it,' Hetty answered dubiously. 'I've never read it. I prefer Joanna Trollope myself.'

'Three girls live there. The would-be suicide, Annabel, is the oldest. Her father bought the flat so the others have to tolerate her,' Christian explained. 'That's not the first time she's tried it. Usually it's such a spectacular and public event that she's bound to be discovered. But one of these days she'll go too far and there'll be a tragedy.'

'She said the man she loved thought she was too fat, and was in love with Flo.'

'Flo's the youngest and prettiest. She's black. Flirty. If I wasn't gay, I could fancy her.' Christian winked, but Markus frowned. 'Shelagh's the one with red hair, from County Wexford. She pretends to be bog-Irish, but actually her family are sausage-barons. Quite wealthy.'

'And why,' Hetty was determined to find out, 'do you call them the Bridget Joneses?'

Markus smiled. 'Because they spend their whole time yearning for men, usually totally unsuitable specimens, never manage to pin one down long enough to marry any of them, are frequently plastered, and seldom take anything seriously for five minutes. Least of all themselves.'

'You're being too hard on them, Markus,' Christian chided. He had opened another bottle and poured it before Hetty could prevent him. 'They're great fun, and quite harmless. You could have far worse neighbours, Hetty. Now, are you going to have a house-warming? And are we invited?'

'Heavens . . .' Hetty considered. 'D'you think I should? Who would I ask?'

'Us, for a start,' the young man said. 'Unless you're afraid you'd catch something nasty from a pair of raving queers.'

Hetty punched his arm playfully. 'Stop it. I've already grovelled and I'm not going to keep on doing it. Should I ask the BJs?'

'Of course. And their men – then you can see what we mean. Send them home at eleven, though, or they'll sleep where they fall,' Markus advised. Then, gently, 'It's a splendid idea. People can easily get lost in flats in London, especially after a crash-landing like yours. You feel like you've been thrown out with no parachute, right? You could stay in night after night nursing your wounds, and never speak to a soul. I know – I've been there. But if you reach out and are friendly, anything might happen.'

'Isn't he wonderful?' Christian cried. 'You see why I worship him? And you'll meet my family when you come to the first night, Hetty. My grandmother adores Markus. There's a little party afterwards. You will come, won't you?'

'Yes,' said Hetty. 'I'd love too. Goodness, aren't you kind? What do I wear?'

The Wandsworth Studios, Rosa said, were easy to find: in the middle of Putney, behind Young's brewery, near the bridge. Hetty, unused to finding her way on foot around London, soon became lost. For over forty minutes she wandered in the area near Putney Bridge, before a traffic warden redirected her. 'Wrong bridge, love,' he said. 'Wandsworth Bridge, that's the one.'

So it was a flustered and hideously late Hetty who eventually trotted into the studios and was nearly knocked over in the flurry of activity.

'Ten minutes!' she heard a gruff male voice call. 'Back on set by four forty-five or we're mincemeat!'

A squat man in tight denim jeans, belly overhanging his belt, pushed past her. Under one arm was a clipboard with pink typewritten sheets, in the other a biro; another pen was stuck behind one ear, under his headphones. A microphone extended under his chin. He stopped, pushed a button on the pack attached to his belt, listened, then barked, 'I mean it!' before walking on.

Suddenly she was grabbed by a whirling figure – wild black hair, red velvet trouser suit, flashing teeth: Rosa, who hugged her vigorously and planted a kiss on both cheeks. 'Mwah, mwah! Hello! It's great you could make it. Did you find us all right?' The energetic life-force did not pause for an answer. 'Your timing's perfect. We've just broken for tea. Come and meet everyone.'

Hetty was half carried along a corridor to a cramped area with banked seats and Formica tables littered with ketchup and vinegar bottles. The air crackled with voices and the hiss of steam urns. Condensation misted the windows, but the smell of baking was cosily welcoming. The canteen was packed with what she took to be the crew – men with half a day's growth of beard, wolfing sandwiches and pastries as if half starved, mugs of tea in their hands; young girls sipped black coffee or Diet Coke. Everyone smoked. In the far corner a family of four were huddled with dazed expressions, teacups untouched. 'Our guests,' Rosa said, in a stage whisper. 'You needn't bother with them, it'll be another bunch next week.'

She propelled Hetty round the room. 'Mike, Gerry, Phil – cameramen. Dave does sound, he's a genius. Bob you've already met, he's the floor-manager. Daisy, Sue, Kate – researchers. The makeup ladies are busy with the next guests upstairs, editors are in the gallery checking the tapes – have I missed anyone?' She clapped her hands and obtained a moment's silence. 'This is Hetty, and she's coming to work for us.'

'Hi, Hetty.'

'Hello, how're ya doin'?'

'Welcome on board.'

The buzz rose to its former volume as each returned to his or her previous conversation.

'Grab a cup of tea, or whatever, and we'll sit in that corner,' Rosa ordered.

Hetty obeyed meekly, but muttered a protest: 'I haven't agreed to come yet. Why did you tell them that?'

'Because I need you, that's why.' Rosa glanced up. 'And you need a job, right? So you could do worse than start here. We've had to sack a couple of youngsters who were misbehaving. Prompting the guests about what to say and adding a few improbable sexual details of their own. Can't have that. A mature person like you, Hetty, even a beginner, who I can trust would be ideal. Not that I can offer you much.'

'I'm not a complete beginner,' said Hetty huffily. The Eurostar with Clarissa suddenly seemed more tempting.

'That's what I've told 'em. You won't let me down.' Rosa drank her tea quickly. 'Yerrch! That's hot. I've burnt my tongue.'

'What does the job consist of?'

'Mostly fixing up the guests. Phone calls, loads of persuasion. Then you take care of them while they're here, don't let 'em get cold feet. Keep telling 'em how wonderful they are, and how their problems will be resolved by their appearing on the telly. Natch. The programme's called *Tell Me All*. It's a sort of true confessions-cum-agony-aunt set-up.

Daytime TV.' She rolled her eyes, as if that explained every-thing. 'Got to fill the airwaves somehow, and we aim to produce programmes of integrity and quality. Anyway, the network seems to agree. We're contracted for next year already – that's why I can put you on the payroll.'

Hetty felt weak. 'What should I ask you? Salary, I sup-pose.'

'You're paid per programme. You'll get fifty pounds a show – three hundred a week. For God's sake, don't go round spouting about it 'cause some of them are only workies.'

'Workies?'

'Work experience. They get zilch. Students, or ex-stu-dents. It's all that's available, and they're glad to get it.' She snorted at Hetty's shock. 'Honey, don't be so green. That's the only way *anything* gets made for TV these days. They'll probably think you're a workie too because you're a mate of mine. So keep schtoom.'

Hetty nodded mutely.

'Now, next week's programmes are just about fixed, but on Monday planning begins for the following week. You could come in then. Nine thirty start. Supposed to pack up by five but it's a bit open-ended. Plenty of nosh on filming days – that's Thursdays and Fridays, we make three shows a day – otherwise it's packed lunch or the pub.'

One of the cameramen – Gerry, Hetty believed – had left the canteen and now returned, shaking his head. 'Camera five's out,' he announced. 'Take a minute or two to fix it.'

'Relax, everybody,' called Bob, the floor-manager.

'Oh, good, we have a bit longer.' Rosa grinned. 'So, apart from needing a job, how are you doing? Haven't seen you in ages.'

Hetty began to insist that she didn't *need* a job, then thought better of it. She needed something to do. The creative cacophony of the studio, though bewildering, was distinctly more to her taste than repeat episodes of Knightsbridge with Clarissa; she could keep up with the one, but not with the other, not indefinitely. It dawned on her that Rosa, in her fast-moving way, was doing her an enormous favour. The least she could do in return was be grateful.

'I'll be fine. Suffering a bit of culture shock at the moment.' *Keep that resolution. Don't whinge. Nobody wants to hear your sob-story.* Hetty put her head on one side and examined her friend. 'Rosa, you look marvellous. This life obviously suits you.'

'Yes, it does. What makes the difference is knowing we've been recommissioned. TV's a hair-raising business. You can produce an award-winning series – and I have – and still come to the last shot unsure if you can pay the bills next month. Budgets are murderously tight, like I said on the phone. But we manage. Struggle from one crisis to the next. What about you?'

'Me?' Hetty's caution came into play. 'The decree absolute is nearly through. I have a flat, not too far from here, so this is convenient. I'm beginning to settle in.'

'Got a boyfriend yet?' Rosa nudged her arm. 'Go on, you can tell me. I won't let on.'

Hetty covered her embarrassment with a short laugh. 'Everyone thinks I should no sooner have got rid of one man than be haring off after another. What is this?'

It was Rosa's turn to seem shocked. 'You're not about to turn into a nun, are you? Because I don't recommend it.'

'I'm not about to haunt street corners saying, "Hey, fella," either. Or go night-clubbing with people half my age.'

'But the sex!' Rosa hissed, loud enough for the two men at the next table to hear. One snickered but kept his back turned. 'Won't you miss it?'

Hetty shrugged. Even if she were to confide in Rosa, this was hardly the moment.

'I mean, I don't know what it was like between Stephen and you. He seemed a hunky guy, but one never can tell. But if it was okay, then surely you'll get stuck in soon as possible? And if he wasn't up to much . . .' Rosa nudged her again. 'You're not past it. Not by a streak. Believe me.'

One of the cameramen twisted round and peered at the two women. 'It gets better with age, like fine Cognac,' he remarked, and made kissing noises with his lips.

Rosa made a face. 'Buzz off, Phil, this is women's talk. Anyway, you're married.'

'Never stopped him before,' guffawed his companion. That must be Mike, Hetty worked out by a process of elimination. Phil muttered something the women could not catch. Mike found it wildly funny and spluttered into his tea.

'You can take my word for it,' Rosa finished loftily, so that the entire room could hear, 'it gets smaller with age. Like their brains.'

There was a bus back, which she would be able to use regularly, but for the moment she would walk in the gathering dusk. Past a smattering of Italian, French and Indian restaurants – this was hardly a gastronomic wasteland. More bookshops, a children's clothing shop, a bicycle store crammed with parts, its window obscured by tyres in neatly tied bunches like a Victorian child's ringlets. An old-fashioned ironmonger's with a tin bath and tools and faded signs for Eveready batteries. A video shop: she was tempted to enter, then made her second resolution of the week.

Rather than sit morosely in front of the telly night after night, as Markus had warned, it would be better to join the library. She had said it to her mother and Sally as a joke. But her mind did cry out to be filled, and not with more Delia recipes. Could she aspire to read a book a week? Where should she start? Fiction? Biography? It was ages since she had read anything remotely improving or note-worthy. What might somebody like Markus read, that she could chatter to him about without seeming a complete fool?

Hetty stood outside the biggest bookshop and examined the contents of the window. Shortly after, she resumed her walk up the hill towards the common, with a copy of Pinter's plays and *Bridget Jones's Diary* under her arm.

It felt like a step forward. Her spirits were high as she approached the block of flats.

A house-warming. When? Who?

Markus and Christian, obviously. The three BJs, and their men, if they would come. Mrs A. Her mother, and Sally and Sally's Erik, though he didn't attend family functions. Perhaps he could be persuaded for once. Hetty felt a fresh curiosity about him. Her son Peter, if invited, would plead too much on at uni. Rosa, and Clarissa and Robin. Larry and Davinia, though they would act superior all evening. Heavens, that was eighteen people already. Mr and Mrs McDonald, as a courtesy. Twenty.

How much would twenty people drink? A case of twelve bottles, maybe? Hetty calculated, then recalled Annabel and the empty vodka bottle, Christian and Markus polishing off a single bottle with her help in less than half an hour. Her mother, Sally and she had got through two and a half.

Twenty bottles, then. Thirty?

Should she make a fruit punch or mulled wine? That was the done thing in the countryside, to welcome guests after a chilly walk. She glanced up at the lighted windows above her. A punch did not seem right. Thirty bottles it would have to be, and Oddbins would lend her the glasses.

'And what do I serve to eat?' she asked aloud. Mystery upon mystery. What would sophisticated young, and older, Londoners expect?

A footfall came on the path. It was Markus, muffled up against the cold, a preoccupied frown on his face. 'Beg pardon?' he said, fumbling with his keys. 'Hello, Hetty.'

'I was wondering,' she mused. 'I will have a housewarming. How about three weeks on Sunday? My pay cheque comes then. But food. Do I spend the whole day cooking?'

'Mercy, no. If it were me, I'd have oodles of decent plonk and a few peanuts. Christian wouldn't argue with the first, but he'd think nuts were distinctly *infra dig*.'

'What would he prefer? I'd like to please.'

'Dim sum, probably.'

'*Dim sum?*'

'Yes. Don't be so terrified, Hetty. You'll get them in Sainsbury's.'

The replies came back, on the answerphone, or via notes pushed under the door.

'*Annabel, Flo and Shelagh are delighted to accept your kind invitation. And belated thanks for saving me from death – should've said so before. Not known for my manners. Likely blokes are Richard (he was the one who came in the ambulance), and probably Stuart and Ted. But it could change. See you!*'

'Hi, Hetty. Larry here. Thanks for the invite. We're over-whelmed at work, so please count us out. But we haven't forgotten you're coming to us. Be in touch. 'Bye . . .'

'Clarissa calling. How sweet – a flat-warming! Sadly, Robin is speaking at a weekend seminar and wants me with him, so no good for us. When are you coming to Lakeside? Give me a buzz . . .'

'Lovely idea. Thanks. Can I bring Thomas? D. Archibald. P.S. Do you need any help? I'll come half an hour early.'

'Hello, Mum, Sally here. You're branching out a bit, aren't you? You've got me worried. Who're you going to invite? You can't just ask your old Dorset friends. D'you have anybody else? Anyway, I'll support you. Ring if you need me.'

'Markus and Christian are honoured at your splendid invi-tation, and will be there on the dot. Is it bring-a-bottle?'

Hetty calculated. That would produce a kitchenful of unmatched wine. She preferred to be the hostess: buying her own would give her some control over events. The Shiraz Cabernet had been delightful. So had the Moselle her mother had drunk at Bruce's. That would do. A case of each, and a few spare.

'Hetty. Your mother. Terrific – I will delay my trip to Florida. Can't imagine why I'm going, I hate mosquitoes. I may have an escort – nobody terribly grand, one of your father's old cronies. Shall I suggest he bring somebody along for you, too?'

CHAPTER SIX

Having a Party

Would they come?

The flat was pristine; the heat had been on, then turned down in case it got too stuffy. Perfumed candles were lit on the mantelpiece, their flames flickering over the little ornaments. The Lladro statuette was adorned for the occasion with a blue ribbon around her neck. White wine was in the fridge, three bottles were uncorked on the table with the glasses, washed and wiped. Mrs A – Doris – was pottering in the kitchen. A bowl of hyacinths added to the fragrance. Thomas the cat had appropriated a chair and curled up to sleep; ginger hairs scattered with every breath. Hetty heard him purr.

The CD player murmured Enya: suitably anodyne, Hetty hoped. She dried her hands on a tea-towel, checked around. The dim sum (if Markus had said spring rolls and bits, Hetty grumbled inwardly, she would not have balked) sat on baking trays ready to be popped into the oven, or on Pyrex dishes for the microwave. The house did not run to steaming bamboo baskets tonight.

Sally would come. Hetty wondered about the boyfriend. Her daughter was so cagey about Erik. He did exist: he was not a fantasy of Sally's. Hetty had glimpsed airmail letters postmarked from various parts of the globe, and accepted that he was constrained by his career in the airline industry like Sally. But her daughter did not keep a framed photo by her bed, and never spoke of long-term plans.

'He's probably married, and stringing her along,' was the main conclusion Hetty could arrive at, in the absence of further information. How little she knew of her daughter, of what inspired or drove her, if anything. The girl kept things close to her chest. That hurt.

An icy sliver of melancholy entered her soul. Peter was away, almost a grown man, and though dutiful – as his grandmother had remarked – was never likely to be a dear friend to his newly single mother. More tactful than his sister, he would avoid taking sides, and probably slide away from either parent. He would go his own way, as he had been brought up to do. Would that make him a selfish adult? His easy manners Hetty recognised: they might have been inherited from his father or herself, but they made him pliant, and thus not available. Sally was less sunny, more introverted. If additionally she was willing to let a man walk all over her . . . Hetty sighed. That was hardly a recipe for a contented life. Was she about to admit that her daughter was not a great success emotionally? Was that Hetty's fault too?

The doorbell rang to interrupt her reverie. Hetty leaped to switch on the oven and tore off her apron. In the kitchen, like the sprite of the hearth, Doris hovered with a proprietorial air. The turban had been discarded revealing dangling earrings and a fussy perm, which did little for her appearance, but she had donned a flowered frock, cheerful and brassy.

'Hey! Happy house-warming! Mwah, mwah!'

Three girls and five men bounced noisily across the threshold, four carrying bottles of wine and one, Christian, a bouquet of flowers, which he thrust into her hands. 'May you have good fortune in your new home, Hetty.' He smiled down at her, with the slow bob of the Adam's apple that made her gulp. Then he busied himself arranging the blooms artistically in the other gift they had brought, a Finnish blue vase.

Annabel was still in black, garments too tight for her *embonpoint*. She resembled an overstuffed sausage, the type that hangs in glistening rolls in French delicatessens. Wholesome and worth eating, but a trifle overpowering. She loomed over Hetty; she must be five feet ten and over fifteen stone.

Annabel gave her rescuer a bear-hug. 'Thank you for saving my life! God, was I a pig. Sorry you found me like that. Next time I'll puke on my own doorstep. Where's the bottle-opener?' And she was gone.

'Hi. I'm Shelagh. That's Flo. Thanks for asking us. Have you got any music? We can bring over some CDs to dance to, if you'd like.' Shelagh had a mass of extraordinary flame-coloured hair that was confirmed by her pale skin and freckles to be entirely natural. Even in the dimmed light her eyes were a bewitching green. She spoke in a high lilt.

'Maybe later,' murmured Hetty. Dancing? That was not quite what she had had in mind. 'Who are the boys?'

'Oh, yes.' Shelagh did not seem troubled by the lack of introductions. She pointed at the young men who were now casually opening bottles and pouring drinks. 'Making themselves useful. Richard you've met – he was the one Annabel was breaking her heart over, but he's after Flo.' Shelagh grinned. 'For the moment. But I'm working on him. I've told him he doesn't need to kiss the Blarney Stone, but he should see the Wicklow mountains. He says he may come in the summer.'

'You mean, you're all in love with him? With the same chap?' Hetty's eyes rounded.

'Not exactly in *lurve*,' Shelagh drawled scornfully. 'Annabel's the one who's in love with him. It's a gross turn-off for a fellow like Richard. Commitment isn't his scene.'

'Isn't he in love with Flo?'

'Not him. He's only ever been in love with one person.'

'Who's that?'

'Richard? Himself, of course.'

Two glasses of wine were thrust into their hands. Before she could speak to the young man who had produced them, he had vanished back into the throng. The other two remained anonymous.

'So why – forgive me being nosy – are you all three so besotted with Richard?'

'Oh, but he's a catch, isn't he? And *fabuloso* in bed. Or so I've been told. On the other hand, you'd want to check that out for yourself, wouldn't you?'

The doorbell went twice; the nearest person answered it. A timid couple, one of whom Hetty recognised as Mrs McDonald, tiptoed in, jostled from behind by a portly gentleman with a moustache booming greetings, who was completely unfamiliar. Behind him, however, were Hetty's mother and Sally.

'Darling!' Peggy was being helped out of her coat by the moustachioed gent. 'I've brought the Colonel. You do remember him, don't you, darling? He and your father were adjutants together in Egypt.'

Hetty politely composed her face, but could not recall having seen the mottled jowls and beetle brows before. 'Nice to be here,' he called, glancing over his shoulder. He pronounced the word 'hyar' with some flourish. 'Your mother's a splendid woman. D'you know we're going to Florida together?'

'No, I didn't,' Hetty told his retreating back. Who was this man?

The smell of baking pastry began to waft from the kitchen. Doris had told Hetty firmly that she would like to make herself useful. There was a yowl from the corner and a cackle of laughter. Someone had inadvertently sat on Thomas, who fled in disgust under the sofa.

The doorbell rang once more; Hetty reached it first. Rosa burst in, hair flying, a bottle wrapped in silvery Cellophane with ribbons in her hand. More mwah-mwahs ensued. Hetty reflected briefly that she had not been kissed so much for years. It was rather pleasant.

She fetched a glass of wine for Rosa and refilled her own. 'Golly, everyone's come. I can't believe it,' she said.

'Well, I must admit, you've made lots of new friends already,' Rosa said, peering round the now crowded living room. 'Fast mover. Who'd have thought it?'

'It's misleading,' Hetty confessed. 'About half of them, apart from family, I've never seen before. For example, one of those boys is Ted, and one's Stuart, or at least I think so, but I couldn't say which is which. Or who each is with. And that's Mr McDonald who lives downstairs, but that's the sum total I can tell you about him: tonight is the first time we've met. And as for the Colonel –'

'The Colonel? Which one is he?'

Hetty saw that Rosa was casing the joint in a highly practised fashion. She pointed. 'He's with my mother. She's seventy-three. Can you credit it? Arrives with a bloke I've never heard of before, out of the blue. Heavens, look at him.'

The Colonel's hand was patting her mother's bottom while he knocked back an entire glass of white wine and smacked his lips.

'Beefy piece of meat. You should be thrilled for her,' Rosa chided.

'I'm a bit startled. One doesn't quite think of one's elderly mother as a sex object.'

'Ask her for her secrets. Is she on HRT?'

'My mother? I haven't the foggiest. It's not the sort of subject we'd have talked about – before.'

'Are you?'

'Sorry?'

'Have you been through the change yet?'

Hetty felt her knees wobble. She drank more wine to steady herself. 'No, not yet. Everything seems to be working normally.'

'God, then you could still get pregnant. You'll have to be careful.'

'Rosa, I have no plans to –'

'*You never know.* Women get pregnant in their fifties. Even without fertility treatment. Anyway, I wanna give you one piece of advice you'll thank me for. When the hot flushes come, don't put up with them for a minute. Not one minute, d'you hear? You get straight down to your doctor and you *demand* HRT. If yours won't help, I'll give you the name of one who will.'

'But don't they say – the side effects?' Hetty was wilting under the onslaught.

'Sure. The best. The juices keep flowing and the skin's soft as a baby's. Here, feel.' She offered her forearm; Hetty prodded it tentatively. 'Made me a new woman. The libido's up and running.' Her eyes roved and settled on Christian, who was talking animatedly to Flo and Shelagh. 'Now, who is that stunning Adonis over there?'

'He's an actor. Christian Devenish. Lives upstairs.'

'Oooh! I wonder if he'll come on the programme.' And with that Rosa was off, nostrils flaring, a greyhound after a hare.

Mr and Mrs McDonald were standing quietly together by the wall. Hetty took a bottle and topped up their nearly full glasses.

'Thank you so much for coming. I wanted to get acquainted, and this seemed the easiest way.' She shook hands with them, formally. His was cold and bony, his wife's plumply soft.

'It was kind of you to ask us, Mrs Clarkson. We can't stay, we don't have a baby-sitter.' Mrs McDonald's speech was richly accented, and she spoke so low that it was hard to understand her.

Hetty bent closer. 'Are the children all right? D'you need me to pop down and –?'

'No, they'll be fine. They're watching the telly and eating a Chinese takeaway. Bit of a treat for them. And they know where we are.' Mrs McDonald smiled faintly.

They were not – odd, exactly, Hetty reckoned. A mite out of place, maybe. The wife was about five feet four, dumpy, plain, with a careworn face. The husband was Hetty's height and thin, his face shadowy. He might have been slightly younger than his spouse – under forty. He wore a cheap grey suit, a blue shirt and tie. Both, indeed, had dressed up, a compliment to her. Perhaps they were not asked out much.

'Are you both from up north?'

'We are. From Cathcart. Glasgow, that is.'

'Have you been down here long?' The conversation had a forced quality, but Mrs McDonald did not appear ill at ease. Her husband said nothing; his eyes darted, but his mind seemed partly elsewhere. The pair stood so close that they gave an impression of being joined at the hip, needing no contact with anyone else.

'About three years. We've been married seven; the children were born in Scotland. We came down here for the work – my husband's a lorry driver.'

'Oh.' Hetty felt puzzled. 'Were there no openings for lorry drivers in Scotland?'

'Long-distance. He couldn't get home nights. But we're getting used to London. Better now the children have lost their accents – they don't get teased so at school.'

'Well! If ever I can help . . .' Hetty stopped. That was unwise. She did not intend to get stuck as a regular baby-sitter, not for complete strangers, though the children had been well behaved when she saw them.

'Thank you for that, Mrs Clarkson, but we're okay. We don't go out often. This is quite a treat for us too.'

On the other side of the room Sally was signalling for her attention. One of the men – Stuart? Ted? – was trying to chat her up, an approach clearly not to Sally's taste. Hetty moved adroitly away from the quiet couple, as she had begun to dub them, but not before adding, 'Enjoy yourselves. Food's coming. And please call me Hetty.'

Sally pursued her into the kitchen. With Doris's help, Hetty transferred the hot pastries and dumplings to platters and thrust one into her daughter's hands, along with a wad of napkins. 'Go serve,' she ordered. Sally pursed her lips and did as she was told.

Doris's eyes followed her in curiosity. 'She's not much like you, your daughter, is she?' she said.

This was not the time for confidences; in any case, Hetty knew that her worries about Sally would have to be resolved with the girl herself, if at all, and with no one else. 'Too darn like her father,' she replied briskly. 'Sorry. Shouldn't have said that. Had two glasses of wine. Goes to my head. Isn't it awful?'

'Have another.' The old lady grinned. 'You're much more relaxed. Doing you good, it is.' She peeped round the door. 'Is that your mother? I'd like to meet her.'

'Oh, yes. Excellent idea. Remiss of me. Wait.' Hetty grabbed a second tray and sailed out into the room. Was it her imagination, or had the music changed? Madonna, maybe, or an imitator. Not one of her own. The noise level was higher, too: everyone, apart from the silent McDonalds, seemed lively and happy. The eats were vanishing fast – she should have bought more. Eight empty bottles already! Everyone would soon be pie-eyed. Oh, well, that was the objective.

Her mother was leaning against a table edge, elegantly displaying her figure in a maroon Jean Muir dress and jacket. The Colonel was half bent over her and appeared to be whispering something entertaining in her ear. Hetty smiled sweetly, took her mother's arm and led her towards the kitchen. 'You planning to marry him, Mother?' she asked urgently.

'Heavens, no. What a barmy suggestion.' Her mother's laugh tinkled out.

'Why? What's so barmy about it? He seems quite besotted.'

'So he should be. But for one thing, he's only a half-colonel. Your father was two ranks up. And if I remarried, I'd lose my pension. We'd have to manage on his alone.'

'Oh! That matters, does it?'

Her mother shrugged. 'Don't be snotty, dear. Believe me, a lot of pensioners live tally. In unholy unwedlock. Creature comforts matter more when you get older. Anyhow, this way he keeps his teeth in in bed.'

I am learning, Hetty reflected grimly, a great deal about my mother I could not have imagined. Am I like that? Am I to become like that?

There was no time to ponder further. Hetty introduced her widowed mother to her widowed neighbour and left them chatting merrily to each other. She suspected that she herself might be one of the topics of conversation, and moved away.

'Mum!' It was Sally. She had hardly touched her wine and had a gloomy expression. 'Who *are* these people?'

'People,' said Hetty vaguely, waved a hand and drank another half-glass. The wine was super; it had been a wonderful choice. 'C'mon, Sally, loosen up. You should be enjoying yourself.'

'*You* obviously are,' said Sally, but she did not smile. 'What are you up to? I thought you were down in the dumps, what with the divorce and that. Beginning to appreciate what you'd given up. But here you are, giving a frantic party and surrounded by half a dozen chaps young enough to be your sons. What's going on?'

'Nothing,' Hetty answered, testily. 'They're just acquaintances. I'm not about to start an affair with any of them. Why should you assume I have my eyes on anybody? Don't you trust me? Anyway, some of them are gay.'

Sally stared hard out of the kitchen at the gathering. The lights had been turned down further and several guests had started to dance. 'Oh, I get it. You're going to be a fag-hag, Mother. A fine life that'll be.'

'What's a fag-hag?'

Sally grunted. 'Why don't you ask one of them? Look, I have to go – I have an early call tomorrow morning. Don't get yourself arrested.'

Hetty turned her back, suddenly furious. It was plain that she had not brought Sally up to have impeccable manners; and now it was too late.

Rosa was back, her arm entwined round Markus's.

'Darling! You didn't tell me you knew Markus Krushnikoff! Heavens. He tells me he lives nearby.'

Markus had evidently been economical with the truth. Hetty decided not to betray him. 'That's right. We bump into each other out on the street, don't we, Markus?'

'But have you seen his plays? The *Antony and Cleopatra*? The *Britannicus*? He's marvellous. Hetty, you're so lucky – what circles you move in!'

Markus blushed and rubbed his hand over his non-existent hair. He murmured modest dissent, soon detached himself and returned to watch over Christian, who was in deep debate with Stuart – or was it Ted?

'I haven't managed to get to the theatre much, recently,' Hetty said to Rosa. 'I used to go with my hus – *ex*-husband. Not sure who I could go with now.'

'Why? What would you like to see?'

'The new Pinter. I've been given tickets for the first night. Christian's in it.'

'Oo-oo-ooh! Those tickets are like gold dust. You seriously looking for a taker?'

'Er – yes, I am.'

'Can I come?'

'If you'd like to. But are you sure you want to come with me?'

Rosa gave her arm a squeeze. 'You bet. And is there a boozy knees-up afterwards? Are we invited to that, too?'

Hetty nodded, dazed. 'At the Savoy, apparently.'

'Yippeee! Then we'll get dressed in our glad-rags, and we'll whoop it up. Cinderella, you *shall* go to the ball.'

It was after ten. Several of the guests had bade farewell and slipped away. The McDonalds had vanished discreetly, Sally had gone. Doris was washing up, humming to herself and swaying her hips. The others seem to have settled to some solid drinking and slow dancing. The Colonel and her mother were in the centre of one knot. Christian was still engaged in earnest conversation, trying to explain a point with much exaggerated waving of his elongated white hands. The two young men who were arguing with him had still not been introduced to Hetty, nor did they seem to feel any need to meet their hostess. Perhaps they were uncertain who was responsible for the event; it didn't seem to matter to them. Rosa tapped Richard on the shoulder and was soon sashaying smoochily with him coiled about her, while Annabel, her back to the gathering, steadily demolished the remaining food.

Markus returned. 'It's a super party. Would you like to dance, Hetty?'

'Lord, I don't – I can't remember how . . .'

He laughed indulgently. 'Come on. You'll be safe with me.'

They moved to the edge of the dancing group and he took her in his arms the old-fashioned way, one hand on her waist, the other holding hers high in the air. He moved with grace, lithe and fit. Hetty was taken aback and had to concentrate. 'You're very good,' she puffed. 'Sorry. I haven't danced with a man in years – only my ex.'

'I started my career as a dancer,' Markus said. 'I still go to classes, once or twice a week. With a young lover, I have to.'

'You don't have anything to worry about, surely,' Hetty murmured, her tone wistful. 'Christian adores you. He said so.' Her head was full of wine and warmth. What a pity this lovely man was in love with somebody else: it was like dancing with a girlfriend's husband, a source of mingled delight and regret.

'But I do have to worry. There's a twenty-year age gap, for a start. When I met him he was a mess – that bit's true. What he didn't say was that I had to teach him everything. I was a sophisticated, experienced homosexual; he knew nothing about himself or his sexuality. He had been in a clinic, had been self-mutilating. But now look at him. He's a success, confident and utterly beautiful. I don't think I can hold on to him much longer.'

The pace had not slackened, but the ice had re-entered Hetty's heart. 'Is that why he presses you to come out?'

'It's his way of testing me, yes. He gets angry at what he regards my lack of support for the cause. But it would be natural for him to find men closer to his own age. He's propositioned often enough. The theatre is a queers' paradise.'

'And he – does he go chasing men?'

'I don't think so. But he might.'

Markus sounded so sad that Hetty pulled back and gazed at him. 'What would you do if . . . ?'

'God knows. I might ask Annabel over there for some tips, then do the job properly.'

Odd people. In Dorset the chat would have been about lobelias and the special offers at the garden centre. Hetty shook her head, a little too vigorously. 'No, you can't. Don't. Come and talk to me instead. Cry on my shoulder. Life goes on. It must.'

'Such wisdom, Hetty. Have you learned that already?'

They danced without speaking for a few minutes. As the tune changed to a slower tempo Markus pulled her closer. She felt quite drunk but, as he had suggested, quite secure in his arms. He would not lie to her. With her, he was not playing a game.

'Markus, can I ask you something?'

'Go ahead.'

'What's a fag-hag?'

He burst out laughing and stopped dancing. 'Why? Where did that come from?'

'My daughter. What does it mean? Come on, Markus, I'm a sea-green innocent. You taught Christian – you can teach me.'

He started dancing again, and this time they moved easily together, though it was becoming extraordinarily difficult to control her feet. 'Well, Hetty, it means a woman who likes to go round with homosexuals. Sometimes that suggests she is not interested in sex. But she likes to be seen with men, as a kind of cover.'

'What's wrong with that?'

'I'm not sure anything is *wrong* with it. It has the

advantage, of course, that she doesn't see the men she's with as sex objects – provided she accepts that they are not pursuing her for sex, either. Some women, unfortunately, have a mission to convert men like us. They argue that if a man can be persuaded to be gay, he can be unpersuaded. It can be a rotten business.'

'It must be quite nice, not to be seen as a sex object,' Hetty mused. The room was moving round, faster than their dancing could account for. 'Golly, I do believe I'm pissed . . . Nice feeling. Not a sex object. Not to have sex on the brain. I'm supposed to be like that, apparently. To think naughty thoughts all the time. Everyone says so.'

Markus was chuckling. 'Sex does matter. Most people can't imagine life without it.'

'Um, most people in this room. That's what couples are for. Had plenty of it, in my time. Husband was a big randy bloke. But what I want – what I'd *really* like . . .'

'What's that?' Markus smiled. Hetty had the fuzzy impression he was holding her up.

'I'd like,' Hetty said with heartfelt emphasis, 'to be seen as a *person*, first and foremost. A human being.'

'Yes,' said Markus. '*In vino veritas*, perhaps, eh, Hetty?'

'A person. Not a blob of flesh. Not sex-mad. Gotta brain . . . A person . . .'

But she was sliding gently from his arms and to the floor, a blissful smile on her face, her eyes closed.

Markus and Christian conferred, lifted her on to the sofa and covered her with a duvet. Thomas the cat emerged and curled up by her knees. The company then carried on dancing, till the wine was gone: Rosa with Richard, Stuart with Flo, the Colonel with his lady and with Doris, alternately; Markus with Doris and with Hetty's mother, with Annabel and, at last, as the candles burned low, with Christian. Then they stacked the empty bottles neatly, left the dirty glasses in rows in the kitchen, blew out the guttering wicks, turned out the lights, and shut the door behind them.

CHAPTER SEVEN

Morning After

The racket resembled power-drills blasting inside her head. Her mouth was coated in rusty brown fur. Hetty coughed and rolled over. What was she doing on the sofa? And what in God's name was that din? Why wouldn't it stop?

The phone – *the bloody phone*. Hetty staggered to the other side of the room, her eyes half shut, dragging the duvet with her.

'Darling!' It was Clarissa. 'How did the house-warming go? Was it a great success?'

'Erggh,' said Hetty, and coughed. 'Just a minute.'

The tinkle of running water from the tap was like surf pounding a beach. She forced herself to drink two glasses, ignoring the squawking from the phone. 'Yeah,' she said, into the mouthpiece. 'Clarissa, what's your cure for a hangover?'

'You have a hangover?' The voice was astonished.

'Either that, or a brain tumour.'

'Hair of the dog, Robin always says.'

'Eh?'

'Have another drink. A whisky. D'you want me to come over? Is the place a mess?'

Hetty forced her eyes to open and peered slowly around. 'No, tidy. Tidier than before.'

'Sounds like it was some party.' A grunt came from the phone. 'Better than the boring function we went to last night. Coronation chicken! I ask you!'

'My mother's got a boyfriend.'

'What did you say? How do you know?'

'They were here. Smooching. My mother looked a million dollars. Not giving up her pension; though.'

'Hetty, you're not making sense. Stay there, I'll be with you in an hour. Take two aspirin and go back to bed.'

'Not been to bed . . .' Hetty replied, but the phone had clicked. She sat down on the floor and pulled the duvet carefully over her shoulders. 'Ooo-ooh . . .'

Clarissa arrived, full of solicitude, curiosity like an aura. Her eyes goggled at the bottles, the empty glasses and plates. The revellers' consideration had not extended to washing up; perhaps, however, their hands had been so unsteady that it was better they hadn't.

'How many people did you have here?' she demanded. 'An entire army?'

'Feels like an army inside my head,' Hetty muttered. ''Bout twenty. Less. Boy, can they *drink*.'

'You too,' commented Clarissa. 'I've never seen you like this.'

The aspirins were having a soothing effect. 'I used to be the maestro. Now I'm one of the players.'

'Come again?'

'Couldn't disgrace my lovely husband, could I? I never drank much. He did, sometimes. Had to put him to bed. He felt sorry for himself for days.'

'Hetty, I don't like this.' Clarissa had filled the washing-up bowl, removed six rings, the charm bracelet and the Rolex, and began to sluice the glasses. 'Are you going to make a habit of drinking yourself into a stupor? And did I catch you saying that you didn't go to bed?'

'They put me on the sofa,' Hetty admitted. 'Slept it off there. Don't nag, Clarissa. I'm feeling lousy. It's my life, anyway.' She giggled. 'Lot more fun than rubber chicken, as you said. Or compared with Hoovering up round Stephen and Peter.'

Clarissa stood, one hand on her hip, a tea-towel in the other. 'You'll be back. Not with Stephen, maybe, but with another chap in a beautiful house with a garden big enough to keep you busy and a four-wheel drive in the garage. My image of you, dear girl, is on your knees in the shrubbery putting in bulbs, not on the floor with your head in your hands. We *have* to fix you up, Hetty. Otherwise – just look at you. You'll be going to the dogs in no time.'

But Hetty was sliding back into sleep. 'Not dogs,' she mumbled. 'Cat. Named Thomas.'

'Who? What did you say? Thomas? Who's he? Is he married?'

Hetty reawoke, still horribly dehydrated, her tongue sour-tasting and too large for her mouth. This time she was in her bed. It was dusk. The phone was ringing once more. She sat up cautiously.

Clarissa had moved the new vase with Christian's flowers to the bedside. On the table a wrapped package suspiciously like a small box of Quality Street had appeared, with a card: 'Thank you. From Jane and Andy McDonald and family.' Other than that, there were no thank-you notes, no other acknowledgements. It was as if the event had vanished completely from the memories of all the participants. Except hers.

The phone stopped, then began to trill once more. She trudged across to pick it up.

'Hello?'

'Oh, hi, Hetty. Is that you?'

'Who else would it be?' Her head still hurt, but the thudding was more muted.

'Don't be like that. It's Larry. Sorry we couldn't make it to your drinks thingy.'

He and Davinia would have stood out like sore thumbs, Hetty thought murderously. Larry would have engaged in vociferous argument with Christian, would have insulted Markus and have belittled Rosa's work on daytime TV – if she hadn't tried to get off with him first, in which case Davinia would have brained him with the nearest Moselle bottle. Had it been known they were coming, her mother would have arrived alone: the Colonel would not have been let loose anywhere near their inquisitive gaze. And Sally would have commiserated with them about Hetty taking leave of her senses. She herself would probably have behaved with her previous decorum – which is to say, would have drunk little, been a matronly dampener on other people's spirits, and been left at the end with a sensation of something missing. Instead of which –

'Sorry, Larry, I have a stonking head. What did you say?'

'You poor thing. Coming down with 'flu, are you? There's a lot of it going round. Look, we were wondering. Christmas and New Year we're heading to the cottage. D'you want to come?'

Larry had used his share of the legacy on their father's death to buy a farmhouse near Chichester. Hetty's had paid for a conservatory, which meant it was now gone.

'I'm not sure. What exactly are you planning? Lots of people down?'

'No,' Larry drawled. Hetty had the impression that he was not levelling with her. 'Boxing Day, yes, and the New Year weekend. But Davinia could do with some help kitchen-wise, and you are always *so* good with the children. When we go out, I mean.'

'How kind of you to think of me, Larry.' Hetty paused. 'Hope you don't mind if I say no.'

'But what else would you be doing?' Larry wheedled. 'Your first Christmas since the divorce? You can't spend it on your own. And you'd be doing us a favour.'

'I realise that. I don't particularly want to spend it baby-sitting, either.' Hetty was surprised at her own tartness. 'I'm sorry. My sense of familial duty is drying up. I'll come down for the Boxing Day bash, if you'll have me, then go straight back.'

'I'm not sure,' Larry was dubious. 'I'll have to check with Davinia. We were rather counting on you, Hetty, now you've nothing much else on.'

'Right. Understood. Sorry I can't help out.'

The conversation ended. Hetty sat staring at the phone for several minutes with the request, its implications and her refusal still ringing in her ears. Then she blew a raspberry at the unprotesting instrument, and went to make herself a cup of tea.

'I can't go on! I can't! I can't!'

The chubby woman, her breasts bulbous in a scoop-neck top, bare legs blue and mottled in spiky-heeled shoes, bottle-blonde hair straggling from an insecure topknot, dabbed furiously at her eyes and left panda-like smudges on both cheeks.

'But why not? You've got it pat. And you'll look smashing on the box. Think of it – your friends will be so envious,' Hetty cooed, and squatted down beside her.

'They won't. They'll laugh at me.' The woman sniffed. 'I mean, they don't know I'm a kissogram, do they?'

'But that's the whole point. You're a kissogram who wants to give up for the sake of your little girl. That's your dilemma. Everyone will admire you.'

'You think so?'

'I'm sure of it,' said Hetty, with every scrap of sincerity at her command. 'People will stop you in the street and con-gratulate you. They'll say you're a terrific mother.'

The woman pondered, then heaved herself slowly to her feet and tugged the micro-skirt down over thighs dimpled with cellulite. She hiccuped.

'Come on. I'll take you back to Makeup. They'll soon have you at your best. You don't want people to see you upset, now, do you?'

Gently but firmly Hetty propelled the reluctant guest out of the studio. Behind her Rosa, clipboard in hand, mouthed a frantic 'Thank you.'

A few moments later Hetty returned as the woman, her

Pan-stick reapplied, tottered on to the podium for the sound check.

'Well done,' came a chuckle at her ear.

'I didn't do much, Father Roger,' Hetty answered. 'Bit like trying to get a naughty child back to school.'

'Ye-e-es, quite.' Father Roger tweaked his cassock. He was of medium height and indeterminate shape under the black serge. His robe was not the badge of a particular order, Hetty had ascertained, since he was High Anglican, not Roman Catholic. His head was almost bald, his jaw clean-shaven. His brown eyes twinkled and his expression, as usual, shone with bonhomie. 'Have you seen the next one?'

Hetty consulted her notes. 'Aimée and her mother. The child who wants her belly-button pierced?'

'And Mother says no. If I wasn't a priest, and a believer in the essential goodness of all mankind, I'd have that child whipped.'

'Makes you glad you never had them?'

'Rather.'

Father Roger was the permanent member of the panel on *Tell Me All*, and something of a media star in the capital. He was joined by various minor celebrities, mainly from soap operas, of varying loquacity and perception. The presenter was a lofty young man who played with his tie and had never acknowledged Hetty's existence; he was, it was said, destined for higher things.

'I love the way you deal with them,' Hetty confided. 'And you're so sharp sometimes. You get away with it when others wouldn't.'

'I didn't intend to reduce that stripper to tears, but she was a prize fool,' Father Roger grunted. 'Fancy! "How am I to tell my children that they have four different fathers? I'm so ashamed!" Idiot. If it worried her that much, she should have stuck with one chap. Or used contraception. As for keeping it a secret – I mean, Hetty, they act like this is a private conversation, don't they?'

'And the day after it's broadcast they'll wish they hadn't come near us.' Hetty was laughing. 'All human frailty is here. But that stripper wasn't so dumb. Crocodile tears, I reckon. She had a knowing air about her.'

'Precisely. She was touting for business. See how she leered at the camera? Vanity, thy name is woman. Harrumph!' And he scuttled away to take his seat on the set.

Most of the 'guests' of the programme were self-referred. They came in answer to advertisements placed in various free newspapers round the country. Others, especially those with disabilities, were recommended by interest groups. Hetty had been moved by the young woman recovering from ME, who had haltingly explained what the condition had meant to her. Others were more sly, less genuine. The skill, she had discovered, was not in persuading guests to appear: on the contrary, the dottier their situation, the more eager they could be. The British disease, from the vantage-point of the broadcaster, was exhibitionism – 'My husband is sleeping with my mother' cases were two a penny, had Rosa allowed them anywhere near the studio – but shaping issues into dilemmas that could be argued about and engage audiences was less simple.

'Who's on this afternoon?' a voice hissed in her ear. It was Kate, the chummiest of the researchers, a tall girl in spectacles.

'The jazz player,' Hetty hissed back.

'Oh, God, not him.'

'You know him?'

'Sort of. I used to work on *Kilroy*, and he was on that.

And he's been on *Vanessa*, and *Good Morning*, and *Thursday Night Live*. He makes quite a career of it. They do the rounds, you know.'

'Makes a career of it? What d'you mean?'

'Two hundred and fifty pounds fee, he said, or he wouldn't appear. But he does give a superb performance. Same every time, but totally reliable.'

'And his dilemma is never resolved?'

'Never. He's so convincing – what is it? Ah, yes. "I'm so gorgeous the women are all over me. How do I fight them off?" or some such.'

'D'you think he's gorgeous?'

'Me?' Kate snorted. 'You've got to be joking. The only person round here I think is gorgeous is Rosa, but she prefers the camera crew. The tattier the better. Heartbreaking.'

The jazz player was in his mid-thirties, had been married twice and was now, by his own claim, footloose and fancy-free. The name he wished to be known by was Al. He was in a corner of the canteen, showily playing snatches on a tenor saxophone to one of the servers. Chatting her up, at a guess. Hetty examined him from a distance. He was losing his hair and had grown the rest longer to compensate. The blond locks curled, quite fetchingly, on his shoulders. The black leather jacket, navy open-necked shirt and red neckerchief gave him a louche air. His legs were thin in their black corduroy trousers.

He immediately caught her eye. 'Eddie, isn't it?' he called. 'Are we on yet?'

The server slid regretfully away. The jazz player put down his instrument and patted the seat beside him. 'Come and keep me company,' he invited. 'I get nervous.'

Hetty grinned. 'What, you? A professional performer? I hear you've done this once or twice before.'

'Yes, well.' His face was shifty. 'I explained that when we talked on the phone. Did I get your name right?'

'Hetty.'

'And your phone number's . . .' He quoted it correctly. 'I never forget a phone number. Especially when it belongs to an attractive lady.'

'You flatter me.' Her tone was faintly sarcastic, but he seemed to take it as flirtation.

'A lovely dame like you must have lots of fellas wanting your private number. I bet you keep 'em hanging on, don't you?'

She did not answer, though the temptation to put him in his place was strong. Yet what was his place? Should she tell him she was not available? What was the language for that? She could say she was married, though that was no longer true. She could imply she was spoken for, but doubted she was a good enough liar. Instead she smiled and tried to look enigmatic. His snigger suggested she had not entirely succeeded.

'D'you like my music, Hetty?' He stroked the saxophone.

'I liked listening to you. I can't claim to know much about it.'

'Well, now, you could learn. If I were to call this 'ere number and invite you out for a drink some time, would you slam the phone down on me?'

'Of course not.' This was real devotion to duty. She could maintain the pretence at least until his piece had been satisfactorily recorded. He was wearing a scent, an aftershave or spray, reeking of eucalyptus. It made her nose wrinkle.

'Then I'll do that.'

'I think I'm a bit old for you, Al,' Hetty excused herself.

'No, you're not. Don't talk like that. I *love* mature women.'

'That shows you have discrimination and taste,' Hetty replied drily. She checked her watch. 'I'd better get you and your horn into Makeup. You'll be on in a minute.'

He rose and lunged. She turned her head sharply sideways; he managed nevertheless to plant a wet kiss, not on her lips but on her burning cheek. The eucalyptus was excessive and made her want to sneeze. 'Nice, huh? More where that came from. I'll ring you.'

Rosa had been held up in the gallery, checking rushes. As the programme ended she joined the crew in a briefing session for the next day's shooting. The hair was wilder, the black skin shinier and healthier, the energy more exuberant than ever. This time she was wearing an orange silk minidress. Her legs were still those of a twenty-year-old. She reminds me of the liquorice sticks we had as children, Hetty thought: so delicious you could eat her.

'Hey! What a life!' She squeezed Hetty's arm affectionately. 'You enjoying yourself, hon? You seem to be making out okay.'

'I'm making out, fine,' Hetty answered. Was this another new language? 'I love it.'

'You're brilliant at the job. The guests like you and trust you. That's always a plus.' Rosa gave her a flashing smile. 'I forgot to thank you for inviting me to your party. It turned out quite a night, didn't it? *And* since . . .'

'Since?'

Rosa nudged her playfully. 'Oh, sure. You know. Richard.'

'You've been seeing Richard?'

Rosa giggled. 'Yeah. Seeing quite a lot of him. *Terrific*

body. Pecs like ski jumps and a butt like two walnuts. And nuts like . . .'

'I can imagine. But I'd have thought he was a bit young – for us, I mean?'

'What? Six or seven years' difference? Don't be so old-fashioned. Listen, Hetty, he may be kidding those teenagers in the next-door flat that he's only thirty, but he's closer to our age, believe me.'

'Another guy who makes a career of it,' Hetty commented, cautiously.

'Say again?'

'Mid-forties, still playing the field. Never stops long enough for anyone to catch him. Has a harem on the go, almost. What's the correct description? Serial philanderer?'

'Perfect. An experienced sexy bloke who's *not* after my money. Who could ask for more?'

Hetty laughed, then turned away. Rosa's riposte seemed too ready an acceptance of standards sharply lowered. *She* could ask for more. A lot more. And could manage with much less. But Rosa's pleasure in life infected her, and left her pensive.

CHAPTER EIGHT

Home Truths

The nights were drawing in; the shortest day loomed. Hetty and Doris sat in the latter's kitchen comforted by a pot of tea. In the garden of The Swallows a few hellebore flowers peeped out under the sodden bushes, pale heads nodding like forlorn refugees. Out of the window, Hetty saw Thomas sniff the pathetic clumps with lordly indifference.

'Doris, what do people do round here for Christmas?'

The old lady considered. 'Carol concert and Midnight Mass, if you're religious. I go to St Veronica's. It's that trendy vicar – Father Roger, that's him. Barrel of laughs. The jokes he tells from the pulpit – he's on telly, did you know?'

'Father Roger? Yes, he's on our programme.' Hetty explained the connection.

Doris gaped, suddenly respectful, then wily. 'D'you ever get spare tickets for the audience?'

'You can come every week, if you like. We're having awful trouble getting enough bottoms to fill seats. These days, appearing on television doesn't quite compete with staying at home to watch it, apparently.'

'Ooh, yes! I'd love to. Can I bring Thomas?'

'No!'

Doris poured another cup of tea. Her hand slid to the pocket of her apron. 'I could tell your future in the tarot cards, if you like,' she offered. She put the pack on the table.

A chill touched Hetty around the nape of her neck. 'Have you second sight, Doris?'

'Maybe,' the old woman said. She began slowly, deliberately to shuffle the cards, their colours vibrant under her thick fingers. 'My grandmother was supposed to have Romany blood. But, then, they said that of everyone in the East End when I was a kid.'

'The answer to that one's no, too, Doris,' said Hetty reluctantly. 'I wouldn't feel comfortable. If our future were set in the stars, or in the cards, there'd be no point in us trying to do better, would there? Anyhow, I'm not sure I'm ready to know what Fate has in store for me.'

'Not sure I believe it either,' Doris answered, her eyes lowered. 'But when you hear some people's misfortunes, however much they've tried, you do wonder.'

Her voice had such a hollow note that Hetty stared at her. But the moment had gone, and the cards had been returned to their hiding-place.

It was acutely embarrassing, particularly when the guest was a distinguished, smartly dressed man, who sat, bemused but patient, as Bob the floor-manager ran his ragged troops through their paces.

The four rostrum cameras were trained on the rows of seats. Most were empty.

Instead of serried ranks of enthusiastic supporters, only about thirty people had turned up, mainly a minibus-load of pensioners from a Darby and Joan club. Most of those seemed too far gone to follow a single word. Several shoppers had been dragged from the street with the plea that they need only stay for half an hour to rest their feet, then have a cup of tea – *after* the recording, not before. Three drunks had slouched in from the local pub. A trio of giggling gum-chewing schoolboys in multi-coloured windcheaters three sizes too large and huge trainers, unlaced and loose, were the sole occupants at the back. The entire 'audience' was bunched together in the middle of the rows to make it appear to the cameras that the studio was packed.

Bob was squinting upwards at a screen. 'No,' he squawked. '*Don't* stare at the monitors – look at Johnnie there.'

The presenter waved a languid hand. Every eye swivelled naturally to Bob, the speaker, except those already shut. The shrunken crone in the front row was dozing and threatening to slide off her chair. Bob prodded her tentatively with his foot; she revived with a snort. He leaped sideways at the boys. 'And no waving your arms or pulling faces, either.' He scowled. 'Why aren't you at school, anyway?'

'Baker day,' the boys chortled in unison. One started blowing lurid pink bubbles. 'We're let off early.'

'What's a Baker day?' Hetty saw that Bob instantly regretted asking, but the boys were happy to enlighten him.

'For training our teachers. To give 'em some ejjicashun. So they can teach us be'er.'

'Is it effective?' Hetty asked under her breath, then gazed askance at the restless imps. 'Not a chance.'

'Everyone ready?' Bob demanded. 'Eyes on Johnnie. Big smiles, come *on*.'

He danced on the spot, clapping his hands over his head, the clipboard papers flapping about. One leaf detached itself and floated to the floor and he scrabbled to catch it, cursing. The audience stirred, shuffled and clapped in a desultory fashion.

'No, no. That won't do. You're watching the best programme on telly! You're going to be on telly yourselves!'

That did it, though it took two more attempts before Bob was satisfied. The required noise level was achieved eventually by playing the first tape over in synch, so that it sounded as if double the numbers were present. Thus encouraged, the boys and the drunks whooped and hollered, though he would not permit them to stamp their boots. 'The set'll collapse,' he explained ominously. The boys glanced down anxiously.

'Okay. On your feet. To your left – one, two, three, go!!'

The entire crowd rose, collected itself and its belongings and shuffled ten paces to the left, then with much grumbling (and a few guffaws from the boys) settled itself once more in front of a different part of the backdrop.

Bob pointed at Johnnie. 'Again! Big smiles! And let's hear you!!'

The drinkers indulged themselves, this time, in hearty cheering. Bob's eyes lit up. 'That's more like it. Once more!'

Hetty found herself observing the guest sitting pensively on set, miked-up and ready. He was a banker in his forties, with a tanned, handsome face and a trim haircut silvering above his ears. He had told Kate, who had handled the contact, that he was agonising whether to give up the financial world in order to follow his dream, to be a writer. Nicholas was his name. Father Roger thought he was a bit of a poseur.

Hetty had taken his part. 'A man like that,' she had

argued, 'would have to be very brave to abandon everything and reach out for the unknown. It's admirable.'

Such a decision, for a man, had parallels with her own in divorcing Stephen and quitting the cosy world of marriage and coupledom. Maybe Nicholas, too, felt he had little choice, if restlessness had come to the fore. But the future would still be a shock. His security would vanish, all previous points of reference be destroyed. He would need every scrap of self-confidence to survive.

In herself, the ache for security was vividly present, reawakened each Sunday evening as she sat down to sort out her bills. At the council of war Sally had painted a gloomy scenario: a reflection of her own fears, perhaps, or of her unsatisfactory experience so far. Clarissa, also, had common sense on her side. Marriage was a meal ticket. It had been wonderful not to worry about money, to spend whatever was necessary, not to puzzle why her bank account emptied so fast. Stephen was not the only one spoiled under the old regime. She had been too, and she missed it.

A man like Nicholas might be totally sympathetic. Hetty began to examine their guest with greater interest. He did not seem like a poseur – Father Roger could be too worldly wise altogether. Did Nicholas have a wife or partner? Was he in any way available? His personal details were on the computer; she could bring them up without revealing her reasons to anyone. That would also give his home phone number.

She watched Rosa dashing about: the lady exuded *joie de vivre*, though there was no suggestion she was in love with this Richard. A great sex life, it was no more than that. Nothing would come of it, but although she felt superior, Hetty could not suppress a niggling desire to follow suit. Sex with a masculine man. A professional, a lover who could make a woman's body sing. Pecs like – what had she said? Oh, lucky Rosa.

Hetty checked herself. She was *not* in the business of chasing men. So soon after the break-up it did not seem either dignified or a responsible way to behave. Not least, because it takes an age for scar tissue to heal. The rebound from an unhappy marriage was probably the worst possible springboard for a relationship.

Pity . . .

Bob was still leaping about but with relief on his features. He had persuaded the able-bodied audience, who were wearying of the game, to rise and move twenty seats to their right. Johnnie was standing before them on the balls of his feet, facing camera one, and was reading from autocue the bouncy words of introduction to *Tell Me All*.

Suddenly Bob screamed like a banshee, yelled, 'Stop, stop,' and lunged at the nearest schoolboy, dragging him out by the scruff of his neck. 'I saw you, you horrible insect. Get out, and your friends with you. *Now.*' He stood panting and running his finger under his collar. The boys hooted, made obscene gestures and slouched to the exit.

'What were they doing?' Hetty whispered to Kate.

'Mouthing FUCK at the camera. Right behind Johnnie's head. Appropriate, somehow.'

'Larry and Davinia have asked me to have a word with you. They're terribly keen that you should go there for the holidays.'

The takeaway curry from the shop by the station had been an experiment. Not entirely successful, Hetty decided, as she nibbled the remaining poppadum. The excruciating

Delia had a recipe for curried beef in yoghurt and another for Sri Lankan egg with garlic, root ginger, turmeric (Sainsbury's had it), Madras curry powder and creamed coconut. Maybe that would be a better bet next time Sally came. She poured the rest of the chilled Riesling into her daughter's glass. 'Larry and Davinia want a chief cook, bottlewasher and baby-sitter for those two horrible little boys, Sally. I'm not going.'

'Heavens, Mum, what has got into you? And you're being unfair. *They* are only trying to be supportive.'

How liberating wine is, Hetty reflected. 'Rot. I've said I'll go as a house-guest, but not otherwise. That flattened their enthusiasm.'

'But what else will you do?'

'Not sure. Maybe not much, other than go to church. I don't intend to start cooking a turkey. Or to feel guilty, whatever decisions I make. That I have promised myself.' She eyed her daughter. 'What about you?'

'Well, Dad says I can spend Christmas in Dorset, if I want. He and – they will be having a few friends round, nothing elaborate. He says you'd be welcome.'

'How very cordial.' Hetty was aware that her tone was curt.

'He told me, when she wasn't listening, that he was dreading the holiday. It'd remind him of the kind of get-togethers we used to have.'

'Oh, my. Does that mean the new girlfriend can't cook?'

'It's not that. She has a name – Natalie. They want to be civilised, honestly, Mum. You wouldn't consider –?'

'I would not. I couldn't. Worse than Larry's, that'd be.'

There was a silence. Hetty reopened: 'You haven't answered me. Where will you and whatsisname be over the holiday? Incidentally, am I ever going to meet him?'

'Erik'll be in Sweden – that's the roster. I could volunteer for holiday duty, I suppose. Triple pay, plus days off in lieu.'

'Doesn't sound too exciting.' Hetty guessed that Erik would be with his family, and that Sally knew it. His wife? His children?

'No, well, it isn't.' Sally drained her glass and ignored Hetty's second question. 'Men! I despair, sometimes, Mum. That's why I'd much rather you had a proper Christmas, either with us at home or with my uncle and aunt. Peter'd come, instead of going to his pals. Maybe we could persuade Grandma to stay as well, and Larry and Davinia might pop in with the boys before they go to Chichester. That'd be great.'

'It'd be a disaster, Sally.' Hetty suddenly felt sorry for her wistful daughter. 'We'd fight or get maudlin or paranoid. Your dad would creep around not sure whether to show off his new love or hide her. That's not fair – I'm sure she . . . *Natalie* is quite, er, nice. The village would be *agog*. And my brother! God help us. Larry and Davinia would carp and fidget, their boys would vandalise something – they're incapable of walking past an ornament without touching or a blank space without scribbling on it. I'd end up in tears. Nobody'd eat the bloody turkey – nobody in our family likes turkey anyway, never did.' She paused for breath.

'Don't,' Sally begged. 'It's so ghastly. My whole life is disintegrating.'

I am responsible for this, Hetty thought. Her voice softened. 'Poor baby. I hadn't realised how devastated you'd be. I assumed, with you being older, that you wouldn't be affected, but that's not so. Is Peter the same?'

'No, not him. Water off a duck's back. He has plenty of mates. They'll be delighted to have him.'

Hetty cleared away the plates and discarded the uneaten food. 'I'm not averse to advice, Sally,' she ventured quietly. 'What – apart from going backwards – do you think I should do? Not just Christmas, that's of minor importance. Generally.'

'Golly.' Sally cradled her almost empty glass. Hetty wondered whether to open another bottle of wine; she had laid in quite a substantial stock, with the help of Malcolm Gluck and *Superplonk*, but a glance at her daughter's woeful face decided her against it. There was a limit to the volume of *vino veritas* a person could take, especially from a virtual stranger.

Her daughter sighed. 'Being on your own isn't normal. I still think you should aim at finding another chap. Maybe not next week, I grant you. And p'raps somebody different from Dad, who won't let you down. But you'll need to take action, now.'

'In what way?'

Sally's eyes roamed over her mother. Hetty felt uneasy under the scrutiny. She went to the mantelpiece where she twiddled the glass perfume phials, which she had come to think of as representing her various options. One had got broken at the house-warming: repaired, it was covered in cracks, its surface misshapen with tiny beads of glue.

'Come on, Sally. What exactly do you have in mind? If I'm to go chasing men, as you seem to think I must, what steps do I take? Go to an agency? Answer adverts?'

'Something else first.' Sally seemed to wish she had never started. Then she gulped down the remaining wine and spoke in a rush. 'Forgive me, but at the moment you wouldn't attract a blind man at midnight in a dark alley, Mum. Look at you – you're two stone overweight and your roots are showing. You need to get fit and firm. More like Grandma. Maybe she can fix you up with one of her friends. Or on second thoughts,' she had caught Hetty's glare, 'maybe not. But you see what I mean?'

'I do,' said Hetty frostily. Her mind was racing. 'I did ask. Heavens, we've had more conversation, shared more – what can I call it? intimacy, I suppose – in the last few months, Sally, than ever before. Life since my divorce is turning out more a voyage of discovery than a shipwreck.'

The girl kept her eyes averted. 'Sorry. That was rude of me.'

Hetty touched her hand. 'I love you, Sally, and I want to be close to you.'

'Me too, Mum,' was all her daughter could manage. I didn't even teach her to say I love you, Hetty reflected sadly.

'Tell you what, Sally, how about a few days at a health farm?'

'Exactly. That would help.'

Hetty took a deep breath. 'We could kill two birds with one stone, and neither would be a turkey. How about we take a double room, you and I, over the holiday, and go together? Do you think we could get along?'

Sally began to cry. She touched her mother's hand. There was a long hiatus, during which Hetty could hear only the beat of her own heart and the damp gulps of her daughter.

At last Sally gave a short, rueful laugh. 'Why not? Yes. We can *try*. At least I could keep an eye on you. I'll make it my Christmas present. How about that?'

CHAPTER NINE

Sex and the Single Girl

'Hi. Al here. We met when I was on your show. How are you? Listen, I meant it when I said I'd like to see you again. You're a foxy lady, y'know? Come and have a drink with me. Call me . . .'

'What on earth would a man like that see in a woman like me?' Hetty pondered. What does he mean by "foxy"?'

She stood in front of the mirror, the full-length one attached to the wardrobe door, and made an honest appraisal of herself. Sally had been brutally accurate. Two excess stones – which would not be shifted by four days' indulgence at a health farm. She lifted her sweater and prodded her midriff. Her fingers sank into yielding flesh. Allure and flab were mutually incompatible. But the prospect of sweating it out in a gym or joining the morose joggers who trundled every evening around the common filled her with dread.

'I think I'll get a bike,' Hetty resolved, without any great conviction. A bike could take her to the studio, and offered potential at weekends: Richmond Park and Wimbledon Common were within reasonable distance. Box Hill – no, *not* Box Hill. Hampton Court: yes. In the spring she could take a picnic and a novel. That would keep her out of trouble. Or were bikers attractive men? Might she meet someone?

'Stop it,' she rebuked herself, and twisted sideways. The bulge of her backside brought a wave of despair. Did she want it even larger, more muscular? 'Weight Watchers,' Hetty told herself gloomily. '*And* the bike. Oh, Lord.'

She played Al's message again and, after a moment's hesitation, wrote down the number. If desperate, she might use it. Desperate for what? Hetty turned her back on the mirror. What could Al give her that she didn't have already?

Sex . . . What was on offer was a night in the sack. With a new man. Maybe lots of nights in the sack. Nothing else: no commitment, no promises of undying love. Sex, pure and simple, and with a younger, slimmer man, who was clearly well up in the sensual arts. No more and no less.

Her body thrilled to the idea. Hetty pulled up the sweater once more, and ran her hands over her breasts in their Marks and Spencer bra. To her surprise, her nipples stiffened at once. She reached back and unhooked the bra, pulled the sweater over her head and looked at herself. Then she ran her hands again over her breasts, pressing and squeezing, as a man might. Her body tensed and she gasped. 'Good Lord,' she murmured. 'I *do* miss it. Didn't think I did, but I do.'

In the early days of their marriage their love-life had been hectic and sweaty. She and Stephen had explored together with manuals. They read the *Kama Sutra* and, with much laughter, tried the positions. They teased each other about how many times they could perform, until the night he ricked his back. After that they had settled into a comfortable regime, as most married couples do.

When had it started to fade? Hetty reached for her bra and sweater and dressed pensively. On the shelf stood photographs of those happier years, of herself with Peter and Sally as small children. As she had become engrossed in motherhood, as Stephen made enough to buy first a house in Notting Hill Gate (it was not so fashionable in those days), then the property in Dorset, her eyes had been taken off the ball. The solidity of their marriage had not been in question but that *urgency* had no longer been present. They no longer had to prove anything to each other. Occasionally, Hetty wondered if her husband wasn't taking too much for granted. Once, after a speedy early-morning session, he had left the bed and trotted to the bathroom. A few minutes later she had glimpsed him through the door, seated on the lavatory, engrossed in the business pages.

But as their friends' partnerships broke up and the Clarksons' proved more durable, she'd reminded herself she had a lot to be thankful for. Sex wasn't everything. Middle-aged people did not expect to be sexual athletes. A man over fifty had less *oomph*. Except that he was secretly devoting an increasing proportion of his *oomph* to another woman, wife of a neighbour, while contriving to keep his wife on board. The strong marriage in which both had basked had become a romantic fiction.

Now, nothing. No sex of any kind with anyone. Hetty sighed, and rubbed her thighs. A warmth she had almost forgotten was rekindled; it chafed and throbbed. She bit her lip, pressed her knees together. *Celibacy.* A cruel, unfamiliar word for something so intimate. So barren. So unaccustomed and uncomfortable.

Her reaction intrigued her. The warmth between her legs, the twinge in her groin, meant that she needed sex. It would be miserable to live without it indefinitely. Celibacy did not feel natural. Not for her. Sleeping alone was not a problem. She was working so hard at the studio that afterwards she was not much use for anything in company other than to drink a glass of wine, or possibly see a movie at the cinema across the common. Doris was happy to oblige for either, or her mother or Sally, though Sally could be a morose and uncommunicative companion. Probably for the same reason: the Britannia job was punishing.

Absentmindedly Hetty pottered about. The orderliness of her home soothed her. The bed was made as she liked it with four big lace-fringed pillows; cosmetics and face creams were arranged neatly on the window-ledge beside a pot of anemones and a doll from Tahiti, a gift from Sally. Her clothes, such as they were, hung in mute rows in the wardrobe, not flung about collecting fluff and making the place untidy. In the kitchen, plates were stacked by size in the cupboards, a clean National Trust tea towel was draped over the sink, her favourite brand of ground coffee sat in the canister. The air was fresh: there were no overflowing ashtrays. How on earth would she cope with an invasion, for any reason, by another human being?

But the sex, the sex. What was the answer to that? Al, or someone like him? A more refined creature – Nicholas, whose details still nestled in the computer? Or a man she had never met – via an advert, say, in a respectable newspaper?

It got dark so early. Hetty went to the window to draw the curtains. Down by the common, which she could just glimpse, the street-lights were coming on. The great stretch of windswept turf was supposed to be unsafe at night, though Hetty had walked across it several times without being approached. It stood to reason: the hooded loiterers, she guessed, were seeking other men.

A jogger bounced by on the far side of the road, a young blonde female, her pony-tail swinging, eyes half shut. Headphones protected her ears from the cold; the thin black wire flapped down her back to the Walkman hitched to her belt. What was she listening to? Bach? Oasis? Maeve Binchy? *Teach Yourself Japanese?*

The light from the doorway of the flats caught an aureole of golden hair. She would know that glorious head any-where, even from the back: Christian, his hands thrust deep into the pockets of his leather jacket. He did not glance up. His show was a success; he would have to leave for the the-atre soon. Was he going shopping?

As Hetty watched idly, her hand on the curtains, she saw Christian stand at the roadside, waiting for traffic to clear. Then he crossed over and strode purposefully towards the shrubbery on the northern side, as if he knew what he was looking for.

'Julia Roberts may be a pretty woman, but she's a stinker as an actress.'

'Yes,' Hetty answered cautiously. 'But what wouldn't I give for a face like that?'

'Looks aren't *everything*. But I grant you, they matter.'

Hetty and her mother were walking back after the film on the well-lit pavement along the south side of the common, their arms linked against the chill wind. Peggy's stylish high heels clicked along the paving stones next to Hetty's mute flatties. That made the older woman two inches taller, and a great deal loftier and more confident.

'Mother,' said Hetty cautiously, 'when Dad died, what did you miss most?'

'Let me see. It's ten years ago. First, friendship. I was dreadfully lonely. We'd hardly spent a day apart in thirty years, other than when he was on active service. When he retired, we set about enjoying ourselves. His passion was following the tracks of ancient battles – Alexander, the Crusades, Wellington. Mine was following him, guide-book and maps in hand. It was fascinating. And lovely to share in a man's hobby: most men don't want their wives with them, but he did.'

'You were an intelligent companion, Mum. D'you still take an interest?'

'Not so much. Robert,' the moustachioed colonel, 'was in the Far East. Prisoner of war. I don't think he wants to see the swamps of Borneo ever again.'

'So how did you fill the gap?'

'Kept myself busy. Joined everything in sight. Took up golf, but it bored me rigid. Terribly boring people play golf, you know. Tried a bit of sailing, hated getting wet.'

'You never considered getting a paid job, did you?'

'No. It was different for my generation. We avoided going out to work, if we could. That was a last resort, and a negative comment on your husband's income.'

'And pension.'

Her mother smiled in the dark. 'And pension. I feel so sorry for the girls today, don't you? They feel they *must* work, that they'll lose their identity if they don't. Then one day the biological clock's ticking and they're thirty, forty. No babies. No husband. Only the wonderful career, which by then they're sick of. Poor things.'

'My friend Clarissa would agree. While I value my hard-won independence, she urges me to find a bloke who would keep me in luxury. Candidates galore, she says, though she hasn't come up with any names. But it'd feel like putting myself on the market. Akin to prostitution, almost.'

Hetty thought again fleetingly of Nicholas, the would-be writer, and his hesitant manner as he explained on camera why he had become dissatisfied. Independence mattered to him, too. He was more genuine a seeker than most on the programme. If, the day after the broadcast, a telephone call came from a competent professional adviser, he would hand in his notice without ado and bury himself in his laptop.

'Marriage was always a market,' her mother observed. 'At least we recognised it as such.'

Hetty waved her hands. 'But we can have it both ways. Women your age worked during the war – you had no option. At demob, wives were sent back to the kitchen – no option, again. But in the sixties we were the first girls to take advantage of university education, in big numbers. We had careers *and* we had families. We could have both.'

'You didn't. You chose to stay at home, like me. You sound regretful.'

'No. I could have carried on at the BBC. But I queened it in Dorset, Mother. I had my own little realm. Small beer, I know, compared with Stephen's responsibilities in an international firm. But there were days when I think he envied me none the less.'

'Women's lib wasn't all it was cracked up to be,' said her mother, sagely. 'Those feminists never seemed to me to be very happy, despite all their posturing.'

Hetty frowned. 'I don't know any feminists. Rosa's not an

activist but a sexy lady. Sally would be the closest, I suppose. She might say that happiness had nothing to do with it. Equality is a principle.'

'Happiness has everything to do with it. And if you can't achieve happiness, serenity is a fair substitute,' Peggy said, and squeezed her daughter's arm. 'Who wants to be equally miserable?'

They walked on in silence. Then Hetty tried again. 'Did you miss – anything else?'

'Like what?'

'Oh, *you* know.'

'Oh, that?'

'Er, yes.'

Hetty's mother laughed. 'Rather. Big man, your father.' There was another thoughtful silence. 'That's another stupid myth, that ladies my vintage didn't enjoy it. It depended on your luck, whether you had a sympathetic and skilled partner or not. I became a fan of Queen Victoria when I read that she had been warned, after her ninth child, that she was risking her health if she had any more. "Does that mean no more fun in bed?" she asked the doctor. Splendid woman.'

'D'you reckon she had it off with John Brown?'

'Oh, absolutely. Now there was a he-man. Especially if he looked anything like Billy Connolly in the movie. Did you see his –?' They giggled together.

'Does it – ah – improve as you get older?'

Her mother laughed. 'No, darling. It gets harder. For the men especially. It's a fact that most men over the age of sixty have prostate – waterworks – problems. And do avoid a chap on beta-blockers, unless you want a quiet life.'

'There are new drugs . . .'

'Viagra? Oh, sure. Recipe for a heart-attack. Anyway, they

don't help the rest of the time. The Colonel is a sweetie, but in Florida he spent most of his days asleep under a palm tree. Some Lothario *he* turned out to be.'

The dark created an envelope of intimacy. The two women walked steadily, their gait strikingly similar despite the different footwear. They did not look at each other. 'I never imagined you like that. My mother. It feels strange, almost wicked,' Hetty said.

'Every child believes its parents couldn't possibly have done it, every parent thinks their children absolutely shouldn't,' Peggy murmured. 'My mother never told me anything – one simply didn't mention it.'

'*We* don't talk about it. This is the first time we've ever broached the subject – realistically. I'm an adult, and so are you, but we still find it awkward . . .'

'What is it you're trying to tell me, Hetty?' Her mother stopped, concerned.

Hetty paused, then shook her head. 'No, nothing. It can be hard, living without a man. That's all. But I'm managing – somewhat to my own surprise.'

'Early days yet.' Her mother's eyes showed her curiosity.

'Early days. But I'm not going to be passive: I shall make things happen. Watch.'

Rosa picked up the dark green gherkin with a suggestive grin and popped the end in her mouth. 'You could try one of these,' she said.

Hetty flapped a hand helplessly and spluttered into her Diet Coke. 'Oh, don't, Rosa. You'll give me hysterics. You have such a filthy mind.'

'I have not,' Rosa responded, in mock indignation. She had suggested a pub lunch: it was a non-filming day, when

the tempo was slower. The studios had been booked by
other programme makers who had commandeered the canteen. Hetty and the researchers were crammed into a
crowded office, rented for the duration of the run. That
encouraged them to get out and about, Rosa had asserted:
guest contact was best done in the guests' own homes, not
down an impersonal phone-line.

'So how'm I doing?' Hetty asked.

'Well, Mike and Phil both think you're terrific. Bob is
wearing his heart on his sleeve for you. Kate thinks you're
cute. You're doing okay, Hetty.' Her eyes were alive.

'God, you've got sex on the brain today. I've told you, I'm
not in the market.'

'Not now or not ever?'

Hetty sighed. 'Lord, is it showing? The nun's habit is not
exactly me. Stephen and I got on quite well in that direction.
I did like it.'

'Most people like it.' Rosa was on her second pint of
Carling Special; Hetty had tried the strong lager, but had
found a single half set her head spinning all afternoon.

'I don't think so, Rosa. Lots of women loathe the physical
side, especially if they've had a bad experience.'

'Or if they've never met a man who's good at it.' Rosa
smacked her lips. 'Ho! Ho!'

'Can't take you anywhere.' A group of men at a nearby
table were ogling them and chuckling. 'I did wonder
whether I should try answering an advert or two. A few
phone calls can't do any harm. If they sound awful, I don't
have to meet them.'

'Yeah, brill. You could land yourself a couple of hot dates,
if nothing else.'

Hetty ignored Rosa's nudge. 'What do you watch out for

when you meet a stranger? How can you tell if he's going to be both nice and, well, capable?'

'Hell, Hetty, that's the oldest question in the world,' Rosa replied. 'You were married. You must know the signs better than I do. What are you after? D'you want to fall in love again and get hitched? You want him wealthy, tall, cultivated, what?'

'I don't know,' Hetty confessed. 'But it's ages now.' Her voice trailed off.

'Since what?'

'Since – since last time.'

'Oooh, I geddit. You're missing the sex, aren't you? That's natural. Healthy lass like you.'

Hetty nodded miserably. 'I feel such a fool. I'm a grown woman with a job I love. But something is definitely amiss. I feel – edgy. I'm beginning to dream. I had to wake myself up this morning, otherwise . . .'

'Lucky you. Wet dreams are wonderful.'

'Rosa! How can you?'

'As I take it,' her friend offered, 'you have several options. Apart from accepting when Artful Dodgers like Al call you, of course. You could do worse.' She began to tick off points on her fingers. 'You could certainly answer an advert. Or go to an agency. Or just let it be known that you're on the lookout – that can be surprisingly effective, though if you find the perfect man, do let me know.'

'How come you know about Al?' Hetty was mystified.

'Him? He calls everybody. Me, Kate, the girls. He took the phone number of that stripper, but he's on a hiding to nothing there – her husband'd razor the pair of 'em.'

Hetty stared gloomily into her glass. 'You don't believe the perfect man exists, do you? I thought that was a notion we discarded with our navy-blue school knickers.'

'Often the same night. Schoolboys! Acne, bad teeth and BO. Too much Old Spice, yuk. Plus a lot of fumbling in the dark. One laddie used to count out loud – he never got past five, then it was finished. No, I *don't* think so. But hunting for the perfect man is one of life's great games. It's the only search that counts.' The men nearby were listening intently. Whenever Rosa paused, they burst into barely suppressed guffaws.

Rosa picked up the last pickle and put her head to one side. 'You could explore one other possibility, Hetty,' she said.

'What's that?'

The shiny wet vegetable was wiggled provocatively back and forth. Then Rosa lowered it beneath the table, spread her legs, threw her head back and grunted loudly and rhythmically: '*Oh! Oh! Oh!*'

The male drinkers were transfixed. Rosa returned to the present with a hoot. 'That *always* works, Hetty. Though I wouldn't recommend it *quite* with a dill pickle.'

Near the pub where she and Rosa ate was a busy shopping centre. It was convenient to pop into during the lunch-hour for odd items or at the end of the day. Hetty was impressed by how many shops stayed open late and seemed to think nothing of providing a full range of services even as the streets emptied and commuters headed home.

She strolled about one damp afternoon, aware that she was searching for something but unsure what. Fresh fruit, a slice of chicken pie for supper, a bunch of daffodils were safely in her bag. She turned a corner and halted before a window painted matt dark blue all over so that not a chink of light could emerge from inside.

'ADULT SHOP,' the lettering stated. 'ITEMS ARE EXHIBITED HERE WHICH MAY OFFEND. PERSONS UNDER 18 NOT ADMITTED.'

'It's persons under eighteen who need this help most,' Hetty muttered. Not her kind of place at all. But, as she had realised in conversation with her mother and Rosa, big gaps existed in her knowledge. Maybe she should persuade Rosa to come here with her for a laugh. Maybe not. She gathered her courage and pushed open the door.

A blast of hot air hit her from an overhead blower; garish spotlights made her blink. A camera swivelled to examine her. There were no other customers. Hetty hid her mundane shopping behind her coat and stepped inside.

The sight that greeted her took her breath away. Straight ahead, ludicrous in the small space, was a six-foot blown-up plastic model of a woman, blatantly anatomically correct, trussed up in scarlet and black lace underwear. The crotch of the panties was open; shiny nipples protruded from slits in the bra. The hands with their red-painted fingernails displayed more underwear in jewel colours, vivid scraps of fabric leaving little to the imagination. Hetty had to squeeze past to get further into the shop.

On the far wall, on a sheet of silver paper were arranged a collection of whips, manacles, chains, studded dog collars and gloves and other leather gear. Facing her were several bookshelves and an array of well-thumbed magazines and videos. On the floor stood a three-foot-high erect phallus in the same salmon-pink plastic as the blow-up doll, but exaggeratedly ruched and lipped in purple. Nearby was a parody of a tinsel Christmas tree, its branches adorned with condom samples in blue, green, red, and Dayglo yellow, with knobs and prongs, 'guaranteed to keep the lady screaming for more'. They were, a scribbled note said,

available in ten different flavours from strawberry to chocolate mint. Some played musical tunes on ejaculation. Hetty
gulped.

'Can I 'elp yew?'

The thin girl at the counter, her open mouth masticating
gum, eyes hidden under lashes encrusted with violet mascara, barely glanced up. She was flicking through a magazine
of colour pictures of naked men. Hetty kept her eyes averted
from the multiple erections and gestured dumbly round the
stuffy room.

'Admirin' Mona, was yer?' The girl chewed. 'The doll. We
call 'er Mona. If you push her belly-button, she moans. We
got a male version too, if yer int'rested.'

'Merciful heavens,' Hetty answered weakly. 'Can I just –
browse?' It was a far cry from Rosa and her gherkins. Or was
it?

The girl shrugged. 'Yeah, course. I'm goin' off in a minute,
at six. The manageress'll take care of you, if you need anythin'.'

'Thank you.'

Hetty walked, nonchalantly, she hoped, towards the
bookcase. It contained a section of new books and many
scruffy paperbacks with torn covers. Bondage seemed to
play a large part in the fantasies of the shop's literate customers. On the bottom shelf were a grubby boxed album of
Robert Mapplethorpe photographs, a heap of old girly cal-
endars, scores of glossy postcards by photographers with a
stocking fetish or a taste for the grotesque. Some of the poses
looked painful, in Hetty's opinion. Is this what turned
people on?

A glass-covered stand contained odd-shaped implements.
It was a moment before Hetty could identify them, then she

gulped again, twice. A faint mewing sound escaped from her throat. Battery-driven or mains, smooth or ridged, in sizes from six inches up to a monster of over a foot long and two inches thick. Surely those were not for *real*.

'You'd do yourself an injury with one of those,' she remarked aloud.

'Nah. Completely safe,' said a familiar voice behind her.

Hetty whirled round. The girl had been replaced by an elderly woman, dumpy and short, her grey hair in tight curls about her ears. Coral red lipstick, haphazardly applied, covered her mouth; spots of rouge turned her cheeks into a painter's palette. Metallic earrings dangled in the harsh light. The teeth were strong and square, in a slight leer, until the manageress took in her customer. Both gasped.

'Hetty!'

'Doris! God, Doris, what are you doing here?'

The old lady's manner became shifty. 'I work 'ere two days a week. Pays the gas bill. They gets busy towards the weekend.' She became more officious. 'Was you looking for anything in particular?'

But Hetty had fled.

Hetty sat on the edge of the bed, lifted the whisky glass to her lips and drank. She shook her head as if to disperse the alcohol more quickly, then poured herself another. The ice clinked invitingly. The door was shut, the answerphone switched on, though at ten at night she was expecting no calls. The bedside light's pink shade cast a rosy glow over the duvet, the pillows, the library copy of Anaïs Nin, the washed fruit in a bowl. And the copy of *Hot Sex* left on the studio canteen table, which nobody had claimed.

The door of the wardrobe was open, so that the tall

mirror reflected the bed. So she could see herself, but nobody could see her.

She took off her clothes with calm deliberation, let them fall unhindered to the floor. And sat facing the mirror. It needed more whisky: she had never done this before. Never *needed* to before. She drank and tossed her head, and giggled at the sight . . .

Her breasts were round and full over a curving belly. The thighs, head on, were almost circular, the knees dimpled. Two stone too much. Never mind for the moment: no one else was watching. She breathed in, held her breath until she could see the thump of her own heart under her ribcage. She pressed her fingers over her heart, then slid them to her right breast, and tweaked the nipple, sharply.

The pillows made a mound for her head, so she could lean back and still see herself. The thighs elongated, the tyres of fat disappeared and became smooth. Her feet were in good shape, the toes tiny and pink. Without any hurry, she opened her legs. The hairy bush was dark and luxuriant; Stephen used to remark on it. She smiled. He used to start her off by putting his fingers – *here*. She pressed, then settled back, lifted her heels on to the edge of the bed.

And began to rub. It was moist inside the bush: surprisingly so, but then she had been *thinking* about this the entire evening. Ever since returning from the sex-shop and the startling encounter with her downstairs neighbour. The shop could not help. No one could, not tonight. She had to do it herself.

And doing it herself . . . was a curious sensation. Heady. Not bad. Her two middle fingers slid up and down, up and down. It was great to move at her own pace. The flesh was swelling and hot to the touch: it guided her where to go, easily. Not too rapidly, steady. Not heavy, just rhythmic, up and down, in and out. Not dirty, not pornographic. As good as eating chocolate, but a great deal less fattening.

With her other hand she massaged her breasts till they almost hurt, pinched and tugged the nipples as if they were being sucked or nibbled, rubbed her abdomen. Deep in her pelvis muscles stirred, something almost forgotten . . . Her heart seemed to have shifted to a location down between her legs and was pounding, strongly. This was almost better than with Stephen: by now he would be grunting in her ear, his eyes shut tight, and she would be concentrating on ensuring that *he* was enjoying *himself*. Her own needs would have been secondary.

Oh! It was beginning to happen. 'Oh!' Hetty yelped. Her hand flung out and nearly knocked the lamp off the bedside table. It connected with an object. Not a book. *The right shape*. God in heaven. Did it fit? It did . . . *Marvellous*.

In and out – there was a spot inside her that responded intensely . . . the G-spot, wasn't it called? 'Oh! Oh!' Waves and explosions swept over her and she shuddered, appalled and delighted. 'Oh, my God . . . oh, this is fantastic. *Oooooh*.'

It was like being carried off on a magic carpet, swooning in the delirium, disorientated but utterly joyous. Uplifted and panting, her body shuddered . . . Her arms clasped about herself, a broad smile on her face, she flew . . . and at last, lay still.

If she had missed sex, she had found an answer – one answer, at least.

She half sat up and regarded herself triumphantly in the mirror. Her hair was tousled, the skin over her breasts and throat mottled and flushed. 'Yes!' she exclaimed, in plea-sure. Orgasm was achievable: men were not absolutely necessary. She lay back, reached for a peach and began to eat it greedily, letting the juice run down her chin.

Then she pulled the duvet over herself and fell into a deep, dreamless sleep.

The only casualty was the banana, which she found, bruised and blackened, under the bed two days later. Next time, she would have to ask the greengrocer for the green ones. As firm, and as hefty, as possible.

CHAPTER TEN

A Warm Bath

A l was being a pest. Or was he?

'Come on, Eddie, I'm keen to see you. What are you up to New Year's Eve? I'm booked to play at the Millennium Club – that's near Trafalgar Square. Come and see me. Nothing too grand, but I'd be pleased if you would.'

This invitation was couched in quite formal terms. Hetty wondered if he had phoned everyone he had met on *Tell Me All* – and his other programmes – with a similar request. His tales of females fawning over him sounded hollow. Maybe she would be doing him a favour, not vice versa. And, although a Christmas of self-indulgence loomed at a health farm with Sally, New Year's Eve was blank as yet in her diary.

Why not? She left a message on his machine, spelling her name, and felt oddly pleased with herself.

*

'Right,' said Rosa, 'let's look at these ads. Time to get you started.'

She and Hetty were seated, their feet tucked up under them, in her cubby-hole office. The computer screen had been unused for some while; Hetty noticed that the screen-saver message urged, *'Keep it up – don't stop now – think of the money!'*

Hetty sipped a diet drink. 'Ugh. This stuff is disgusting, even if it does have only one calorie,' she said. And, 'I had thought about it. But what sort of sad geeks put ads in newspapers? Or answer them, come to that.'

'Geeks like you,' said Rosa robustly. 'Have you any idea how many are lurking out there, Het, single but not satisfied with being single? Men and women. Men especially. Thousands of them. It's a modern phenomenon.'

'I'm not dissatisfied. And I'm not too sure about this. Supposing they start making obscene remarks?'

'You should be so lucky. But if it happens, you shriek loudly enough to deafen the guy and slam down the phone. And don't start giving your address. Take a positive view, Het.'

'No harm trying, I agree. I'm not totally averse to an evening out with somebody glamorous. Or even vaguely attractive. Pass me that paper.' Hetty decided not to mention Al. 'These used to be called lonely-hearts columns, didn't they? Heavens, it's mostly blokes. You'd think men would have no trouble finding partners.'

'How do you figure that?'

'Don't men still take the initiative? Make the running? It's much trickier for a woman in a pub, for instance, to approach a man she quite fancies and start chatting him up.'

'Not these days. You're showing your age. The lads are

often far more timid. And so many blokes are complete workaholics, they're slaving late at the office, or are forever on an international flight that arrives after midnight. They never get time for a proper social life, though they'd like one. Otherwise –'

'– they wouldn't need the ads.'

'Correct. Now let's see who's in this week. We can listen to the browse lines as well. At the very least, it'll be a gas.'

The two heads bent over the folded newspaper as Rosa wielded a highlighter pen.

'How about "Educated male, divorced, blue eyes, slim, good appearance, tactile, sensual, wide interests, WLTM" – that's would like to meet – "similar, very warm female, for fun times." Not terribly original. "For fun times" – they all say that. It means they have no strong tastes, or they don't get out much.'

'Or they're indecisive. But I'd far rather a chap know what he wants.' Hetty pulled a face. 'Tactile and sensual, eh? Wants a "very warm female" – what's the code there?'

'Making it clear. He wants sex.'

'Oh.'

Rosa giggled. 'Doesn't turn you on, then?'

Hetty shook her head. 'Not a lot. Allied to the fun times bit, he sounds excruciating. What's next?'

'Aha! "Age/colour/size/status immaterial."'

'In other words, he's desperate.'

'Probably a chap who's tried many times before, and hopes for loads of replies rather than just a few.'

'Cheapskate?'

'Yeah.' Rosa pursed her lips. 'Maybe there's another clue. If age is immaterial, his probably isn't. In most of these ads the vintage is stated – forty-three in that one, sixty in another. If this babe doesn't give it, there's an obvious reason why not.'

'What's that?'

'He's old. Probably a lot more than sixty. I wouldn't touch him.'

'Older than sixty? Good Lord.'

Rosa nudged her. 'But if he can still get it up, he might be just what you're looking for.'

'Or he could be decrepit enough to be my grandad. No, thanks,' said Hetty sourly.

'Would you fancy an intellectual?'

'I might. What does it say?'

'"London publisher, tired of conversation with neighbour's dog and occupying his bed like a starfish, WLTM sensuous, very intelligent woman, seeking deserving man. London/South East area."'

'Let me see that.' Hetty peered at the page. 'Might be worth a call, anyway.' She made a note.

'Very intelligent probably means he's an intellectual snob. An arrogant bastard. But I agree, one to try. The one below is far more specific. "Funny, unconventional, kind man, forty-two, non-smoker, IQ a hundred and forty, seeks similar woman to share life and times." What's your IQ, Hetty?'

'Haven't the faintest. Not sure I want a love-match built round IQs. And he's a bit young for me, don't you think? Ah, he lives in Inverness. That lets me off the hook.'

'There's a skier your age wants an attractive, intelligent, passionate woman.'

Hetty rested her chin on her hands. 'I'm beginning to understand the terms. "Sensual" means sex, please. So does "passionate" or "tactile". If it doesn't say "slim", he isn't.' ('And may not be, even if he claims he is,' Rosa reminded her.) '"Well-built" means fat, period. "Distinguished" means grey-haired. "Sincere" means he isn't – or why say so? Sincerity is a quality most people take for granted. "Adventurous" means – what?'

'Into S and M, in all probability.' Rosa rolled her eyes. 'They're not likely to put "Bull whips and chains preferred" in the ads, are they?'

'"Down-to-earth widower –"'

'Means rude sod. Won't modify his language or his manners for a lady. Take me or leave me, he's saying, which is why he's reduced to putting in an ad.'

'"Easy-going, fifty-five, GSOH, WLTM female similar, for relationship, age unimportant . . ."'

'For easy-going read idle. GSOH means good sense of humour, usually, and often implies it's missing entirely. He's retired and bored to tears – but if he had any interests he'd mention them, surely. Tedious old slob, I'd say.'

'I quite like the "Welsh, handsome has-been, sixty-four, seeks educated woman to cuddle up to",' said Hetty, with a smile. 'At least he's being honest.'

'Umm. But you can see why they lie,' Rosa pointed out. 'If he called himself "a Welsh dragon, breathing fire, fit and active, seeking a willing soul-mate to tie to my rock", he'd have dozens of replies.'

'Stop!' said Hetty. 'Before my courage fails entirely, let's call a few. Can I use this phone?'

'Sure. I'll allow you a quick ten minutes. Those special numbers charge at a pound a minute. You can run up a helluva bill.'

Rosa patted Hetty on the back, and soon left her to it.

A week later Rosa asked Hetty about progress. Hetty flipped

back through a notepad covered in scribbles and phone numbers.

'Mixed. You were spot on about the guy for whom age was immaterial. He'll be seventy-three next birthday. He is old enough to be my father. But you have to admire his nerve. He seemed sparky on the phone, but I decided against. I'd prefer someone closer to my own generation.'

'Wise. Next?'

'The easy-going fifty-five-year-old asked me out for a drink. I was quite hopeful, till he started asking what I would wear. He was insistent on my coming in a dress. I told him that wasn't the height of fashion any more and I'd rather wear a trouser suit, but he seemed most put out. Said he didn't like women in trousers. If we'd carried on talking, he'd have been demanding I turn up in stockings and high heels. So you were wrong, he does have some ideas. The problem is, they're set in aspic.'

Rosa's eyes were dancing. 'A gentleman with taste. Did you crack any more codes?'

'Did I ever. "Romantic and sensitive" means divorced and wants to moan about how badly his ex treated him. Over the phone, to a complete stranger. Aren't they dopes? A lot of selfish little boys out there, I reckon.'

'Go on. Did you try the publisher – the one who's fed up talking to the dog and sleeping like a starfish?'

'Him!' Hetty snorted. 'I did, but it took an heroic amount of effort. The recorded message he left, in which they're supposed to fill in details, simply said that everything was in the ad. So I told him I was in broadcasting, and I tried to make my own reply bright and amusing. When he called back his manner was brusque, but I put that down to shyness. Then he had to stop talking abruptly as his other phone rang.

That happened three times. You'd think he'd put the other one on hold, wouldn't you?'

'Did you arrange to meet?' Rosa wriggled with curiosity.

'That was the daft bit. I wasn't keen merely to chat aimlessly, though many of the blokes are content to do just that – makes you wonder what they're up to while they have a pliant female safely miles away on the other end of the phone.'

Rosa mimed an obscene movement till Hetty slapped her hand. 'Drop it. It's enough of an advance for me even to make the calls. Don't put me off.'

'I'm all ears.'

'If I'm going to make progress I have to meet real flesh and blood. So I started dropping hints, like getting together for lunch in town on a non-filming day. He barked that he never ate lunch. Then how about a glass of wine one evening? But no, he hated town and left to go home to Mill Hill as soon as possible. Did he enjoy the theatre, I asked? No, he hated the theatre, hadn't been in twenty years. I began to feel stumped.'

'Did you give up?'

'Not yet. Don't go too fast. I asked him then what *he* wanted, and how he thought we might meet – over the holiday, say. And he answered, "I could offer you a cup of tea and a piece of cake. How about this afternoon? Could you come to Mill Hill?"'

'He didn't!'

'He did. So I thought, sod him. *That*'s why he's occupying his bed like a starfish. And I said goodbye.'

The two women chuckled together, but it was clear that Hetty had drawn a blank.

'It made me think, Rosa,' she said slowly. 'There are

thousands of singles out there, as you said, men and women. Lots of them, I'm now convinced, are basically decent. Most subscribe to the principle that coupledom – a man and a woman – in love, gazing adoringly into each other's eyes over a candlelit supper is the ideal. Some just want to fantasise, and not to meet. A few are more cynical: they want a one-to-one, but they want several of them. Or, whatever they'd prefer, they're chary of commitment.'

'As you are, in fact, at present. But you're capable of love, and many of them aren't.'

'It's a strange world. Quite extraordinary. So many facets of it that I knew nothing about when I spent my afternoons pruning the hedges in Dorset.'

'You could always,' Rosa drawled, 'put an ad in yourself.'

'Mmm . . .' Al came to mind. 'Let's see the New Year in first.'

'A happy New Year, then, Het?'

Hetty gathered up her notes for the next recording and tapped the list of guests, then the folded newspaper. 'Happier than this lot. *Moderately* happy. That'll have to do.'

Season of goodwill. A battered holly wreath was nailed on the main door, slightly askew: Doris's doing. It looked as if it might have been saved since last year. On Doris's window-ledge, Christmas cards kept company with an electric candelabrum that switched itself off and on incessantly. Thomas had acquired a red ribbon and a tinkling bell on his collar: he must have been catching mice or small birds. He did not have a festive demeanour, but prowled crossly about the damp garden, instincts thwarted.

Hetty had not dared go near Doris's corner of the shopping centre again, or knock on her door to explain.

Explanations that made sense and did not reek of humbug would have been difficult. Instead she scuttled inside the block each night, trying not to notice if the rosy face was peering out at the sound of the key in the lock. The call inviting her to the ubiquitous cup of tea did not come. Maybe the sex-shop was extra busy and required Doris's services. Hetty wondered, irreverently, whether its customers were also offered a cup of tea. Or something stronger.

The estate agent had hinted that the block had some odd residents. Was he aware that the teapot-wielding occupant of number one had more than a passing acquaintance with dildoes and penis rings? Maybe he was himself familiar with the shop's contents. He could hardly have avoided the self-appointed concierge when checking the empty flat. Doris could not have resisted *that* temptation.

The gentleman friend, Jack, had never materialised. Did he exist? Or was he, like Rosa's perfect man, a figment of the imagination? Maybe he too visited the shop. Hetty began to laugh. Could it be that Doris's unusual proclivities, suggested by those rouged cheeks and dangling earrings, had once extended to other types of customer? Though probably not in a respectable location like The Swallows. Maybe Jack had been a client of another kind. Or the estate agent. Or both.

Rosa was rushing to finish the series in time for the winter break. After each day's wrap Hetty was drained of energy. It was ages since she had worked so *hard*. It was still fun, but the gilt had gone off the gingerbread when she realised that a typical fifty-hour week brought in a mere six pounds an hour before tax and insurance. Once the series was in the can, there would be no holiday pay or retainers. Hetty began to understand why the young researchers had turned gloomy during programme forty. Recommissioned or otherwise, they would have to manage on their meagre savings till the next round started in February.

Other people, meanwhile, were celebrating the year end rather more thoroughly. The three BJs were out partying every night, a bunch of mistletoe slung rakishly low over their doorway. Their ability to leave a trail of human debris continued to amaze Hetty.

The Sunday morning before Christmas, as she returned from the newsagent's with a double edition of the *TV Times*, she was about to let herself in when there came an intermittent moaning from the steps above her head, out of her sight. Cautiously, the bulky newsprint clutched under her arm, she tiptoed up to investigate.

A young man was sitting on the stairs, his head held in his hands. From his chest issued soft growls. He sounded rather like Thomas in a bad mood. He wore no coat, gloves or scarf, but was in shirtsleeves and tieless. He was shivering violently.

'Hello,' said Hetty. 'You okay?'

'What? Where, in God's name, am I?' The young man had a superior accent.

'Clapham. Is that where you want to be?'

'Clapham? God!' And he rolled over and put his head between his knees.

He did not look like any of Christian and Markus's circle, Hetty decided. Markus was in Leeds supervising what he called 'an intellectual pantomime', while Christian was playing to packed houses and was in all probability fast asleep in his own bed.

'Are you with the BJs – I mean, the girls in number four?'

The man groaned, as if such a proposal were utterly out of the question. 'Who?'

'Ah – Flo and the other girls.'

The haggard boy opened one eye and peered out between his fingers. 'Flo? Florence, do you mean? Don't abbreviate, it isn't smart.'

Hetty nodded.

'Black?'

'Yes.'

'Frightfully attractive, if you like that kind of thing.'

'I – I guess so. She has plenty of admirers.'

'Well, then, I could be in the right place. What time is it?'

'Nearly eleven.'

'Saturday or Sunday?'

'Sunday morning. Eleven a.m.'

'Christ!' The boy sat up and scrabbled about wildly, clutching at his shoulders and open neck as if bewildered about the lack of jacket and tie. He twisted about and found his wallet in a back pocket, yelped in exaggerated relief, and jumped up.

'Watch it!' Hetty warned, for he was swaying.

'Father's expecting me at Simpson's. Oh, God, he'll kill me. The state I'm in . . .' And with that, he took the steps an alarming two at a time and vanished out into the cold air.

Hetty knocked tentatively on number four. It was several minutes before Flo, sleepy in a pink silk wrap, opened it a crack.

'Did you lose a young man?' Hetty enquired. 'Tall, skinny. Well spoken.'

'Hooray Henry, you mean?' Flo was having the same trouble focusing her eyes as the boy. 'God, Hetty, he didn't pee on your doorstep, did he? That's his usual trick. Where is he?'

'Gone to meet his father,' Hetty told her, then realised

that this message could be misunderstood to suggest the
boy had died. 'His real father. At Simpson's.'

'He insisted on coming home with us, but only after he'd
filled his car with petrol. It must have taken ages. We gave
up on him.'

'He drove in that condition?'

'Yeah, sort of. His daddy's a judge. Henry thinks he can
do whatever he likes. Master of the universe, him. Sorry,
Hetty.' And the door was closed.

The *Big Issue* seller had a mournful air. Hetty had purchased
the magazine from him more than once and had been
intrigued at the content and quality of its articles. A whole
world existed with which she had had little contact: urban,
decayed and self-pitying. The society she had previously
kept had been exactly the opposite.

'Terrible weather,' she said, as she gave him the pound
coin. What did one say to a homeless man? The weather
must matter more to him than to most.

He pulled indifferently on the stub of a hand-rolled cigarette and tossed her a copy from a pile protected by a
flapping plastic sheet. The greasy jacket was no cleaner than
before, though its design had altered. Did he wear his
clothes until they were too dirty even for him, then swap
them in their entirety for a new set?

'Can I buy you a cup of tea?' Hetty said, on impulse.
'There's a café opposite.'

The man scratched his tousled head, eyes averted. He's a
marginal improvement on Hooray Henry, Hetty thought,
but not much. What possessed me . . . ?

'Yeah, why not?' The vendor tucked plastic over the pile.
'You're right, it is fucking freezing.'

The two crossed by the zebra to the workmen's café. In a few minutes the man was wolfing down bread and butter and a vast slice of apple pie to go with the tea. Hetty sipped hers, fascinated and repelled. Behind the counter the owner, a small moustachioed Greek with a mournful expression, eyed them curiously.

'Fuckin' great, missus,' the vendor said, and wiped his mouth on the back of his hand. The intonation was Liverpool. The fingers and nails were blackened with grime and endless contact with nicotine. A damp odour wafted from him, but he had shaved within the last two days and the hair was not too matted. Despite the no-smoking notice, he took out a tin and began to roll a cigarette, shakily placing the orange fibres of tobacco one at a time in the flimsy paper.

'You're not supposed to,' Hetty pointed.

'Fuckin' rubbish.' He licked the gum, pulled a stray bit of tobacco out of one end and tucked the meagre cigarette behind one ear. He pronounced the expletive 'focheen,' and seemed incapable of uttering a sentence without it. Hetty decided to treat its use as the equivalent of a stammer, and ignored it.

'What's your name?' she asked.

'Me? Brian.'

'Brian what?'

'Brian fuckin' nothin'. None of your business.' But he grinned. 'No offence.'

'No offence taken. How long have you been selling the *Big Issue*?'

Brian considered, squinting up at the ceiling as if the answer was scribbled in its cracks. ''Bout six months. Fuckin' ages.'

'D'you enjoy it?'

'It's a livin'. Of sorts. I get 'em fifty pence each. Anythin' I make over that is mine. A fuckin' fortune.'

'Where do you live?' An idea had begun to form in Hetty's mind, to do with *Tell Me All*. Cleaned up, Brian might be moderately presentable. He was certainly less of a fraud than the superannuated strippers or the media professionals like Al.

'Hey, what is this, missus?' He had smeared tomato ketchup on two slices of bread and made a sandwich of it. Now he paused with the thick doorstep half-way to his mouth. 'You some kind of fuckin' social worker, or what?'

'No. I work in television. Have you ever been on TV, Brian?'

'No. Fuckin' 'ell, who'd want me?'

'It pays, you know. A bit more than you'd make selling magazines,' Hetty ventured.

'What would I have to do?'

'Tell your story, explain how you need help, how you want to get back to normality.'

'Oh, yeah. An' then what?'

Hetty was stumped. *Tell Me All* had no follow-up system; indeed, the team studiously avoided contact with its guests – victims – after the broadcast. Only if a complaint was made was any kind of investigation warranted. As long as it could be proven that every participant knew exactly what they were agreeing to (and had signed to that effect), and since all had stuck tenaciously to their tales of woe however unlikely, no complaint had been upheld, so far. The entire crew, however, was perpetually on the lookout for authentic oddities, Hetty included, though she had offered Brian tea without any ulterior motive.

'The idea,' Hetty said slowly. 'is that you tell your story, as I say. About a million people tune in every day, and the best episodes are repeated. Someone might be watching who could advise you.'

'Only if they can make me a millionaire, missus!' The man cackled, then coughed and banged his chest. Muttering to himself he retrieved the cigarette from behind his ear and, with a belligerent oath towards the counter, lit up. The proprietor slid away.

'Would you want to be a millionaire?'

A blob of ketchup had spilled on the table. He traced a circle with a grubby forefinger. 'I was, once,' he said, or at least, Hetty thought she'd heard it, but could not be sure. He looked up, his eyes dull. ''S not worth it, missus. But thanks, anyway.'

'Merry Christmas,' Hetty said, and rose, feeling obscurely humiliated.

'Oh, yeah,' Brian laughed, 'merry fuckin' Christmas.'

The notice near St Veronica's advertised four special services including Midnight Mass, and three carol concerts. Trust Father Roger not to do things by halves, Hetty reflected. He had handed out flyers and pressed everyone: 'Bring your family, whoever. On Christmas Eve we have mince pies and sherry. Do come!'

But by Christmas Eve she would be at the health farm with Sally so it was on the Monday beforehand when, muffled up against the cold, she caught the bus.

It felt almost a lark, going out to a strange church, alone, simply for the heck of it. In Dorset she had been a server and had done a stint on the parochial church council. There church attendance for families like theirs was virtually *de rigueur*. It would have been more of a statement *not* to go. With a guilty start she recalled the two gay teachers who had attended on Sunday mornings, regular as clockwork, for years. She had never exchanged more than a cool nod with them. Why on earth had she bought Brian a meal? Maybe it was the time of year, some vestige of the Christianity she had once taken for granted. But religious feeling had had little to do with it. Freed of some of her former prejudices – wrenched from them, rather, in the case of her new friendship with Markus and Christian – she was beginning, tentatively, to challenge a few more.

What a mixed collection of motives, she teased herself as she alighted from the bus. You're becoming quite devious. Once, you were a nice woman, if instantly forgettable. Is this a change for the better – or worse?

The church was brightly lit: ablaze with candles, and tinsel, and shiny green holly with fat red berries. A huge decorated tree dominated the entrance. Mistletoe like a pearly fountain hung from a rafter. Beneath, arms outstretched, was a beaming Father Roger. 'Hetty! Darling lady! How wonderful. Oh, do come here.' He pulled her sideways. 'I won't have the tree and mistletoe inside the body of the church – far too pagan – but that doesn't mean I can't take advantage. Mwah, mwah!'

Hetty dimpled. 'Happy Christmas, Roger.'

He was already transferring his attention to the next arrivals and waved her inside. 'Sit anywhere. And, mind, I want to hear you *sing*!'

Hetty paused in pleasure at the end of the nave. St Veronica's was a Victorian stone edifice of no great architectural merit, but it had the grandeur and self-confidence of its builders. Every cranny was adorned with flowers and greenery; the air was heavy with the smell of lilies, and of the incense Father Roger was partial to using in some quantity. His congregation could forgive him: his exuberance and commitment filled the church and the offertory plates, despite the popish smoke.

'Hello. Didn't expect to see *you* here.' It was Doris, dressed in an old coat, a headscarf over her curls. Gone were the lipstick and rouge; if the earrings were still a feature, they were hidden.

Hetty hesitated. Doris patted the pew. 'Come and sit down. Starting in a mo.'

The whole gathering heaved to its feet as the procession, with Father Roger, several acolytes with silver-plated crosses held aloft, the churchwardens and the entire surpliced choir strode in.

> *Hark, the herald angels sing,*
> *Glory to the new-born King . . .*

Something was let loose in Hetty. She opened her mouth and sang with enormous relish, savouring the glorious verse and the exquisite melody. When the trebles began to soar with the descant, she followed them, note for note.

> *Once in Royal Daaa-vid's city*
> *Stood a lo-o-owly cattle shed,*
> *Where a mother laid her baby . . .*

Hetty felt a surge of emotion. *Laid her baby*: the sweetest moments had been when the children were small. Little bodies, warm and pink after their bath, asleep on her shoulder. There had been no question about it: then, she had been in charge, her role supreme, in her arms the greatest achievement any woman can know – her own child.

She glanced sideways at Doris and was surprised to see silent tears trickling down the lined cheeks. As they sat for the readings, Hetty whispered, 'You all right, Doris? Anything the matter?'

'Nah.' The voice was muffled. 'Christmas. I'm a sentimental old eejit. Be a pal – take no notice.'

Hetty fished in her pocket and found a clean handkerchief. Without a word Doris took it and blew her nose.

Heads bowed for the Lord's Prayer. 'Give us this day our daily bread,' Hetty prayed, with some fervour. Not far beneath her surface lay the ingrained middle-class fear of getting into a mess. Singledom, above everything else, meant insecurity.

'Forgive us our trespasses . . .' She hadn't committed any. Not yet. Or had she? Brian, maybe, though intruding on his grim day wasn't a trespass, was it? Was she being a busybody? Might she trespass with Al?

'For ever and ever, amen.'

Hetty stayed kneeling for a moment longer, sunk in rather muddled reflections.

'You taking the bus back?' Doris's tone was noncommittal.

Hetty pulled on gloves and buttoned her coat. 'I was, yes. You going home?'

Doris nodded. 'Let's go. There's one on the hour, if we don't dawdle.'

Once installed on the narrow seats of the bus, their coated arms and thighs touching, the slight frostiness of an hour ago was unsustainable.

'Doris,' Hetty started, 'tell me not to be nosy, if you like, but what on earth are you doing in that shop?'

'Obvious, innit? I work there. Pays well. And they need a mature woman: the youngsters don't last five minutes. The customers keep propositioning them.'

'Ugh!' Hetty shuddered.

'You should talk, you were a customer,' Doris replied briskly. 'Or would've been, if I'd stayed in the back another minute. The good girls go off in a huff, see, saying they didn't realise what they'd let themselves in for. The rest accept an offer and vanish. We're forever training replacements. It's quite technical. Got to know your stuff.'

'I'll bet,' Hetty murmured. Her curiosity surfaced. 'And will you be seeing your gentleman friend over Christmas?'

'Jack?'

'Yes.'

'No. New Year, maybe. He goes north this time of year. To be with his wife.'

'Oh.'

The bus rounded a corner. Hetty continued, 'What does he do for a living, Doris?'

'Jack? He's a businessman. He was a police officer.'

'What kind of business?'

'Him? He owns the sex-shop. He owns three. Quite a little money-spinner, they are. Now, are you coming in for a cup of tea?'

'A health farm?' Her mother had sounded dubious. 'With Sally? That's mighty maternal of you, Hetty, but it wouldn't be my preference. And *Sally* doesn't need to lose any weight.'

The last comment, Hetty thought, had been a mite too barbed. Clarissa had been more supportive. She had recommended Hoar Cross Hall as better value than the grander establishments near London, though less likely to secrete recuperating celebrities. Springs in Bedfordshire, or Champneys, it had to be, if one wanted to bump into the likes of Roger Moore or Shirley Bassey.

'I would find those two depressing,' Hetty said glumly.

'Why?'

'Because they're both older than me and still stunning.'

'Well,' Clarissa had added diplomatically, 'make the most of it, darling. I recommend the aromatherapy, a hot seaweed face-pack, and a foot massage.'

Rosa's response had been predictable. 'Joy! You jammy devil. Can you squeeze in a third? I'll sleep on the floor. No? *Shame.* Anyway, make sure you go to every single class. The instructor might be just what the doctor ordered . . .'

Sally had already checked in. She had explored the handsome manor house and its wintry gardens, and had familiarised herself with the timetable. Her manner was uncertain and a little awkward.

A few hours later, Hetty was naked, wrapped in thick towels, lying on her front on a padded trolley with a wide hole for her bosom and a narrower one for her face. In a towelling robe on another trolley was a floppy Sally, who had volunteered to go first.

'Aaagh!' Hetty squealed.

'I apologise, Mrs Clarkson, but your shoulders are a mass of knots.' The masseuse was a hefty woman dressed in white from head to toe. Sleeves rolled above the elbow revealed forearms like hams and fists like mallets, which were now kneading Hetty's neck. A prison wardress from a Soviet gulag was the image that came to mind. 'Do shout if I'm *really* hurting you.'

'Ooof!'

'What have you been doing? Sitting in one position all

day and no exercise? No wonder. There!' And the heel of a beefy hand was ground into a recalcitrant spot.

Hetty sagged limply. 'No exercise.'

'No excuse,' said her torturer. 'Roll over.'

Later, in the hot whirlpool, Hetty gingerly tested her shoulder. 'It does feel looser,' she admitted, 'but I'm glad there's only time for one massage. Unbelievable.'

Sally spread her arms, held on to the bar and lifted her feet in the rushing water. 'Great idea of yours, Mum,' she said. 'You do seem more relaxed – compared with when you first moved into your flat, anyway.'

'Absolutely. You said then that I should turn tail and scoot straight back home.'

'Umm . . . I didn't believe you'd last a week. You've proved me wrong. So far.'

Hetty kicked up her heels in the hot stream. 'God, I could get used to this.'

'You don't miss the old life? I thought you'd be in tears every night, to be honest.'

'I've been so busy. Earning a living is a great antidote. Not had time to miss anything.' Hetty glanced sideways at her daughter. 'Except you, of course. And Peter. He seems to have grown away from me completely. He's sent a Christmas card, but that's it.'

'Not lonely?'

'Nope. Made friends. Every day brings something new. Look, I'm turning puce.'

'I only wondered, after the failure of your marriage . . .'

'I don't see it as a failure, Sally. It succeeded, after a fashion, for quite a long stretch.'

'But you failed. Don't you *feel* it, even a bit? Isn't that what most women would feel, if their man goes off?'

Hetty held still. 'D'you know, Sally? Six months ago a comment like that would have made me weep. Of course, you have a point. A woman always asks herself if there was anything she might have done differently to save the marriage or to prevent it going wrong to begin with. That's how we're brought up.' A sudden anxiety flashed into her mind. 'Sally, did I bring you up like that? D'you tend to assume, if a relationship isn't going well, that it must be your fault? For not pleasing your bloke, say.'

Sally shrugged. 'A bit. I'm not terribly good at picking them in the first place.'

'Is your current chap married?'

'Yes.'

'D'you want to talk about it?'

'No. Not yet.'

'It is a chap – not a woman – is that right, at least?'

'Lord above, Mum. You *have* been widening your scope. No, he's male, though there are moments . . . Men are so complicated.'

Hetty moved to the cooler part of the bath, swam a little, testing the freshly supple shoulders. Then she returned and put an arm round her daughter. 'I won't push. I've not the most tactful soul. But I grieve, Sally, for the mistakes I've made. I wasn't brilliant at picking, either. As it turned out.'

'Maybe we're better off without them.'

'Men?'

'Men.'

In the distance a bell rang; supper beckoned. Hetty hauled herself out with a sigh. Swathed in white robes, hair dripping and expressions pensive, the two women left wet footprints, similar in shape and size, on the edge of the pool.

CHAPTER ELEVEN

Ring in the New

New Year's Eve. The Millennium Club, near Trafalgar Square. To join in, watch and listen as a saxophonist performed, a man whom she had met properly only once.

What to wear? The weather report said the night would be freezing but dry. The club might be very warm, and she might be asked to dance, in which case she had made up her mind to try it, and not to care if she made a fool of herself. She would need a clutch bag, to be kept with her at all times. A coat not worth stealing from the cloakroom. And enough money tucked down her bra to get a taxi home.

Hetty had not made calculations of this kind for over two decades and was amused even as she fretted. Who was she trying to satisfy? Al, who couldn't even get her name right? Al, who hadn't bothered to dress up even for his appearance on television, but who reportedly was delighted with his efforts on the show? Nor was anyone likely to attend who knew her. It was her first visit to the club – to any club, for years – and the management probably wouldn't give her a second glance.

'I can please myself,' she told her image in the dress-shop mirror. She could ignore the slight excess of weight, the roll of podgy fat that disappeared if she held her breath. 'For the first time in God knows how long.'

It was a peculiar experience. Before, she would have dressed hurriedly as Stephen barged around the bedroom hunting for the tie and socks that she had set out on the bed, and which inevitably he had managed to cover with his jacket. On completion she would seek his approval, and automatically obtain it; that was hardly surprising, as her main objective in life, then, had been to please Stephen. She had assessed everything with his eyes. It had not been necessary to develop her own judgement or taste.

'In fact, I have no idea what my taste is, or if I have any,' Hetty answered herself, *sotto voce*. 'What would I wear in my dreams? Chanel or Yves St Laurent? Monsoon? Zandra Rhodes? Would I go for Vivienne Westwood?' She stopped. 'Maybe I already look like Vivienne Westwood. The designer, not the clothes. Oh dear.'

The assistant was a tubby woman in a buttoned suit. 'Modom looks de*laigh*tful,' she said eloquently. 'Ay think the blue suits Modom rather better than the red.'

The blue dress swirled, its spangled hem dashing against her calves. It tantalised and swished. It fitted without wrinkles and was ten pounds cheaper. 'I'll take it,' said Hetty, and her eyes sparkled.

It also felt strange to be going somewhere smart alone. Coupledom ruled socially; singles stood out, forlorn and awkward. Hetty had overcome her fear of entering a pub or a wine bar by herself, but had quickly decided that, in any case, pubs were not her natural stamping ground. If a movie appeared that she was keen to see, she would propose it to friends, but did not take their refusal as a veto; she would march across the common for an early-evening showing, and be delighted with herself for doing so. Theatre tickets came unbidden via Markus and Christian, who ensured an enthusiastic welcome. Many of their circle were not in couples either: she felt at ease with them. Since most were gay, she was not forced to endure any ham-fisted chatting up.

But this New Year's Eve jaunt was different. She would be chatted up by Al. His pals were almost certainly hetero, and some would be on the lookout behind their escorts' backs. A club was a place for getting off with someone, wasn't it? Should she have asked Rosa or Sally along for protection?

Rosa would not have protected her for five minutes. She would have raised that beautiful nose in the air, literally, and sniffed. Then she would have gone haring off in the direction of the first man who took her fancy. At some point she would have pinched Hetty's arm and hissed that she and whoever were leaving, and that much would be revealed, with giggling and rolling of eyes, in a day or so. Hetty would have wished her luck, and have been left wondering once more what Rosa's secret was, and whether she truly wanted to emulate it.

Sally might have accepted. The boyfriend Erik was back in the UK, but her daughter's glum demeanour hinted that he was attending to other duties besides flying. Hetty had considered the matter with some care and felt selfish for not inviting Sally. But the fact was, she would not have been the greatest company. She would have resisted any attempts by jolly men to partner her, and – Hetty could easily picture it –

would have sat, smoking, a half-full glass to hand, gloomy and forbidding. Had Hetty tried to enjoy herself – by accepting an offer to dance, or by getting carried away a little – Sally would have muttered a barbed comment to put the man off, and possibly Hetty too.

As she tried bits of jewellery against the cocktail dress, Hetty's eye caught the assemblage of family photos on the bookcase. Sally was no longer the gawky girl, knees over-large on thin legs, hiding behind her mother. The cheeky shock-haired child who had been Peter had vanished for ever. It was not easy to come to terms with these changes: her children were, effectively, people she barely knew. Neither she nor Stephen had expected their absent offspring to call daily or even weekly, nor had they phoned their own parents very often. But to think of a daughter as a social companion, albeit a rather prickly one, was definitely an unaccustomed proposition.

It was apparent that Sally, too, was struggling to come to terms with Hetty's altered state. A contradiction clouded her attitudes. On the one hand she obviously wanted her mother to remain Mum, the central rock of the family, immutable and asexual. On the other, if that were not possible and her mother was to consort with new men, Sally would have to cope with Hetty becoming a sexual creature once more. If her own private life was foundering that could open up fresh resentments. Children, Hetty admitted ruefully to their childish faces in the photo frames, could be a pain.

Too many complications. Coping with her own minor crises was quite sufficient. Sally could stew, just for tonight. Hetty had determined to make the most of an unusual opportunity and to follow where it led.

*

Taking the tube into town at nine in the evening was an
adventure in itself. She was surrounded by youngsters, in
groups and, inevitably, pairs, bundled up in fleeces, scarves
and woolly hats, heading for the conviviality of Trafalgar
Square. An energy flowed from them, from their never-still
bodies, the vibrancy of youth in a celebrating city. Some
had started their indulgence early. Opposite, a smelly alcoholic lurched and sang snatches of an unintelligible song, his
hand grasped round a bottle in a paper bag. He was observed
with mute disapproval by a gaggle of Japanese tourists. At
the far end of the carriage somebody was strumming an ill-
tuned guitar. All humankind, it seemed, was on its way into
central London, in a rattling carriage stained by old graffiti,
their feet half hidden by litter, faces creased in anticipatory
smiles.

'Happy New Year,' Hetty said lightly to the drunk, as the
train halted at her stop.

'Urkk,' he belched, and leered at her.

She found the club without effort and presented her
ticket. It was larger than she had anticipated, rather better-
appointed, with flashing pink neon over the entrance. The
bouncers were enormous: two huge men in their thirties,
one black, one white, both shaven-headed with skulls
bulging through shiny skin, their steroid-enhanced chests
draped in frilled evening shirts, tiny dickey-bows like red
ticks at their throats. But they were polite enough and
unhitched the tasselled cord to let Hetty through, while
keeping others at bay.

Inside, the noise was deafening. Dozens of tables were
ranged in tiered semicircles around a small stage. Every surface was painted matt black, but silver tinsel had been
wrapped round railings and light-fittings. Strobe lights

played over a raised platform where a handful of couples gyrated to recorded music. Blue laser beams shimmered over the scene. It was extremely hot. She deposited her coat, touched the money in her bra, renewed her lipstick and was shown to a table near the side of the stage.

'You came! Terrific.' Al was in black tie, his hair tied back neatly. Working clothes. The effect was oddly demure.

It was too noisy to have a proper dialogue. He leaned close and screeched into Hetty's ear, 'We're on at ten thirty. Order yourself some dinner. Put it on the tab. The bubbly's coming. Have a wild time!'

A basket on the table was full of silvered hats and party poppers. She tried on a crown, which fitted, and practised making the party poppers reach out to the next tier. In a moment she was joined by a florid man in a fancy brocaded waistcoat accompanied by a younger, buxom blonde in a low-cut sequined dress. 'Hi! I'm Ted,' he mouthed, 'the band's agent. This is Mandy.'

Hetty shook hands and began to explain. Ted cut her short. 'Yeah, we know. One of Al's pals. He usually has a couple of birds floating about. I must say, he's gone up a notch with you. Very nice.'

He and Mandy selected party hats and put them on roguishly. The elastic cut into fleshy cheeks; they looked like a pair of well-fed clowns. Ted's attention was immediately engaged in ordering the meal. Hetty turned to the blonde. 'You in showbiz too?' she asked.

'In a manner of speaking.' The girl simpered and waggled her shoulders so that her substantial breasts wobbled. I've made blancmange like that, Hetty thought. She raised an eyebrow in friendly enquiry. The girl leaned across the table, threatening to spill the blancmanges out of the dress entirely. 'Escort agency,' she hissed, with a wink.

Hetty glanced at Ted, who was pressing twenty-pound notes into the waiter's hand. 'Got a good customer tonight, then?' Hetty hissed back, woman to woman.

'Oh, yeah. He's a regular.' Mandy patted her cheeks. 'Warm in 'ere, innit?'

The standard of discourse was not going to rise much higher than that, Hetty guessed, but she did not mind. The champagne was served with a flourish in a bucket full of ice. A plate of savoury pastries was plonked down. As the cork was popped by the grinning waiter and poured overflowing into Babycham-style glasses, cries and whoops came from nearby guests and glasses were raised in mock toasts.

Hetty took a long swallow and let the bubbles get up her nose. 'You celebrating anything in particular?'

'Nah,' Ted answered. He pulled Mandy to him and kissed her wetly on the mouth, then patted her bosom proprietorially. 'I've asked 'er to marry me a dozen times an' she won't. I'll keep poppin' the question, though. Maybe she'll say yes tonight.'

Mandy pushed him off and picked up a canapé. 'Oh, you,' she gurgled. 'Why should I want to marry you? Anyway, you're already married. Best you stay that way.'

'I love the wimmin,' Ted confided. Trails of streamers covered his jacket. 'Been married four times, so far. Twice to the same woman, that's the current one, but we don't get on. Can't live with 'er, can't live without 'er.'

'Expensive, I'd have thought,' Hetty said, with a smile.

'Oh, God, tell me about it,' Ted answered. 'There, they're starting.'

An MC in a midnight-blue tuxedo and pink shirt jumped on-stage, trailing a microphone. The voice boomed, tables and plates rattled in sympathy. 'Ladees and gennlemen! The Badger Boys and Lindy present their New Year spectacular! A big hand, please!'

The band consisted of six musicians with a singer. Al was in the front row, saxophone in hand, a silly hat on his head, a garland of tinsel round his neck. He fiddled nervously with the stops, blew through the reed, pinched his nose. He seemed a more diminutive personality than close to in the studio. They struck up vigorously, a tune that began by resembling 'Bye Bye Birdie', but which was soon lost in syncopations and jazzy improvisations. Ted was tapping on the table with a spare hand, a lit cigar jauntily in his mouth. The other hand was under the table, hidden from view.

The meal arrived, large platefuls, an avocado with smoked salmon to start, followed by Ted's choice of steak and oyster pie with all the trimmings. A special menu, she was informed: on normal band nights it was chicken in a basket. It made for a heavy meal, especially washed down by the champagne. A second bottle was cooling in the bucket.

The music had changed to a heated version of 'Ol' Man River', laid down to a thumping beat. Feet planted wide apart, Al forced riffs through the horn, his cheeks distorted and purple. The singer, an anorexic girl in black, alternated with wordless warbles.

'Yeah, my man!' Ted urged him on, between mouthfuls of suet pastry. The cigar was employed like a baton, keeping time, its swirling smoke creating a bluish fug through which Mandy's sequins, the brocade waistcoat, the laser lights flickered hazily. The noise from nearby tables had grown to a crescendo; despite the amplification, it must have been impossible to hear any melody at the back of the club.

Hetty's eyes began to water and her ears rang tinnily as the notes reverberated off the walls.

'Shape of a tit, this,' Ted announced between numbers, the glass held up between forefinger and thumb. 'Some French king's mistress. Madame de Pompidou.' He nudged Mandy. 'We prefer 'em bigger these days, don' we?'

Mandy buried her face in her glass and gulped her drink. A dribble fell on her dress and she prodded herself. 'Oops!'

It was not done to dance during the main band section, Hetty saw. At the side of the stage people were on their feet, clapping and swaying, engrossed. Her brain was swimming; the noise was horrendous, a cacophony of jangled sounds, Al's saxophone shrieking above the rest, the girl singer yodelling in another key. Hetty could not tell whether this was deliberate or not. She could make no sense whatever of the music, other than the thundering beat laid down by the flailing drummer.

To loud cheers, a big clock with spangled hands was lowered from the ceiling. It showed five minutes to twelve. Around the club people were swaying in time to the beat, arms round each other, glasses in hand. A man walked casually in front of her view. If she stayed seated she would be unable to see anything. She rose, and tried to join in the general merriment, wishing she did not feel quite so sober.

A woman at a nearby table threw streamers in her direction. Giggling, Hetty seized a handful of party poppers and fired back. Behind her somebody was spraying a can of fluorescent goo that snaked across bare shoulders, ice buckets and the remains of dinner. A lighted sparkler was thrust into her hand and she was urged to wave it.

'Ten! Nine! Eight!' Hetty chanted with the rest and waved

her sparkler obediently. She blinked furiously in the smoke and heat.

'Three! Two! One! *Happy New Year!*'

Ted and Mandy fell into an embrace, eyes closed, their mouths chewing hungrily at each other, Ted's paws massaging her sequined bottom, though he retained a firm grip on his cigar.

On all sides strangers were kissing and hugging. On another tier a conga had started. Someone grabbed Hetty and planted a smacking kiss on her lips, then the would-be Don Juan passed swiftly down the aisle and embraced every female within reach. He was gone so quickly that she had only the faintest impression of excess Brylcreem, aftershave and tobacco. It could have been anybody.

'"Should auld acquaintance be forgot . . ."'

Hands were grabbed, a disjointed line formed. Hetty twisted round to find Al, but he was still on stage, blowing as if his soul depended on it. She opened her mouth and tried to sing, but found she was hoarse from the shouted exchanges earlier. Her throat hurt. She felt slightly sick.

When she turned to sit down again, Ted was still munching his blowsy escort, and had one hand thrust down her dress. Hetty lifted her glass, cleared a piece of streamer from the stem and finished the flat champagne. She knew what to do next.

Quietly, without disturbing the writhing lovers, she tiptoed slowly away. Al was still totally absorbed in the love of his life: his music. She collected her coat, left a tip and walked out into the chilly night.

Crowds of youngsters were milling about, their breath white on the frosty air. Black-helmeted police officers on horses, their mounts' eyes protected by plastic blinkers, stood guard at the entrance to Trafalgar Square, exchanging banter with the more boisterous visitors, warning off those laden with bottles and six-packs and instructing everyone to keep moving. Hetty let the sharp chill clear her befuddled head. The cigar smell clung to her skin; her nose wrinkled in disgust. Stephen had smoked them at banquets, the kind of event she used to attend to support him. But now that she had a choice, she found them neither sophisticated nor alluring.

The multitudes were strolling somewhat aimlessly past the National Gallery, away from Nelson's Column, as if they sensed that the party spirit was somewhere nearby, if only they could find it. The fountains were boarded up: the crowd's disappointment was tangible. Any wildness was elsewhere; under the watchful eyes of the police the behaviour on display was sedate and good-humoured. Hetty let herself be carried along and offered no resistance.

She found herself on the steps of Leicester Square station and was informed that the last tube was leaving shortly. 'I might as well go home,' she told herself, a trifle miserably.

As the carriage – a replica of the scruffy one that had brought her, but now knee-high in litter, including beer cans and hamburger wrappers – careened towards her stop, she leaned her hot face against the window and gazed at the blackness beyond.

Why had it not worked? Why had she not been – engaged? Would it have been better if Al had been at her elbow, had carried her off to dance, been solicitous and attentive? He had been utterly engrossed: he'd probably not noticed yet that she had left. It was as if he had paid court all night to another woman and had ignored her, though since he'd made it clear he would be working she should have expected nothing else. How very *vexing*. At least he hadn't let her sit on her own. Ted and Mandy, however, had hardly been the most scintillating company.

'I don't like jazz. I didn't know that before, but I do now,' Hetty told her jerky image in the grimy window. 'I don't like smoky atmospheres. And I'd rather have a conversation any day. Or night. Preferably with someone intelligent.'

She coughed slightly. That appeared to rule out Al.

By the time she emerged from the tube station with a straggle of other late passengers the night had grown colder. A scruffy youth was tugging half-heartedly at the handle of a cigarette machine. The sleepy attendant wished her goodnight and a happy New Year, then turfed out the youth and dragged the folding gates closed behind him.

Any New Year resolutions? Only those that had emerged in recent weeks: to carry on as she was, not to look back, to regret little, apologise when necessary, mope seldom, and learn something from everyone she met. To keep trying new experiences, regularly, and not to be fearful of disappointment. To lose some weight, take more exercise. Take *any* exercise. On yer bike.

To chase men? To be chased by them — better men than Al — and let them catch her?

The year before, her mind had been blank. Asked what she wished for, she would have replied in terms of the health and happiness of her family, and continued peace and prosperity for the world. Her own positive ambitions had been non-existent.

She trudged away from the lights of the station, head down, gloved hands thrust deep into her pockets. The common was dark and bleak. Any men seeking love out there tonight would have to be quick: there was little shelter to be had from the gusty wind.

One of the street-lights was out. At its base, someone had dumped a bundle of rags that straggled across the narrow pavement. Hetty went to step over the heap, and inadvertently prodded it with her foot. 'Hey! Wotcher fuckin' doin'?' The voice, slurred and guttural, came from the depths of the bundle.

Hetty hesitated. 'Sorry. Is that you, Brian?'

'Who de fuck's that?' The bundle struggled half upright. A filthy head gazed blearily about. From the battered nose came a trail of dried blood. There was a powerful odour of cheap liquor.

'You okay? Can I get any help?'

She wasn't sure how she would fetch assistance other than dialling 999, and the emergency services would not be ecstatic about a liquor-sodden vagabond early on New Year's Day.

'Bugger off. Fuck you. Fuck you all.'

The figure slumped back. A dark stain began to appear on the trousers; the acrid stink of urine sullied the night air. Hetty trod daintily around the body, relieved that he was alive, and walked on quickly.

A taxi, empty, but with its light off, slowed down at her side. 'Looking for The Swallows, Miss,' the driver said.

'Next corner, first block,' she answered, lost in her own reverie.

Her head had cleared, though the tinnitus still buzzed loudly in her ears. What a rum evening. Not a disaster, just not quite what she'd expected. Too much like hard work. Not to be repeated. Not every negative event was as gentle, she reflected moodily. Still, she had learned a lot from tonight: that she could look attractive when she chose despite the unwanted plumpness, that she could hold several glasses of champagne, that her presence did not spoil other people's fun. And, now, that she could resist the temptation to be a Good Samaritan. Other people had rights, including Brian, which included the right to be left alone, to go to hell in their own way.

Time was when she could not have imagined leaving a man lying in the street. It didn't happen in the countryside, or not much. The victims would be known, and would be carried by their drinking buddies to a place of safety. She had heard that pedestrians were more at risk on a night like this than drivers, not least because so many of them were on a blinder. Had Brian tried to cross the road, an unwary motorist would not have stood a chance. It was probably the end Brian most wished for himself. She hoped, when it came, it would be easy.

The taxi was waiting outside the block of flats. The cabby was smoking and listening calmly to the chatter of Radio Five Live.

'Busy night for you?' Hetty asked.

'Yeah. An' if this lady doesn't hurry up, I'll be off. I've got three more fares waiting.'

Lady? Was Doris about to go out on the razzle? The three BJs had left early that afternoon, laden with bags and bottles for a location some distance away, so it could not be them. Hetty's brain was too weary to puzzle. She fumbled for her key.

The door opened suddenly.

'Oh!' Hetty stepped back in surprise.

She was confronted with a tall figure, a woman. A full

head of flowing black hair. Elaborate makeup, glitter eye-shadow and a Cupid's bow of glossy lipstick. As the extraordinary apparition pushed wordlessly past, Hetty took in diamanté earrings, a quilted velvet coat with a narrow waist and a fur collar, fishnet tights with perfectly aligned seams on muscular calves, and shiny high-heeled shoes.

Who the hell was that? Hetty wondered groggily. Looks like a dog's dinner. She shook her head. It was time to start minding her own business. Another resolution for the New Year. Head drooping, she climbed the stairs to bed.

CHAPTER TWELVE

Seizing Control

In the garden, snowdrops had given way to clutches of erect daffodils, like platoons of royal trumpeters heralding the imminence of spring. Under the oldest trees, crocuses doggedly pushed gold and purple silk through the mud. The afternoons were no longer so brief, nor so dark.

Hetty stood in front of the full-length mirror, stark naked. 'You are fat,' her eyes told her with brutal exactitude.

'So what? I'm comfortable. Mature. Carry the marks of a fully lived life. Motherhood. Pregnancy. Nothing to be ashamed of.' Her shoulders shrugged, attempting disdain.

'Take a handful of those folds around your waist.' Her hands did so, reluctantly. 'Let's be honest about it. They aren't round your waist. They're several inches below. Any more, and your pubes will disappear for ever.'

'That's unkind. And irrelevant. Appearance is the least important thing about a person. Personality counts for far more. Who wants to look like a bimbo, anyway?'

'You did, once. What makes the first impact? What we *see*.'

'I'm feeling defiant. And feminist. Fat is a feminist issue. We don't have to conform to that skinny Barbie doll image men think they prefer. They don't anyway – they like us plump. And I don't judge people on their appearance. I'm not so shallow.'

'Yes, you are. Yes, you do. Christian, for example. Even Rosa. Your own mother.'

'*Ah* . . . Okay, so first impressions do count. But what's truly important is how a person does her job and relates to other people.'

'Now you're talking complete rubbish. How she relates, as you put it, depends on how she looks. Instant assessments are made before the subject has opened her mouth. Tells you loads in a few seconds. And often there isn't a second chance. Not for somebody like you, anyway.'

'What do you mean, somebody like me?'

'*Look at you*. You're a grey-haired, flabby, turkey-skinned fifty-year-old. And you're *fat*. Past it. Period.'

'I am not past it! How dare you? I have years ahead of me.'

'But you *look* past it. That's the whole point. Geddit now?'

Hetty was silenced. She continued to palpate the flap of podgy flesh that was her belly, lifting it up and down like a mini-apron. 'Well,' she said, 'I won't do anything drastic. I'm not having it cut off, and I'm not going in for liposuction.'

'You can't afford either,' said the inner voice smugly.

Hetty turned sideways, holding in her abdomen. She closed her eyes, clenched her fists and let her stomach muscles relax completely.

'Go on. You have to know the worst,' came the accusatory whine.

Hetty opened her eyes, then quickly shut them again. The profile that had greeted her had a pronounced curvature with a distinct gravitational pull downwards. 'God,' she groaned, 'I could be six months pregnant with twins. Oh, that's awful.'

'Absolutely.' The voice was triumphant. 'Progress! The first step to redemption is to recognise that a problem *exists*. You've been in *denial*. That has to *end*.'

'Oh, piss off,' said Hetty, and reached for her clothes.

'They are all mad. I swear it.' Rosa mimed tearing out her hair, then pulled the two top pink sheets from her script and melodramatically ripped them up. 'They promise to perform, and we send a car for them to effing Sunderland, agree a fee over the odds and they arrive with every item of kit. So why back out at the last minute?'

Hetty sighed, and read from her notes: 'Mistress Delilah, aged twenty-eight. Telephone number at the dungeons, et cetera, and bleep. "I have been working as a dominatrix for four years and love my work. I'm twenty-eight now. I can't work as a dominatrix for ever and am frustrated that I'm not doing something as creative as I'd like."'

'"Is it about time I got a proper job?" Yeah, yeah,' Rosa grunted. 'Have you seen the trunkload of stuff she brought? We should've sent a van, never mind a Ford Mondeo. The whips and chains, the straps – heavens. Her dressing room could double for the tack shop where I went riding as a kid. And the penis restrainers – ugh! Some poor bugger must have a pathological need to be chastised if he's going to wear those.'

'Were you honestly going to let her show one on screen? It's hardly family viewing.'

'Too true. We're nowhere near the nine p.m. watershed. This series is likely to transmit just after nine *a.m.* So you're right, we haven't a snowball's chance in hell of getting away with it.'

'But you'd still like me to try to persuade her, with everything toned down a jot?' Hetty was smiling broadly.

'We'll have to. Spent a chunk of budget on her and can't waste it. Tell her to lace up that revolting rubber body-shaper two inches higher, and make sure her knickers aren't showing. Superglue her nipples inside that basque, if necessary. But get her on this set if it kills you, Hetty. You have five minutes.'

The canteen was unusually crowded, with a queue at the tea urn and some bickering over the cakes and pastries. A stranger, a short wide man in a blue T-shirt, trod on Hetty's foot and muttered an apology.

'What's going on?' she asked Kate.

The researcher pushed her spectacles up her nose. '*Star Style*. They've taken the big studio. Very popular – four million audience, and it's repeated. Have you seen it?'

Hetty had to confess she hadn't. Working on television herself left precious little time for watching it, especially during the day. In any case, her determination not to spend hours passively ogling the box was bearing fruit, as she had begun to plough happily through the later novels of Jane Austen. Joanna Trollope had been long abandoned.

'It's a makeover programme,' Kate explained. 'They take two ordinary people, friends or a couple, and redo the lot: hair, makeup and clothes. Quite clever – the result is usually a transformation.'

'Probably choose 'em grotty to begin with,' Hetty said. 'It's the sort of thing I might almost have volunteered for, in the old days, with my husband. Though I'm not sure he'd have been vain enough to do it.'

'Um,' said Kate, noncommittally. 'It's normally harder persuading men. Women are no sweat – they queue up for the free beautification and ignore the ritual public humiliation. But men are far more wary.'

'Yet they need it more than we do.'

'D'you reckon? I'm not an expert on men. They all look alike to me.' Kate's eyes were roving towards Rosa; her face assumed a hangdog expression.

'Oh, sure, especially in middle age. Women make more effort. The men let themselves go. Men in their fifties can be ghastly.' Hetty was aware of a tinge of insincerity in her voice. What was it? Wishful thinking? Was she still arguing with the mirror?

'If you say so.' Kate sounded doubtful. 'Not many women are as adorable as our beloved producer, at any age. With respect. You don't think she might be a teensy-weensy bit bisexual, do you?'

'Not a chance,' laughed Hetty, and squeezed Kate's arm.

Hetty cursed as she tried, but failed, to stop her fingers straying to the turkey-and-Brie-stuffed croissants. The receptionist appeared in the doorway and called to her, 'A young lady's arrived, says she knows you, but she's not on the list of guests. Says she's your daughter.'

'Sally? What's she doing here?' Hetty felt anxious and hurried into Reception. But Sally was grinning broadly, and seemed rather pleased with herself.

'Hi.' She greeted her mother with a brief kiss. 'Hope you

don't mind. I wanted to tell somebody quickly.'

'*You're pregnant.*' It came out like an accusation. Sally blinked, astonished.

'No, of course not. Not much chance of that. No, I've got a new job. Sorry to barge in. Can I tell you about it?'

Hetty led the way back into the canteen, found two polystyrene cups and poured coffee. The crew of *Star Style* were drifting back to their studio. The short man was talking in a corner. According to Kate, he was the producer.

'So, shoot,' Hetty said, in her best television manner. They sat opposite each other. Sally's hair was blonder than before and layered neatly, in place of the rather careworn disorder, replete with split ends, of the days at the health farm. 'You've had your hair done. It's lovely. Did it cost a fortune?'

Sally rolled her eyes. 'Mayfair. A hundred quid including highlights. But I'll have to get used to the expense. Gotta go upmarket for the world's biggest airline, haven't I?'

'British Airways? Is that the job?'

'Yes!' Sally was clearly delighted. 'It was time for a change, Mum. Charter holidays to Ibiza were getting me down. The passengers, not the crew – they were fine. But, ugh, the drunks guzzling the duty-free and goosing us, and horrible kids running around being sick. I was threatened with a bottle last month, though we pinned down the guy quickly – he was in no shape to stand, let alone fight. He ended the flight in handcuffs. I've often felt I could do better. So I'm upgrading. Going for the hot shots. I'll be doing business class from here on, mainly on transatlantic flights.'

'Businessmen? They get drunk too, you know.'

'At least they tip well. And, you never know. I might get to meet Mr Right.'

'On a plane?'

'Sure. It's eleven hours to San Francisco. Maybe I'll get to join the Mile High Club.'

Hetty had read the term somewhere, but couldn't be sure. 'What d'you mean?'

Sally's peal of laughter rang out. 'You mean you don't know? You *have* led a sheltered life. It means sex in the stratosphere. Lots of people manage it. You'd be surprised. One pair called me over recently on a flight to Athens and asked for permission to make love under a blanket. I ask you!'

'And you'd like to be one of them,' Hetty responded drily, though she had no wish to dent her daughter's new-found enthusiasm. 'I *did* know – I'd just forgotten. Not the sort of thing we discussed at the parish council.' She checked the clock. 'I must go. I am thrilled for you, and especially pleased that you wanted to come and tell me. Last time you did that, you were eleven and you'd come first in the art exam at school.'

They were interrupted by the man in the blue T-shirt. He introduced himself as Tom, then, eyes flitting from one to the other, said, 'I hear you're mother and daughter. You can see the resemblance.'

'We are,' said Sally.

'Ever been on TV?' the man asked.

'No,' came from them both, Hetty cautious, Sally intrigued.

He took a greasy wallet from a back pocket, extracted a card and addressed Sally.

'I work for *Star Style*. We're forever on the lookout for interesting couples. People our audience could relate to. You two'd do great. Pretty young lass – our stylists could make you stunning. And your mother here, very typical of our viewers at home. Middle-aged – know what I mean? A makeover'd do her the world of good, and it's free.' He waggled a hand. 'You get to keep the clothes and the cosmetics. Give it some thought, and let us know.' He hurried away.

Sally's eyes shone. She began to chatter about the possibilities, then stopped. 'Darn. I don't suppose I should. Not with a new position. My employers mightn't like it.'

Hetty snatched the card. 'Typically middle-aged. Huh!'

'Well, you are. Face it. But I can suggest somebody you should do it with. Someone a lot older, who could help put you in a favourable light . . .'

'Who?'

'Granny. *Your* mother. And wouldn't she just steal the show?'

She had missed a bus, and began to walk. As she headed away from the studio, Hetty's route took her past the bicycle shop half-way up the hill. It was still light. Slightly puffed with the mild exertion, she gazed idly in at the window, through the rolls of tyres that hung about the door frame like ringlets, past the tattered advertisements for ancient brands of batteries.

She peered inside. The shopkeeper was tinkering with a bicycle which sat helpless, upside down on its handlebars. The man was tall and spare in a blue overall, with steel-rimmed spectacles. Beside him crouched a skinny cyclist in green Lycra leggings. The bike's complex gear system had them scratching their heads.

There was no harm in looking. The interior was crammed with frames, tyres, handlebars, saddles, chrome pipework, silver and red headlights and reflectors in racks. Clothing in every garish hue was piled higgledy-piggledy on shelves, hung from the ceiling and tacked to the walls. The smell of rubber and lubricating oil enriched with a faint tinge of sweat stirred her memory. It was thirty years since she had ridden a bike.

'Hello. Were you interested in anything?'

'Maybe,' said Hetty. 'D'you sell second-hand bikes?'

'We do. A ladies', was it? A road bike? You'd need a twenty-inch frame. Let me see.'

The biker righted his machine as if it weighed almost nothing, opened the street door and left. Her last glimpse of him was of a stick-thin praying mantis crouched over the handlebars, helmeted head down, buttocks pumping from a standing start uphill. He had not registered her existence; she could not fail to admire his.

'What is the bike to be used for, miss?'

'To and from work, mainly. And perhaps to go to the leisure centre for a swim. It's a bit far to walk and I should feel guilty going by bus,' Hetty said shyly.

The man smiled. 'Any cross-country?'

'Absolutely not. The roads are bad enough,' Hetty answered. She smiled back.

'Safer than the roads, it is.' He took off the spectacles and wiped them on a clean corner of his apron. 'Wait till you've tried Putney high street in the rush-hour.'

Hetty made a mental note not to.

The rest of the walk home seemed further than usual. Three buses came and went before she could get to a bus stop. But from tomorrow onwards, when her chosen steed would be ready for her, the journey would be half an hour shorter.

Should she get green Lycra leggings? Now, or wait?

*

'Darling Hetty! You came to my gig. Hope you enjoyed it. Dying to see you again. My agent Ted says you're gorgeous, he says it was all he could do to keep his hands off you. I said, "Lay off, the lady's mine." So how's about it? When do I get to toot my tin horn for you again? I'm appearing on Sunday . . .'

Hetty frowned. It was the third message Al had left. In none had he apologised for leaving her to her fate on New Year's Eve. In his own eyes it was obvious that he had behaved impeccably. His tone betrayed puzzlement as to why she had left before the end of the night; he assumed that perhaps she had not been feeling well, which she took as a euphemism for having drunk too much. The comment from Ted, so patently false, must be intended as a compliment. More strange language.

But her presence had been an irrelevance to Al, to Ted, to Mandy and everyone else in the night-club. They had barely noticed she was there. It was not stupid to suspect that, if she were to accept further invitations, the pattern would repeat itself. Not only would she have to endure the incomprehensible caterwauling that passed for music – and pretend to love it – but she would be an adjunct, ignored by her host until it suited him, with no guarantee even then that he would pay her much attention.

Since she had not hung around, what might have happened afterwards was a mystery. Sex, probably. That in itself would be a welcome and positive act, even with Al, assuming he was competent. She had to break her duck, sooner or later: it might be easier with a man with little emotional baggage. But before that? Jazz players drank, and took substances, and smoked cannabis. Was she expected to be a good sport and join in that, too? Should she? She'd draw the line at hard drugs. If that's what it took for him and his ladies to get high, they could count her out. Cannabis *maybe*. And what if Al took it for granted that she was a sophisticated type. Perhaps he liked group sex. Suppose Ted and Mandy got involved too?

Hetty's fingers paused over the erase button. What did a man like that see in a woman like herself – fat and middle-aged, as the mirror, her daughter and practically everyone else kept telling her? Except that she had glowed that night, had been glamorous and excited. Ted's compliments had the ring of truth. She had not disgraced herself.

Was he the sort of man who didn't give up, who assumed all women found him irresistible? That's what he'd claimed on the show. It could explain why he was so casual about the niceties. Yet, in fact, she had been the sole female groupie present.

Al was younger. A younger lover was not such a crazy idea. If she could keep him satisfied. *That* would make Sally's eyebrows shoot up into her fancy new hairdo. It would be something to boast about to Clarissa. And Rosa would be agog.

From her meagre acquaintance a few conclusions could be drawn. Al was a big kid, a one-track-minded adolescent engrossed in his own talent. If she did want to sleep with him, she would have to do the chasing.

'One thing's for sure,' Hetty told herself, '*I* am not fixated on *him*. And I'm not quite desperate enough. On the other hand, waste not, want not.'

She pressed the button for the next message, and gaped as it played.

'*Oh, hello. Not sure I've got the right number. If it's Hetty Clarkson, then this is James Dolland. Your brother Larry suggested I call. We were at school together, remember? I work in*

*London during the week. Larry thought we ought to renew the
friendship. My number is . . .'*

'Goddamn!' Hetty swore.

Her brother was matchmaking. How dare he? Her brow
furrowed. James Dolland. Had he been in her class or
Larry's? Which school? She cudgelled her brain to remember, but came up with a complete blank. Whoever he was,
he had not made much impression on her at the time. Maybe
he had improved. Maybe he was splendid. Especially if he
did not like jazz.

Hetty made a note of the number. But she did not call
back. It would not do to appear too keen.

The sound equipment was giving trouble and the crew had
been given a hour off. Hetty found Rosa in the tiny office,
engrossed on the Internet.

'What are you doing? Researching for guests?' Hetty
asked.

Rosa pointed at the monitor. 'No, I'm playing hooky.
Every so often I call up one of the interconnect services.
Chat rooms for adults. Meeting places, if you like. Lunatics
unlimited.'

The cursor was blinking; letters flickered into a line.
Hetty drew up a chair. 'What's this guy asking – what size
shoe you wear?'

'He's from Basingstoke. I've told him five and a half, and
he says that's too small.'

'Maybe he's a chiropodist.'

Rosa blew a raspberry. Hetty tried again. 'Or a foot
fetishist.'

'Usually, that sort prefer *small* feet. Toes like nipples.
Little toe like a clit, as one of my lovers once said. That's

why they like to suck them. I think this geezer wants a tall
partner, and doesn't like to come out with it.'

'Why not? He can't see you. You could lie, Rosa.'

'If he were tall himself, he'd say so. That means he isn't.
And I don't fancy a dinky guy who wants a big lass with
boobs that can bob about on the top of his head. Maybe he's
so petite he just wants to burrow his noddle inside my – what
the hell? Let's tell him to push off, and we'll try another.'

Hetty was amazed. She did not have a computer, though
she was accustomed to using one in Dorset. For the time
being, she had no need: letters could be written by hand, and
phone calls sufficed for most purposes. She also feared getting lost on a global network and running up vast phone
bills. Rosa, however, was a competent surfer.

'Here's one! Look.'

The screen said, 'Hello there. Are you
shapely? Beautiful? Looking for a new man?
Tell me truthfully. How old are you?'

Rosa tapped in, 'I'm Rosa. I'm five foot
five, nine stone, and in my adorable forties.'

'That *is* a lie,' hissed Hetty. Rosa hushed her.

'Perfect. My name's Ian. I live in
Watford. What would you say to a slim,
handsome 28-year-old who's into older
women?'

'I'd say, keep talking, Ian. Tell me
about yourself.'

'I can see you. You're fabulous. I'd
like to put my big cock into your cunt
right now. It's huge. I've got it right
here in my hand. Are you juicy?'

Rosa and Hetty squealed and clutched each other. Hetty's
chair threatened to collapse. It was several moments before
they could stop shrieking with laughter, wipe their eyes and
whisper to each other.

'Oh, sod him,' said Rosa. She tapped in, `What's the
matter with you? What a rotten way to say
hello to a respectable lady you've never
met. Can't you do better than that?'

There was a pause. Then came, `That's the nicest
response I've ever had. Sorry. SORRY. Can
we start again?'

Her mother was elated. 'Are you sure *Star Style* want
me?'

Hetty decided to be diplomatic. She was unsure how her
mother might take her substitution for Sally. 'You know
how vague these things are. Nothing's fixed. But if it does go
ahead, then we make the programme in Wandsworth. It
takes less than an hour – it's made as broadcast, virtually.
And you get to keep the outfit.'

'I've seen the show on TV. But they won't try to make
idiots of us, will they?'

'As far as I can tell, it's entirely above board. And if
anyone's going to end up a fright, it'll be me. You'll be the
picture of elegance.'

'Thank you, dear.' Hetty's mother was nothing if not gra-
cious. However, a *coup de grâce* was not beyond her. 'When
is it? Not for a couple of months, I suppose?'

'That's about right. I can tell you nearer the date.'

'Oh, splendid. And that gives you a bit of time too, Hetty
dear.'

'Time for what?'

'To lose some weight. You want to be at your best, don't you?'

The smiling, slim woman in the narrow leg trousers and cropped top pointed at Hetty. 'And why are you here?'

Hetty took a deep breath. 'Because everyone I know thinks I should be chasing men, and that it'd be a lot easier if I shed a stone. Or two.'

Titters ran round the room. The massive woman to Hetty's left clapped her hands together: her billowing thighs wobbled in unison.

It had taken more than two hours of pleading with herself, sitting on the bed in an unlit room as the dusk gathered, before Hetty had plucked up enough courage. The slimming club was in a local community hall. She knew the location: she passed it every day on her way to the bus stop. It was unthreatening, ordinary, inoffensive. The moments had ticked by as she sat frozen. Why was it such a struggle? Why couldn't she simply shrug, reach for her jacket, and march out into the night to the club? What battle was going on inside her that made her legs so leaden, and forced her instead to enter the kitchen and raid the fridge?

The confrontation with the mirror had become a daily event. Her resentment at being categorised on her appearance was real and sound, but infuriatingly irrelevant. It might have been acceptable had she aimed at earning her living as an academic, say, or in circumstances where homeliness was a virtue: for example, working with small children. And she wasn't gross, just pleasantly plump. But in the television world it was a disadvantage. Not that Hetty planned to perform in front of the camera, but at the studios she was surrounded by beautifully dressed girls skinny as beanpoles, who did have such aspirations. The male presenter had a habit of not so much looking through her as *round* her. She was in danger of becoming a non-person.

But there was more to it. The word 'victim' floated into her brain. Victim of what? Of the world's superficiality? Of the sardonic, dismissive glances that came in her direction, that took in the spreading hips and sagging jawline, and relegated her to the lower depths of whatever hierarchical system they had in mind?

Victim of her own stupidity. Of self-indulgence. Of a yearning for an easy way, when there was none. Self-pity oozed invitingly like an old scab asking to be scratched, and begged to be soothed with a Danish pastry. The results produced more self-pity. It was a vicious circle that ended up weighing two stones or more, then sat like a retread tyre slung round her middle.

She did not have to be a victim. It was up to her.

'I have to take back control of my life,' Hetty added quietly, but the instructor's questing finger had moved on.

The community hall suffered from a lack of finance, but was in constant use. The parquet floor was dusty and broken in places. The blackout curtains had not been renewed since the war and not cleaned, at a guess, for decades. The chairs Hetty recognised from her youth: tubular steel with frayed canvas seats and backs, and loose screws at the edges to catch unwary legs and fingers. They smelt musty. But the walls were alive with children's paintings from the nursery and playgroup: Ailsa and Ibrahim had been busy in the park, Sonali and Karim's offerings of buses and cars were wildly exuberant. Along one wall danced a cheerful alphabet, each letter illustrated with an animal or household object, so that a smiling Cat chased a nappied Baby, a Giraffe galloped before a Hand, a Sock and a Teapot were gaily intertwined. The celebration of childhood lifted Hetty's spirits as she had waited in line to join. She clung to that feeling as she read the club's booklets, and tried to concentrate.

The hall was full. This club was popular, with over a hundred in attendance each Monday evening. Ten minutes after the time the club was supposed to start Hetty had tentatively crept through the door, to be greeted by a barrage of chattering voices. Mostly women, of every shape and size, some vast, some black, many young, a few older than herself. A select few, slim and smug, flaunted gold cards, proof of success. The two men present sucked in beer bellies, examined their record cards with hopeful expressions and did not stay for the pep talk. Nobody took much notice of her; established members were comparing their week, congratulating each other on pounds lost, ruefully or with outbursts of hilarity. As Hetty watched, one woman jumped off the scales with a delighted squeal and hugged the instructor.

'It'd be nice,' Hetty ventured to her obese neighbour, 'if we could do this by ourselves. Stay under control without help.'

The woman was in her fifties and must have weighed twenty stone. Her immense bulk, spread across two chairs pushed together, had a liquid quality as if held together only by the envelope of her skin. A husky chuckle heaved from the depths of a multiple hairy chin. 'I put it on in company, and I'm getting it off in company. Take me another year at least. But it's shifting, thank God.'

'How much have you got to lose?' Hetty asked in awe.

''Bout ten stone more,' wheezed the woman affably. 'Lost three already. It's going at about three pounds a week at the moment. Later on it'll slow down. But by then I'll be able to walk a bit, and we'll get a dog.'

'Doesn't it make you slightly cross,' Hetty ventured, 'that we're judged so much by our appearance in modern society?'

The woman raised an eyebrow. 'If I cared how I look, I wouldn't look like this, dear.'

Hetty was abashed. The woman patted her knee. 'Doctor told me I had three months to live. I ran a chip shop and used to demolish five fish-and-chip meals a day, mega portions, plus hamburgers, saveloys, the lot – they called me the Human Shovel. Tried every quack cure – mouth wired, my stomach stapled. I'd lose some, it'd go back on again. Heavier each time. Then Marge stopped me in the street.' She indicated the instructor, who was speaking to a squat Asian woman in a sari. 'She said she'd been almost as big as me once, and she could help me. No potions, no hospitals. So I upped and sold the business. And here I am.'

Hetty was silent. By contrast, her own agonising seemed pathetic. She examined the instructor from a distance, then realised with a jolt that the nearby blown-up photo of a barrel-like woman in a flowered print tent must be the same individual.

'Oh, no. Hetty?' A young voice groaned behind her. It was Annabel, in black, her clothes still too tight for her, with her usual mournful air. 'What are you doing here?' she continued as she plonked down hard on a vacant chair, which sagged alarmingly. 'You don't need to slim.'

'I do,' said Hetty firmly, with missionary zeal. 'It's going to take me ages. Then I intend to keep it off. I have a choice. Do I want to be a middle-aged frump, past it, or a vibrant single woman starting out afresh?'

'Come again?' said Annabel.

Hetty giggled. 'What about you, Annabel? How's the love-life?'

'Ghastly. Non-existent. That's why I'm here. D'you think she'll tell me to stop drinking?'

'Mmm. Possibly to stop drinking so much.'

Annabel was dubious. 'Not sure I can cut down, honestly. I mean, if a girl calls a halt before she's finished the bottle, her friends'll think she's on the wagon.'

'Diet Coke?' suggested Hetty.

'Yurrkk!' said Annabel.

The instructor was standing in front of them. Her narrow hips failed to fill out her blue trousers; her wrists were bony, the fingernails almost bloodless. 'Courgettes,' she said.

'Pardon?' asked Hetty. She had missed the first part of the woman's remark.

'Courgettes. Vegetables. They have no calories, provided you cook them according to the booklet. Very tasty.'

To Hetty, courgettes were a tedious watery nothingness at which both Stephen and the children had turned up their noses. She pondered, then shrugged.

She would try courgettes. Why not? They might, at any rate, make a solid change from bananas.

CHAPTER THIRTEEN

Valentine

Tomorrow it would be Valentine's Day. A Sunday.

Nothing had arrived in the post. Not a card, not a letter. Hetty unlocked the postbox and cleared out the plain envelopes with their window labels. Nothing handwritten. She opened them over a meagre breakfast and coffee: two offers to lend her up to £15,000, the information that her name was in a draw for a car provided she attended a presentation on time-share in Sicily, and a coding notice from the Inland Revenue.

There was no reason to expect any cards. Al, who might have been idiotic enough to send one, did not have her address: the liaison had never progressed that far. James Dolland probably didn't have it either. Once, a person's phone number had been regarded as private information; now it was the first detail anyone expected, while an address had receded to a hinterland of greater intimacy. In any case, all James wanted was to make contact. A Valentine would have been inappropriate. Next year? Maybe.

Last year had been different. A fancy lace-frilled card had materialised on her pillow, and Stephen had been effusive with a hug. Her response had been more modest and stilted. At lunchtime on the day (it had been a Saturday) they had gone to the village pub, only to discover that the dining room was packed, and since Stephen had forgotten to book, they had had to wait. As they had sat, drinks before them, for more than an hour, conversation had waned. By the time they had been served a limp prawn cocktail, overdone roast beef and soggy trimmings, a barren irritation had set in on both sides. Most of the meal had been eaten in silence, punctuated only by brief comments. It had been a relief to get home. Hetty had then pulled out the ironing board, Stephen had switched on the television and promptly fallen asleep. Later she had heard him murmuring on the phone. She had wondered who he was speaking to, but did not ask.

But at least there'd been that card in the morning, and the hope, as ever, that their love might recover. It was the same belief that had deceived her for years. But here in The Swallows, nothing. Loneliness and melancholy lay in wait in the little jam-pot, the single teacup. Hope, that gentle protector, was spread too thinly for comfort.

Hetty finished her toast and found herself staring blankly at the plate. She moved; a fuzzy image reflecting her red sweater moved with her, but the dish's crumb-ridden surface could give but a blurred impression. Someone alive was nearby, the plate said, but ill-defined and unrecognisable. Someone who did not receive Valentine cards. About whom nobody cared.

A tear fell on the plate, then another. Hetty wiped her

eyes with her fingers. She let herself cry, just for a moment. Then, swiftly, she gathered up the crockery, knife and spoon and swept them into the sink.

On the phone, Mother waxed excited and schoolgirlish.

'I've had my invitation from *Star Style*! They say to come in my everyday clothes, and not to worry about getting my hair done or anything special. What do you think?'

'The idea is to transform you. They need a clear "before", I suppose,' Hetty answered.

'But I can't turn up in old trousers and a pinny, with my hair a mess, can I?'

Hetty had a sudden picture of her mother dressed like the domestic version of Doris. 'You could, but it wouldn't be the authentic you,' she admitted. 'Don't overdo it. They may make some unkind remarks to start with.'

'Such as?' Her mother's voice betrayed concern.

In reality, since Hetty still had not found time to watch the video of an earlier show, she hadn't the faintest idea. But it seemed wise to dampen her mother's enthusiasm.

'Such as – they would describe you, for example, as a mature woman.'

'Oh, really.' Her mother sounded offended. 'In that case, dear, how would they describe you?'

This was the best way to tackle it. Seize the day, or whatever. Gather ye rosebuds. If Sunday – Valentine's Day – was to be rescued from self-pity and disaster, then an excess of zeal on her new bike would serve as well as anything. Hetty shifted the gears to a lower notch and pedalled furiously up the steepest part of West Hill towards Tibbet's Corner. The heavy gravel surface of the A3, designed to reduce skidding in the wet, was gruelling to two-wheel users. But as she reached the top without stopping, she congratulated herself on progress made so far.

At first, cycling had been a refined system of torture. Leg tendons and muscles ached maddeningly the next day. To her surprise, so did her shoulders and wrists, till she caught sight of herself in a shop window, hunched over the handlebars like a mad crow or a Valkyrie. Whenever she remembered, she would sit upright, and flap one hand then the other to relieve the tension.

She rode alone: to the studios during the week, and out, more ambitiously, at weekends on those days that, like this one, held no promise of other entertainment. The option of joining a club had entered her mind but had been dismissed. It was grim enough coping with new acquaintances at work and in her personal life, without adding another element that might be competitive and raw. In any case Hetty soon came to enjoy her own company, especially in fair weather. This was almost the only extended period when she was on her own and not tired out. Mostly, the rides felt like an escape.

She halted cautiously at the main roundabout. At ten thirty on a brisk Sunday morning not much traffic was about. Her return route through Kingston later would be busy and she could expect to encounter irritated motorists stuck in bottlenecks, who would refuse to make room on the near side for a cyclist to pass.

Then it was over the main road and on to Putney Heath, and a clean breeze in her face. Although she had initially feared going off-road, the bridle-paths of the heath and of Wimbledon Common a couple of miles further on were a great attraction. The nearer, northern part was scrub, gorse and uncut grass, with a sweep of open land near the wind-mill full of yapping Labradors and ill-parked jeeps. Closer to Wimbledon itself, mature woodland took over. There, she would be riding squishily along muddy paths deep in mouldering leaves, accompanied by magpies, jays and the occasional robin. Grey squirrels would perk up, their paws like tiny hands possessively clutching nuts, and eye her passage. There were worse ways of spending a spare couple of hours.

Hetty accepted that she probably looked odd. A scarf constantly threatened to unwind and fly off. Her knuckles were frozen despite gloves. She was hardly a proper sportswoman, but that was not her objective: the aim was to increase her fitness level, not compete in the Tour de France. Or appear in *Zest* magazine or *Here's Health*. Hetty had never summoned up the courage to buy the green stretch leggings, though her thighs and buttocks were soon tightening up nicely. She did, however, return to the store and braved the shopkeeper's amused expression to buy two sets of padded shorts. Saddle-soreness was *not* on the agenda.

On one issue, the man had been spot on. Cycling round south London was a nerve-racking terror. It felt, and probably was, horribly dangerous. Hetty suffered a hot flush of shame as she remembered how often, as a car driver, she had failed to notice a biker, who had had to swerve as she pulled out. Now, she saw, cyclists were invisible to most motorists, even if they were sporting, as she was, a Dayglo jacket with their lights switched on. Cars and vans respected vehicles big enough to do some damage, and no others. A two-wheeler was no more than a gnat on the skin of a rhinoceros.

In her new guise she began to harbour uncharacteristically uncharitable thoughts about school runs. Four-wheel-drive monsters too large for suburbia with screaming infants in the back, driven by harassed mothers in desperate need of a cigarette and a coffee tried pitilessly to force their passage, with dire consequences for anyone in their path. The biker's viewpoint was several feet more elevated than theirs: Hetty could see trouble coming much earlier than they could. Traffic round a corner, an elderly person trying to cross, a milk-float about to pull out. There was no point in shouting: no one could hear. Again and again the car would screech to a halt, the driver would lower the window and let loose a stream of invective, the cyclist would fall off and get the blame.

On the other hand, bikers were hardly blameless. As she paused at traffic lights *en route* to the studio, Hetty found herself categorising riders drawn up alongside.

The cycling buff, exemplified by the praying mantis in the bike shop, was less common than she had supposed. As lean and taut as his machine, often a racing model bristling with accessories, he would glide silently to a stop in front of her, and be a hundred yards down the road again before she had managed to place a foot on a pedal. Invariably they were male, with narrow hips and ribcages lifting through silky fabric. They sported gloves like knuckle-dusters and toe-guards like sabre handles: their saddles were fearsomely pointed, the handlebars slung low and held like machine-guns. Some, she suspected, given their style, must be into sado-masochism with a vengeance.

Then there were the commuters. Some, however, unlike herself, made no concessions to their mode of transport. Amongst the girls helmets were *infra dig*: loose untied hair streamed behind and whipped wetly into the eyes when it rained. Skirts flapped at ankles and threatened to get caught

in the spokes or chain. A handbag was often slung precariously over one shoulder, a carrier bag balanced on the front.
As traffic lights changed they wobbled menacingly. Hetty
gave them a wide berth.

A third group came into view on a route near a major
construction site: the Lads. Everything about them
announced their unwillingness to be cyclists. The battered
bikes sagged unhappily like ancient mules under their riders'
considerable weight. Their knees stuck out at an angle from
seats set too low, as if comfort adjustments were disdained.
No nonsense about protective headgear or warning Dayglo
troubled the Lads' brains. Instead, the trademark was a
mortar-encrusted donkey jacket. Beneath the jackets, and
increasingly visible as the weather grew warmer, pale buttocks heaved up over their jeans. As she waited patiently for
the lights to change, Hetty was mischievously tempted to
pinch the bulging flesh, but reckoned they could outride
her.

'I wouldn't have thought you guys would enjoy cycling,'
she said one morning.

'Too bloody right,' one answered, wiping his nose on his
sleeve. 'Lost me licence, didn't I? Get it back next year,
though. Then you won't see us for dust.'

She was close to the windmill now. A dog barked excitedly in the distance. Above, the strengthening sun turned
the bark of upper branches to gold and sent slanting shadows through those darker, mysterious corners of the
common yet to be explored. She lifted her head and sniffed
the air, almost animal herself. A feeling of joy, and of serenity, seeped through her, as her system settled rhythmically
into the exercise.

As open land gave way to trees, she was forced to pedal

more gently. In the bushes to one side, low down, came a commotion; she slowed, and a small leggy animal, a young deer, trotted across. The long fronds closed behind it, leaving only a trail of pert footprints in the mud. Could it have been a muntjak? Hetty waited, fascinated, but no more followed. This was a moment to savour, and she breathed deep, taking in the budded trees, the freshness of the new grass, the blossom starting in the hedges, the pale warmth of the sun on her back.

Unbidden, the picture came into her mind of Clarissa and her bags of shopping, and of Sally serving gin to jaded businessmen on a plane. Her mother might well be sinking a G and T with a half-sozzled colonel on a cut-price romantic weekend. Rosa could be anywhere, with anyone. Al, having blown his soul into his saxophone, was in all probability snoring in some seedy bedroom, his head pillowed on someone's bosom. The three BJs would be out cold, and so too would Brian, the seller of the *Big Issue*. She had not seen him since New Year's Eve. Father Roger would be active in his pulpit. Larry and Davinia were almost certainly eating more than was good for them, and snapping at their children. Were she still married herself, she might have been basting a Sunday roast, a meal that would have been praised but not appreciated. Or sitting, desperately trying to think of something to say that would not lead to a row, in that stuffy mock-Tudor pub with Stephen. Neither proposition, it came to her, was something she desperately missed.

She would ride through Wimbledon, in no hurry, and window-shop. Then she would head home, buy croissants and orange juice in the café that was open on Sunday, plus the newspapers, and spend a lazy half-hour soaking in a soapy tub. She might amuse herself with the contact ads, might even ring a few that caught her fancy.

If this was to be her lot for a while, it would serve. A muted rapture, perhaps, but tinged with a sense of well-being. On the whole, she felt content.

On her mat was a small brown box, with a red ribbon tied in an elaborate bow. No name or details were written on it. Intrigued, helmet in hand, Hetty picked it up and fished in her pockets for her keys. Her limbs felt numb and weary, but not painful. Later, she would sleep soundly, and wake refreshed and fulfilled.

The phone began to ring as she opened the door. Wiping grime from her face, she picked it up. 'Hello?'

'Is that you, Het? Glad I've caught you in. Have you got your diary handy?'

Hetty took the handset away from her ear and stared at it. 'Who is this, please?'

'Hetty! I know it's been a while since we spoke. Larry. Your loving brother.'

'Larry. Yes. Hi,' she replied, without enthusiasm.

'Davinia and I have been talking. Sorry about the mix-up over Christmas. We should have realised you wouldn't want to babysit, having so recently left all that behind you. Might be different when you have grandchildren, hey?'

'That's okay, Larry. I wasn't in the mood.'

He paused as if expecting her to apologise and offer help in the future. The screeching of the two monsters who passed for infants in Larry and Davinia's household was unmissable in the background. She resisted the temptation without a qualm.

'Right. Fine,' he continued uncertainly.

'So what exactly were you and Davinia thinking, Larry?'

'About you. How are you getting on?'

'Great. I've just been on a bike ride. I need a bath.'

'A bike ride? What – on your own?'

'On my bike, Larry.'

'Yes – er, I see. Well, look. What we thought was this. You shouldn't be on your own. It's not right.'

Hetty sighed audibly but did not answer.

'See?' Larry had apparently taken the sigh as forlorn agreement. His tone became eager. 'We want to try and help you, sis. So we're at last organising that dinner party we promised. Sorry it's taken so long, but you understand . . .'

'Did you give my phone number to James Dolland?'

Larry snickered. 'That guy we were at school with? We met up at a client's and got talking about you. He used to be quite keen, he said.'

'I can't remember him at all,' Hetty said, crossly. Her muscles were starting to stiffen. 'Please, Larry, I'm sure you mean well, but I'd rather you didn't hand out my number willy-nilly. Even if he was passable as a schoolboy, who knows what he's like now?'

'I know,' said Larry triumphantly. 'He's in good shape, honest. I wouldn't pick a turkey for my own sister, now, would I?'

Hetty stopped herself giving a tart reply.

Larry continued, 'Anyway, we're going to arrange this dinner party for you. James has already said he'll come. How about . . .'

Several minutes' negotiation ensued, until Hetty ran out of excuses. A date was fixed. Ten minutes later she was up to her nose in perfumed bubbles and watching the mud of the ride floating off as planned, but the atmosphere had been soured.

Who was James? She could not put a face to him, nor had his voice, brief on the answerphone, rung bells. He had called only once, and she had not called back, though some instinct told her she ought to. She was not entirely hostile to the man. About him, indeed, she had no feelings whatsoever. It was the manner in which the contact had been made that was depressing.

'You ought to be grateful.' The trenchant, supercilious voice was hovering over her navel. It was her own, that infuriating *alter ego* that had tormented her into both cycling and the slimming club. Hetty groaned, and sank lower into the tub.

'Here are your friends and family, concerned about your welfare, trying to ensure that you aren't condemned to a lifetime of solitary misery.'

'That's not what they're up to,' Hetty retorted. 'And I am not lonely, or at least not often. The tears at yesterday's breakfast were a blip.'

'You should be delighted that they're flinging desirable male company at you,' the voice lilted, menacingly.

'I don't need it.'

'You sure?'

Hetty considered, tossing the flannel from hand to hand. The very idea of her family as matchmakers was excruciating. If she were to make progress, she would rather do it at her own pace, and under her own control.

The voice wheedled, 'At least you'll acknowledge that your brother means well?'

'Him?' Hetty snorted. 'I doubt it. He never means well, pure and simple. He doesn't like anything untidy. He hates it if anything unexpected breaks cover in case it'll bite him. My unusual state – or, at least, Larry and Davinia'd regard it as unusual – would niggle at him till he had to do something. I'm in a defective condition. He sees it as his familial duty to put me right.'

'Hetty, you need all the help you can get.'

'Do I? The term "control freak" could have been invented for Larry. He and Davinia are bad news. They're militant marrieds, though they've never gone near an altar.'

'Ah, loving coupledom. They've been together ages. You're not knocking it now?'

'Not at all. But I'd love 'em more if it wasn't so blatant. Their version – their unmarried state – is just a fad. They're slaves to the *mores* of Fulham and Chelsea. It's *far* smarter for Larry to introduce Davinia as "my partner" than as "my wife".'

'Perhaps they'd claim that a piece of paper, or vows in church, don't make a marriage,' opined the voice unctuously.

'I don't believe it,' Hetty muttered. 'As and when their circle of friends head for legality, they will too. Avoid the stampede? Not join the uncommon herd? You've got to be joking. They won't be the first but they would never be the last.'

Hetty brooded as the water began to cool. What Larry and Davinia couldn't cope with was any notion that their fashion-driven lifestyle wasn't for everybody. Since they saw their choices as both necessary and sufficient for success, so must everyone else, and it followed that alternatives implied failure.

'I am not a failure!' Hetty told the bathroom ceiling fiercely. 'And I won't have my prat of a brother telling me so. Damn his eyeballs.'

Her toes, pale and white-nailed, wiggled their agreement

at the far end of the tub; the mountains of her knees and her hilly breasts wallowed in sympathy. The bump of her belly disappeared when she sucked it in, the water swishing merrily into the hollow. It was like a new landscape, one entirely private, about to be invaded by her brother, trailing in his wake potential lovers, men whom *he* regarded as suitable.

Invaders were to be repelled. Hetty skimmed the soap into the sudsy water by her feet and made a splash, like the puff of smoke after an explosion. It was heartily satisfying. She giggled, retrieved the slippery missile and threw again. Who was to object? Soon the floor was awash with foam and puddles, and her hair was soaked.

She heaved herself from the water and reached for a towel. Two towels, then four, warm and cosy from the heated rail. The sodden bathroom could take care of itself. Swaddled like a Roman, she stumbled into the kitchen and poured a glass of wine from the bottle in the fridge. Outside it had begun to rain, and she was hungry.

Till Larry had phoned she had been at ease. The best defence to his onslaught, however, was obvious. She would go to their precious dinner party dressed to the nines, elegant and feminine with 'happy' written on her face. She would flirt with James and any other man present, as might be expected of a single woman in her position – her *unfortunate* position. She would allow herself to be patronised by her brother and sister-in-law, and try to be good company.

And she would keep her temper, and her own counsel.

It was not till a while later that Hetty rediscovered the cardboard box under the helmet and gloves; not till she had dressed, finished the wine and was drowsy and content.

Who might have put it there? Somebody who knew her

address, certainly. The ribbon suggested it was a gift, of sorts. Not chocolates: the box was too utilitarian. She shook it experimentally and heard a clinking noise. Metal? Electrical? What could it be?

Inside was tissue paper and an illustrated card. Hetty began to laugh.

New stock for Valentine's. Thought you might like a free sample. I put batteries in. Enjoy yourself. Doris.

The glossy leaflet dubbed it the 'Passion Orgasm Kit'. Hetty gingerly picked up the translucent bobbled, ribbed and spiky attachments, then pressed the switch and rubbed the multi-speed pink gadget experimentally against her arm. It made her skin tingle. 'Seven and a half inches,' she murmured, glancing at the leaflet. 'Now, Doris, are we being pessimistic, or isn't that a bit *small*?'

CHAPTER FOURTEEN

Stepping Out

Clarissa's voice sounded odd. So did her request. 'I need some moral support. Be a pal, Hetty.'

Hetty pulled a cushion off the sofa on to the floor and sat on it, her legs tucked under her, the phone cradled in her lap. The attempts at slimming seemed to be working, but at the end of a busy day left her weary. She was not sure what reservoir of energy remained to cope with Clarissa's moral needs, whatever they might be.

'I can't do it alone. The thought fills me with panic,' Clarissa continued, in a wail.

A great yearning came upon Hetty to put the call on hold and retrieve a hidden packet of chocolate digestives. She gritted her teeth. 'I'm listening.'

'You know that big modern building near you? Further down your road. Swallow House, it's called.'

'Yes – a posh old people's home, isn't it? I've walked past.'

'Very posh. Better carpeting than I can afford. And they keep it so hot! Their heating bill . . .'

'Clarissa. What has their heating bill got to do with your moral dilemma? You don't have to pay it, do you?'

'What? Well, yes, in a manner of speaking. My aunt, Auntie Millie, my father's sister. Widowed twenty years ago. She had a mild stroke recently and decided to give up the house in St John's Wood.'

'I see,' said Hetty, who didn't quite. An image of the biscuit, the chocolate melting temptingly, shimmered in the air before her lips. She swatted it away.

'She's taken herself off to live in Swallow House. It was the only place – she was adamant. Robin and I help with the fees. So the hotter it is, the twitchier I get. It's understandable,' said Clarissa grumpily. 'She's a nice old dear, quite civilised. Doesn't ask for much and talks sense when she wants to. I try to keep her sweet.'

'And that means?' Hetty was beginning to guess.

'Oh, Hetty, I find it so tough going on my own. Not that the home is smelly or disgusting. It isn't – it's more like a five-star hotel. But all those old people! They're like dodgems with their wheelchairs – and those steel things they push around, like mobile crash barriers . . .'

'Zimmer frames?'

'Yes. And they make me shiver – age spots and turkey skin and scrawny ankles.'

'You are being unkind. We'll all be like that one day,' said Hetty severely.

'Exactly. I can't bear it. Vacant mad eyes. And death everywhere, lurking round every corner.'

'But your aunt isn't dotty, is she? You said she was nice.'

'It's the others. The whole atmosphere. Gives me the

creeps. Last time it was as much as I could do to stay half an hour. Auntie Millie was most put out. She's hinted since that if I don't visit properly, she'll come back from the other side and haunt me. She's into astrology and I believe her. Please, Hetty.'

'You want me to go with you?'

'Would you? You are a darling. Oh, Hetty, you've saved my bacon. When?'

'I was rather wondering,' Father Roger twinkled at her, 'whether your attendance at the carol concert and your lusty singing might be more than a flash in the pan, Hetty.'

You are an incorrigible rogue, Hetty said to herself. In another incarnation you were a medieval barrow boy, or a ticket tout for Shakespeare's Globe. You're a salesman at heart, even if you're selling salvation. Or the hope of it. 'Roger, you could sell fire extinguishers to the devil,' she replied, with a smile.

'I'm to take that as a compliment, I suppose.' The priest laughed. 'But you haven't answered me. You have the makings of a splendid choir member. Given that our Anglican congregations are becoming ever more ancient and decrepit, rather like our church fabric, the quicker you accept your fate and come the better.'

'I'm not sure. I may occasionally. But more for sentimental reasons rather than out of belief. I don't feel any great sense of commitment.'

Father Roger tucked his hands inside his voluminous black sleeves and rolled his eyes in mock horror. 'Commitment? Stuff and nonsense. Come because you enjoy it.'

'Aren't you supposed to say something like, "Christ was

committed enough for you, it's the least you can do in return"?' Hetty chided gently.

'No.' Father Roger shook his head vigorously.

'Why not?'

'Because it puts people off, that's why not. It's preaching. I *loathe* preachers.'

They were standing at the side of the set while Dave the sound man fixed the small clip microphones on to the clothing of the next pair of guests, a brash young couple. The man, Gary, wore white jeans and an Arsenal top, the girl a low-cut tight sweater and a miniskirt, and silky black hair down to her waist. Their swagger showed they knew their good looks; their motive for participating must be their almost tangible vanity.

A great deal of giggling ensued as the girl was required to push the clip up under the sweater. Hetty reckoned, from what she could see, that the proprieties were being observed, but the girl squealed provocatively. Her boyfriend sat back on his rump, legs splayed wide before him, and encouraged her by uttering mild threats at the sweating Dave. Job done, Dave retreated, red-faced and muttering.

'Now there's commitment for you.' Father Roger nodded towards the young man. 'Says he loves Arsenal more than anything – more than his girl, more than his job.'

'They're a fine pair,' Hetty agreed. 'They deserve each other.'

'Quiet, please. We're rolling,' called Bob, the floor manager. He waved Father Roger to his seat on set. 'And, remember, this is *family* viewing.'

In a moment Gary was pouting archly at the presenter. 'It's like this, see,' he was explaining. 'I'm in trouble with Darleen here. I do love her, and she knows it, but I love my

Arsenal more than anyfink. An' they'll be playing a cup-tie in Amsterdam the weekend it's her birthday. And she wants me to take her to Paris instead. An' I can't, I can't.'

'Could I ask,' Father Roger leaned forward, his body language almost as macho as Gary's, 'what is to stop you going to Amsterdam on the Saturday night with your mates, and then joining Darleen in Paris on the Sunday for her birthday?'

'Nah, I'd be smashed,' said Gary.

Darleen nodded energetically. 'Anyway,' she sniffed, 'that wouldn't prove he loves me, would it? An' he wouldn't turn up. I could take myself off to Paris an' spend all that money, and I'd be sitting at a restaurant on me tod till it was time to head home. No thanks.'

'How is it at home?' asked the other panellist, a soap actress of no great brain.

'Well, bit weird, really,' the girl admitted. 'See, my half of the bedroom's normal. His is in the Arsenal colours. An' the bedspread, his half. All over.'

'What, red and white strip wallpaper?'

'Yes.'

'Carpet?'

'Yes. He used carpet squares. Done 'em quite fetching.'

'But, see,' the fan broke in, his face serious, 'I couldn't cope wiv *her* taste, could I? I mean, a pink fluffy bedspread and thick pink shag pile an' flock wallpaper. Stuffed toy animals. So she has her half the way she likes it, and I have mine.'

'And do you have Arsenal posters up?'

'Yeah, but she's got Robbie Williams. Or rather, she *had*. Opening his flies. I said I'd leave unless she took that down.'

'I understand entirely.' Father Roger oozed synthetic

sympathy. 'A strict demarcation line. And you live the whole
of your lives like that, do you? How long have you been
together?'

'Five years,' the two said proudly, in unison. They held
hands and gazed fondly at each other. He flexed his thighs
and rose slightly in his chair, sucking air into his nose like a
gorilla on heat. She tossed the silky black mane back from
her face and dimpled.

The soap star, whose spectacular but speedy amours, usually with other women's husbands, often featured in the
tabloids, sighed romantically. 'Do you see yourselves staying
together, having children, maybe?'

'Oooh, yeah,' the girl said, and snickered. She tugged his
hand. 'An' you do too, Gary. You've said so.'

'Only if they're boys,' her boyfriend said stoutly. 'Then I
can take them to watch Arsenal.'

'Oh, you are a bleedin' horror,' the girl yelped. 'An' what
about my bleedin' birthday, then?'

A screech came from Bob, the floor manager. 'I said
family viewing. *Cut*. Can we do that again?'

The recording finished almost on schedule. Though the
football fan and his girlfriend caused much grief before
their piece was acceptable, the pallid teenager who featured in the second half of the show was given short shrift.
He had been put in charge of a girlfriend's cat while the
friend was on holiday. She was due back the following
week. The cat wandered, as cats will, and had been run
over and killed. Should he come clean and tell her, or buy
a new cat and hope the hapless owner could not tell the
difference?

The soap star, it turned out, was a feline fanatic. The

owner would *know*, instantly, and be devastated. Her solution was for the youth to meet the girl at the airport with a contrite expression and a box under his arm. And a tiny winsome kitten inside the box.

'Right, that's a wrap,' said Bob with a grateful sigh. 'Same time tomorrow, boys and girls. Thank you all.'

Father Roger lingered with members of the audience. He was handing out cards with pictures of St Veronica's inset with a photograph of himself and signing autographs. Hetty watched him as she shooed people out.

He caught her eye, winked, then excused himself and came back to her. 'You don't approve,' he said.

'It's only–' Hetty stopped. 'You're a rum sort of priest, Roger. Do you ever stop working?'

He considered. 'No. But then I love what I do.'

'A calling.'

'Ye-e-es. I certainly felt called when I was a young man. Can get wearisome sometimes, when parishioners roll up in numbers with their disasters – real-life ones, not the minor stupidities we've had today. Confession is the penance of High Church ministers. After dealing with half a dozen impending broken marriages in one evening, I do feel a little drained.'

'When do you do confession?'

'Mondays and Wednesdays. After choir practice. Too often at the moment it's members of the choir. They tend to assume they can sleep with each other with impunity, that their misbehaviour is somehow Teflon-coated, simply because they met in church. I tell them it won't wash in a divorce court and they must make up their minds. Awful!'

Though he was shaking his head with a twinkle in his eye, Hetty sensed that he was more deeply upset by such adulteries than he might admit. 'And you're inviting me, a single divorced woman, to join in?' she countered wryly. 'Don't worry. If I do come, I'll leave the surplices alone. But it sounds, Roger, as if you need a break. What do you do when you're free?'

'Sleep. Read. Eat.'

Hetty wondered what made her ask the next question. She had not planned it. A priest had never figured in her potential list of companions. Nor, even in fantasy, as a possible lover. He was a celibate by choice; she was not about to challenge that. Perhaps that was why he intrigued her. She noted that he had not said, 'Pray.' That fitted with his generally secular approach to the programme as well.

'D'you ever go to the theatre? I get tickets quite often. One of my neighbours is an actor. Might you like to?'

A fleeting wistfulness crossed his face. He opened his mouth as if to refuse, then chuckled. 'What a lovely idea,' he said. 'Nothing frivolous, mind. Since you don't plan to become a regular attender *yet*, I can say I'm still trying to persuade you.'

She should not make assumptions. 'I can always get an extra ticket, if there's somebody – ah, a special friend – you'd like to bring along too.'

He drew himself up. 'I am wedded to Mother Church. At least, in theory. A kind offer, but no, no one skulks in the shadows. Though the diocese is threatening me with a curate, God help me. They say a helper will take the burden off my shoulders. Add to it, more like.'

'Male or female?'

The priest crossed himself. 'I am in their hands. I'll resist to the last minute. I don't care what goes on under the cassock, Hetty. It's the prospect of having another human being endlessly at my side, whimpering and pinching my elbow, that puts me off. At least now, when the grumblers have gone, I can sit and enjoy my solitude.'

'The job's getting to you. A night on the town will do you good.'

'Dear girl, you're on.'

They chose a Friday afternoon, when *Tell Me All* finished early. Clarissa crashed the gears and swung the Volvo back into the street as Hetty fumbled for the seatbelt.

'I have insisted to Robin that the next car must be automatic,' Clarissa grunted. 'Cheaper in the long run – I've wrecked three clutches. Now, how *are* you?'

'I'm okay.'

'No more drunken orgies, I hope?'

'It wasn't an orgy, Clarissa. It was a house-warming. And it was months ago already.'

'It sounded to me,' Clarissa disapproved, 'as if you have some strange neighbours. I should be very cautious.'

'Unconventional. Not what I was used to, I grant you. But fun.'

'Huh! Flotsam and jetsam. Nothings and nobodies. Hetty, darling, you can do better than that. Now what else have you been up to?'

'I joined a slimming club. Bought a bike.'

'God! Whatever for?'

'To try and keep fit, to get me to work quicker.'

'You'll arrive looking a fright, and you'll get killed. Can't you afford a car?'

'I can, just, but I don't want to. Anyway, parking round here's a nightmare.'

'You're mad. And you're getting madder. How can you

possibly manage without a car? Come to that, what about the other necessities of life?'

'Such as?' Hetty had found the seatbelt clasp at last and snapped it closed as Clarissa slammed on the brakes at a zebra crossing. They rocked forward.

Two harassed mothers with pushchairs and toddlers straggled over the crossing. Both women were pregnant. Clarissa pointed. 'What they've got that you haven't? A man and a home. Have you found yourself another chap yet?'

'What?'

'Another man. Have you got yourself fixed up? A boyfriend?'

'No.'

'Why not? Aren't you trying?'

'A bit.' Hetty briefly described the episode with the adverts. 'I'm not their type, I guess. They see me in fishnet tights and high heels, or else they only want to chat on the phone. Or they offer nothing but a cup of tea. Maybe when I've got trim my talent-spotting will improve.'

'I hope so. It's been ages, Hetty.'

'But I'm perfectly content as I am.' She said it defensively, but as the words came out she realised it was not altogether a lie.

'Oh, rot. You *say* that, but you can't possibly be.'

'*Why* can't I?' A hint of rebellion entered her tone.

'Because men are essential. We're sociable animals, Hetty. We mate, we're bred to live in pairs. You'll go barmy, or strange, without a chap in tow.'

'I went a little strange when I had one,' Hetty ruminated. 'I lost my identity completely. These days I occupy much of my time finding out who Hetty is, and what she is capable of.'

Clarissa sniffed. 'Spare me. I know what you need, and so do you. Here we are.'

Clarissa was right about the home at least. Deep-pile Wilton in lilac welcomed their feet with an eerie sponginess. Hot air and neon hit them as the automatic doors slid open, as if they had entered a hermetically sealed netherworld. Muzak – a version of Bach, or was it Burt Bacharach? – caressed their ears.

A tiny old lady in a cream trouser suit scurried up to them, a clipboard on her arm. 'Visitors! Hello. Who are you looking for? I can take you there. This place is such a rabbit warren. We like to make everybody welcome. Tea is at three thirty in the coffee shop to the right on this floor. Our sale of work starts on Friday, in the annexe. The Mayor is coming – isn't that wonderful?' She paused for breath, her eyes wide and anxious.

'Millie Curtis, please. Can I ring her room?' Clarissa had a terrified expression and reached behind her for Hetty's hand.

'Millie? No, she won't be in her room. I shouldn't try there. I saw her ten minutes ago, heading for the library on the second floor. She'll be going to the book club. Take the lift – to your right, then left . . .'

They followed instructions. As the greeter's voice hallooed after them, 'Have a nice day,' Hetty could feel Clarissa shudder.

'It's something else, this home,' said Hetty warmly, in an effort to cheer up her friend. Both had removed their coats and were carrying them over their arms, along with the bottle of Bristol Cream and a bunch of spring flowers that Clarissa had brought. 'Is it as superb as this only on the ground floor, or is the rest equally luxurious?'

'Like a stick of rock. The same right through, except the top floor is even hotter,' Clarissa answered grimly. They found the lift, pressed the button and were transported silently and sedately to their destination.

It took a few moments to locate the library. From inside came a babble of voices, then a shriek. 'Well, I hated it! Hated it, I tell you! Boring as hell. Nobody lives like that.'

'*You* didn't like it because there was no sex.'

'Precisely. What's the point of describing adultery and broken promises and such – the plot was fine, I grant you – if the action stops at the bedroom door?'

'You are beyond redemption. You'd rather have those sleazy parliamentary novels. Plenty of red meat for you in those.'

The speakers were seated at opposite ends of a large table in the middle of a room lined with filled bookshelves. One was a bosomy body in a tweed suit, her left hand adorned with rings, the other ringless, stick-thin and reedy, as if the faintest wind would blow her over. Hetty learned later that these were respectively Phyllis and Moira, both in their eighties, retired headmistresses of rival girls' schools. Phyllis, the tubby one, was the fan of explicit fiction; the writer under discussion, Hetty saw, was Maeve Binchy.

As Clarissa flinched in the presence of so much aged flesh, Hetty gazed about. Every one of the ten or so residents present wore spectacles; two were also using magnifying glasses. One old lady was bent double with a dowager's hump. Her nose almost touched the tablecloth, but her expression was alert and interested. Two participants, a grey-haired man with a patrician manner and a short, shapeless woman in a Crimplene dress, were in wheelchairs. The two other men present were shrinking before the machine-gun onslaught of the teachers. The table with its white cloth and china crockery was set for tea.

'Millie?' Clarissa asked uncertainly.

A rangy individual in the far corner perked up. She wore what was evidently a Chanel suit in dark red and a great deal of shiny jewellery. 'Clarissa! You've come. Lovely. Everybody, this is my niece. And you've brought sherry! Quick, Phyllis, phone the kitchen for some glasses. How *delightful*. And your friend – who is this, dear?'

Introductions were made as the tea trolley arrived laden with fruit-cake and sticky pastries, pushed by a rotund black woman with a huge smile. The glasses were soon filled and refilled. The conversation became noisier and more animated. Space was made for Clarissa near her aunt, and for Hetty beside the old gentleman in a wheelchair.

'I'm Hetty,' she addressed him. He was sitting bolt upright, silvery hair framing a still handsome face with a square jaw and beetling eyebrows. The hair was cut long so that it touched his shoulders and, with the bottle-green velvet jacket and bow-tie, gave him a Bohemian appearance.

'Professor Bernstein,' he answered, and shook hands. His speech had a soft slur. No first name was offered.

Hetty helped him to tea and held the cake plate for him to choose. 'Professor of what?'

'Fine art. Slade. London University,' he said. He pointed at her empty plate. 'Not eating?'

'I'm dieting. Or trying to.'

He tipped his head back and examined her frankly, up and down. His brown eyes were fierce under the brows. Hetty crossed her legs, uncomfortable at his scrutiny.

'You have a Rubenesque figure. Womanly. Don't lose it.

You would make a splendid life model. Most women these days are too thin.'

'Er, yes. Thank you,' said Hetty. 'Tell me about the club, Professor. When does it meet?'

'Last Friday in each month. We choose an author. Usually by a process of the lowest common denominator. I suggested the Hilary Spurling biography of Matisse but nobody was interested. Maeve Binchy is not my cup of tea, either, I'm afraid. But, then, neither was Jeffrey Archer.' He half closed his eyes and sighed.

'Do you do the classics?'

'We do anything Phyllis and I can persuade them to do,' the Professor replied. 'We make endless deals. They can have Deborah Moggach next month, for example, provided that after that it's Michael Wood on Alexander. I have the video of him, which is a great incentive – some of them prefer to read their books on TV. More politicking goes on in this room every month than in the Doge's palace.'

He opened his eyes again and stared at her, as if suddenly aware of her presence. 'What are you reading right now?'

'*Pride and Prejudice*,' she answered instantly. 'And I've got the video, too.'

He laughed then, a sweet, sad sound, as if he did not laugh often. 'You remind me of my wife,' he added, but did not elaborate.

Hetty glanced around. The room was full of chattering noisy residents, most of them disabled, each in need of assistance for the most personal and intimate functions. Yet they were arguing convincingly and to the point, managing at the same time to cram in enough tea, sandwiches and home-made cakes to put a school cricket team to shame. Clarissa was the only person present who, jammed up against her aunt (who was ignoring her) and Phyllis (who was slamming *The Glass Lake* down furiously on the table, as if she wished to brain someone with it), seemed ill at ease.

Hetty found herself smiling, and turned again to the Professor. 'They seem happy,' she remarked.

'That's deceptive. Not one soul would be here if they had the choice. But we haven't. Take me. I had a stroke. Would I truly prefer to spend my last days with people I've never met before, whose tastes and ideas may be a million light years from my own? But I can't manage in a normal house any more, so here I am.'

Hetty hesitated, then decided to be nosy. 'What about your family?'

'I'm a widower. I have one daughter. She married against my wishes, and we are not close.' The old man's mouth clamped tight shut and he stared ahead of him.

It was safer to return to generalities. Hetty gestured discreetly at the lively room. 'This is not quite what I anticipated when I said I'd tag along with Clarissa,' she observed. 'I reckon you're being too hard on them, Professor. You could make new friends. They're a bright lot. They still have their marbles.'

'Don't be so surprised at *that*. Senility is not the main scourge of ageing for most of us. One person in five over eighty goes peculiar, but the other four stay mentally competent. Jenny there, who is so bowed with osteoporosis, is ninety-two. She ran a multi-million-pound business and has buried three husbands. She writes poetry. Phyllis and Moira between them compile the home's newsletter – far snappier than the *South London Press*. They pinch the crosswords from back copies of the *Times*. We get slower and more forgetful, maybe, but that's all. Don't patronise us, Hetty.'

'I'm not. I'm correcting my own ignorance.' It had to be a self-selected group; elsewhere, out of sight, must be many others whose grasp of reality had long vanished. Hetty wondered whether to apologise, then saw that the Professor was not angry. Emboldened, she tried another tack. 'Do you get lots of visitors – former students and colleagues, perhaps?'

'A few. I'm old, Hetty. So are they. They die. Or get so decrepit, like me, that they can't visit either. I do use the phone a lot. And e-mail and the Internet are a blessing.'

A sudden vision of the Professor indulging in Rosa's chat room came to Hetty's mind. She dismissed it, but not before a naughty giggle escaped from her lips.

The Professor bridled. 'What's so funny?'

Hetty was about to demur, then explained in a low voice. The Professor chuckled. 'I shall have to log on to that,' he said.

A possibility was forming in Hetty's mind. It might be dismissed out of hand but there was no harm in trying. 'Professor,' she said slowly, 'this club is more fun than I've had for ages. I have some spare Friday afternoons. Suppose I came regularly? I'd love to learn more about books, and maybe I could make myself useful, pushing wheelchairs, or whatever. It's about time I did some volunteering. And maybe I could be your ally.'

'In choosing authors?'

Hetty nodded.

'An excellent notion. And afterwards, if you do that, you could come and have a glass of good wine with me before I go in for supper. I like you.'

The tea was being tidied away. Phyllis tapped her saucer with a spoon for attention. 'Now, are we clear? Deborah

Moggach next time, concentrating on *Close Relations*. We'll set up the video, then we can compare the televised and printed versions.'

'She pontificates as if she's setting us all an essay,' Hetty hissed to the Professor. It was his turn to nod, and half smile.

'It's horrible! It's dirty! Three in a bed,' protested Moira. 'Where's the literature in that?'

Jenny, bent almost in a semi-circle by her bowed spine, uncurled herself with great effort and glared at the scrawny spinster. 'I had assumed,' she said, in a startlingly resonant voice, 'that we were all *grown-up* here.'

'Hear, hear,' came from round the room, and 'Rather!' and 'Good for you, Jenny!' The matter was settled, with Moira fluttering back into her seat abashed, Phyllis triumphant, the two silent old men somewhat flushed with anticipation, and Clarissa's aunt asking in a loud squawk what had been decided.

Hetty rose and shook hands with the Professor as a porter came to take his chair. She left Clarissa with her aunt and went to find the volunteer organiser. It was soon arranged. In a trice a roomful of new acquaintances, people of whom she could make no pre-judgements but would have to take on their merits, had entered her world – or, rather, she had entered theirs.

The Professor in particular, with his vigour and intelligence, had intrigued her. And the way he had swept her up and down, as if sizing her up sexually. The idea was preposterous, but she did not feel disgusted. Instead, those dark eyes under the fierce brows had paid her a heady compliment, to which she was not immune.

*

When she got home the answerphone was blinking.

'Hi, Hetty. Al here. *I'm playing a gig near you this weekend –
Brixton. Not as salubrious as New Year's Eve, but they're a
great bunch. Don't be put off by the neighbourhood – Brixton's
cool. Will you come? And party with us afterwards?*'

Hetty took off her gloves and coat, and put the kettle on.
Then she came back to the phone, picked up the handset
and dialled. It was the first time she had responded quickly
to one of Al's calls. With relief she heard a recorded message:
'Al here! I'm not far away, so leave a message, or try my
mobile . . .'

'Al,' she said firmly. 'This is Hetty. Please stop phoning
me. I came to one of your gigs, but I don't want to come to
any more. Jazz isn't for me, sorry. I don't need it, don't like
it, and don't want it. Forgive me. 'Bye.'

CHAPTER FIFTEEN

Larry's Party

Hetty stood in front of the mirror, holding the blue cocktail dress from New Year's Eve. It would fit well now that she had lost a few pounds. 'I absolutely don't want to go to Larry's party,' she said, as she zipped up the dress. 'I am sick to death of pseudo-friends trying to push me around.'

Her reflection in the mirror frowned. 'You're being too hard on them,' it chided. 'Davinia's not so bad. Better than him, in many ways.'

Hetty shrugged, perplexed, as she applied her lipstick. 'She must be doing something right. This is the longest he's stayed with anybody.'

'Or maybe,' her *alter ego* suggested cruelly, 'he's getting too old to move on.'

Hetty clipped on her earrings and reached for her coat. 'Thanks. I'll keep that by me, as my bigger, *older* brother tries to re-order my life. I do wish he wouldn't.'

'Maybe he'll resist the temptation . . . ?'

'Larry? *Larry?* You must be joking. Here we go . . .'

The long-promised, long-delayed dinner party for Hetty was to be mid-week at the house in Fulham. That required mini-cabs, but in turn that meant she could drink. With a determined air Hetty paid off the scruffy cab with its unshaven driver, picked her way through tightly parked Audis and BMWs, and rang the doorbell.

'Hetty! Mwah, mwah!' It was Larry, in an open-necked navy shirt and too much Hugo Boss aftershave. He held her by the shoulders at arm's length. 'It's yonks since we've seen you, sis. You're thinner. You okay?'

'Yes, well, I've been trying to get the weight off,' said Hetty.

'Weight is *very* ageing,' Larry agreed, as he led her into the narrow hall and took her coat. He patted his midriff. 'Ought to lose a pound or two myself, eh?'

If the correct reply to that was 'No, Larry, you're magnif-icent as you are,' Hetty was not about to oblige. The doorbell rang again. She waited patiently to be shown into the living room and offered some hospitality.

'Aha! Nicholas!' Larry hooted the name as if it carried a spell. Hetty edged out of the firing line as a large camel over-coat was flung at the coathanger rack, and found herself at the top of steps leading into the warmth of the kitchen.

'Hello, Davinia. Smells wonderful.' Hetty handed over the bottle of South African Shiraz, which was accepted without thanks and placed next to two other assorted bottles on the dresser. Larry and Davinia would not leave the wine selec-tion to chance.

Davinia was bent over a bubbling pot, tasting and

seasoning. She was a busty, handsome strawberry blonde with hair that normally swung about her ears, but was now fastened in an untidy topknot on top of her head. Since her neck was a little too thick, the style did not flatter her. Her manner was sub-Roedean overlaid with Sloane. 'God! There's too much coriander in it! I told him not to be so heavy-handed.'

'It'll be great, I'm sure. What is it?'

'This? Only a soup. Carrot and coriander. Or supposed to be. *I* don't think carrot soup is such great shakes – I mean, we're not *peasants* – but it's dead easy and these days everyone eats it. God, why do we give dinner parties? If you serve something classy, like oysters, half the guests turn up their noses and say they're kosher or organic or have an allergy. And you plan and plan, then somebody announces they've gone vegan.' She eyed Hetty with suspicion. 'You haven't, have you?'

'I eat most things. Especially *your* cooking, Davinia. Can I help?'

'You could cut the bread.' Davinia waved at four French baguettes and a breadbasket. Hetty searched through drawers for a sharp knife and started to cut the loaves in rounds.

'No! Not like that. So old-fashioned, Hetty. Split them down the middle, lengthwise.'

There was a distinct danger of being mistaken for the maid. Hetty sliced the loaves as instructed as Davinia banged and clattered. Then she wiped her hands on a tea-towel, smoothed down her dress, and sidled out of the kitchen towards the living room.

'I want you to meet Nicholas, Hetty. A colleague from work. Be sweet to him. Remember, this party is for you,' Larry hissed.

A tall man, dressed in a dark Armani suit, striped shirt and silk tie, held out his hand. 'Hello. So you're the famous sister?'

Hetty nodded meekly. He was tanned and pleasant-looking, a glass of red wine in his hand. Then she blinked. 'Don't I know you from somewhere?'

'I don't think so . . .' Nicholas began. Then he stopped. His hand flew to his mouth. He leaned forward. '*Tell Me All*?' he asked in a low voice.

Hetty nodded. This was the same Nicholas with a well-paid job in the City, who dreamed of throwing it all up to become a writer. The Nicholas whom she had considered, fleetingly, as a potential partner for herself, but had never followed up. A failure of nerve, perhaps, or a perverse irritation with all those who were so insistent that she could not survive alone.

Larry was glancing quickly from one to the other. 'You've met already?'

'Kind of,' Hetty replied. She waited till Larry had scuttled away once more to answer the door. Then she turned her attention more fully to Nicholas, and noted that the description on the computer of a rugged-looking man with fair hair and brown eyes was accurate. He was – *nice*. 'The programme you're in will be broadcast in a fortnight or so,' she told him. 'Kate or one of the other researchers will contact you.'

'And the day after I'll be famous, I suppose,' Nicholas murmured.

'You'd be surprised how many people watch it.' Hetty was unclear whether this would reassure or worry him. 'It might be wise to cover your back. At work, I mean. You did imply you were on the point of resigning.'

'I'm in a bit of flux at present – that wasn't flannel. It's a secure income but, as I said on the programme, I have found myself so restless.' He smiled, a slow gentle smile, and seemed to gaze deep into her eyes.

Hetty felt herself become flustered. 'Umm . . . Your employers might not take too kindly to that. At worst, you could find yourself out on your ear.'

Nicholas gulped half his wine, moodily. 'Television – it's so immoral. Or do I mean amoral? I hoped I might get some in-depth analysis. But it's just entertainment, isn't it? The schedules dish up endless makeovers – people with problems, rooms, gardens, even pets. You claim to resolve their dilemmas, but it's illusory.'

'It's what the viewers want. I shall be taking part in a makeover myself shortly,' she told him, and outlined the theme of *Star Style*. 'I must be crazy. I don't approve of us judging everyone on their appearance. There's illusion for you. And I share your distaste for the letdown afterwards.'

'You do? Surely what happens afterwards, to your victims, is of no concern to you programme makers.'

'I'm a mere researcher,' Hetty responded crisply. 'And we do try to persuade participants to weigh the consequences. They never listen, of course. What about yourself, why did you agree to appear?'

'It was Davinia, actually,' Nicholas said lightly. 'She convinced me. I don't think she knew it was your series. But she said it'd do no harm. It'd make my boss realise I meant it. They'd see they need me. She says the most likely outcome is promotion.'

'Oh, really?' Hetty could not help sounding waspish. Best to change the subject. 'Have you known them long?'

'Years.' Nicholas's glass was empty and he examined the

dregs. Then he barked, 'I say, you haven't got a drink. What would you like? Red? White?'

'Same as you,' said Hetty, glad that someone had noticed at last. Nicholas marched off, seeming to know his way about.

A clatter in the hall announced Clarissa and Robin, and Hetty's mother, who had arrived on the doorstep at the same moment. Robin and Larry had kept in touch since college days. The table in the conservatory was set for eight, so that left only James Dolland still missing.

'Darling!' Clarissa enfolded her in a bear-hug, then, as Larry had, examined Hetty from head to foot. 'You're getting . . .'

'Thinner, I hope,' Hetty forestalled her. 'It's deliberate, so don't tell me I was perfect before. If anybody's going to make me over, I'd rather do it myself.'

Clarissa looked mystified, as Robin took their coats. 'Don't forget what I said in the car. Larry explained when he rang. Tonight could be the start of a great adventure.'

'Clarissa –' Hetty tried to protest, but Robin had returned: Robin, bluff, red-faced and exuberant, who put his arm round her and gave her a breath-crushing squeeze.

'Hello, Hetty old girl. You surviving? Never mind, it won't be long.'

'What won't be long?' Hetty felt herself begin to burn.

'Oh, *you* know. Larry's told us. He feels so responsible for you. Couple of likely lads for you to check over tonight. Not one but two. Take your time. You gotta start somewhere.' And he gave her another gasping squeeze.

Hetty spluttered, but he and Clarissa had swept into the further reaches of the living room, where introductions were made with Nicholas. Hetty's mother emerged from the kitchen and gave her a kiss. 'Dinner will be edible, if nothing else,' she announced to her daughter. 'The tyranny of the committed cook! Come upstairs while I say hello to my grandsons.'

Hetty wondered privately why her mother had been invited, if the objective was as blatant a matchmaking – or meat market – as Robin implied. Perhaps she was an obvious adjunct at an event involving her two children. It would have required a decision, and not a pleasant one, to leave her out. Her mother's tact in not bringing an escort – in being *Mother* – was noteworthy, but not entirely plausible. Maybe she was in on the conspiracy as well.

The two women traipsed up six flights to the top storey. The house was badly organised, dark and cramped: bathrooms were not next to bedrooms, windows gave out on to blank walls, store cupboards spilled open with laundry cast higgledy-piggledy over the stairs. Not for the first time Hetty pondered the values of those who paid over half a million pounds for a property arranged on four minuscule floors with naught but an attic for the surly nanny and nowhere to park the Alfa Romeo.

A racket came from one of the bedrooms. Two small boys in the latest *Star Wars* pyjamas were hurling pillows at a television. They were surrounded by a dozen snack packs and Fanta bottles; crumbs littered the duvet. Behind them a computer screen flashed with repetitions of a game involving a great deal of kicking and slashing of opponents. This was the bedroom of the older boy, similar to his brother's next door.

'Isn't that *Lock, Stock and Two Smoking Barrels*?' Hetty asked, astonished. 'Bit grown up for you – should you be watching it?'

'Bang! Pow! Gotcha,' was the reply. Neither child acknowledged the visitors.

'Say hello to your grandma,' Hetty suggested. 'And your Auntie Hetty.'

'Yeah! How many's that? I counted fourteen dead bodies,' one shock-haired infant challenged the other.

Hetty tried again, but it was apparent that in the children's world, adults intruded only if they were armed with pump-action shotguns and litres of fake blood. After several more attempts and anodyne remarks, the women crept back downstairs.

'Yours were better behaved, even at that age,' was Peggy's comment.

'It's unacceptable,' said Hetty. 'What kind of kids are we producing?'

'I blame television,' said her mother knowingly. Hetty bit her lip.

It was possible that James had appeared in their absence: Hetty was in no hurry to find out. 'How's the Colonel? Still going strong?'

'Still asleep, more like,' was her parent's answer. Peggy, as elegantly dressed as ever, straightened and rubbed her back. 'It's a nuisance. Do I want him at it morning, noon and night? I should be relieved if he dozes off at the drop of a hat.'

Hetty giggled. 'Maybe we should get Larry to pair *you* off with some of his pals, instead of me,' she mused. 'I feel most uncomfortable about tonight. I wish everyone wouldn't keep trying to stuff me into a mould of their own manufacture. Why do I have to be like everyone else? I *am* changing – changed a heap since I bought my flat – but at my own pace.'

'You could have refused the invitation,' her mother said.

'Not without causing a family row. I'd have preferred it if Larry and Davinia had asked me round after the divorce. Then, I needed every ounce of support. Maybe that's exactly why they didn't. Brother dear took his time, but then he wouldn't be put off.'

Her mother touched her arm. 'We all want you to be happy, Hetty.'

'Oh, don't you start too. I *am* happy. More or less. For the moment, anyhow.'

But for the moment it was easier to scale down the resistance movement and go with the flow. As the doorbell rang again, Hetty was well into her second glass of red wine, and was watching amused as her mother flirted mildly with Nicholas. He did indeed seem familiar with the layout: when the Celine Dion CD ended, he casually slipped another into the midi-system.

Davinia appeared, pulling off a plastic pinny emblazoned with the Naked Chef, and urged them to the table. It was stylishly set, Hetty had to admit, and must have taken hours to do. Davinia, a devotee of *Harper's and Queen* like Clarissa, had probably copied a photospread. Cutlery and Venetian glassware gleamed. Each napkin was folded in a winged shape. In the centrepiece purple nasturtiums and cornflower heads floated fetchingly in water at the base of frosted blue candles. The lights were dimmed, the candles lit. The glow over the blue tablecloth, silver napkin rings and gilt-edged white Thomas china was seductive, if contrived.

The seating-plan must have been the source of some dismay to her host and hostess. Two couples, no fewer than four singles. Hetty could just imagine the arguments: it must have felt so untidy. The guest of honour, Hetty, was seated with her back to the french windows, with Nicholas to her left and Robin to her right. Larry was too far away to chat to but winked at her infuriatingly. Next to Nicholas was Davinia. The City man was pouring wine and chatting graciously. He was undoubtedly at ease.

And opposite her, in a fluster because he had so nearly been late and ruined the meal, was James. James Dolland, he of the phone call, of the totally forgettable features. Hetty smiled politely, half rose, shook hands. Davinia was busying herself ladling soup; Clarissa's eyes locked on Hetty, to catch her immediate reaction.

James. Pleasant enough, Hetty decided. About five foot ten, a little heavy for his height, smooth-shaven, a bit jowly. Greying at the edges, his hair might once have been quite dark. In a lightly pin-striped suit, with a blue shirt, a club tie. From the way he was breaking his bread roll and talking too fast, he was highly nervous.

'So, do you remember me? I was in Larry's class at school.'

Hetty let her gaze drop demurely. 'It was a while ago, James.'

'Well, I remember you. Larry's little sister. You had pigtails and scraped knees.'

'That's because my brother was forever pushing me over. If not him, then his gang,' Hetty reminisced. She reached for her glass, her third. 'Hope it wasn't you, James.'

'Me?' The idea appeared to floor him. 'No, I didn't go round knocking girls over. Not my scene, even then. I was a shy boy.'

Not setting me on fire now, either, Hetty reflected, but suppressed it. She smiled her way through the sour-tasting orange soup, leaving as much as she dared in the bowl. Only

Larry ate it with gusto. Peggy helped clear the plates. Davinia
brought in a large leg of lamb garnished with rosemary and
smelling strongly of garlic to cries of synthetic delight; the
platter was placed in front of Larry. He wielded the carving
knife with a wide flourish and less skill, the embodiment of
a *paterfamilias*. Roast potatoes, roast fennel and peppers,
cauliflower and broccoli, sauceboats with thin winy *jus* and
redcurrant conserve were passed around. Mint sauce, it
appeared, was too *infra dig*.

The noise level increased. Larry was telling a complicated
tale to Robin whose jocularity and rotundity waxed with
every mouthful. Mother was listening, a sliver of vegetable
on her fork, a faraway haze in her eyes. Hetty realised, with
a wistful pang, how pretty her mother was, despite her age.
Or perhaps because of it: that understated elegance had not
come easily or soon. Nicholas was leaning close to Davinia,
murmuring so low Hetty could not grasp his words. Clarissa
was offering James fresh English mustard, spooning it on to
his plate with a flick of her wrist. So that's how you flirt,
Hetty observed. But this guy needs more than mustard.

'Hey! That's mine! Give it back!'

A screech came from the stairwell, followed by a series of
bangs and crunches, as if two bodies were being flung
against each other and the staircase. There was a crash of
splintering wood, then another, louder bang, and a squeal of
pain and rage.

Davinia dropped her napkin. 'Now what?' she yelped,
and ran out of the conservatory. She returned in a moment,
panting hard and dragging the two boys, one by the arm, the
other by his Darth Vader pyjama bottoms. The smaller one
was clutching a lurid plastic tommy-gun, the other the video
in its box.

'You give the bloody nanny the night off, and see what happens,' she fumed, to no one in particular, though the accusation could only be directed at Larry. She shook the infants like wet puppies. 'I told you two not to watch that crap. It makes you hyper. Encourages you to thump each other.'

'Hello, kids,' Larry greeted them mildly. The other guests sat frozen, unsure whether to react or offer advice, except Robin who continued to masticate steadily and Clarissa who sipped her wine, her eyes alight.

'They've done it this time,' Davinia said crossly, dropping the children in a heap on the carpet, where they continued to tumble about and hit each other with balled-up fists, though to no apparent effect. 'They've broken a piece of the banister. The beech part you had restored last year. It'll cost a fortune to have it mended.'

'No, it won't.' Larry eased back in his chair. 'I'll have a go at it tomorrow. Nothing a nail and a bit of wood glue won't fix.'

'Are they okay?' came doubtfully from James. The boys had rolled over and were pummelling each other under his feet. He shifted his chair.

'Oh, yes. Indestructible. Boys will be boys,' said Larry. Then, somewhat reluctantly he stood up, grabbed each infant from under the table by the scruff of its neck, and hauled them out of the room. The guests could hear Davinia mutter crossly to him, 'Next time, we get rid of the kids. There's a limit,' before the two partners resumed their seats, full of fluttering apology.

'Do you have children?' Hetty asked James.

'Yes. Grown-up, now I'm afraid.'

'Mine too. Nineteen and twenty-three. Quite an

achievement to get them off our hands, isn't it? Though I miss them.'

'You have children that age? I'm surprised.' James was almost smirking. Hetty sighed. Since he knew her year at school – and the same went for him: if he was in her brother's class then he was fifty-three or thereabouts – there was no mileage in pretence.

'Started young. You too.' Now *that* was flirting. Hetty felt a twinge of shame and pushed it away. She ploughed on, feeling a total amateur. 'My view is that we're lucky to be mature people. We've experienced the most important elements in life – marriage, kids and so on. I'm glad I did, but I don't want to mourn what's past. Or to repeat the exercise, necessarily. Maybe I'll try pastures new.'

'Footloose and fancy-free, then?' He *was* smirking.

'In a manner of speaking.' Hetty considered whether she was simply too sober to relish this man's conversation and drained her glass. 'Could you pour me some more?'

As the meal proceeded the wax candles dripped slowly into the water to make blobby islands. The candlelight flickered through the red wine: she could easily have spent the evening twiddling the fluted glass, fascinated, paying no attention to those around her. It was proving difficult to find topics of conversation to share with James. If Markus had been here, she'd have interrogated him about his latest theatre project, even if much he said was over her head. Doris would have offered gossip from the neighbourhood; Father Roger would have told tales of his parishioners, or what the bishop was getting up to, or the latest synod fuss. The BJs would probably have gurgled through conquests and lost loves, real and imaginary. Rosa would have been telling dirty jokes by now, and would leave with at least one of the men hanging on her arm. Even Sally was a worthwhile companion in private, though still morose and withdrawn in public.

Getting to know a new person was not easy. Hetty sat up straight and gamely tried again. 'Do you go to movies? What did you see most recently?' she asked James.

'We don't get to see many films where we live,' he said, then coloured. 'I mean,' he stammered, 'I don't see many films.'

'Aaah.' She let the vowels emerge slowly. 'Who's *we*, James?'

'I live in the countryside,' was all he would add. But Hetty had arrived at her own conclusion. In a minute James had excused himself and gone to the bathroom.

Clarissa leaned across the table. 'How're you getting on?' she demanded.

'I think he's married, Clarissa,' Hetty mouthed.

'So what? He wouldn't be here alone if he was *happily* married,' came back the swift reply. 'He'd have brought his wife. He's available, I'll bet.'

Hetty groaned, and subsided. James, looking sheepish, slid back into his seat.

Pudding time. The doors to the kitchen were hauled open, the lights switched off. Then came a *zizzzz* and suddenly the conservatory was ablaze, as the sparklers on top of the *bombe surprise* caught alight and fizzled brilliantly. 'Oooh!' and 'Ahh!' greeted the sight, as Larry and Davinia carefully shuffled their display before their guests. There was nowhere to put the tray on the crowded table, so it was deposited precariously on a bookcase. As the dessert was spooned on to plates, gobs of meringue and ice cream dripped unheeded on to the leatherbound books. On future visits to this house,

Hetty realised, the stained spines would serve as a reminder of this night's curious ordeal, and as proof that the volumes were for show and seldom for reading.

She toyed with the dessert, she listened to James, debating with herself whether to make more effort or not. It was one thing to resent the matchmaking. It would be another to reject the match out of hand. Hetty had neglected Nicholas: he might be a livelier companion. When she twisted about to speak to him, however, he was gazing fondly at Davinia, bent over the *bombe*, her hair tumbling over her flushed face.

'Lovely meal,' Hetty commented, fork in hand. The meringue had not quite set and slid in slimy whiteness about the plate. Hetty remembered what uncooked eggs can do and deftly extracted the ice cream and sponge. 'Hasn't Davinia done well?'

'She's a lovely girl,' Nicholas murmured, rather drunkenly. His face was blotchy and he had loosened his tie, though that air of well-meant niceness had not forsaken him.

Hetty glanced sharply at him. 'You been friends how long?'

'Depends what you mean. 'Bout a year, properly.'

Hetty explored. 'She and Larry seem well suited. A highly successful couple.'

'He's a lucky man. He doesn't know it.'

'Oh, I think he does. He is my brother.'

'No.' Nicholas spoke with asperity. The object of his devotion was out of earshot at the far end of the table, offering seconds. 'He does not appreciate her qualities. He expects her to behave entirely as a traditional wife. And that's wrong for her.'

'It is?'

'Yesss.' His speech was slurred. 'She's a terrific girl. It's a tragedy. Getting dragged down by dome-est-iss-itty.' Completion of the word clearly gave him some satisfaction and Nicholas repeated it to himself.

'I've always considered them quite a conventional pair,' said Hetty cautiously. 'They are much agitated about my being out on a limb, at any rate.'

'She used to be a model. A beauty,' said Nicholas mournfully.

This was too juicy to miss. Hetty's sense of mischief surfaced. 'So, if you decide to quit the City and become a writer,' she whispered, 'what will Davinia make of that?'

'She says I should go for it. No more being tied down and miserable. No more commuting. Freedom!'

'And what about the children?'

'I don't have any. Or I do, but my wife has them. Nothing to do with me, now.'

'I meant *hers*.'

Nicholas gave her a bleary glance, reached for his glass and drained it. 'God-awful little monsters,' he said. With that at least Hetty could agree. The man had taste.

The guests rose from the table to the buzz of a whirring dishwasher. Liqueurs, brandy and vodka made their appearance in the living room with the coffee. Hetty settled for a Drambuie on ice and was soothed by its chilled sweetness. James, to her relief, began to converse on the sofa with Robin.

She headed upstairs to tidy her hair, and halted outside the bedroom door.

'Well, you *should* be worried about her,' came Clarissa's loud voice from the bedroom. 'She has started hitting the bottle, you know.'

'Nonsense!' came her mother, robustly. 'She's coping far better than I expected.'

'She's terribly lonely. You can see it in her eyes.' Clarissa was fierce. 'Look at the way she was chatting James up across the table tonight.'

'James? Did she? I didn't check.' Her mother laughed lightly, as if the idea was extraordinary. Hidden from their view, Hetty pressed her fist to her mouth.

'Desperate for a man. Any man, if we're not careful. Poor Hetty. I feel so sorry for her.'

'That's admirable of you. And you her best friend.'

Hetty was shaking, her emotions boiling within her. How dare they? Clarissa especially. What right had they – or anyone – to discuss her as if she were a three-legged dog or a threat to polite society? She fled and hid behind the first door she came to: the bathroom. She locked herself in. With friends like that, who needed anyone?

Yet she had gone along with it, this flirtation with James. It would have been rude to ignore him, but she had persevered and tried to get him to relax. That had led to his slip about the cinema, but at least she had a clearer picture. Larry must be aware of the wife in the countryside, surely? Odd that her brother, so bent on seeing her coupled once more, was casually willing to forget the potential damage to another couple. Or maybe Larry was so eager to reform her that he hadn't given it a moment's pause.

Should she walk out now? Hetty seethed, and held her temper only with the greatest effort. She washed her hands, twice, and twisted the towel till her knuckles went white. She banged her palm furiously on the porcelain and wished she shared the vicious destructive tendencies of her nephews.

Above the bath, on a shelf, sat an array of scent bottles and jars: Allure and Dune, De La Renta and Fifth Avenue, relics of countless duty-free trips. They recalled the antique perfume phials on her own mantelpiece, those mute witnesses to the choices originally facing her. Some had been rejected – such as getting perpetually drunk or eating herself silly. Or turning tail and running back home, or succumbing to genteel poverty. Some she had avoided, so far: becoming depressed or making a career of crying for help, though that message had not been received by either Clarissa or Larry, it seemed.

Hetty screwed up her eyes and tried to remember the other options, taking dabs of Davinia's perfumes with shaky fingertips. She had indeed found a job and a church and some voluntary work, though the book club with its raucous discussions on sex was distinctly unexpected. That left chasing men, or being chased by them. Or both.

At last she peered out: the bedroom opposite was silent and empty. She reeked, powerfully. As she splashed a final dash of Davinia's Passion on her hot brow, she pointed crossly at the mirror.

'Don't you say a word. I will do my best. But do they have to be so dull? Or married? Or mad? Are there no normal, kind, friendly, attractive *unmarried* men out there?'

'No,' replied the image bluntly. 'Make do with what's on offer. It could be worse.'

She started to descend the stairs, conscious of being a bit wobbly. They had had a lot to drink: the empties must come to over a dozen bottles. At the corner of the half-landing a door was slightly ajar. As she passed, it was closed from inside by a foot. But not before she had caught a glimpse of a man in shirtsleeves and Armani trousers in a clinch with a tousled strawberry blonde.

From the kitchen came a yell and a loud oath. Clarissa's squeal rose above the commotion, but there was giggly collusion in it rather than real fear: 'Gawd, he's passed out. Daft old bugger. I warned you you'd had enough. Robin, do get up. Don't make such a fool of yourself . . .'

The future head of chambers was sprawled on the floor amid the debris of dinner, eyes shut tight, bald head pink and shiny, knees tucked up almost in the foetal position, like a beached walrus. His expression was merry and he was gurgling gently. 'Don' wanna get up! Better down here . . . tired.'

'Is he ill?' Hetty asked. 'Should we fetch a doctor?'

Clarissa prodded him with her foot in distaste. 'Not the first time he's done it, won't be the last. He calls it "letting gravity take hold".' She bent over and yelled, 'Robin, darling, you're a fat slob. I'm going to get the car and bring it round. You'd better jump to it, 'cause I'm not carrying you.'

The walrus hiccuped from its prone position, grunted and began to snore.

James was at her side. 'Mmm, you smell gorgeous. Delightful evening, wasn't it?'

'Er, yes,' said Hetty. Her head was starting to pound. Bed would be a good idea. But *alone*. Taxi first. Where had she left that card?

'I have your phone number, Hetty. Larry gave it me. If I contact you again, maybe we could have a meal together?'

'Er, yes, if you like.' Hetty was too weary to argue. James squeezed her hand and looked smug; he turned aside to speak to Larry, as if to report success.

Her arm was suddenly grabbed from the direction of the pantry, and she found herself held tightly by Davinia, jammed up against stone-ground flour and jars of guacamole, out of sight of the other milling guests.

'You didn't see anything,' came a fierce whisper.

Hetty was unclear whether this was a statement of fact or a plea. 'Not sure I know what you're talking about, Davinia,' she answered hesitantly.

'Me and – you know. You won't let on, will you?'

Despite her headache, Hetty found herself inquisitive. Did she mean Nicholas? 'You two an item, then?'

'Sort of. Nothing serious. Don't fret – I shan't be leaving your precious brother.'

Hetty was sorely tempted. 'Dear Davinia, you and Larry so deserve each other.'

Davinia shrugged: she obviously took the remark as a compliment. Hetty did not elaborate. The puzzle was how Nicholas, earnest and well-meaning, could have let himself get embroiled with this household. Davinia must have hidden talents.

Time for coats, for hugs, for goodbyes. The minicab was even dirtier than its predecessor, its driver more evilly villainous. The alternative was to stay over in the spare room. Home, however, was a bare ten minutes away. If the cabby tried anything, Hetty would be too far gone to care.

'So, sis, enjoy yourself?' Larry was as overbearing as ever, though his eyes were drooping and bloodshot. He sniffed, twice.

'Rather!' she answered gaily. 'It was kind of you both. I'm so grateful.'

He leered. 'Made any conquests? James is impressed. You might have tried harder with Nicholas but, then, he's the sensitive type. According to Davinia, anyway.'

'He was charming.' She struggled into her coat, then looked her brother straight in the eye. 'I'm fine, Larry. I appreciate your concern.'

'Nah. You can't be. Not till your love-life is restored. A new chap. And you need the whole hog, sis. A house, garden, the lot.'

'Like yours?' she asked, archly, then regretted the implied sarcasm. Not that either Larry or Davinia had caught her mood. 'You do have a super home, honest. And the boys,' she added hastily.

'Thanks, sis.' He preened, and kissed her cheek. His breath smelt of garlic and brandy. 'We've got everything a man could want here. A woman too, if she's got any sense. Keep in touch.'

'I will. And thanks.'

CHAPTER SIXTEEN

In Style

The reception at the Wandsworth studios was a square lobby bland with beige paint, low sofas, overlarge dried flowers and dusty foliage in brown pots. The area was a familiar stamping ground to Hetty. Here daily she would greet guests, soothe their neuroses and nurture them like a mother hen till it was time for their performance. It was strange to be the guest herself for the recording of *Star Style*, dressed down in jeans and a baggy sweater.

'Good Lord, Mother! What have you done?'

Hetty stared in disbelief as her mother came through the door. Peggy was blonde. Not an understated ash tint, but a bold yellow colour. Like a canary.

The new Goldie Hawn patted her hair nervously. 'You don't like it?'

'I'm not sure.' Hetty circled her cagily. 'I'm not used to having a vibrant sexy lady as a parent. You put me to shame.'

Peggy shrugged. 'I figured if I was going to be on TV I'd

better make a splash. I could not – could *not* – obey that
instruction to start off ordinary. I tried a new hairdresser
yesterday, but she overdid it. It *is* a bit bright.'

'You make me appear positively dowdy. What colour will
my hair have to be if I'm to compete – fuchsia?'

Peggy found her lipstick and compact and checked the
frizz, her confidence intact. She wore the same elegant
maroon Jean Muir dress and jacket as at Larry's party. 'Aren't
you excited?' she trilled.

'No,' Hetty said shortly. 'I can't imagine what made me
agree to this farce. It's a load of trivial nonsense. I must have
taken leave of my senses.'

'But made over, you'll look fabulous, dear,' her mother
soothed. 'Won't you find that a simply magical experience?'

Hetty began to say 'No,' again, then settled for accepting her
mother's enthusiasm. 'I wonder, genuinely, why I did agree to
it. Perhaps because it's telly, and I work in the business: it
would have been churlish to refuse. They caught me at a weak
moment when Sally had dashed in to tell me about her new
job. I was feeling magnanimous. Or maybe my battered vanity
surfaced, what remains of it. Hope I don't live to regret it.'

'Why should you, dear? Both yours and this are splendid
programmes.'

'Thank you. We try. But *Tell Me All* isn't intended to
make them look good on screen, as *Star Style* is. As some
people arrive it dawns on them that, for all their boasting or
whingeing over the phone, it's entirely another matter to go
on TV and expose their privates in public. Some have the wit
to fast forward to the day after transmission.' And some
haven't, she said to herself, as Nicholas floated into her
mind.

'I feel *sorry* for a lot of them,' her mother said, stoutly.

'Like the woman who suffered from blushing. Father Roger was too unkind to her. Suggesting that if she hadn't announced the fact to the nation, nobody would have noticed.'

'But that was true. She was no more a blusher than I am. What kind of strange personality is so keen to be on the box that she makes out she has a major disability?'

'And that lady you had with the awful pimply teenagers who wanted to spend their grandfather's legacy on CDs and a Gameboy, when she offered to put it away for them. I had no doubts which side I was on.'

'The law, unfortunately, was on *their* side,' Hetty answered. 'And Grandad knew he was making mischief when he wrote that will. He probably died laughing.'

'I've made my will,' Peggy said suddenly. 'You're in it, of course.'

'Don't talk like that. You'll be around for years yet.'

'I hope so. But in case. Have you made yours?'

Hetty was startled. 'I honestly hadn't thought about it. Enough to cope with, living from day to day.'

'You should. If you fell under a bus without one, it's a terrible wrangle for those left behind. And the taxman could get his sticky fingers on what's left. Take my advice.'

Hetty gazed at her mother with renewed respect. 'Good Lord,' she said again, and was silent.

'Ah! There you are!'

A short, solid woman bustled towards them. She wore a tunic-style trouser suit in a shiny grey fabric; her stout figure was without discernible bosom, waist or hips but bounded with energy. Half-moon spectacles were perched on a snub nose. Steely hair fell in a straight fringe over the forehead. The eyes were brown and darting.

'I was wondering where you'd got to. My name's Alexandra Hillary. C'mon, Hetty. You can find your dressing rooms. You're in Three. Is this your mother? She's next to you in Four. Quick! Quick!'

'We've been waiting twenty minutes,' Hetty mumbled, as they trotted along after the steel-grey dynamo.

'Silly girls. Not you – the researchers. We've just had a celeb on, Jason Donovan, and they're still gaga with excitement. I'm so glad you agreed to appear, Hetty. You understand the problems of getting good guests. We're all paranoid about fraudsters, but for us the difficulties are obvious: finding people who won't act like scared rabbits, who'll smile at the right camera, and who won't take offence at the results. Like you.'

'Absolutely,' Hetty muttered. This was beginning to feel like a moral obligation.

Ms Hillary stopped dead before the dressing rooms and her two guests cannonaded into her. 'Go in and get undressed. Down to pants, tights and bra. There should be robes on the door – clean ones, I pray. We'll be along shortly with the blindfold.'

'Blindfold?' said Peggy blankly.

'You have to be blindfolded,' said the steel magnolia firmly, 'so that the first time you see the outfit we've chosen for you will be *on air*. When you shout, "Oh! That's wonderful," it'll be hunky-dory for real.'

'Yes, I see,' said Peggy doubtfully. 'What happens while we're blindfolded?'

'We try the kit on.' Ms Hillary chuckled wickedly, as if explaining to condemned prisoners how the trap-door worked. 'No cheating – you mustn't peep. We've had loads of practice. Then, once we've decided, we can press the outfit or shorten hems or whatever, so it'll be perfect at the *dénouement*.'

'And do we go on – in our bra and dressing gown?' Peggy shrank back.

'No, no. Who gave you that idea? In those things you're wearing now.' She gestured with mild distaste at Hetty's jeans, then stared at Peggy's hair. 'D'you mind if our stylist takes that down a couple of shades or so? Or streaks it, perhaps?'

'Why? Don't you like it?' Hetty's mother sounded affronted.

'Oh, it's terrific. For our purposes. That colour is excellent for "before" – it'll be splendidly *loud* under the lights. But you want to end up much improved, don't you?'

The noise in her mother's throat was suspiciously like a protesting growl.

The dressing rooms were tiny and smelt of talcum powder and spray deodorant. Keys in hand, mother and daughter entered and, calling through the thin walls to each other, made themselves ready, as lambs to the slaughter.

A tap came on Hetty's door. Without further ceremony it was flung open. Three frantic girls rushed in, their arms laden with clothes concealed in opaque plastic wrappers, with bags from Harrods, Fenwicks and Peter Jones. In a trice Hetty's head and face were swathed in a chiffon scarf, her eyes covered by a stiff black blindfold.

She was helped clumsily to try on several pairs of trousers then a blouse and jacket. Much discussion ensued in heated whispers.

'Mind that zip. It's a bit tight. Did you say you were a size fourteen, Mrs Clarkson?'

'Those trousers don't hang properly. Her thighs will rub

together as she walks. And the jacket's not long enough.'

'Try the other one. That'll cover her bum. Ah, much better.'

'Shoes. The Manolo Blahnik? Why not?'

'Bit posh to go with a Bhs suit, don't you think? Oh, well, if you say so.'

'Try the leather skirt – or PVC?'

'Nah. Mutton dressed as lamb.'

'Okay. Jewellery?'

'Nothing too flash. She can't take it. Restrained. Yes, that'll do.'

Sleeves and legs were pinned to the correct length, shoes and accessories selected. The team vanished, instructing their victims to dress as fast as possible.

Hetty emerged, flustered and annoyed, from the head-scarf. How dare they? And yet, the comments, she guessed, had not been meant as insults. With so many programmes to make each day under pressure, the girls would simply forget that a human being was suffocating under the blindfold, with burning ears. She resolved to swallow her dignity, concentrate, and learn whatever she could. If she had any plans to go chasing men, even the remotest stirrings, the knowledge might prove invaluable.

Another girl tapped on the door, entered, and introduced herself as assistant floor manager. Her manner was harassed; twice, messages on her radio interrupted her flow. Hetty's dismay increased with each bleep. The girl's task was to outline the choreography required on set. Dazed, Hetty began to share her mother's empathy for the stream of guests appearing on her own programme. The process was bewildering, and seemed to have precious little connection with the job in hand. What difference did it make if she stood still for a count of three, or forgot and turned left instead of right?

'We make it as broadcast. Thirty minutes in total. No retakes if we can avoid them,' the AFM explained. Hetty started to tell her that *Tell Me All* was run on the same lines but the girl was not interested. 'We do six shows on the trot,' the girl interrupted. 'You're the second today. So we have to get a move on if we're to finish by seven.'

'So you're going to finish our hair and faces in – what? About twenty minutes?' Hetty was incredulous. The outcome might be trivial, but the input was highly skilled.

'Yah,' said the girl, with a world-weary grin. 'The professional stylists are fast movers. Wait till you see them. Best way, actually.'

'I suppose so.' Hetty was struggling with buttons. 'Tell me, should I know Alexandra Hillary's name?'

The girl took a step back. 'You mean you've not heard of her? Golly, we have punters dying to come on, just so they can have her attention. She's editor of *World Chic*. British edition. She's really cool, yah.' The girl's voice betrayed reverential awe.

'Yah,' Hetty echoed, uncertainly. 'I mean, yes, I see. Do I go to Makeup now?'

The ASM reached out and tweaked Hetty's everyday sweater disdainfully. 'No. You'll do as you are,' she announced. 'Follow me.'

Accustomed to the modest proportions of the *Tell Me All* set, Hetty was amazed at the sheer size of the studio that greeted her. It was enormous. Ten cameras, including a sweeping eye on an extended tendril, covered the whole arena. Along the whole of one thirty-foot wall, banks of seating were crammed with the audience who sat clutching handbags and coats on their knees and talking excitedly. No artificial padding filled out this show: the public wrote in considerable numbers demanding tickets. Hetty wondered fleetingly if it might be possible to borrow a few when their own attendance was thin. And maybe, just maybe, some of this crowd might have true-life dilemmas they'd love to share? A little networking after the recording might be useful.

Somebody on the second row waved at her. 'Yoohoo! Hetty!' The rouged cheeks and dangling earrings were unmistakable.

'Doris! What are you doing here?' Hetty leaned hurriedly over the front row.

'Come to see you pampered up. How did you get on with my prezzie?'

'You're a naughty lady, Doris,' said Hetty severely, but her mood had lightened considerably. She turned, and felt set for whatever fray would ensue.

A very tall man, perhaps six feet five, loped on to the set, beautifully dressed in a tailored suit with a modish knee-length jacket and a mauve shirt and tie. Already made up, he was fiddling with his earpiece and adjusting the radio pack on his belt. He appeared to be talking to himself, nodding and gazing about, then pointed, listened and moved four steps forward. The audience's chatter quietened, and they observed his antics intently. This was Simon Darling, heart-throb co-presenter with Ms Hillary.

Hetty waited pensively with her mother. The set was in two halves, mirror images of each other. On each part, assistants were hurriedly checking the sinks and makeup sections, laying out sponges, brushes, tissues, cotton-buds, towels. The steel dynamo was fidgeting at the back, flitting about with garments on hangers and deploying hats, shoes and handbags on stands tastefully underlit with bluish light. The catwalk in front was covered in silvered tiles. At each end was a vast poster-sized board emblazoned with the *Star Style* motif in sequins. The effect was garishly jolly, like a tatty circus.

'Where are the big mirrors? For the – ah – *dénouement*?' Hetty asked.

The AFM's voice over the loudspeaker announced, 'Two minutes.'

'Over there.' Simon Darling adjusted his tie and indicated. 'The posters. When we twist 'em round, you'll see what we've created. You'll adore it, I promise you.'

The next half-hour went in a whirl. Hetty and her mother were pulled behind the set, combed and brushed, for their 'before' appearance. Alexandra Hillary patted Peggy's canary coiffure with unfeigned pleasure. Her own had acquired purple streaks that made her witch-like.

'And today,' a voice boomed, 'we meet a wonderful mother and daughter team, both with new lives, who sought our advice. Will you *please welcome* Hetty Clarkson and Peggy Morris!'

To loud cheering and whooping from the audience, Hetty and Peggy were propelled from behind into the whitest light Hetty had ever experienced. She was immediately certain it could not be flattering. Simon Darling leaped up to them in turn, his teeth flashing. Under the Pan-stick he was sweating.

'Peggy! You look wonderful! You're an army widow, isn't that right?'

Hetty's mother simpered as if to the manner born. 'I am, Simon – a merry widow . . .'

'And you, Hetty! You find yourself on your own too?'

'I do,' Hetty said, and tried hard not to sound peeved. She set her lips in a cheesy smile. Why, oh, why had she agreed to do this?

'When we've finished with you, they'll be queuing up! You ready, Hetty?'

'Yes,' answered Hetty, through gritted teeth.

'And your stylists today are . . .'

Each participant had a different pair. Hetty's makeup artist was small, sandy-haired and American with a high fluting voice. Whether he was nervous or for some other reason, his hands shook violently as he dabbed and powdered Hetty's cheeks. Alarmed, she wondered how on earth he was to avoid poking the mascara wand into her eye, and offered to do it herself. The hair stylist was older, calmer. A lean man in a charcoal grey suit and tieless shirt, he chattered gaily, *sotto voce*, as he snipped and pampered. 'Your hair's not bad,' he commented in one ear. 'Your mother's – oof! Does she always wear it like that?'

Hetty tried to shake her head. 'Bit of an accident.'

'I'll give you my card. Let me attend to it properly for her. Tell her to come to my salon.' His voice was seductive.

'Where is it?' asked Hetty hopefully. That might make a splendid birthday present for Peggy.

'Mayfair.'

'And what would you charge for the works? Coloured, trimmed, the lot.'

'That depends. A time-served stylist and colourist, average-length hair? In the region of a hundred and twenty pounds.'

Hetty gulped. 'And if you were to do it yourself?'

'Aha. Bit more than that. Two, three hundred. But I'd do your mother's half-price, just as a challenge.'

'Er – thanks.'

The portable camera swooped about her wet head, examined her fingernails as they were being manicured, her eyebrows as they were plucked, focused on her double chin. Simon Darling gambolled determinedly from one woman to the other with increasingly vacuous questions. The audience laughed indulgently and clapped at every sally. Hetty kept smiling, though her jaw muscles were beginning to ache. This excruciatingly cheery simper was deeply alien to her. Not for the first time she felt a sense of relief at earning her living behind the camera, rather than before it.

It was almost over. More speedily than she could have imagined, the snipping had stopped and hairspray hissed in her eyes. Now came Ms Hillary's moment. The mauve-streaked fringe flapped puckishly about her brow, the shiny suit swished like aluminium foil. A witch from *The Wizard of Oz*, Hetty decided groggily. Was this fashion?

'Now, *Hetty*,' Ms Hillary commented portentously to camera, 'is short – about average height for her age group, certainly. And she would be the *first* to admit she does not have the *ideal* figure.' ('I'm dieting. And getting there,' Hetty muttered furiously.). 'So *I* suggest – trousers, which are *so* slimming, and an extra-long jacket, to hide the *bumps*. And, of course, to lift the whole outfit, these three-inch high stilettos.'

Hetty's heart sank. She had not worn high heels in years – not since her twenties. The lonely-hearts advertiser's hinted request for them had immediately painted him as dotty. Could she cram her spreading, be-corned toes into such instruments of torture? Would she fall over and make an utter fool of herself? If that happened, would they halt the recording and do it again? Suppose she broke her ankle? *Was any of this worth it?*

She and her mother were bundled out to the back of the set as mood music and jungle drums rumbled. A clock could be heard ticking loudly – only thirty seconds were allowed for dressing. Her mother's hair was now a soft peach tint, but fluffed out like a Joan Collins wig; her makeup involved a lot of blusher and pink lipstick.

'Have they made me a complete freak?' Peggy hissed. Hetty, her face buried in a beaded T-shirt, could not reply.

Assistants were shoving them into clothes, pulling down jackets, pinching earlobes with earrings, fastening chromed collars, the latest in jewellery. Hetty's feet were thrust stockingless into the stiff distorting cages that passed for shoes. 'Christ,' she groaned, as one toe stuck through a metal grille. The jungle drums grew deafening. The *tick-tock* boomed overhead. Buttons and buckles were frenziedly fastened, zips secured. 'Breathe in, Hetty,' commanded her mother.

'And *here we go*!' came Simon Darling's voice, like an avenging angel on Judgement Day.

Tall, slim, in a cream silk dress and jacket with an enormous cartwheel hat trimmed with feathers, her fluffed-out hair dazzling, the pink lipstick a-shimmer, Peggy walked regally down the catwalk and into the limelight. On cue she stopped, twirled, sauntered, showed off the lining of the jacket. The applause was admiring and sincere.

Then came Hetty, trying hard not to trip in the metal cages, her calf tendons protesting with every step, the trousers' belt digging into her midriff. It was an enormous struggle to stay upright without holding out her arms for balance. To do so and keep smiling was almost beyond her.

Then, to trumpets, the great posters were reversed into gigantic mirrors. Both women could see themselves as others saw them.

'Satisfied?' the image smirked at Hetty.

The hair and face were vaguely familiar and, in a tarted-up way, not unattractive. But though the navy striped trouser-suited female who gazed back had the same body and the same slack-jawed mouth half-open in astonishment, the personality had changed beyond all recognition.

'That's not me,' said Hetty promptly, while grinning gamely.

'But is it how you'd like to be?' The image seemed anxious.

'No. I don't think so.'

'Why? What's wrong?'

'Nothing's wrong. It's just that . . . I'm not sure. She looks a dog's dinner.'

'But come on. It's great. Different, anyway.'

'Granted. I've gained a lot from this. My mother's having a whale of a time, bless her. But for me? I still don't accept that appearance matters that much. Al didn't seem to think so, and James was more taken by that mix of perfume. I'd hate having to go through this palaver whenever I wanted to poke my nose outside my door. And I'd rather be with people who appreciate me in other ways.'

'Huh,' said the image huffily. 'No pleasing you, is there?'

In a few moments the show was finished, the closing credits rolled to triumphant music and they were hustled out. Behind them assistants scurried on stage as the sinks and worktops were wiped down. On the side the next pair, an elderly art teacher and his wife from the wilds of north Cumbria, waited hesitantly, their expressions betraying mixed fear and disbelief.

Doris had extricated herself from the audience and rushed up to Hetty with a hug. 'Terrific,' she said. Then, in a stage whisper, 'All you need is some decent frilly under-wear and you'll knock 'em dead.'

'Indecent, I think you mean,' Hetty murmured, but not loud enough for her parent to hear. The entire outfit was hers now. The suit was worth keeping, and the T-shirt, though it cut under the arms. The belt could be undone a notch. She kicked off the shoes and stood barefoot with them in her hand. An idea occurred to her.

'Here,' she offered Doris. 'These are murderous machines, but with a pair of fishnet tights they'd suit one of your kinkier clients down to the ground. D'you want them?'

Doris giggled. 'Nah, you keep 'em. They make you look proper nifty. You never know when they'll come in handy, now, do you?' She squeezed Hetty's arm. 'I did your cards last night. Guess what?'

'I'm not sure I can bear it, Doris.'

'Good stuff. A man. Several men. You're in for a whopper soon, you'll see.'

CHAPTER SEVENTEEN

Sex Fiends

'He didn't like it, you know.'

Sally and her mother were at an outside table in the Oblivion wine bar, SW4. The evening was warm, with the breeze of early summer. Full-leaved trees on the common hung heavy beneath the traffic dust, bees thrummed lazily in nearby gardens over the exuberant first flush of roses. The tube station was spewing out tired customers whose step picked up as they headed home.

Hetty sipped her chilled Chardonnay. The Swallows had been a forced purchase and she could not have imagined, then, ever being truly at ease in this urban cocoon. But she had chosen well, perhaps instinctively. The location had its charms.

Her attention returned to her daughter. 'Why should your father have any views on my appearance on *Star Style*?' she enquired, slightly cross. It was too pleasant an evening for a confrontation.

'He still feels concerned for your welfare. At least, that's how he put it. There was a lot of comment in the village and he was ribbed. You had altered. You'd have turned up your nose before at a trouser suit – remember swanning about in flowery dresses by Laura Ashley? He was worried you'd made a fool of yourself.'

'I was never slim enough to do a trouser suit justice.' Hetty smoothed down the wrinkles in her Levi's. Under the denim firm muscle flexed, the legacy of riding her bike. 'Do you agree with him? That I made a fool of myself?'

'Not exactly. To be honest, you looked splendid. But you didn't seem keen.'

'I wasn't,' Hetty said. 'You grandmother wowed everyone, as you said she would. She's an example to us all. I kept the outfit and will wear it when the opportunity arises. Not with those damn shoes, though. But I was not comfortable. To me, the show glorified the wrong values.'

'Two million people saw it, you told me.'

'Two million people with nothing else to do but watch daytime TV. Whose heads are shallow and empty. Or maybe they're not. Maybe I simply want more than the casual approval of strangers.'

The two women drank companionably. Hetty saw Markus emerge from the station with an attaché case. He was too far away to notice or speak to them. Hetty summoned her courage. She did not want to discuss Stephen, but it was clear Sally did. 'Not sure I'm after your father's approval, either. How is he?'

'You interested?' Sally's eyes were owlish.

'No. Yes. We knew each other for such a big chunk of our lives. I hope he's happy.'

Sally pondered. 'I don't believe he is, entirely. The new

girlfriend is a poppet – sorry, Mum – but perhaps she didn't realise she was taking on a middle-aged man.'

'Tell me more . . .' Hetty buried her face in her glass and suppressed a giggle.

'I shouldn't – Oh, what the hell? You're both grown-ups. He's been complaining about a bad back, visiting an osteopath, that sort of thing. Fretting that he might have a touch of arthritis. It may stem from . . . trying to do too much.' Sally was also giggling now.

'It's odd,' Hetty reflected quietly. 'It's a year since I knew we couldn't stay together, and I had to make plans to get out. Eight months since I came here. I never thought I could have talked about him objectively, without terrible anguish. He's just another ordinary human being. He used to be the centre of my little universe.'

'Healing process,' said Sally. 'You're more in control, you have friends, you have loads to occupy you. So he's receded. Shrunk. To something more manageable.'

'Makes me feel almost guilty. Aren't I supposed to rage against him still, and seek revenge? I ought to hate the girl-friend and be madly jealous. Instead, to all intents and purposes, I'm indifferent.'

'You're not a bitter sort, Mum. You're too *nice*.'

Hetty frowned. 'Don't count on it. There are moments . . .'

'Go on.' Sally drained her glass, her face alight with curiosity.

'Oh, I don't know.' Hetty backed off. 'Bits of my old lifestyle I do dream about, sometimes. Money is a struggle but, then, I had it so cushy before. I don't miss the house as such, but I do miss the space. And the calm satisfaction of weeding the garden and having time to watch what I planted growing, and the smell of fresh linen in the cupboard after wash-day. I don't get any of that now. And gifts from Doris may be entertaining, but they're no substitute.' She had regaled Sally with the encounter in the sex shop and its aftermath.

'You're getting ready.' Sally's tone was teasing.

'For what?'

'Boyfriend. No, I mean it. Your confidence has increased. And you've . . . changed. Yes, that's it.'

'Changed? Apart from losing that flab, and chuntering round on my bike, and going to a few movies with you?' Hetty's reticence surfaced. She was not about to tell Sally about James. Not yet.

'You've moved on, Mum. In my eyes, and in other people's as well. Though I doubt if Dad has any idea. To him, you're still the same as you were. He's the one with guilty feelings. He's convinced you must be desperately miserable and can't possibly cope.'

'He's wrong about that.'

'So was I,' Sally admitted generously. She gazed out over the common, eyes screwed up as if choosing her words with care. 'Seeing you on that weird programme, and here in this wine bar, and in your flat that you've made so cosy, and plain busy, like at the studio when I called in, that made me think. Gave me quite a jolt, in fact. Just as you now see Dad in perspective as a human being, that's true for me about you.'

'What are you trying to say, Sally?' Hetty's voice was gentle.

'I'm not sure quite how to put it. It's taken me a while, but you're not just Mum any more to me. You're a *person*.'

'I always was a person, you know,' said Hetty gravely.

'No, you weren't. You only existed as a reflection of Dad,

Peter and me. We were a rotten, selfish little bunch. We never considered you, and your needs, for a second, and maybe you didn't have any, except us. But you're a real person, you're Hetty Clarkson, not merely an adjunct of our family. Dad doesn't know it, Peter never will, but I do. And I like it.'

'Heavens,' Hetty muttered. Then, 'Whose round is it? I could use another.'

When she returned to the flat the answerphone light was winking.

'Hi, Hetty. James here. It was great to meet you at Larry and Davinia's. I wonder – I work in London all week and it gets a bit dull in the evenings. Might you be free? Dinner somewhere in town? Do call . . .'

'You live in London all week, and in the countryside at weekends,' Hetty commented coolly, 'and you don't go to movies. Pity.' A movie escort was not required to churn out sparkling conversation: a dinner companion was.

The answerphone crackled at her. 'He could be useful practice, Hetty. Go on. Nothing ventured, nothing gained.'

'Early signs of madness,' Hetty chided herself severely. 'First the ruddy mirror tells me what to do, now it's you.'

'There you are!' the answerphone squeaked derisively. 'Talking to yourself when you could be meeting a respectable bloke. And a slap-up meal into the bargain. He *wants* to see you – that's a mark in his favour. Stop dithering. Make a date.'

Hetty went to fetch her diary, and did as she was told.

The *Tell Me All* set was particularly noisy and disorganised. A gaggle of athletic young Australians in T-shirts and cut-off jeans were milling about, five boys and two girls, banging awkwardly into cameras, their big feet tripping over cables. It was decided eventually to select two, Clive and Mark, for the show and seat the rest in the audience. Their bulk filled out the depleted numbers superbly.

'They're a collection of complete wankers,' Father Roger hissed to Hetty.

'Roger, shame on you. You shouldn't be using bad language.'

'Oh, I won't. Rest assured. "Twats" isn't allowed on a day-time show either. But I should be able to get away with "prats". Nobody these days knows what it means.'

'And what's that?'

'Buttocks.'

'You're kidding.'

'I'm not.'

The Australians had a tale of woe. Seven of them rented a three-bedroom flat in Earl's Court, the centre of expatriate Ozziedom in London. Two shared each room – the girls were together – and one had the lounge, which was also the communal living area with the television and a pair of beat-up sofas. Hetty had visited it in the course of her research. Her nose had wrinkled at the mixed odours of dirty bed-linen, cigarettes, lager and aftershave. She hoped Peter lived better at college, but suspected not.

'The problem,' Clive drawled, 'is that we rub along brilliantly, except for him.' He jerked his thumb at Mark, at his side. The accused slid lower in his chair.

'I'm perfectly reasonable,' he protested. 'Just 'cause I have to be in work for seven each morning . . .'

'He wants us to clear out of the lounge by nine each night,' Clive finished for him. 'And that means, no telly, no mates, unless we go out. And we aren't all City slickers, like 'im. We can't afford to take over the pub every evening. Anyway, we each of us pay towards the telly. It's not his exclusive property.'

Mark, it transpired, operated on the trading floor; arrival at seven was the latest he could manage, since much of his activity involved deals with Australia itself and the Far East. 'They'd like me there twenty-four hours,' he commented gloomily.

'They pay you enough to get your own place,' Clive prodded him.

'Saving,' was Mark's reply, with an expressive shrug.

'An' what's more, he's got both the girls after him. You can't do that with flatmates,' Clive continued, a trifle pompously. 'You have to get on. It's making the atmosphere poisonous. We told him to leave, and he won't.'

'Ye-e-es,' murmured Father Roger, as the camera switched to him. 'Well, Mark, when you reach your first million, you'll be able to buy the whole house, won't you?'

The smirk on the young man's face suggested that the notion had occurred to him. 'It's owned by an Ozzie, yes,' he answered.

The presenter peered at them. 'So what's the solution, then?'

'I suggest you take off elsewhere with one of the girls, shack up together, and then you'll only have to pay half-rent,' Father Roger answered smoothly. 'And, given your remarkable charm, Mark, you'd make not only her but lots of people very pleased.'

The boy sat up and preened. In the corner Hetty covered her mouth.

'At least they're genuine,' Rosa remarked, as the recording

ended. 'You couldn't fake that kind of prissy jealousy. Lucky girls. Mark's a dish, isn't he?' She pointed to the next guest. 'Not sure about him. You and Father Roger will have to check him out.'

The man was of medium height with glossy dark hair: dyed, probably, though it looked his own, not a wig. He was dressed in full Scottish regalia with a tailored kilt, woollen socks with a dagger, a silky-haired sporran across his groin, the whole topped off with a black velvet jacket, silver buttons, ruched collar and lacy cuffs. He stood, legs akimbo, a swagger about him, as if about to break into 'Scotland the Brave'.

'Overdone it, hasn't he?' Hetty commented.

'Okay for Burns' Night. Or to make a point. But what point?'

The case was not one of Hetty's. 'What's the matter?'

Rosa consulted her notes. 'He says he's bisexual. Fifty-two years old. Wants to settle down – claims he's had enough of playing the field. The dilemma is, who should he choose as a permanent partner? A woman or a man?'

'Blimey,' Hetty said. 'Most people don't have the option.'

'Trouble is, I don't believe him. Given the God-awful mess with *Vanessa*, we can't be too careful. Being taken off the air because we're using fakes is *not* in the game-plan.'

'Maybe he's sick of sleeping like a starfish? This could be his free advert.'

'Could be. I wouldn't have any objection. With a get-up like that, he'll be great on screen. So I'd like you and Roger to find out.'

'How?'

Rosa became vague. 'He'll be going back to the dressing

room – I've given everyone a twenty-minute break. Get in there and see what happens.'

Hetty refreshed her hair, sprayed a little *eau de parfum* on her throat and wrists and tapped on the door. Without waiting for a response she pushed it open and peeped in.

'Gordon, isn't it? I need to fill in a few details about you. My name's Hetty.' She smiled beguilingly and tapped her clipboard.

He held out his hand. His voice was deep, a Scottish burr that, if false, took some skill to create. 'Pleased to meet you. You understand my little difficulty, don't you? A lovely mature woman like you.'

Hetty steeled herself to go on smiling. After *Star Style*, anything in that line was easy. 'I do. I need to flesh out a few facts. You have had women friends, haven't you? Am I right in thinking you were married once?'

'Married twice,' he corrected her smugly. 'Adorable ladies, both. The first when I was in my early twenties. The second, ten years ago. That lasted longer than any of my other – ah, liaisons. But they both finished for the same reason.'

'And what's that?' Hetty enquired brightly.

'My fondness for young men,' he said, and winked.

Hetty gulped. The guest was perched on the end of the sofa-bed, a meaty fist on each knee. As Hetty let her glance drop, he twitched up the kilt so that his bony kneecaps were exposed. And then a slice of thigh. And–

Gordon was parting his legs, inviting her to look up between them. What did Scotsmen wear beneath their kilts? Hetty decided hastily not to find out. She stepped back, scrabbling at her clipsheet. 'Right, that's fine. Thanks. We'll call you in a minute.'

Outside, Rosa caught her arm. 'Well?'

'He's a creep, but he's not messing with us. At least, as far as women are concerned.' She paused. 'And warn the gallery. Keep the cameras away from his hairy legs.'

Hetty stood aside as Father Roger gathered up his cassock, crossed himself with a theatrical gesture, tapped on the same door and was admitted. She and Rosa strolled down the corridor, looked in on the makeup girls, then went for a cup of tea.

In a few moments there was a commotion, a banging of a door and a loud curse. Father Roger, his face flushed, came hastily down the corridor into the canteen. From behind him floated a whinny of high laughter.

He clutched the counter, swaying. Then with a shaky hand he helped himself to tea and a biscuit, and sat opposite Rosa and Hetty. Both women were agog.

'Shoot: is he gay? Bisexual?' Rosa asked.

Father Roger's eyes flickered from one to the other. 'I don't know why I do this job. It's not as if you pay a fortune. And I don't earn any Brownie points in heaven.' He broke the digestive biscuit and made a great show of dunking it in the tea until it disintegrated and fell in. He groaned.

'Is he for real? I have to know. Or some out-of-work actor or agency freak pulling the wool over our eyes?' Rosa demanded.

'He's a sex-mad fiend. Poor women, when he gets his hands on them.'

'Poor men, too?' Hetty asked.

Father Roger nodded vigorously. 'He tried to grope me. Nearly succeeded. An actor wouldn't do that. He'd draw the line at a priest. Unless, of course . . .'

'Go on.'

'Let's just say he picked the wrong priest.' And he cracked his knuckles, one by one, with a relieved chuckle. But his face was pale.

Afterwards, in the small office with the flickering computer screen, Hetty touched Rosa's arm. 'Did I miss something?' she enquired.

'Mmm?' Rosa was preoccupied, scrolling down lists of guests for the following day.

'Father Roger. Is he gay?'

'Dunno. He's never said so.'

'But he hinted. That a priest might enjoy that sort of thing.'

'Why don't you ask him?'

Hetty was shocked. 'I couldn't. Not straight off.'

'Why not? I expect he's been asked crazier things in his time. He's hardly a sea-green innocent, or he wouldn't be on this show. We may not be cutting edge, but we're not exactly *Songs of Praise*, either.' Rosa glanced up. 'What is it? D'you fancy him?'

'A priest? Heavens. I hadn't ever seen him as a possible.'

'Why not? He's a man. Got all the right equipment, as far as I know.'

'Because I've naturally assumed he's celibate. In the Church they're either married to worthy types with an appropriate number of children, or they're out of it, aren't they? None of the Churches approves of hanky-panky without a sacrament. As Roger himself would say.'

'My impression is that he's maybe not that keen on sex,' Rosa mused. 'He works like the clappers, and doesn't relax much. In love with his job? Some people have other priorities. Some – and maybe Roger's one – shy away from relationships of any kind. They're happier with books, or whatever.'

'Relationships can be a pain,' Hetty observed drily, 'especially starting from scratch.' Something in her was dreading the forthcoming supper with James. Twice she had resisted the urge to call it off.

'So maybe you're the girl for our Roger, hey?'

'Me? You're joking. Life as the wife of a rural dean? No way. Friend would be as much as I could aspire to,' Hetty answered briskly. 'Anyway, I've got myself a hot date.' She told Rosa briefly about James, playing down his weekend activities.

'Good girl,' Rosa enthused, and squeezed her arm. 'Just as I was about to drag you into a dating agency. Go for it. And once you're off your mark, if he's no earth-mover you can keep an eye open for something better.'

'Ye-e-s.' Hetty sounded uncertain. The mixed metaphors were confusing. 'Chatting up blokes. Me, in my fifties.'

Rosa chortled. 'Nobody said the sex manuals are written only for twentysomethings. We are where it's at, darling.' She halted. 'Talking of sex manuals, I could lend you a couple of crackers. Fully illustrated. Might help.'

'Rosa, you're a doll. Let's hope James won't need them. I'll keep you posted.'

'Good evening.'

So formal. Hetty shook hands.

James bent down and kissed her jerkily on the cheek. 'Glad you could come.' He seemed shy, even more so than at Larry's party. Hetty examined him under her lashes. From the grey suit and slightly creased shirt, he had come straight from the office and had not had time to change, or had not thought to. He was carrying a leather briefcase, which he deposited in the cloakroom. She had dashed home from the studio and donned the *Star Style* trouser suit; a few more pounds off since the date of recording meant that it fitted well and flattered her.

They stood awkwardly, unused to each other's presence, until the waiter, lanky, narrow-hipped and superior, unbent long enough to show them to their table.

Minimalist décor, again. Bleached linen, steel, glass, blond wood. No adornments on the walls, the windows frosted so that they could not see out. On the table, a bowl of salted green pistachios in their shells. No water, no breadsticks. Nothing to fiddle with.

'I trust you like Japanese food?' James said.

'I've never tried it, in truth. I've never been to Japan. I've never been here,' Hetty had to confess.

'This is part-owned by Robert De Niro,' James confided, as if that were a major recommendation. 'It's Japanese-Mexican.'

'Oh.' Hetty was puzzled, and decided to show it. 'What does that mean?'

'Raw fish with chillies. Extraordinary.'

Hetty was quelled. Neither appealed, much. Japanese-Mexican must be popular, however; the place was filling up with young diners, mostly dressed minimalist-style, the girls in floaty fabrics, the boys in open-necked shirts and pale slacks. By contrast she and James looked overdressed – and old.

His conversation was as stilted and as formal as his greeting. Hetty, however, had learned a great deal at the studio and had become adept at setting the nervous at their ease. She drew him out on his job, on his journey to work, on what he enjoyed on television, though it was an effort to remember what he said and not to repeat the same question. But he looked all right, she reflected; she was not ashamed to be seen with him, and he was gazing at her quite raptly as he spoke.

But what exactly was she doing here? Hetty stopped herself asking straight out whether he was, indeed, married. He did not mention it. That was confirmation enough: a free man, a divorcé, say, would have promptly bemoaned his availability, and might have spent half the evening complaining about his ex to boot. If she were searching for another partner, a replacement for Stephen, then James's status mattered. Danger lurked: James would not have sought her company, she a single woman, unless some fragility or chill had seeped into his home.

On the other hand, a bit of *fun* could do no harm. A torrid affair was unlikely, on current estimations, but that was fine too. If she was going to break her duck soon, she couldn't be too choosy.

What if they were observed by somebody who knew one or the other of them? 'I suppose we ought to say,' she whispered, 'if we're seen, that we're business acquaintances, celebrating the completion of a successful deal.'

James nodded. He seemed taken aback. Maybe the subterfuge was beyond him.

After an inordinate delay the waiter drifted back with two glossy menus. Hetty asked for a glass of water. She had skipped lunch and was hungry. Another ten minutes elapsed. With a start, Hetty realised they had been sitting there nearly half an hour but no one had yet taken their orders. 'The service is a bit slow,' she commented.

'We were in luck getting a table,' was the answer. 'It is the hottest spot in town.'

'Not in the kitchen department,' Hetty said under her breath. The salted nuts were making her thirsty and her stomach was growling. The water had not materialised. 'So, what do you like doing, when you're not working?' she asked, then wished she hadn't. A simple enough question, it could too readily invite unwelcome confidences.

'Oh, you don't want to know,' James murmured, and blushed.

'I do, indeed,' Hetty fibbed playfully.

'I go round the country,' he began. Then, 'No, you'll laugh.'

This sounded intriguing. 'I won't. Cross my heart.'

'I go trainspotting.'

She burst out laughing but at his hurt expression covered her mouth. 'What – with a little notebook?' She wanted to add, 'And an anorak?' but stopped herself just in time.

'Of course. A portable computer, actually. Quite modern these days.' James wriggled his large bottom on the hard minimalist chair. 'The railways of Britain are our lifeblood, our arteries – the industrial revolution, social history, all that. When you see a big DMU churning out thousands of horsepower, with hundreds of holidaymakers or commuters depending on it, it's fantastic. And steam engines – d'you know the great ones from the thirties still hold the long distance records?' He burbled on, oblivious.

'I'm planning a trip on the French TGV,' Hetty interposed mischievously, when he paused for breath.

'Oh, *them*,' James said scornfully. 'They're quite impressive, but we invented the locomotive, not the French. They can't take that away.'

At last the waiter returned. Hetty asked politely what he recommended.

'Black cod cured in *miso*, speciality of the house,' he purred. 'Or you could have the *omakase*.'

'What's that?'

'Pot luck to you,' was the reply. 'Chef decides what you eat. That's a fixed price.' He pointed. Hetty saw '£60 per head' on the menu, folded it and put it down.

'I'll have what you suggested,' she said weakly. 'The cod.'

But when the purple slabs of raw fish came, swimming in an excess of fiery sauce, Hetty could only toy with it. Her guts wrenched at each overseasoned sliver; the Pinot Noir selected by James was ruined by the battleground of flavours on her tongue. She struggled for a while, then pushed her plate away.

'Do you think we could get some bread and a salad, maybe?' she asked.

'What? Oh, yes. You should come with me, Hetty. There's a big bank-holiday event coming up at Whitby. The sight of twelve or twenty of those magnificent workhorses in steam! It'll stay with you for ever . . .'

A black-suited male receptionist eventually responded to his beckoning finger.

'Everything all right?'

'No,' Hetty muttered. 'I think our waiter's forgotten the bread.'

'We don't have bread here, madam. This is a Japanese restaurant.'

'Oh. Then something hot and filling – a plate of noodles, perhaps?'

'No noodles.'

'But if it's a Japanese restaurant –'

'No noodles. Our chef from the royal house in Kyoto won't serve them. I could bring you some rice.'

'Yes, please. And water. From the tap. In a jug.'

But he had swept away. The bowl of rice, when it eventually arrived, was sticky, hot, blessedly unsalted – and tiny. Hetty hungrily polished off the contents and called the man back. 'Another, please. Just the same.'

'You're supposed to eat it with a main course,' James said knowledgeably. He was steadily demolishing plate after plate of unidentifiable mauve and green flesh: Hetty could not tell if it was fish, fowl, vegetable or what. He held out a slice in his chopsticks towards her, the black sauce dripping onto the spotless tablecloth. 'Fresh tuna. Do try.' She shook her head with a sickly grin. 'Best Japanese food I've ever tasted,' he commented. Her distress seemed to pass him by completely.

At last the meal was over. Coffee in diminutive cups, acrid and strong, was poured. Hetty's head was swimming with the wine and the edgy chemistry of salt, chilli, fish oils and caffeine on an empty stomach. James smiled and patted her hand.

'Hope you enjoyed that, Hetty. You're super company. You really listen to a chap. Terrific.'

'Doesn't take much to please him.' The voice inside her head sniffed. 'Maybe he's more thrilling on a windswept platform. What a bore.'

James paid the bill, rose, retrieved his briefcase, then followed her downstairs to the street. The night air hit her like a slap in the face and she staggered. He reached for her arm. 'Had a bit too much to drink, old girl? Come on, I'll put you in a taxi.' He darted about hopefully until a black cab stopped for him, then hesitated. Hetty must have appeared doleful: at the last instant, he clambered in himself. 'Can't let you go off like this. You don't look too well. I'll see you home.'

At the door of her flat he made no move. She pecked him on the cheek and squeezed his hand. 'A very – unusual dinner, James,' she said wanly. 'Thanks for taking me.'

He dimpled. 'A pleasure. You're lovely. Let's do it again.'

A wild notion occurred to her. Romantic progress, given James's culinary preferences, would be slow and agonising, if left to him. But he was a decent enough chap. He would pass for what she still had in mind. She was not about to give up. 'If you don't expect too much, James,' she said, 'you'd be welcome to eat here. Pot luck, it'd have to be, whatever the chef decides. Is that okay?'

'Oh, rather,' he gurgled, and planted a salty kiss on her mouth. 'I'll phone you.'

She climbed out and waved as the cab reversed and returned in the direction it had come.

'Oh, Lord,' she said. ' I hope you're worth it.' Then she tiptoed round the back of The Swallows behind the bushes, stuck two fingers down her throat, and was thoroughly and satisfyingly sick.

CHAPTER EIGHTEEN

Breaking a Duck

The book club were in a tetchy mood. Hetty could not figure it out, until she realised that, despite their protestations, the members had not enjoyed the latest author, crime writer Ruth Rendell. Their disappointment was almost tangible.

'Something about her characters,' Moira mused, with pursed lips. They had been concentrating on *Keys to the Street* and *The Crocodile Bird*.

'You can't complain about the sex this time.' Phyllis pouted. 'There isn't any. Buckets of psychological mayhem, but the action stops at the bedroom door.'

Thin, wan Moira crumbled a rock cake and lifted fragments into her mouth. In the time it took her, Hetty noted, her stout friend had demolished two large scones with jam and cream, and two cups of tea. The ascetic Moira's cup was hardly touched.

Jenny, the oldest member and osteoporosis sufferer, raised her head with an effort. 'The problem is, none of the characters is warm or kind, with the exception of the child in *The Crocodile Bird* and the girl Mary in the Regent's Park novel. And they're for the chop the whole way through. The stories are gripping – but you feel it's a world turned upside down. Clever stuff but cruel, heartless.'

'Should suit us, then,' the Professor murmured. He spoke to Hetty out of the corner of his mouth. 'The world we live in here. It's topsy-turvy, don't you think? The sharpest are the most bowed down, like Jenny. Or tied to a bloody wheelchair, like me. Those with the most fluency have the least to say.' He glanced in the direction of Millie Curtis, Clarissa's aunt, who was chattering on with total conviction, even though it was clear to everyone else in the room that she had not read the texts.

Hetty had missed a couple of sessions through pressure at the studios. She nibbled a biscuit. It was a pleasure to be with the club again, to hear the shrewdness from the depths of those ample cardigans. Human beings, indeed. Plenty to be found here.

'How did you get on with Beryl Bainbridge?' she asked. The Professor chuckled.

'They adored *An Awfully Big Adventure*. It's set in the repertory theatre in Liverpool where the author was a stage-manager, so we swapped tales of amateur and school dramatics. *Master Georgie*, I fear, was a bit beyond them. Mostly, they debated Miss Bainbridge's views on accents. That was within everyone's capacity.'

'She criticised the Scouse twang, didn't she?' Hetty racked her brains. 'Said you have to drop it if you want to get on. Took elocution lessons when she was young.'

'Everyone did, then. Good vowels were the hallmark of a lady. Or a gentleman.'

'But if you needed lessons, then presumably you weren't a real lady.'

'Absolutely. But the delightful Miss Bainbridge was the product of a home that fell tragically below its pretensions. People were far more conscious of class than now.'

Hetty recalled Larry and Davinia's street. 'Today it's the BMW convertible that says you're smart. Or the Audi TT Special with its year-long waiting list. Or liking Japanese food with a Mexican slant. Not your accent.'

'If my television and radio are any guide, a regional accent is *de rigueur* these days.'

'That's quite true,' Hetty told him. 'When we're deciding on guests for *Tell Me All*, it helps if they're Geordies or Welsh. Provided they can make themselves understood.'

'I don't know what the world's coming to,' the Professor continued, teasing. 'You can't even hear a cut-glass accent on Radio Three these days. As for Classic FM . . .'

'Snob,' grinned Hetty, and poured him another cup of tea.

The session was drawing to a close. A flurry of argument developed over the next two authors. As the choice fell on Michael Dobbs and Jilly Cooper, the Professor protested. 'I come to this meeting for intellectual stimulation, not to be fed commercial pap,' he grumbled, but nobody was listening. 'Whatever next?'

Hetty pushed his wheelchair back along the corridor. 'You're too hard on them. Not everybody has an IQ of a hundred and fifty,' she chided. 'I haven't, for a start. I love Jilly Cooper. And we can watch *To Play the King* on video.'

'Allow me to confess I've never read either. No doubt

they're fine enough, and popular. I'm no literature buff, but we should always aim higher, Hetty. Trying to grasp what is unfamiliar and difficult never killed anyone.' He wagged his finger. 'The trouble today is that people have become mentally idle. They won't strive. The end result is what's called dumbing-down.' He was riding a favourite hobby-horse. 'Everything's supposed to conform to an easy norm. But diversity, my dear, is the spice of life.'

Hetty agreed fervently with that, and described to him in the lift her unhappiness with the makeover mentality of *Star Style*. 'Ah, but, Hetty,' he cajoled, 'the impression you make visually does matter.'

'Not that much,' she objected.

'It does to an artist. You forget who you are talking to,' he said. They had reached his room. On previous occasions she had deposited him, ensured he was safe and then left. But now, 'A glass of wine, dear girl?' he asked, as he unlocked the door.

Hetty did not hesitate. He indicated the cupboard, where bottles were laid in rows on a rack. 'There's a Pauillac, top right. Don't shake it.' She found the corkscrew, wiped glasses and poured. Then, cradling a full glass, she gazed about, and was overwhelmed at what she saw.

The room was a generous size, the metal hospital-style bed with its sling hoist dominating the centre, but with space around it for the wheelchair. A bay window overlooking the garden filled it with soft light; dust motes danced in the air. Low shelves crammed with books and art magazines lined two sides. In corners on stands, and on the bookshelves, were small sculptures, some of which looked unfinished: one was recognisable as the Professor's own head. But the glory was the pictures. Several substantial oils

in ornate frames, mostly modern, faced the light. Pastels
and acrylics, charcoal drawings and a few water-colours
jostled for position. Another wall was crammed with dozens
of coloured prints, some pinned with thumbtacks, others in
simple glass frames. Not a spare inch showed. In many, the
subject was female, and nude.

He followed her eyes. 'Picasso – I met him several times.
That small one was a gift but, then, he was so prolific. The
Degas is a favourite, and the Modigliani. His work was
banned because he dared to show pubic hair, but his women
are so elegant and alive. The Seurat is charming, isn't it?
But they pale into insignificance beside the master.' He
pointed. 'Renoir. See? The blonde bather. That's his wife,
with those adorable breasts – you just know he had kissed
those nipples, and what pearly skin! He painted women as
they should be painted. Curved, fleshy, like ripe peaches. So
good you can taste them. So full of love, every brushstroke.
You can tell he adored women.'

Hetty was dumbstruck. A row of prints showed women
lying on sofas or posed in landscapes. 'Velázquez – the
Rokeby Venus. Titian – the Venus of Urbino. Isn't she gorgeous? He was still painting perfect women when he was
over eighty. Giorgione – the way they posed the left hand
makes us snigger today . . . looks as if she is playing with
herself, doesn't she? But what an exquisite face. The
Venetians worshipped beauty. Rubens – *Venus and Area* –
extraordinarily erotic. Most of his nudes are too fat for
modern taste, but over there is Helena Fourment his wife,
naked beneath her fur coat – so tactile. Can't you just feel
the contact of her skin and her fur? Such generosity of heart,
Rubens. That one's Ingres. And here's Manet's *Olympia* –
that caused a scandal, because she's so real, her expression

so challenging. He never again chose the female nude for a major work. Maybe he felt he didn't need to . . .'

Hetty listened avidly, desperate to remember. The Professor talked enthusiastically, then touched her arm: 'We gaze and turn away, and know not where,/Dazzled and drunk with Beauty, till the heart/Reels with its fulness.' He smiled. 'According to Byron, *Childe Harold*.' She nodded, and bit her lip, her glass untouched.

He swivelled his chair and directed her attention to another series of prints. 'Raphael's *Three Graces* – he painted a naked Venus in the Vatican, in Cardinal Bibiena's bathroom. Must have been some talking-point. That one's the *Allegory of Passion*, Bronzino. Very sexy – see how the nipple is tweaked?' Hetty touched the print with her fingertip. The leer of abandon on the figure's face made her recoil.

He whirled round. 'You know the secret of the *Mona Lisa*, don't you?'

She shook her head, fascinated.

'Leonardo revealed it to Correggio. He said to look at women in twilight: he'd studied scientifically the passage of light around a sphere. That's why Leonardo's depictions of breasts and thighs are so sensuous, as in his *Leda*, even though he was not himself sexually attracted to women. The painting's lost, but the drawings are still extant.'

Hetty moved towards the modern works, many of which were sketches or pastels. The Professor spoke of his personal acquaintance with many of the artists and their circles. He launched into anecdotes of sessions with this or that celebrity, dinners and alcoholic evenings spent on Tuscan and Provençal hillsides, lectures given, students shared. The names were known to her through press reviews of important exhibitions, though she would have been at a loss to discuss their output.

She tried to calculate. He could not be more than eighty, and thus born after the end of the First World War, so his claims made him either exceptionally precocious or a bit of a tale-spinner. Or maybe, as an old man, what he had read or heard and what he had done himself, had begun to merge in his brain as reminiscence. Hetty decided at once not to correct or question him.

'I've got hundreds, but mostly in storage. Like children, you never want them to leave home. I had more at my studio, but that's gone. Some of the paintings dotted around the corridors here belong to me. At least I can have the pleasure of seeing them on my daily jaunts, and so can others. My little battle against mediocrity.'

One of the small statues caught her eye. It was a bronze about a foot high of a child dancer, her toe extended, her head bent as if checking the twist of her shoe ribbons. The style was graceful and unmannered. Cautiously, she ventured: 'That's wonderful. Is it by Degas?'

The Professor smiled. 'Not officially.'

'What do you mean?'

'Oh, Hetty, the insurance would be astronomical. Officially, most of what you see are reproductions, or copies, some of which I made myself. The bronzes are castings, of course, and there may be dozens identical. But you may take it that if the master himself made a casting, he would sign it.'

'It's extraordinary,' she said, as if to confirm that she grasped the issue, 'that a copy, however beautiful in its own right, has so little value.'

'Ah, but put a copy and an original together, and you can tell. Not least, because the original usually has an unfinished air.'

She must have looked puzzled, for he added, 'When we

create a work of art from scratch, we experiment, we cross
out, we redo, we paint over. The copy lacks all these imper-
fections. Real life, like art, is full of errors. But that's what
makes it unique.'

'So the copy's a makeover,' Hetty murmured.

He chuckled softly, but did not reply.

'What will you do,' she asked, 'when the time comes?
Leave them to a museum?'

'Probably. I daren't let on to the management, but one or
two here are quite valuable. If anyone was aware of it, they'd
be in a bank vault. And that would be a tragedy.'

Hetty drank quietly, letting the beauty of the images and
the owner's delight in them flow over her. Stephen's taste
ran to Russell Flint and Monet's waterlilies, and no further.
Prints were purchased for their potential value, and to match
a colour scheme; her ex-husband and his friends would have
found the Professor's passion embarrassing.

He had not referred to one part of the collection and she
came round rather pointedly to look. Like many of the other
paintings the subject was a female nude: some full-length,
on a scarlet sofa, others only of the back or buttocks. Many
were sketches, others varnished and framed. On closer
examination they seemed to be of the same person, a lithe,
buxom girl with blue eyes and luxurious dark hair.

'Who did those, Professor?'

He drank his wine with a mysterious air. 'Try and guess.'

Hetty peered closer, moving across the pictures to let the
light fall on them. The canvases had no signature. 'Sorry. But
they are terrific. Even I can see that.'

'You like them?' He seemed pleased.

She bent down and looked more intently. 'Yes,' she said
finally. 'Like the Renoirs, there's a real appreciation of the

female form. Hope that doesn't sound too pretentious. I'm totally out of my depth. But, yes, I like them very much.'

The Professor laughed. 'I knew I could trust you in my den here,' he said indulgently, as if it had been a matter of argument. Perhaps it was: his reputation around the home was as a prickly curmudgeon. Hetty had heard that staff were not amused by his manner; the dust suggested that the cleaners found the images disturbing. He put his glass on the bedside table and cavorted jerkily in the wheelchair. His face was flushed.

'But who did them?'

'I did. They're mine.'

'Oh! I didn't like to ask if anything was yours, but I'm delighted. They're fabulous.' She straightened up. 'Who's the model? Anyone in particular?' Yet, even as she enquired, she knew the answer.

'My wife.' His face became grave. 'My muse. After she died, I stopped painting.'

Somewhere downstairs a radio was playing, with snatches of indiscernible music. The hiss of the lift mechanism came from along the corridor. Hetty refilled their glasses, then sat on the edge of the bed, kicked off her shoes and tucked her feet up under her.

'You must have loved her very much.'

'I did. She had an ethereal beauty, but earthy with it. When I first met her she was sleeping with Augustus John. He went through his models like a knife through butter. A paintbrush in one hand and his prick in the other. But he never cared about them as people. The moment I set eyes on her I adored her.'

Hetty felt her throat constrict. 'You were so fortunate, to have such love.'

He grunted but did not answer. He seemed lost in another world, his eyes on the creamy-fleshed girl on the claret sofa. Then he swung round. 'You, Hetty. You remind me of her. I've told you. The way you hold your head. The way you pause before you say anything. The way –'

'Stop,' Hetty said, as calmly as she could. 'That's your imagination playing tricks. I'm not her. But I'm proud that you make the comparison.' She drained her wine and stood up, found her shoes. 'This is a treasure trove,' she added. 'I feel privileged. Can I come again?'

He reached out his hand to her, slowly. 'Yes. Of course. Darling Hetty. Come again.'

Just as she was about to put the basted lamb in the oven, a hand tapped at the door.

'That can't be him already, can it?' She brushed her hair out of her eyes. The clock said another half-hour yet. She still had time to put on her makeup. In any case, this wasn't the street bell but her own.

It was Doris. In her arms was Thomas, with a lecherous glint in his eye. The old lady peered in, her curiosity palpable. 'I smelt something delicious coming from your kitchen. It's right above mine. And I thought, Why don't I see what's going on?'

'I'm cooking, Doris. Can't stop right now.'

Doris was not to be deterred. She stuck her nose around the door and half insinuated her stout body and Thomas after it. A shower of ginger hairs rubbed off on the lintel. Hetty flapped a tea-towel. 'No, Doris,' she said firmly. 'Tomorrow.'

'Ooh, you gotta fella coming,' Doris judged expertly. 'Special guy, is it? Special date?'

Hetty was unsure whether James would count as a special anything, but she was determined not to spoil the roast for a ha'porth of idle chatter. 'Yes, it is a chap. And, yes, I do want to feed him properly. Especially after the last meal we had together.' The sentence was uttered with deep sincerity.

Doris's eyes narrowed. 'D'you want something to slip into his drink? To help out?' she offered. 'Make a roaring success of the evening.'

Hetty pushed the door so that it bore down on her nosy neighbour. 'Go,' she commanded. 'If anything comes of it, you'll be the first to know.'

'You wearing something nice from the shop?' Doris persisted.

Hetty was, indeed, dressed in new black lacy underwear under the simple skirt and black scoop-necked sweater. 'Scram, please.'

Doris leered as the door closed. 'I'll be listening . . .' was her parting shot.

Half an hour later, with the meat safely in the oven, the salad prepared, the Beaujolais opened and the white Burgundy (if he preferred it) chilling in the fridge, with her hair and lipstick set, Hetty's heart thumped as the doorbell announced a visitor. Quickly she dabbed perfume behind her ears, pressed the intercom button and opened the door.

'James!' she cried, as if he were an unexpected delivery.

He thrust a bouquet into her hands – bought, she noted, from the ready-made bucket at the florists' by the tube station. 'Hello, Hetty.'

The awkwardness was still present. More so, as if each knew that the dessert tonight might be more than the fresh pineapple with kirsch waiting on the sideboard.

Corks were pulled, wine poured. The table in the living

room was prettily laid: a blue cover underneath, covered by a *broderie anglaise* cloth inherited from an aunt, so that the petal shapes showed through. Napkins folded in a wing shape. Two wooden candlesticks bought at a sale of work at St Veronica's, carved napkin rings to match. The second-best dinner service from Dorset. Yet, brave as the show might be, the table set for two had a melancholy feel.

'That's because you've not done this before,' whispered the candlesticks. 'When your mother or Sally or Doris comes, you don't take this amount of trouble. We're new. We've never sat in on your tête-à-têtes. Not even with those who love you.'

'You're trying to impress him, that's what,' the soup tureen slurped, as she set it down. 'Why him? Does he matter more than anyone else you've ever had in this flat?'

'What are you up to, Hetty?' the curtains hissed as she drew them across the fading dusk. 'What do you want from him? Are you being quite fair?'

'I want,' Hetty told the bread silently as she sliced it Davinia-fashion and put it in a basket, 'what I can't get from those others. Not love. Friendship and company, maybe. But what's missing is – well, you know.'

'We know,' chorused the cutlery, and winked roguishly as she lit scented candles. And it seemed to her that the table rocked once in sympathy, and wished her luck.

'I hope you like carrot and lemon soup,' Hetty said brightly, as she ladled it into the bowls and offered the bread. If carrots featured at classy Davinia's, maybe they'd do the trick for her.

James had brought with him a hearty appetite and not much conversation. The soup, bread, and butterfly lamb with rosemary disappeared in substantial quantities followed by seconds, and another bottle was half emptied, before he appeared to relax. He took off his jacket and hung it on the back of the chair. 'Brought you these,' he said, and fished in his inside pocket. He handed her a pile of leaflets. 'I'm not just into trains, Hetty, I'm a supporter of the Tramway Museum at Crich. It's in Derbyshire. I don't suppose you've ever been there?'

She agreed that she had not. He leaned across the table, his pink jowls wistful.

'Would you like to come? Maybe mid-week. Or if you've got some holiday due.'

'But, James,' she said quietly, 'what about your family? Don't they expect you to be with them?'

His eyes dropped. He fiddled with the leaflets. 'Yes, well,' he muttered, 'they're not keen.'

'Ah.' Hetty cleared plates and rinsed them moodily under the tap. Did this mean the evening was about to come to a full stop? She returned to the living room and carried the platter of pineapple to the table.

His eyes lit up. 'I'll say this, you're a fine cook, Hetty.' His voice betrayed surprise.

'Why shouldn't I be? I had enough practice. The secret's to keep it simple. If you want fancy fare, there are so many restaurants here in London.'

'Mmm, that's true. I'd love to take you back to that Japanese place, and introduce you to their special sushi. Sorry you were a bit peaky that night.'

Hetty allowed her gaze to stray over James, to evaluate him more objectively. Not tall. Not fat either, though he could lose a few pounds, and exercise might tighten that saggy chin. He still had most of his hair, although the shade was more bleached and sandy than in a younger man. A speckle of dandruff littered his shoulders. Those were his own teeth. A non-smoker. For a man in his mid-fifties, he was quite passable.

A renewed determination surfaced in her. She *had* to make progress. Chasing men, if she were to indulge herself, required a raft of new skills and resurrected old ones. James, it was now obvious, had every reason to treat her with discretion. If this tryst dissolved into a God-awful disaster, he would not dine out on the story.

'I seem to recall,' she said archly as she poured coffee, 'that you enjoy a glass of brandy to finish off your meal.' She motioned him to an armchair.

'Rather!' he said boyishly. Then, 'Look, shouldn't I help you clear away first?'

She flapped a napkin. 'No, no. Leave it. I'll do it later.' Tomorrow morning, if all went well. The Courvoisier had been a gift from Sally, duty-free, to help her mother stock up. Hetty poured a generous measure then offered, as if expecting a refusal, 'Soda or water? I don't think you take them, do you?'

He shook his head, swirled the brandy round in its balloon and took a long swallow. They must have put away a lot of liquor, Hetty realised. It heightened her awareness of James, of his legs now stretched out lazily, of the quiet room, the littered table, the guttering candles and bits of pineapple skin, which resembled question marks; yet her brain was clear and sharp.

James had started to talk politics, then switched to what was evidently a recurrent grievance about office intrigues and why he had not yet achieved the promotion he deserved. It came to Hetty that his wife was not a great deal of support in his career: the lady did not feature at all in this saga. Not

the kind of wife she herself had been, it was plain – no country weekends entertaining clients or board directors, no
intimate dinner parties at home. Not as she, Hetty, had done
as a matter of course. No wonder Rosa, Sally, Doris, the BJs
found that scenario risible. She must have been mad. It had
given her, none the less, a talent for listening as if engrossed,
and of enabling nervous or tired men to unwind in her presence.

James was burbling on, almost oblivious. He was beginning to relax rather too much. Hetty slipped round the back
of his armchair and knelt down, her face close to his. 'You
poor man,' she said soothingly, in what she hoped was a
seductive murmur. 'It's dreadful when your talents are not
valued.'

'Oh, I wouldn't put it *quite* like that. I do fairly well. But
a man my age should have a partnership on the horizon. It's
not my fault if it isn't.' He seemed about to become maudlin,
and glanced longingly at his empty glass.

Hetty took it from his hand. 'There are other compensa-
tions, James,' she cooed softly, and kissed him.

He tasted of kirsch and brandy, of lamb and garlic and
sweet fruit, as if everything he had eaten had lingered on
some part of his mouth. But I put it all there, she reflected,
and I must taste much the same. She kissed him again.

He appeared startled, as if he had expected to go on rambling, increasingly in his cups, for hours. 'I say, old girl,
that's rather nice,' he said, as if coming up for air.

Hetty was tempted to haul him to his feet by his tie and
drag him to the bedroom. She moved to face him and kissed
him more, putting real energy into it so that he couldn't be
misled. At last he rose, lifted her up and put his arms tightly
round her in a bear-hug. 'Lovely meal, lovely lady,' he

muttered into her hair. 'Mmm, Hetty, you smell good.'

'Wonderful to have you here, James,' she whispered, her throat constricting. What should she do now? She ran her hands up and down the small of his back and pressed him to her. He was slouching a little. Weary? Drunk? It was time to find out.

She pushed him away and flirtatiously began to undo his shirt buttons, slipping her fingers inside. 'I was sitting there, wondering whether you have hair all over your chest, James,' she said lightly. 'A big, masculine man like you.'

He giggled and hiccuped. 'Oooh, yes. Hair everywhere. D'you want to see?'

He tugged at his tie as she undid the rest of his shirt buttons and pulled the shirt-tails out of his trousers. Undressed his upper body was not unattractive. A mite sweaty from the warmth of the room. Hetty found herself breathing harder, her head starting to pound. She pressed her palms over his pectorals; they were fleshy, not excessively so, but not muscular. He wriggled. 'Ooh! I'm ticklish . . .'

'You are? Where? Maybe you'd better show me . . .'

Hetty took his hand and led him, trailing the shirt and tie, into the bedroom. The bedside light was on, but she had set aromatic candles in saucers and quickly lit them. The effect was all one could wish – romantic, glamorous and an open invitation.

'We are a tad overdressed, James,' she said.

'We are, we are. Aren't you a clever woman? I can't get over it, Hetty. So nice, and such a good cook. And now . . .' He giggled again and went as if to hug *himself*.

Hetty lifted her sweater over her head. James gaped: the black bra might be only Marks and Spencer's, but it pushed up her cleavage quite powerfully. Maybe James's sex life was as limited as her own. She prayed he wasn't impotent, but even that she could cope with. As long as he didn't laugh at her. The tinge of melancholy returned, but she shoved it resolutely away and undid her skirt, letting it drop to the floor.

'Tasty,' teased the mirror.

'Ooh!' was James's contribution, as his eyes rounded. He grabbed her, and clutched her to him once more. This time the contact of skin on skin made her tingle. Something twitched, down on her thigh. Then he stepped back, crestfallen. 'I haven't brought . . . any protection, Hetty. I thought this was just for dinner.'

She was prompted to call him a stupid idiot to his face, but instead smiled sweetly. 'No problem. Trousers off.'

He did as he was told, struggling through the comical dance of a man engaged in the impossible task of removing his kit with dignity. He stood upright, this time in striped boxer shorts and navy socks, hands loose by his sides.

'And the rest.'

James appeared to stumble, so Hetty came close, hooked her thumbs inside the elastic of his shorts and kissed his chest as she pulled them down. It was surprisingly easy to do, and as she bent to wriggle them off over his knees and feet, Hetty saw why.

He was indeed hairy – in fact, he was luxuriantly hirsute from the navel down, over a podgy belly. His erection was not in doubt: the man was not impotent. Doris's remedies would not be needed. On the other hand . . .

It was *tiny*. Hesitantly, Hetty touched it, and measured it quickly in her hand. It was about the same length as her little finger, and not much thicker. It was nearly lost in the hairy bush; had she not been looking for it, she might have missed it entirely.

'Oh, do that again,' James groaned, as she stroked his diminutive penis. It wasn't purple and engorged with blood, but pale in the candlelight, though stolidly and proudly erect, like a skinny drummer boy at the end of a line of soldiers.

'Come on, then,' Hetty said, and led him to the bed. In a few seconds, with her assistance, her bra and pants had been fumblingly removed. She guided his hand to her own bush, and waited as he rubbed her eagerly.

'Like that?' he asked, more confidently, and she cooed for answer. He was hefty, on top of her, and breathing more lamb and garlic. The activity loosened a bubble of wind and he belched. 'Whoops! Sorry. You fed me too well.'

For fear of losing it, she kept it in her hand; to lubricate, she licked her palm and wetted it, and he groaned in excitement. Then she commanded, 'Now, James, in you come,' and he obliged willingly.

She could feel nothing, not there. However, she could feel his heavy body wallowing on her, his hot breath on her neck. His eyes were closed and he was grunting, a beatific expression on his flushed cheeks. 'Oh! Oh! Oh!' she uttered theatrically, and 'Oh, Hetty!' he wailed eventually, and slumped down on her, his arms flailing over his head. He grabbed her face and kissed it wetly. 'God, that was terrific!'

'Ye-e-es,' she answered, and wondered whether she should pant in time with his heaving torso. Their bodies were sticking together. Somewhere down there came the faint sensation of a gentle *plop*, but possibly she had imagined it.

As gently and politely as possible, she shoved him off and cradled herself on his shoulder. He put his hand on his chest. 'Oooh! Heart's pumping. Wow! Haven't had proper fun like that in ages.'

Hetty felt suddenly alarmed. She had invited this man into her bed on two assumptions. First, that he was as well equipped as the next chap, second, that his personal life was reasonably sound and that he was merely looking for a bit on the side. Now, she saw, neither was correct. He was not getting his oats at home, and he was woefully under-endowed.

And, what was worse, he clearly didn't know it.

'Hope you enjoyed that as much as I did, old girl,' he said happily and hugged her. His eyes were closed, as if he were in heaven.

Hetty did not have the heart to disabuse him. 'Smashing,' she murmured.

They pulled up the duvet and dozed for a few moments, till Hetty roused herself and picked up the clock on the bed-side table. 'I think you ought to make a move, James.'

'Mmm – can't I stay?' His eyes were still shut tight.

She lifted the duvet and gazed calmly at him. She had not been mistaken: detumescent, it had vanished entirely into his pubic hair. Nor did it show the least flicker of life. 'Only if you want some more,' she said, quietly, half praying that he couldn't hear.

'No, once a night's enough for me,' he mumbled, and that decided it.

Hetty rose and reached for the candlewick dressing-gown on the back of the door. 'It's been super, James, but I have an early call in the morning. And I'm not used to sleeping the whole night with someone. Not sure I'm ready for it yet.'

He was snoring.

She prodded him, and he rolled over. She continued mut-tering as she helped him into his shorts and socks. Then he slumped once more, and she gave up.

Hetty, naked under the dressing-gown, addressed the slumbering form of her new lover. 'Actually, James, I *am* ready, but for something better than this. So you can stay the night and I'll sleep on the sofa – it won't be the first time. But that's it.'

'Lovely,' he mumbled, as she blew out the candles and turned out the bedside light.

CHAPTER NINETEEN

Down the Plughole

'Oh, poor you!' Rosa squeezed her hand. They were in a corner of the canteen, backs to the rest of the crew, with cups of black coffee before them.

'Yes, I did feel rather sorry for myself,' Hetty agreed. 'It was this big.' She held up her little finger and crooked it, then raised it erect and slowly let it droop.

'Couldn't he get it up?' Rosa asked, anxiously.

'Oh, yes, that wasn't it,' Hetty answered, in a stage whisper. Dave the cameraman was staring pointedly in their direction. 'Only you couldn't tell if it was up or down.'

The two women broke out in a fit of giggles, clutching at each other and waggling fingers.

Hetty wiped her eyes. 'And in the morning when he woke up, he complained that it was sore. Can you imagine? *And* he didn't wash up.'

'You know what they say. If you don't use it, you lose it. Maybe he's the proof.'

Hetty collapsed in another paroxysm. 'At least it didn't drop off in my hand. But it looked so fragile . . .'

It was several minutes before either could regain some composure. The male crew were now openly eavesdropping. Rosa put her head on one side. 'I must say, Hetty, you've really altered. No more prim middle-aged matron for you, eh? What happened to that timid little biddy I offered a job to all those months ago?'

'Down a plughole, along with my other illusions, fears and frustrations, I guess,' Hetty answered, marginally more quietly. 'D'you know, I'll be fifty-one next week? And it doesn't bother me in the least.'

'No reason why it should. Going to celebrate?'

'No way. We didn't mark my fiftieth, the big five-oh. From here onwards, I'm going to count backwards.'

'I started doing that years ago.'

'It's not that I'm paranoid about getting older. Not any more. I don't intend to roll over and become a second-class citizen. Not because I've reached a mature age, or because I'm single. There are advantages in both.'

'Quite the philosopher,' Rosa commented drily.

'But so few see it this way, do they? Yet you and I, Rosa, are in the second most rapidly growing group in modern society.'

'Singles. Fiftysomethings.'

'Right. And we're not all – what did Sally say? – SAD, single and desperate. If I were desperate, I'd have stuck with James, trainspotting, miniprick and all. But I'd rather munch a dill pickle any day.' They started laughing again, heads close, Rosa's frizzy black hair and Hetty's streaked brown intermingled like two mop-haired dolls.

'My dope of a brother and his partner will probably think

I'm certifiable,' Hetty continued. 'I haven't dared tell them yet that James and I are not an item. Larry put me under so much pressure, but he has no right. They set themselves up as the perfect couple, but they're far from it. They planned to bring me in from the cold, as they see it. But I'm not cold – or not cold enough to see the Railway King in steam again. So why do I still feel guilty?'

'Were you sweet to James? Polite to him on the phone?'

'Yes. But it's taking him a while to get the message. He feels it was an evening of sheer magic. That's what he said.'

'Dear lamb! Then you've nothing to feel upset about. Tell him your conscience is nagging because he's married – make it clear that the alternative is *not* that he should leave his wife for you. Say you've decided to concentrate on your career. *Whatever.* Suggest to Larry that they try to find the poor baby somebody else.'

'I was half expecting my brother to call me for a progress report. Trouble is, if I tell him the truth he'll be haring off fixing up someone else for me.'

'You could try running a string of men, though it can get complicated,' Rosa said dreamily. 'One for nights out, one to play bridge with, one for romance. Then you can give up searching for the ideal bloke: you exploit the talents of whoever you meet. Doesn't apply to me, natch – there's only one activity for which men are indispensable.' And she mimed a bouncing movement, arms stretched ahead, as if riding a horse.

From behind came a shouted ribald comment, but the women ignored it.

'My friendships are beginning to develop in that direction, now I think about it,' Hetty responded. 'My mother and my daughter provide one kind of loving company, and my neighbours Doris and the lads upstairs another. I'm fond of Father Roger, too, though not sexually – at least, I don't believe he'd respond. I'd like more time to catch up with Christian's current play, but it can be awkward when we're not finished here till seven. Not that I'm complaining,' she added hastily.

'We should have a new contract for you shortly,' Rosa confirmed. 'Four-fifty pounds a week while we're record-ing. Not brilliant, but not destitution, either.'

'I appreciate that. It all helps,' Hetty said.

Rosa stood to go, shaking herself like a young animal. 'You said the second fast-growing group. Where d'you get that info?'

'Kate, the researcher. She's a mine of useless information. You know she fancies you, don't you?'

'I do. You don't need to remind me, Hetty. So what's the other?'

'Old people. Especially centenarians. Everyone's living a lot longer.'

'Yes. Well, I'm glad to wait. A few more years of frisky engagement with the opposite sex, before arthritis and Alzheimer's set in, will do me fine.'

Mention of Larry and Davinia reminded Hetty that, though she had sent a courteous note after the dinner party, some follow-up might be appropriate. As she turned over the Fulham evening and its aftermath in her mind, she realised she had heard no more about Nicholas.

She wandered out into the corridor and found Kate. 'How are the ratings?'

'Not bad. We're getting a regular million. As good as *Trisha*, anyway.'

'That's what we want. Rosa's so professional.'

Kate sighed. 'She is. She creates a pleasant atmosphere. Even though she keeps our noses to the grindstone.'

'I wondered,' Hetty fidgeted, 'whether we got any feedback from programme six. With Nicholas, the chap who intended to throw up his City job to become a writer.'

'There was something . . .' Kate wrinkled her nose to remember. 'A bit in one of the book sections in last weekend's newspapers, that he's been in talks with a literary agent. Rather what you'd expect.'

'Fine,' Hetty answered. 'Thank you.' She turned to leave.

'Why, you interested?'

'No, but I know someone who is. Though if he's going to be penniless, I suspect her ardour might cool quite quickly.'

'Sad, that, women who want a man only for his money.'

'In the case in question it might be a darned good thing.'

Hetty pinned the gilt badge on her lapel, swung this way and that before the mirror and ordered it to be complimentary. Then she picked up her gold membership card and headed for a weigh-in at the slimmers' class.

It had to be confessed that a different woman walked across the common in the summer evening compared to the winter. Both Sally and Rosa had commented. Odd, Hetty reflected, how a woman's self-confidence could blossom again – not easily, it had been a struggle, but so robustly, as if well rooted. Paradoxically James had had a lot to do with it; so, in his way, had Al the saxophone player. The fact that men – *any* men – were attracted to her was a huge morale-booster. And the outward signs, the loss of twenty pounds in weight and the newer, trimmer figure, were crucial. 'You see,' she told the trees, 'the mirror was wiser than me.

Appearance counts. It shouldn't: in a world in which we approached everyone as individuals, with their own special quirks and foibles, it wouldn't matter a toss.'

'Look your best, feel your best,' the trees whispered back.

'And the Professor, too,' she mused. 'Those fabulous paintings, his obsession with how a woman looks. He never once said anything about their personalities. I wonder what sort of girl his wife was? Funny, or serious? Kind, or hard-bitten? Did she take off her clothes for anyone else? Oh, yes, Augustus John, he said. Naïve, maybe? Had a huge effect on him, that's for sure.' She strolled along, swinging her arms.

'What are you chuntering about?' came a voice behind her. 'Slow down, Hetty.'

It was Annabel. Hetty waited till she caught up. The tall, tubby girl was much the same size as on their first visit to the slimming club – five feet ten, or thereabouts, and closer to fifteen stone than twelve, though her substantial frame could comfortably carry the extra weight. If she didn't mind her size – had she enjoyed being big – Annabel would be quite sexy, like Sophie Dahl, or one of the Professor's beloved Rubenses.

'I was feeling pleased with life,' Hetty said, with a smile. 'It's certainly perked up for me recently. How're you?'

'Huh. Frantic. I put on three pounds last week. Three pounds! And I haven't the faintest idea how. This week I've tried to sweat it off – had a long hot bath tonight before coming out. I'm sweating like a pig.'

'What's the weakness? Booze? Biscuits? Mayonnaise?'

'Don't be so smug, Hetty. It's okay for you and your gold pin, you've reached target. You must have tremendous self-discipline.'

'Not a scrap. But it depressed me. I felt I was turning into an old cow. Either I kept putting it on, or I stopped and got it off. It was as simple as that.'

Annabel trudged beside her in silence.

'I haven't seen you and the girls for a bit,' Hetty said. 'How's the love life? How's Richard?'

'Him!' Annabel hooted derisively. 'He went off and found himself someone else. A feisty black lady, works in TV – Flo was furious. But he'll be back.'

Hetty's eyes danced. 'And you? Anyone nice?'

Annabel shook her head. 'I hope I've got *Richard* out of my system. That's a step forward, anyhow.' She brightened. 'What are you doing after class, Hetty? Wanna come round for a drink?'

Hetty had learned to accept what came in her direction: it made for an agreeable if unpredictable diary. 'That'd be great. Shall I bring a bottle?'

'Nah, we got a flat full of alcohol. We laid it in for a party last weekend that didn't happen. If you help us get rid of it, Het, that'll be fewer calories for me, won't it?'

The slimming club was rather less crowded than before. Registrations were at a maximum, Hetty knew, during January, when she herself had joined: fights and broken romances at Christmas brought on New Year resolutions that led to the queues and anguished faces she had become familiar with months ago. The intrepid were still attending doggedly, but others would never return.

The same two men were there, but the beer bellies had shrunk. The instructor was as skinny as ever, still unbelievable as the barrel in the flowered tent of her photo. The Asian lady in a yellow sari was seated on the front row, no longer quite as squat, with another fatter woman, similarly attired, beside her. Possibly a sister: maybe the one had convinced the other to come for mutual support.

On tiptoe in the queue, Hetty searched for the former owner of the chip shop. It took several minutes before she identified her: still very wide, but now stout rather than grossly obese, reading a recipe book, spectacles perched on the end of her stubby nose.

'Hello. How did you do this week?' The standard greeting.

The chip-shop woman screwed up her eyes. 'Hetty, isn't it? I lost another two pounds. That's ninety-six to date. Next week it'll be seven stone.'

'Well done, you!' Another standard.

The woman sighed. 'I'm walking now. I promised myself that at twelve stone I'd buy a dog, but the pet shop said I should be more active first. Otherwise the dog'd suffer.'

'And your target?'

''Bout another fifty pounds. I'll do it, with God's help.'

Hetty patted the woman on the shoulder and went to be weighed. She marvelled at the endurance needed to persist so long, and in the face of such adversity. It had struck her forcibly on her first visit how slight her own problems were by comparison. Now she felt almost ashamed to be present, and said so to Margaret the instructor.

'My dear! No, you must keep coming. For your own sake. And also to encourage the others. To show it *can* be done.' The instructor gave a tough little smile.

Annabel was slumped in a chair. 'Oh, Hetty, I don't understand it. The harder I try, the more I put it on!' she wailed.

Hetty suspected that the girl dieted more in the breach than the observance, maybe one or two days a week, and made up for it the remainder. Perhaps this was part of an unconscious system of self-flagellation: setting herself up to fail. But it was not for Hetty to preach. Instead she took Annabel's arm and pulled her to her feet. 'Come on, I'm thirsty. I'd like to take advantage of your offer.'

'Yeah, right. Let's drown our sorrows, shall we?'

I don't have any sorrows to drown, came to Hetty with a touch of satisfaction. 'What the hell?' she answered. 'Why not?' And they left the community hall arm-in-arm.

At their gate, the initial sign of disturbance was Thomas with his hair on end, back arched, standing square on the doorstep. As Hetty bent to scratch his ears, he hissed. 'My! What's upset you, then?' she asked.

'Those damn girls, that's what.'

It was Doris, with a grim frown and a turban tied roughly round her hair, her hands busy wringing out a sodden dish-cloth. She shook the cloth in the bushes, dirty droplets flying. Thomas fled for cover.

Doris glared at Annabel. 'Hello, miss. Wait till you see what your friends have been up to.'

Behind her in the hall stood Mrs McDonald with a bucket and a mop. The two children could be seen inside their flat, huddling close to their father. All four had wet slippers.

'Oh dear,' said Annabel softly, the colour draining from her face. 'Flo and Shelagh. They're watching videos of *Friends*. They mightn't have noticed.'

'Noticed what?' Hetty asked sharply, as they picked their way over the hall carpet. In places it squelched.

'We knocked upstairs but there was no answer,' Doris called after them angrily. 'It's been coming through the ceiling for an hour. I was on the point of calling the fire brigade. Have you got your key?'

Annabel fished in her pocket then, with Hetty in tow, climbed the stairs to flat four, opposite Hetty's own flat. From within the BJs' residence came the sound of the television turned up loud, and uproarious laughter.

'They've probably started on the vodka,' Annabel explained as she put the key in the lock. 'Tonight's a girls' night in. Flo has decided she wants plaits with beads in her hair. It takes ages. Anyway, they wouldn't hear anyone at the door. If they did they probably wouldn't bother to answer – Doris is so darned nosy.'

'She's probably angling for customers,' Hetty answered, but was met with a puzzled glance and a shrug from the girl.

Hetty and Annabel entered the hallway of flat four. Above the noise of the video from behind the closed living-room door, Hetty craned to listen. The faint tinkle of running water took her to the bathroom. A wall of steam enveloped her and billowed down the landing. Inside, the bath was full, steaming and overflowing. One tap was turned slightly on. Though barely a trickle, the water had obviously been enough to flood the bath and to seep through to the McDonalds' flat below.

Hetty reached across and turned off the hot tap. The scalding metal stung her palm. Beneath her breath she swore. With the back brush she hooked up the plug chain.

'You had a bath before you went for the weigh-in, yes?' Hetty said grimly, blowing on her tingling fingers. 'And naturally you forgot to pull the plug.'

A white-faced Annabel hovered, wringing her hands. 'I was in a hurry. I often forget to let the water out – Shelagh gets hopping mad at me.'

'Costs a fortune. Waste of electricity.' Hetty tried to sound severe, but the girl's distress was almost palpable.

'They won't sue, will they? Don't say it was me, Hetty. Say it was an accident.'

Hetty grunted. The murky water made a noisy glugging as it disappeared, leaving a grey rime around the bath. 'I won't say a word if you clean up here. You're a dope, Annabel, but there's no doubt it was unintentional, as you say. When you've finished, go and apologise to the McDonalds and Doris.'

The bathroom itself was not particularly wet; the water must have found its way quickly through the planking to the floor below. Hetty left Annabel flopped heavily on her knees scrubbing at the tidemark, went downstairs to reassure the anxious neighbours, then returned. At what appeared to be a suitable break in the video programme, she tapped firmly on the living-room door and pushed it open. Inside, the curtains were drawn; the dark room was lit by a single pink-shaded lamp and the flickering screen. Flo and Shelagh were slouched on the sofa, bejeaned legs draped over the arms, their backs to the door.

Flo glanced behind, failed to register that the new entrant was not Annabel, and pushed over a bowl of peanuts. 'Hi, Annie. How did you get on?'

'Annabel put on weight. Again,' Hetty said loudly. Two heads, one red-haired, the other dark, popped up simultaneously. Half of Flo's hair had been put into neat narrow braids with blue beads, the rest stood out in a mass of frizz as if struck by lightning.

'Oh, hello, Het. Nice to see you. Want some vodka?'

Hetty marched over to the video machine and pressed the pause button. Standing crossly, arms folded, in front of the set, she outlined to the two astonished flatmates the disaster that Annabel's carelessness had caused. But it was apparent after a few moments that the girls were more than a little drunk, and unable to focus their minds effectively enough to take action.

'You want us to do anything, Het?' Shelagh drawled. Her green eyes were heavy-lidded. She had begun to plait another of Flo's braids. 'I mean, we will if you insist, but I'm not sure my legs'll do what I tell 'em.'

Hetty sighed. 'No, it's under control. Annabel is responsible, so I'd leave it to her.'

'Right, thanks.' Flo picked up the peanuts bowl again. In doing so she pulled the plait tight. 'Ouch! That hurt. Say, Hetty, you wouldn't like to give a hand with my hair? It takes hours, but the more the merrier, and quicker.'

Hetty relaxed. 'I don't mind. Show me what to do. Annabel did offer me a drink.'

'Help yourself.' Two vodka bottles and several cartons of juice sat on a side table with a metal cooler full of ice. Hetty found a tall glass and mixed a vodka and grapefruit juice. It was refreshing after the tension. She downed half quite quickly.

By the time Annabel returned from her *mea culpas* downstairs, Hetty had learned the rudiments of braiding and, being both dextrous and more sober than Shelagh, had made rapid progress. 'I gather Richard has found himself another love?' she asked guilelessly, as the four of them settled on the sofa and a couple of floor cushions. Flo lay spreadeagled, her head accessible to all three, drinking with the aid of a bent straw.

'Aagh! Richard!' the girls chorused, and Flo made vomiting gestures.

Despite her disapproval of their disorganised, shiftless life, Hetty could not help smiling. 'What about the other fellows you brought along to my party? Ted? Stuart? They seemed pleasant enough.'

More miming.

'Henry?' Hetty was grinning broadly. 'Did he manage to meet his father in time?'

'He got into frightful trouble with his old man,' Annabel confided. 'If you hadn't found him, he'd probably still be out cold on the stairs.' The bowl of peanuts was in her lap and she stuffed a handful into her mouth. 'God, Hetty, tell me to *stop eating*.'

'I think you're fine as you are,' Hetty answered firmly. 'Lots of men would love a lass your shape.' The image of James, prone and content after a single penetration, floated into her mind. 'Especially mature men. You're probably fishing in the wrong pond.'

'D'you really think so?'

Hetty poured herself another drink. 'I can see it now. You should come on our programme *Tell Me All*. The three of you.'

She had their full attention, or as much of it as their condition allowed.

'What'd we have to say?'

'Well, you'd set out your circumstances. In your own words. Three gorgeous young women, yet the lads you meet are only interested in casual relationships. Where might you find real men, who want to settle down?'

The BJs began to twitter excitedly.

'But first,' Hetty continued, 'you'd have to be clear what you wanted out of it. There'd be lots of phone calls afterwards. And the tabloids might get excited, too. You do dream of settling down, don't you?'

'Yes! Yes!' the three girls chanted together.

Annabel turned wistful eyes on her. 'What's it like being married? Having your own home? Your own place, you can turn into a palace, with a smashing geezer rushing back to you every night? Is it absolutely wonderful, like the spreads in *Hello!*?'

'Of course,' Hetty said automatically, then stopped. 'It depends,' she continued more cautiously. 'I mean, you have to consider, do you want children?'

'Yes,' said Annabel, dubiously.

'Eight,' said Shelagh loudly. 'I'd love a big family. My grandmother had eleven, my mother has only me and my brother. Provided I can have nannies too.'

'He'll have to be wealthy,' Hetty pointed out, with a smile.

'Oh, I'll marry for love. Daddy'll make a big settlement, just to get me off his hands,' Shelagh asserted solemnly.

'What about you, Flo?' Hetty asked.

'I'd have Richard, provided I didn't have to share him.' Flo's hair was beginning to come to order; the plaits swung slickly as she shook her head experimentally. 'Not sure about the sprogs, though.'

Hetty saw suddenly that Flo might be a younger version of Rosa. 'You don't feel you'd like kids, Flo?' she asked.

The girl scratched her nose. 'Where I come from, so many girls have babies young, then they're stuck staying in, stretch-marks ruining their figures, when they should be in their prime. The blokes don't turn a hair – "Not mine," they say. Not much future in that. I'd like them *eventually*, I suppose.' She did not sound convinced.

'Did you enjoy your kids, Hetty?' asked Shelagh.

Hetty refreshed her glass a third time before answering. 'Giving birth, no, awful experience. Thank God the memory fades or we'd never have a second. Little babies, yes, when they're well behaved. Mine weren't bad. But after that it gets harder.'

'Whaddya mean?'

Hetty thought about the distance that had grown between herself and her son, and of Sally's years of sullenness, only recently eroded. 'I'm not sure I can say anything very profound. Each family's different. But children can be disappointing.'

'I think babies are lovely! I can't wait!' Shelagh's eyes were shining, though as much with alcohol, Hetty guessed, as with anticipation.

'Then I'd say, pick a man who loves kids too, and who'd make a fine father,' she suggested. 'Not Richard, though you never can tell. But everyone starts off with high hopes for their offspring. Not least, that they'll love their parents and be grateful. It doesn't work out like that.'

'I'm grateful to my parents,' Shelagh burbled. 'They keep me in the luxury to which I'm accustomed!' Annabel giggled and nodded in agreement.

'Do you tell them,' Hetty asked quietly, 'that you love them?'

Annabel shrugged. 'They'd suspect I was after something.'

'You should. Surprise them. The sweetest remark my daughter ever made to me was not long ago, when she said that at last she saw me as a human being. I was so touched.' Hetty was surprised at herself: it was not an admission she had expected to make.

'Would you have wanted to stay single, though, Het?' Flo was curious.

'No. But you learn, after a while, that the fairy-tale's a farce.' Hetty was startled by her own sharp tone. 'Fairy-tale marriages, I mean. Marriage is the most complicated relationship of all. And you alter, over time. The two people who walked up the aisle in white tulle and a top hat aren't the same pair ten years after, with screaming kids and fights over money. Twenty years on, they've altered again. Maybe, after another while, you come together once more, but I can't comment on that.'

'Ugh! I can't imagine what it'd be like to be fifty.' Annabel shuddered.

'When you're fifty,' Hetty said severely, 'you may find yourself sitting with a bunch of twentysomethings hoping they won't make the same mess of their lives you have.'

'You haven't made a mess, have you, Het?' Annabel was contrite, and anxious. 'You look happy. You have friends. You're never in – you're out almost as much as us.'

A similar litany from Sally had struck a chord with Hetty a short time before. 'I don't know how to measure success,' she said quietly. 'It's enough to feel serene, I suppose. Though when you get to my age, health matters too. And the state of your bank balance. It may seem unromantic, but there you are. There aren't any rule books. You have to make it up as you go along.'

Blank looks came from each of the BJs.

'I still dream of the ideal,' said Shelagh. 'Home, children – loads of 'em – and a handsome fellow who adores me. But not yet!'

'I do believe in new experiences, now,' Hetty continued. She could feel the drink talking, her speech beginning to slur. 'I'd try anything once. I used to be so conventional. P'raps I just bored my husband into someone else's arms. Should've been much less hidebound, more adventurous.'

'How about a little adventurous entertainment, then?' Flo had sat up, the hair braiding finished. With the rosy light on her bronze skin, she resembled a young Cleopatra.

'Depends what you have in mind. Have you got a brace of gorgeous guys in a cupboard?' Hetty could feel herself becoming roguish.

'Chance'd be a fine thing. But how about a fizzier way of finishing that vodka? Somebody was boasting about it at lunchtime today. Wanna try?' Flo disappeared into the kitchen. She returned, a grin on her face, braids slapping against her neck. In her hand were four teaspoons and a giant-size box of Kleenex. 'Watch.'

She poured a few drops of vodka on to the teaspoon, bent over, pinched one nostril closed with a finger and lifted the teaspoon to her nose. Then with a snort she inhaled deeply, making a noise like the last dregs of a milkshake being sucked up a straw.

'Yeach!' she squealed, choked and spluttered, and grabbed a handful of tissues. Her eyes rolled right up into their sockets. She staggered and fell on to the sofa. 'Oh! Gawd! That's fantastic!'

As she gasped and rocked, Annabel grabbed a teaspoon and filled it. 'Not too much,' warned Hetty, entranced. But Annabel, never one for half measures, lifted the spoon to her nose, closed her left nostril and snorted vigorously through the other.

'Aagh!' she yelped, and danced about the room, sneezing furiously. Then, standing stock still, eyes bulging, 'Oh, my God! Oh, that's amazing!'

'You must get a hell of a rush,' Hetty murmured. 'Straight into the bloodstream.'

'I guess so.' Shelagh was at her side by the table, as Flo moaned and sneezed while Annabel cavorted helplessly. The remaining teaspoons sat invitingly. Shelagh nudged Hetty in the ribs. 'Go on. I will if you will. Once can't do any harm, can it? It's not cocaine, or anything.'

'Pure stuff, they say, vodka,' Hetty cogitated woozily. 'Only a little. Try anything once. No rule books. Be more adventurous . . .'

Then she and the red-headed girl held their teaspoons in shaky hands and poured each other a few drops each.

'*Now!*' Shelagh called, and Hetty did as she had been shown.

The blast of pain in her nostril knocked her sideways, as if someone had stuck a red-hot poker into the membrane. Her head reeled, and she felt herself sway. Then the rush came, a savage scorching blast, akin to swallowing raw alcohol on a sore throat. Her eyes squeezed shut, she reached too late for the tissues and sneezed a gobbet of vodka into thin air. The pulses in her temples throbbed like crazy. Yet she found herself laughing hysterically, as if some great truth had just been revealed to her.

'Oh!' She coughed, and tried to stop the room swirling.

It seemed to her that Flo, braids trailing, had slid off the sofa, a silly smile on her face. Annabel, predictably, had already collapsed. Shelagh was clutching her, and crying hoarsely, 'Try anything! Ooh, Hetty! Is this better than being married, or isn't it?'

But as her knees buckled under her and she sat down hard on the floor, Hetty did not feel able to respond intelligibly. 'Friends, thash wha counts. Frensh . . .' she began, but did not finish.

And then, with a happy gurgle, she passed out.

CHAPTER TWENTY

Interlude

'Let's take our orange juice out on to the terrace, shall we?'

Father Roger steered Hetty round the concrete pillars of the National Theatre's upper floor. They were twenty minutes early for *Candide*. Below them lay the panorama of the Thames, with the gold-tipped turrets of Victoria Tower, Big Ben and the Houses of Parliament glittering to their left, St Paul's bulbous dome to their right and overhead the London Eye, like a spider's web in the evening sun. On the far bank stood the white wedding-cake edifice of the Savoy and, dwarfed into insignificance, Cleopatra's Needle like a stick of sugar. From a boat by Waterloo Bridge came snatches of dance music and singing. Directly opposite was the back end of the new Charing Cross station, its garish neon reflected in the sluggish river.

They stood for a moment and breathed in the warm air. It

was the second occasion they had been to the theatre together. Hetty had bought the first tickets, for *The Merchant of Venice*; tonight was Father Roger's reciprocal treat. Both plays had ethical themes available for lively dissection over the interval drinks.

It had not been initially in her plan to find out more about him: attending the play was for mutual pleasure, pure and simple. In particular, *pure*. It felt safe, being with a priest, after the machinations of Larry and James and the multiple bared breasts of the Professor's den. On the other hand, Hetty reflected, a man like this might have not only ethical depths but vulnerable shallows. A shiver of mischief led her to explore.

'Balm for the spirit, a lovely evening like this,' Roger continued, leaning his elbows on the parapet. The wind ruffled his blue shirt. 'D'you realise I gave up my turn to hear confession tonight, Hetty? Can't say I'm sorry.'

'Won't they be cross with you?'

'No. Do 'em good to ponder their sins a while longer. Then they might behave.'

'They don't deserve you,' she said stoutly. 'Aren't they supposed to repent, then sin no more? You must find it irritating when they treat you as a sort of therapist.'

'Some of them could use therapy.' His voice was low. 'It isn't a priest they need, it's a consultant psychiatrist. Or a lawyer. Or a few good friends.' Hetty must have pulled a face, for he smiled at her again. 'Having traumas with friends, are we, Hetty?'

'Not exactly. But I do wonder how far one should go.' She blushed, then after mild prevarication told him the story of the BJs, the overflowing bath and the snorted vodka.

Father Roger gasped, then his eyes crinkled, and soon he

was laughing uproariously at Hetty's depiction of the sordid scene. 'You blacked out?'

'Yes, but not for long. I don't suppose there was that much alcohol up my nose – not as much as knocking back a full tot, Russian-style. The best one could say about it is that it's legal. It was like being belted in the face. And the hangover next day was not a sensation I'd repeat, either, even at the risk of losing my neighbours' goodwill.'

Below, the trees on the embankment swelled and fluttered in the breeze, their branches strung with coloured lights. Hetty's inquisitiveness nagged. 'I was expecting you in black and a dog-collar, like last time. Aren't there any rules?'

'None whatsoever, except that a full rig is expected on high days and holy days. One reason why I don't want to be a bishop. I doubt that purple would suit me.'

Hetty gazed over the river, then: 'I don't understand, Roger,' she said quietly. 'A decent man like you. It can be miserable, being at everyone's beck and call, even if you are fortified by faith. Don't you wish sometimes you could lock the church door and go home to your own family? There aren't any taboos about that, are there? You're not Catholic.'

'I am catholic, but not Roman Catholic,' he corrected her. 'I prefer to concentrate on my job. And when I'm not on duty, I have friends, like you, who are kind to me.' He twinkled at her. *Don't be nosy*, his eyes said.

She ploughed on. 'Have you never had – anybody special?'

'Not recently.' He paused, but Hetty did not back off. Then, with a sigh, 'Oh, there was someone, when I was young. But she tried to take more of me than I could give. She wanted me to commit myself body and soul. And I found I could not do that.'

'Did you understand why not? Wasn't she the right person for you?'

'At the time I believed she was. But it was the whole idea of putting another person first. Perhaps, of letting someone get so close. The body did not object, but the soul rebelled. It felt very strange. And it's never happened again.'

'D'you mean,' Hetty persisted, 'that you've never *allowed* it to happen again? Never let yourself go? Suppose one of the choir fell in love with you?'

'That's easy to deal with. I'd be gentle and aloof, as clergy should be. We are aware of the dangers, especially if someone's unhappy.'

'That's not enough.' She pursed her lips. The turn of the conversation was intensely personal, but he was calm, as if he had been expecting an interrogation from her, sooner or later. 'I mean, it's not normal to shy away from human contact like that. Most people are aching for a genuine loving relationship. They'd regard it as a gift from God. Only after they get hurt, as I did, might they be more cautious.'

'Fools rush in?' Roger raised an eyebrow, as if to fend her off.

'Nonsense. It isn't foolish to want to love and be loved. It's foolish not to.' She stared him out, aware that her demeanour was quite fierce.

His shoulders sagged. 'I love my congregation. I love my job, my calling. Doing the TV programme is a bit of leaven amongst the dross: if that went, I should miss it. And when the day is over, I love my solitude. My refuge is in books, or music, or philosophy: the sweet, serene territory of the well-cultivated mind. I fret only that I will never have enough years to sample everything God's world has to show. I will die with libraries unread, languages unlearned. My ideal heaven would be an eternity at the feet of the great thinkers. Does that make sense?'

'Blimey,' Hetty muttered. 'No, it doesn't. Not to me. Ideas can't compare with the richness of human company. I like to be alone, too, but if true love walked in, I don't think I'd push it aside in favour of a shelf full of printed paper.'

'Well, now, Hetty, there we differ. It's probably a serious character defect, but I don't waste hours groaning over it.'

A loudspeaker announced that the play would commence in five minutes. Roger had made no attempt to change the subject. Hetty took her courage in both hands. 'Maybe you prefer to keep your human beings at arm's length?'

He nodded, his face a little sad.

'Don't you miss . . .' she wanted to say 'the sex', but it seemed utterly inappropriate with a priest, even one in an open-neck shirt '. . . the personal contact?'

'The sex, you mean?' He was ahead of her. '*You* can answer that. You live singly, Hetty. And you were married. Don't *you* miss it?'

Into Hetty's mind came the image of the recumbent James, desexed and replete, snoring contentedly. 'There are worse things than no sex, Roger,' she said, with feeling. 'Like hopeless sex. Some people are dire in bed and don't know it. It'd be a cruelty to tell them, and masochism to persist. Especially if they've little else to offer.' Then, more slowly, 'Yes. I really must make an effort. Go to an agency, perhaps.'

She had wandered. What a skilful operator Roger was, to deflect her so deftly from his world to hers. Hetty admitted defeat with a rueful grin and squeezed his arm.

The bells were ringing for the performance. 'Sounds like

a confession you may have to make on a future occasion, dear lady.' Father Roger chuckled as he ushered her inside.

Hetty had seen the Soul Mates agency advertised in the *Evening Standard*. One of its offices was in the centre of Putney; that appealed, as potential dates would not live unrealistically far away. It might also be marginally easier to check their credentials. She rang for an appointment and, rather nervously, went in one evening after work.

The woman seated opposite Hetty was smartly dressed, in a red wool jacket and skirt and black court shoes with a great deal of costume jewellery, and about her own age.

'I'm so glad, Mrs Clarkson,' she said, in a accent that tried to be home counties but had clearly started east of Bow bells, 'that you have come to us. We are the finest in the business, and the most discreet.'

'I'm pleased to hear it,' said Hetty, nonplussed.

The agency office was above a shop. Though the rental might be moderate, some effort had been made with the décor: cream stucco walls, coffee-coloured paintwork, soft overhead lighting and a twirling ceiling fan produced a cool, elegant air. The leaves of the fig tree in the corner were glossy and dust-free, its brass pot brilliant in its lustre; the door-handles gleamed as if they were polished after every client. Behind the desk, the wall was hung with photographs of weddings with couples of every vintage from youngsters to elderly, and many framed letters, presumably testimonials and thanks. Two framed certificates announced member-ship and licences, though of what Hetty was unsure. The wastepaper basket by the counsellor's feet was filled to over-flowing. They must get a lot of weird mail.

'You have to approach these matters with the right mental

vigour,' the woman continued. 'Tell yourself that you *will* find someone, and you will. Start off believing you won't, and it's a self-fulfilling prophecy.'

'Of course.' Hetty sat up and squared her shoulders.

'*Believe*, Mrs Clarkson. Believe in yourself, and in our expertise. Though it may take a little while. We have far more women on our books than men, inevitably. All agencies have. And, I'm afraid, it's less easy to match ladies of – shall we say? – your age.'

'*Why?*' Hetty wanted to ask crossly, but held her tongue.

'. . . as long as you realise it might not happen in the first few weeks, or even the first few months. But if you're patient, we're sure to find you somebody.'

'That's why I'm here. I've tried meeting men on my own, but . . .' Hetty saw the glaze begin over the counsellor's eyes and quickly changed tack. 'But that's in the past. I'm determined, this time.'

'Excellent.' The woman's manner became more confiding. 'You need to understand about our male clients. Very often, they have . . . difficulties. I don't mean sexual hang-ups, necessarily – we try to weed those out at interview. Here at Soul Mates we are *very* thorough. But although they are dedicated to finding a partner, a person like yourself may find that some have commitment limitations.' The last words were pronounced with great care, as if frequently repeated.

'I see,' said Hetty slowly, though she did not quite. 'And the implications?'

'Those may show up only after a relationship has developed. *You* may fall in love, and he may not – cannot, perhaps. So be wise. Keep it light to begin with – don't get too intense. If you run into a sticky patch, men are tempted to give up quickly. On the whole, women don't.'

Hetty blinked. 'Good advice. I'm not a quitter: I have every faith in you.'

But the counsellor had not finished. Perhaps this was a prepared text. 'This is a wonderful sweetie shop for some men, Mrs Clarkson. Males like to try the varieties. Often that's all they do, for years. They are sincere in their desire for a long-term partner – don't get me wrong, they've paid the fee, after all. It's just that they aren't terribly good at coping with the tricky bits. But, meanwhile, we are here for *you* also to choose. We have many successes.' She waved a beringed hand at the photographs.

'Very encouraging.' Hetty fought down any doubts.

'This gent,' the woman pointed at a picture of a thick-set man with a moustache, his arms entwined around a simpering middle-aged blonde, 'was convinced he would never fall for anyone, and now look at him.'

Hetty did as she was invited. The thick moustache was not to her taste, but otherwise she felt a sudden envy. Might she be up there in a silver frame, one day? Was that what she really wanted?

'Now, any more questions? No? Then take this pack and fill in the details. Meanwhile I will trawl through our recent files for some suggestions. I'm *sure* you'll find somebody you like amongst them. *Believe*, Mrs Clarkson. Believe.'

On the table of the Café Pinocchio was a pile of Sunday supplements, baguettes, croissants, butter, jam, coffee-cups and the Soul Mates brochure. Markus and Christian took the leaflets, turned them over and began to read. Within seconds they were both rocking with laughter, nudging each other with their elbows.

'I need your help, *please*,' said Hetty, with as much dignity as she could muster, but she could not stop breaking out into a wide grin. 'I'm deadly serious.'

Sunday brunch at the café had become a regular feature during the summer: a time that was convenient for Christian, often on stage for eight performances a week and, as Markus put it, 'invaluable for getting both of us out of bed and into the fresh air'. Sometimes they would be joined by Doris or a BJ, if any were sufficiently *compos mentis* by noon, or by the men's other acquaintances, who were usually gay. Markus, however, had explained in a quiet aside to Hetty that he preferred to have her as the lynchpin of the table and the other residents; she gained the impression that he was not keen to have competition for Christian's favours from other, younger men.

'All I ask of you,' she continued, snatching back the papers and trying to restore some authority, 'is total honesty. You know how I appear to other people. If I lie or exaggerate, the assessment will be up the creek.'

Christian bit into a *pain au chocolat*. The Adam's apple bobbed up and down. Hetty found it painfully attractive, perhaps because only men had one: it recalled their other appendage, over which similarly they had no control. What a catch he would be for any woman, Hetty judged, if he were hetero. 'It's a deal,' Christian said. 'Which section are we doing first – what sort of person you are, or what your partner should be?'

'Me first. Question one,' Hetty clicked her biro. '"Your character. Do you see yourself as moody, romantic, patient, friendly, considerate, shy, cautious?" Yes, all of these. There's more – "sensitive, conventional, tolerant, impulsive". Yes, to those too. Great – maybe I'm just what the agency needs.'

'Or maybe they're simply lacking in originality. Or mean to flatter you, so you'll fill in the form and send it off with a fat fee,' Markus chipped in. 'You don't need this, Hetty. So artificial.'

'Hush.' Hetty traced the categories with her finger. '"Intellectual, adventurous, adaptable, reliable, practical, ambitious". Not ambitious. Not intellectual either.' She marked those spaces with a firm cross.

'But you are intelligent. Is there a space for that?' This from Markus.

'Not yet. Maybe later.' Hetty frowned. 'Next part. "On a first date, do you expect (a) to be kissed, (b) to be taken home, (c) to be willing to go all the way?" Heavens, I'm not sure I expect any of those. A good dinner, maybe. But sex first time?'

'It can be fabulous,' Christian murmured. Markus snorted.

Hetty ticked (b) as the closest approximation to her usual habits, though she noted the ambiguity: it might mean that the man expected her to offer a bed for the night, rather than his place. 'Now the section on attitudes. How do I answer these? "Do you prefer someone who will take the initiative in social situations?" I like a man to hold open the door, but I'm perfectly willing to pay my share. And book the tickets.'

'I'm enjoying this – it's a form of Chinese torture,' Markus said. 'Go on.'

'"Question eleven. Would your friends call you a perfectionist?"'

'No!' chorused her friends.

'And all the better for it,' Christian added affectionately.

Hetty persisted for several more minutes then laid

down her pen. 'Markus, do they have agencies like this for gays?'

'Sure, but most contacts come through gay bars, or through ads in gay magazines. Lots of people these days advertise in the straight press. Have you tried there?'

'Comprehensively,' Hetty answered, and told them of her earlier attempts at calling advertisers. 'I gave that up as a source of possible admirers. Just too creepy, chatting away on the phone to strangers. Though I do wonder how the starfish is getting on.'

'About a quarter of the Kindred Spirits ads in the *Telegraph* are from gay men.'

'Or purport to be,' Christian took up the theme. 'And you'll find some of the same guys on the common as it gets dark. Cruising.' Hetty saw a look of annoyance cross Markus's face, to which his lover seemed oblivious.

'Going to an agency is probably the safest bet,' Markus said. 'Treat it as a piece of harmless fun. Most of the replies will be ghastly – obvious no-nos right from the start, so don't be disappointed. I'd guess no more than ten per cent could be possibles, some of whom will turn out to be no-nos too. That leaves a handful you should meet.'

'I could, of course, meet the lot.' Hetty tapped her lip with the pen thoughtfully. 'We're promised at least twenty names. Now, that could be hilarious.'

'How many evenings d'you have to waste?' Markus reasoned. 'What if they're bores or – well, what *would* rule them out?'

'Too fat. Too arrogant. Men who could talk only about themselves. Men who go on and *on* about money. Or trainspotting. Or how awful their exes are. Or, I suppose, how amazing the ex was, if that happens. Or if they boast about their conquests – I wouldn't believe them. Anyone gross: bad manners, foul-mouthed, that sort of thing.'

'Quite a list. You have a precise idea of what you hate, which helps.' Markus grinned.

'How about their personal habits? They could be smelly or disgusting. Or diseased,' Christian teased, as Hetty waved her hands in mock horror. 'Wait – have you tried the Internet? At least then you don't have to breathe the same air.'

Hetty described Rosa's games with the chat room and shook her head. 'Not for me.'

'You'll put her off – stop it,' Markus chided. 'The Net can be a disaster too. You never know who you could be dealing with. Murderers, child rapists, the lot. Everyone uses false names. Most are fantasists and liars and, anyway, if they're in Columbus, Ohio, what use is that? But woe betide you if a dodgy one takes a fancy to you. Wrecking your computer with a virus is the least form of attack.'

They were seated at a table on the pavement, taking advantage of the weather. Later in the year, if these enjoyable interludes continued, as Hetty hoped, they would have to move inside. She would make it her business to arrive early enough to secure the table by the window. Gazing at the locals as they collected their newspapers from the shop next door and selected bagels and Gorgonzola wedges from the delicatessen counter was an entertaining and harmless pastime.

A scruffy figure slouched past in what appeared to be several layers of clothes, despite the still-warm sun: an overcoat down to his knees, a knitted balaclava unravelling at the neck, two jackets, more than one stained sweater with a grimy shirt-collar peeping over the top, and – from the torn bottoms – at least two pairs of trousers. He was pushing a supermarket trolley piled high with dirty plastic bags that squeaked as it was shoved hard against the kerb.

'Brian?' Hetty called, and the creature stopped. Christian peered over his newspaper and raised an eyebrow.

'Who's that?' the tramp asked gruffly.

'Haven't seen you for ages. How are you?' Hetty asked. Then, on impulse, 'Would you like a coffee?'

Brian appeared confused at being addressed so normally. Other diners were muttering at him: the odour from his clothes was unmistakable, and there was a faint squelching as he moved. He took a step in her direction then hesitated. 'Awright, missus,' he answered gruffly. 'I could take the price of a cup of coffee, if yer like.'

Hetty found her purse and gave him a pound. 'Still selling the *Big Issue*? I haven't seen you at the station recently.'

'Nah, well, I've been ill.' He seemed embarrassed and shuffled his feet.

'I hope you'll start again. It's a good pitch.'

He looked directly into her eyes, an intense, furious, depressed glare, which made her recoil. Then he dropped his gaze and made to push his belongings once more. 'Fucking interfering bitch,' he muttered, but to himself, not to Hetty. Then, louder, 'Yeah, well, I might. You take care of yourself, missus. Ta for the change.'

And he was gone, the trolley protesting eerily into the distance.

'You do have some odd acquaintances, Hetty,' Markus remarked drily. 'If you were looking for somebody smelly and diseased, he'd fit the bill. Were you seriously suggesting he should join us?'

Hetty pondered. 'You're right. If he'd said, "Don't mind if

I do – move up and make room,' we'd have had a problem. But I feel sorry for him.'

'*You'd* have had a problem. There are limits, Hetty,' but Markus was half smiling.

Hetty sat back. 'D'you know? In my previous life I wouldn't have given him the time of day. Or I'd have crossed the street to avoid him. Don't tell me to be like I was before, I prefer myself now.' She giggled. 'To be frank, in my previous life I wouldn't have been having coffee with you two either, would I? I'd have been scared to sit at the same table, eat from the same plates. Shows you how stupid I was.'

The men did not reply, but their eyes met over her head. Markus handed her the glossy magazine, mutely, as if to confirm that they were still friends.

The street was getting busier. The dog-walking brigade were almost done: they tended to be the earliest out. Families with children were starting to emerge, with toddlers fidgeting in car-seats in double-parked vehicles as their parents collected cakes and ready-filled baguettes for picnics. Hetty was struck by how many of the cars, especially those with older children sitting sullenly in the back, had fathers only: the weekend visit of the divorced man, presumably. She was glad her marriage had lasted long enough for that dismal ritual to be unnecessary.

'God in heaven, who's that?' she whispered, and tugged Christian's sleeve. 'Shush, don't say a word.'

A tall, rangy female stood teetering on high heels, rifling through the newspapers on the stand a few yards away. The mass of glossy black hair was set in a stiff, upcurled style; she wore heavy makeup, black eyeliner and thickly mascaraed lashes. The ruby lipstick would have been excessive at any hour, but particularly on a Sunday morning. Her clothes were black, cinched at the waist and made of some lacy material.

'Why do you ask?' Christian mouthed.

'One of your pals? Anyone you recognise?' Hetty hissed. The woman had finished choosing, picked up a *Mirror* and went inside the shop to pay for it. As she emerged, to see Hetty, Markus and Christian staring over their coffee-cups, she dropped her eyes and trotted quickly away.

'No, not one of ours,' Markus said firmly. 'We do know a few TVs, but not many. They're not usually gay, Hetty.'

'TVs?'

'Transvestites. Cross-dressers. Mostly, they're men who claim to be heterosexual but who like dressing up as women. They're quite often married. And they're not the same as TXs, either – transsexuals. Those people are usually heading for surgery.'

'Oh. Right.' Hetty nodded uncertainly, then craned her neck to follow the receding shape up the hill. 'But I've seen her – him? – before. Coming out of our flats. Let me think – New Year's Eve. In a great rush, dolled up to the nines.'

'Maybe the BJs have some kinky visitors? Or Doris – now there's a lady with a past, you can tell. Has she cast your future in the cards yet? Or the flat upstairs that's always empty – could be them.' Markus laughed. 'Nice to have mysteries, isn't it, Hetty?'

'But who is it?' Hetty broke a bran muffin in frustration. 'Who on earth could it be?'

'How did you persuade them, Hetty? They're terrific,' Rosa said.

On the set the three BJs sat demurely, eyes dancing. Their

choice of clothes reflected their natures: Annabel as ever in too-tight black, Shelagh in a silky suit with a short skirt, the pale-blue colour setting off her flaming hair and milky skin, and Flo, hair braided with silver beads, in a low-cut red sweater and leather trousers. They were rehearsing their dilemma with the male presenter, who was leaning forward eagerly and attempting to pat Shelagh's knee.

'Can't have that,' Rosa commented. 'He'll be in camera view, a big dark blob. Have to tell him to sit back and keep his hands to himself.' She spoke into her head mike.

'Hello, Hetty,' came a male voice behind her. Tall, urbane, charming, this time not in a suit but in a knitted sweater, it was Nicholas, the would-be writer, back for a follow-up. 'We met in Fulham, remember?'

Hetty smiled at him. The computer check had revealed that he was divorced and in his mid-thirties: she had taken him to be older than that, possibly because previously at the studio he had appeared careworn and troubled. Now his manner was almost boyish. His true age might explain why he was of interest to Davinia, but it did mean he was more than a decade her own junior. What Markus would call a no-no.

'So, what did you decide to do?' she asked him.

His gaze was on the girls, as was that of every man on the set. 'I handed in my notice. Fortunately they've been asking for voluntary redundancies so I got a generous package. And I've had several approaches – I could always go back. I'll give myself a year.'

'Anything worthwhile from publishers? I heard you were in talks with an agent.'

'Promising. I have to write a chunk first, then we'll see.' He shrugged self-deprecatingly, as if unwilling to tempt fate.

Then, lightly, he asked, 'The girl in black – the one with the, er, generous proportions. What's her name?'

'Annabel. She's one of my neighbours. She's a lovely lass, but such an idiot. She keeps falling in love with the most unsuitable men . . .' and Hetty outlined the girl's story. 'I told her not to bother slimming – she desperately needs a bloke who can see through all that insecurity to the decent young woman underneath.'

Recording was about to start. Hetty pulled Nicholas out of shot. As they stood close together in the dark, sheltering behind a blackout curtain, a little devil dug at her. 'So how goes it with Davinia?' she asked quietly.

'What do you know about me and Davinia?' Nicholas was guarded, but civil.

'I saw you. That night. Don't worry, I haven't said a word.'

'She was not pleased when I threw up my job. She asked what that meant for her. I'm afraid it showed that I hadn't given her needs much thought.'

'You don't seem too upset.'

He sighed. 'Davinia started throwing out ultimatums and I just couldn't respond.'

'Such as take me but stay with the job?' Hetty could imagine.

'Something of the sort. I won't have much money to fling around – certainly not enough to buy another house instead of my dingy little flat. I already have children to support with my former wife. It gets complicated. Not the right moment to take on further emotional upheaval. It's sufficiently draining, believe me, trying to churn out a thousand words a day.'

'And I doubt if Davinia could assist you there,' Hetty concluded.

In a few moments the BJs' segment was finished. They were replaced on set by Nicholas, who proceeded in a relaxed and humorous fashion to outline the course of events since the original broadcast. Flo and Shelagh were swept off by male researchers and spare crew who had arrived almost from nowhere, leaving Annabel hovering at Hetty's side.

'Well done, you were excellent,' Hetty enthused.

'Glad it's over. I felt such a fool, wittering on about how useless I am at pulling men.'

Hetty pointed at Nicholas. 'You might try him. He was asking about you. He's a friend of my brother's, and quite decent, I reckon. Your luck might be changing.'

Annabel screwed up her eyes. 'Mmm, not bad.' She nudged Hetty in the ribs. 'You can give him my phone number, Het. But don't tell him about the vodka, will you?'

It was late and almost dark before recording was finished. Hetty rode her bike slowly up the hill, feeling tired, her brain empty. The carrier-bag on the handlebars contained a head of celery – intended for a slimming soup – a chunk of ready-cooked chicken, a new library book (she had discovered Mrs Gaskell), and a bunch of yellow dahlias.

Her thoughts, for no obvious reason, returned to the council of war soon after her relocation to The Swallows, at which her mother and her daughter had outlined the various options open to her. The green bottles on the mantelpiece had been shifted about many times since. The dating-agency forms had been filled in and returned. A man had slept in her bed, once, and others might do so in future. Her head was filled with plays and novels, Impressionist and Renaissance art with a particular slant. Her acquaintance was no longer limited to conventional couples. And she was at ease.

It came to Hetty that, if she were ever to share her living space again, it would not be in the all-enveloping manner she had accepted before. She would not cook every evening, for a start; they would eat out far more, or grab whatever was in the fridge. Salads and cold ham were far healthier than hotpot, anyhow. A pear for afters was better than home-made pastry, so lovingly created, so quickly scoffed. How willingly she had slaved, how seldom it had been appreciated.

But the meals were only the start of it. Rather than take responsibility throughout, she would share the load. For example, as household items were used up, it would be a discipline to write them on a list in the kitchen. Then at an agreed point – Friday evening, say – whoever was first home would go to the supermarket. *Not* the same person each time. The Japanese had a word for it, didn't they? *Kanban*. Just in time. Pity that dreadful Japanese restaurant hadn't practised it.

You couldn't teach the members of your family to be helpful by doing everything for them. Being considerate was not catching. Yet, to some extent, her own total commitment to home-making had been stubbornly selfish too. It had given her a task in life. It had stopped her seeking something better.

But the clock could not be put back. The years since her wedding day were not a television broadcast that could be edited or tidied up. The children were grown; she had little doubt that it was too late for Peter. He phoned her occasionally, as he did his grandmother, but he was making his own way without her intervention. Maybe he would be the same, in due course, with his wife and family. If he turned out a self-centred man, that was her fault, but he was beyond reform. That prompted a surge of remorse that she had not made a better job of him, then one of emptiness.

Sally, by contrast, was a bright star. Since their holiday at the health farm they had met and talked frequently. Hetty took care that their hours together should not be a mere unloading of troubles. She always chose somewhere pleasant, often a new venue, to meet up. It amused her that she now deliberately attempted to learn something new regularly, even if only the mistakes of a hopelessly run wine bar. That was the biggest step forward. Before, she would have resisted, and sought only the familiar. What a dreadfully dull stick that old Hetty must have been.

She parked her bike in the cubby-hole under the stairs and locked it. Her body was weary, but with a satisfied streak. It came to her that she would not easily abandon this independence, with its gentle, comforting solitude, this opportunity to rest, to find herself, and to be content. Despite arguing with Roger, she had understood what he meant. If the agency did turn up trumps and produced a wonderful man, she would take some persuading to give up her hard-won freedom.

As she came out into the hallway she was nearly knocked off her feet. The TV – as she now knew to call him – was half running along the corridor. The wig was the same, and the high-heeled shoes: he was surprisingly nimble, given his footwear. He was wearing a red velvet dress, old-fashioned in its cut, with a white lace collar and cuffs and fishnet tights. Quite a wardrobe: almost a ladybird on legs. But Hetty was too startled, and too conscious of the obligation not to mock, to comment. He stopped dead, and stared at her.

'Oh! Hello, can I help you?' Hetty stuttered.

The apparition shook its head and uttered not a sound, but scuttled round a corner out of her sight. Next minute she heard a key in a lock, the murmur of a voice, and a door slammed shut.

CHAPTER TWENTY-ONE

Crossover

'But why,' Sally asked, 'would she want to go to an agency? My mother, touting herself around? Isn't it a bit tacky?'

'Why not?' her grandmother countered. 'Seems reasonable to me. She's fit, pretty and solvent. She's looking rather good, in fact. Sexually capable, not a nun. Not anti-men. But no man in the offing. An agency might turn up trumps. I might try one myself.'

'You're talking about me as if I wasn't here,' Hetty grumbled. The three women were seated on a chequered blanket on the common, late one sunny Saturday afternoon – at least, Hetty and Sally were sprawled out, propped up on cushions taken from the sofa, Peggy had carried a folding chair and arranged herself elegantly on it, ankles crossed. Before them were the Soul Mates folder, an empty wine bottle, a half-eaten packet of Ryvita and the remains of a Brie, oozing in its plastic wrapper.

Nearby, families played mini-cricket or threw frisbees; their whoops echoed on the breeze. A football match was under way, the players scruffy in baggy shorts and tracksuit bottoms, yelling encouragement at each other. Two kites sailed high overhead, their ribboned tails fluttering wildly, controlled by thin youths with serious intent. Over by the pond older men huddled, faces and fishing rods immobile, and small boys pedalled furiously past on brightly painted tricycles.

'I think I might take up rollerblading,' Hetty said dreamily. 'I'm beginning to feel that anything is possible, if only I try hard enough.' She stopped: both Sally and Peggy were staring at her in some alarm.

'I shouldn't,' said her mother firmly. 'Broken ankles. Chasing men is a much healthier pursuit. Now what type of man are you after – what age, for example?'

'I ticked forty-five to fifty-five,' Hetty answered. 'Older than that, and they'll be a bit decrepit – sorry, Mother, but you get my drift. I'm not keen on a chap having a heart-attack on our second date. Younger, and I should feel I was cradle-snatching.'

'If you find one much younger than that, you can send him in my direction,' said Sally.

'And I also thought that if a man that age is happy to meet someone my age he might have some respectable qualities. A bloke in his fifties who goes out with girls in their twenties or thirties wouldn't be my kind of bloke anyway.'

The other women nodded. 'Sleazebags, some of them.' Sally munched a cracker. 'Older men panting after totties young enough to be their daughters. Trying to regain their lost youth. They start off in the departure lounge, flirting with the crew.'

'Do you flirt back?' Hetty wanted to know.

'Too damn busy,' was Sally's response. 'And jaded businessmen farting all night are not the most alluring proposition. We see them at their worst.'

Peggy returned to the theme. 'And what about compatibility, Hetty dear? Did you want somebody like yourself? Or d'you think opposites attract?'

'I couldn't say,' Hetty confessed. 'I'm not too clever at analysing myself, and I'm not accustomed to making such decisions. I go with the flow a bit. I had a real headache filling out the section on preferences. In the end I left a lot of those spaces blank. It'll give the agency wider scope, and I'm curious to see what they come up with.'

'Are you after one relationship, or several?' This from her mother. Hetty blinked, so Peggy expanded, 'I don't mean all at once, dear. Are you searching for a single intense long-term lover, or would you prefer several chaps of varying degrees of intensity?'

'Haven't the foggiest,' Hetty answered. 'I'm not sure mature men are into intensity, or that it'd be terrific if they were. Anyone older is likely to be trailing loads of baggage. I'll have to sit through hours of personal history and moaning about his divorce or whatever. I shall have to make sure I don't do the same to them.' She pondered. 'So, maybe more than one. Though I'm not sure I could manage more than one sleeping partner. Even consecutively, in a typical week. That could be too tiring altogether.'

Three pairs of eyes met, and three women giggled. 'God, Mum, you have come on,' said Sally. 'And I'm glad to hear it.'

'So have you. This time last year you'd have been shocked to the core at the disgusting prospect of your parent stepping out with a stranger, even though you were simultaneously urging me to replace your father as quickly as possible. If I'd taken you at your word, and popped up every month with a new man on my arm, you'd have accused me of being a neurotic nymphomaniac, or desperate. I'm neither.'

Peggy smiled as if pleased with her progeny, and sipped her remaining wine. 'But did you despair, Hetty, of ever finding someone without paying all that money in fees?'

'No. And I do meet men, particularly through the programme. Now that *has* been an eye-opener. They're definitely a bit batty, though. I'm not sure I want to be Venus to an Adonis in a kilt who can't decide whether he prefers men or women.' She told them about Gordon. They gaped in amazement.

'And, of course, anyone nice might be spoken for. Tied up,' said Sally.

'Or lying through their teeth,' Peggy added.

'There is that. I'm wary of becoming too fond of someone I meet socially, or at work, and then discovering he's not available. Or that he regards himself as unencumbered, provided I accept those nights when he's obliged to see his wife. Who, of course, does not understand him. I'm not keen on playing second fiddle to *anyone*.'

'Your self-respect is in fine fettle, then, Mum. Another good sign.' Sally picked up the empty bottle with regret. 'We should have brought another. Still, I've got to drive. But the chaps from Soul Mates could be lying marrieds, too.'

'They claim they do check. I've insisted that I will only meet men who are free. That might give the wrong message – that I'm hoping to get hitched again myself – but I'll risk it. At least I'll have a sporting chance of avoiding complications. I do not wish to feature in anyone else's divorce petition. No, thanks.'

'The best of luck, dear,' said Peggy. 'And now, I'm afraid, I have to get moving. The Colonel is taking me to *Phantom of the Opera* tonight. I haven't the heart to tell him I've seen it three times – he went to such trouble to get the tickets. When you find the guy, Hetty – or, the guys, you could have a whole platoon – do be kind to them. Sometimes they deserve it.'

Hetty did not tell them about the letter. It had come that morning, unannounced, on crisp white vellum, the post-code incorrect, which had delayed it a day. Its four pages were scribbled in a hand she recognised at once.

Dear Hetty,

I hope you don't mind my writing to you. After all those years, I still feel we are close – or should be. We were best friends for such a long time, weren't we? I always said, and I meant it, that I hoped you wouldn't think so badly of me that we could never speak to each other again. But rather than phone, I thought I'd better write.

The main reason is to remind you that Peter is about to start his final year, and has started discussing what to do next. He's already told me he wants to stay on for postgrad, and I've said that's fine. I'll find the money, don't you worry about that. But I hope we'll both be able to go to his graduation ceremony next summer, together. Have you anybody you'd want to take?

How are you getting on? I get progress reports on you from Sally, and she says you have settled in well, though why you should want to live in a small poky flat in south London after the glories of Dorset beats me. I expect you were badly hurt and it must have seemed like a bolt-hole.

*But don't you worry about crime, and not being able to go
out at night? And not having any friends in the area? We
get the latest movies round here now there's a multiplex.
And we did manage to get to the theatre. So I can't see the
attraction.*

*The garden is looking splendid – you'd be very proud.
It's such a pity you haven't had an opportunity to see it
this summer. The climbing roses went mad this year,
and the wisteria was super. I don't have your green fingers but a chap from the nursery comes in to tidy up
once a week: costs me a bit, makes me realise how much
effort you used to put in! Your influence is still very
strong – when he makes suggestions, such as planting
lilac near the knot garden, I want to ask your opinion
first. I wouldn't want to destroy what you created here so
lovingly.*

*This is all leading up to saying that if you ever want to
come and stay here – for a few days, or a weekend
away – let me know. Or bring a friend. You'd be most
welcome. I should enjoy your company again, and talking, like old times. Perhaps you'd let me treat you to
dinner at the White Hart, or somewhere more up-market,
if you'd like. I certainly wouldn't expect you to cook or
anything. And don't worry about Natalie – she might not
be here.*

Lots of love, and do take care of yourself,
Stephen

Hetty read and reread the letter, turning the pages with
shaking hands. 'He's got a bloody nerve,' she whispered to
herself eventually. 'Wouldn't expect me to cook, hey? I bet
he would – there'd be sighs over dinner in the restaurant

Edwina Currie

about how I could do better. If I turned up with a leg of lamb, he couldn't be more pleased.'

That, she felt, was ungracious and bitter. But there must have been other reasons for Stephen to write, nearly eighteen months after he had revealed he was in love with someone else. He was using a kind of code – 'we are close' meant that he could be oblique, but she would still grasp his meaning. So what was going on?

He had no pressing need to write about Peter. The degree ceremony was almost a year off. She would attend, naturally, there was no question about it, and Stephen did not need to be told. So that was an excuse, though 'Have you anybody you'd want to take?' must be Stephen-speak for 'Have you found yourself another man?' Whether she had, or not, was none of his business.

The garden, the 'glories of Dorset': that smacked of emotional blackmail. Look what you left behind. Look what you gave up, and for what? A small poky flat in south London, in which he obviously imagined she was imprisoned by the high crime rate. How wrong he was, how limited by his prejudices. She was half persuaded to write back to correct him on that alone.

But why would he attempt, even subconsciously, to lean on her? What could he gain, especially since she could simply ignore the letter? He was after something. Possibly he himself did not quite guess what. Neither of them had gone in for deep introspection. So his language was friendly if clumsy, the invitation genuinely meant. If she did, cautiously, go for a weekend, he would treat her with courtesy and not humiliate her.

With a friend? That was how the invitation was worded. Then Hetty grasped that a friend would cause difficulties. A woman friend – Doris, maybe – would get in the way constantly, and Stephen would be embarrassed. A man, such as Father Roger, would be even more of an unwanted appendage. A boyfriend was unthinkable, and Stephen did not mean that at all.

He wanted her to come on her own. And Natalie might not be there. Would not be there, was the implication, if Hetty was arriving. So the girlfriend, whom he had not married despite his earlier determination, was not such an absolute fixture.

He wanted her to go back.

'You miserable so-and-so,' Hetty muttered, crossly but with a gulp of pain. 'Can't you leave me alone?'

She reread the pages, crumpled them into a ball, and threw them into the waste-bin, her mind jangling. But she owed him – something, though she was unclear what. So the sheets were retrieved and smoothed out on the table, as Hetty struggled with her emotions. 'If you hadn't misbehaved I wouldn't have left. But that doesn't mean I'm unhappy. Just as I'm getting used to being on my own. Just as I've developed umpteen schemes for surviving alone, away from the world of coupledom. Suddenly you dangle before me the juicy prospect of returning? Of being a cosy couple once again?'

A new skin had grown to cover the scars, but his honeyed words threatened to reopen the wounds. Her former life had not been a failure, but recently she had dwelt relatively little on it. Instead her plans were focused on a different future.

'Just as I'm about to have a bit of fun with a man from the agency, too,' Hetty added wistfully. 'Almost as if you're telepathic. Oh, Stephen.'

At that, she sat down, allowed herself to feel forlorn, and to cry.

The answer to Stephen's letter took her a week to write. Numerous times she sat down with pen and paper, then tore up the results. Eventually she found a card in a drawer from an art exhibition showing a dark-haired pre-Raphaelite woman with a solemn, saintly expression. On the back she wrote, 'Thank you for your kind letter. I'll be at Peter's graduation and will be in touch beforehand. Thanks also for the invite; I may take you up on it. Love, Hetty.' She debated for days with herself whether 'Love' was appropriate, then decided that anything else would sound cold. It was less jocular, and warmer, than his 'Lots of love.' It would do.

It was early evening before she was satisfied and went out to post the envelope containing the card. She was still sunk in thought, head bowed, as she came back up the path and reached in her pocket for the key.

The door burst open and nearly knocked her off her feet. 'Oh!' she cried, startled, and clutched at the wall for balance.

'Oh, sod it,' came Doris's voice. 'Hetty, is that you? Sorry. Come on, we've got to get cracking.' The stocky old woman slammed the door shut behind her and grabbed Hetty's arm, spinning her round in the direction from which she had come. 'You busy for an hour or two? Fine. A bit of moral support would be useful.'

There must be something trustworthy about her, Hetty reflected dazedly, to have so many people demanding her supportive presence. First Clarissa at the Swallows Home, now Doris. What was it? Trouble at the sex-shop? Hetty wondered whether to hang back, but Doris was already hurrying out of the gate and down the road.

'What's going on?' Hetty asked breathlessly, as she caught up.

'Carole's been arrested.'

'Carole? Who's Carole?'

'*You* know. You've seen her. High heels and fishnet tights. Well, *she* knows *you*.'

Was this the young girl in the shop? The description didn't fit. Somebody who'd been on the programme, or who'd applied to appear?

The woman at the café?

'How does she know me?' They were trotting side by side now.

'Dunno. But she mentioned your name on the phone. You're a respectable type, Hetty, so she must have figured you could help.'

Further enquiry or denial seemed pointless, so Hetty asked, 'Where are we headed?'

'Cop shop. Lavender Hill. Take us ten minutes if we walk fast.'

It took all Hetty's breath to keep up with the rapidly marching Doris, whose chin was thrust forward, elbows pumping, as if she were trying to take the lead in a fiercely fought road race. As the older woman had predicted, they soon came to the square grey station on the corner with Latchmere Road.

Without pausing, Doris marched up the steps under the blue lamp and into Reception where she banged on the counter and rang the bell for attention.

'Service here!' she called, as Hetty hovered behind her.

Hetty had not been in this police station before. The posters on the walls were more intimidating than the Dorset versions, with mugshots of a dozen wanted criminals, grubby posters of missing persons (some of whom looked as grim as the wanted men), pictures of stolen vehicles and weapons involved in crimes, and slavering dogs with warnings about rabies. A large notice gave the number of a rape counselling service; another advertised the Samaritans. The place smelt of tobacco, urine and floor polish. The local station where she had once reported a strayed pet, not much more than a detached house in a nearby village, was sleepy and charming by comparison.

'Not the kind of place you'd come to ask the time,' she said to herself.

The door at the back of the counter opened. A heavy-set sergeant in shirtsleeves entered. 'Right. What's up?'

'You've got a friend of mine here,' Doris announced. 'The transvestite. She phoned me.'

'Oh, that one,' the officer said, with deep meaning injected into the words. He began leafing through a day book whose columns were covered in scribbles. He examined Doris and Hetty with interest. 'You together?'

They nodded.

'You two *are* women, I take it?' The gruff voice had a hint of sarcasm. He jerked a thumb. 'Your pal inside is refusing to give her name. His name. Whatever. That's an offence.'

'But that's not why you arrested her,' said Doris, with spirit. 'What's the game?'

'Importuning. Approaching men on the common.'

'In broad daylight?' Hetty was unable to remain silent.

'Two hours ago. Causing a bit of a stir.'

'I'll bet,' said Hetty under her breath.

'Has anyone complained?' Doris demanded.

'Oh, aye. A woman walking past with two small children. Said it made her sick.'

'But Carole wasn't approaching *her*, was she?' Doris had taken over the role of interrogator and was clearly enjoying it.

'No-o-o,' said the sergeant thoughtfully. 'It says here that she was seen talking to several men. They rebuffed her advances and moved away.'

'I'd be astonished if she was,' Doris said decisively. 'Unless she was trying it on to see if they fancied her. She's married.'

'So what?' the officer responded. 'They all are, on that bloody common.'

'Well, chatting up strangers is not a crime, as you well know, Sergeant,' said Doris firmly. 'She didn't do anything really stupid, though – like exposing herself, did she?'

He checked the sheet. 'No.'

'And nor is dressing in women's clothes a criminal activity. Even if you do look like something the cat dragged in. It's a free country. We can wear what we like, as long as the dangly bits are hidden.'

The man's mouth was twitching. 'I can see you know your law, ma'am,' he observed. 'You'd better come and discuss the matter with the prisoner.'

He held open the door behind the counter and ushered the two women inside. Hetty clutched her handbag to her chest as if it were more at risk inside the police station than on the street. Her eyes were wide, her mouth clamped shut.

Down a corridor and through a set of swing doors they came to a row of tattered chairs. More notices on the walls instructed visitors not to spit or damage the furniture. A poster above a payphone advertised a solicitors' help line. The smell of urine was stronger.

Seated cowering on the furthest chair, her back turned to the new arrivals, was the person Doris had come to rescue.

The dress was the black lace Hetty had seen before, but it was torn and there were holes in the fishnet tights.

'Carole!' Doris said, in a commanding accent.

Carole half turned, to show a tear-streaked face, the jowls blackened with mascara, the lipstick spread over the lower jaw like tomato ketchup. The wig was askew and an earring was missing. 'Oh, Doris,' she wailed. 'Oh, I'm such a mess . . .'

Doris rummaged in her handbag and sat down by Carole's side. With a handkerchief she tenderly wiped the stained cheeks and attempted to remove the lipstick. 'What happened, dear?' she asked gently.

'Two men on the common. I was only asking them for a smoke – to see if they'd talk to me as a woman. They decided to have a go instead. Took offence, they said. Some lady yelled at them and they ran off. She had a mobile phone and called the police.'

'That's not the story on the charge sheet.' Hetty was bewildered.

'Well, no, it wouldn't be. I'm not going to press charges, am I?'

'Why not? If they attacked you. You have rights as well.'

'Be practical, Hetty,' Doris advised. 'Carole may come out one day. But not yet. Not while the children are small.' She put a finger under Carole's chin. 'You promised you wouldn't go out in daylight for exactly that reason, too. What's happening?'

'She's taking over,' Carole whispered brokenly. The voice was high and thin. 'I can't help it.'

Doris helped the trembling figure to her feet. The heel of one of her shoes was broken, so walking was tricky. Hetty darted back to the sergeant; and after some discussion and the exchange of a fiver, a pair of battered trainers was retrieved from the lost-property box. She returned with them held out in front of her, like a prize. 'Here,' she said. 'You'll probably catch athlete's foot, but at least we can get you – Where are we going, Doris?'

'Home,' said Doris decisively. 'Where we came from.'

An hour later they were seated in the simple living room of flat two. Mrs McDonald was wielding a teapot, and Carole had vanished into the bathroom. The sound of a shower could be heard for a long time.

'Would somebody mind telling me,' said Hetty at last, 'what's been going on?'

'We're very grateful to you, Mrs Clarkson,' said Mrs McDonald formally. The Scottish accent burred and lengthened the syllables. 'Would you like a biscuit?'

'No, but I would like an explanation. Is that Mr McDonald?'

'It is.'

'And Carole is . . . ?'

'Carole is my husband when he is dressed as a female,' answered Mrs McDonald calmly, as if explaining how the gas meter worked.

'I don't get it,' said Hetty weakly. 'You're in on all this?'

'I am. Always have been.'

'But how long . . . ?'

'It was a couple of months after we were married that I saw Carole for the first time. She wasn't as . . . striking as she is now. I came into the bedroom one evening and found her in one of my nightdresses.'

'Heavens.' Hetty sat back abruptly. 'Weren't you shocked?'

The woman sipped her tea. 'I was a bit green, then. I

wasn't sure whether to be shocked or not. I didn't know anything about it.'

'So it's been like this' – Hetty struggled – 'the whole time you've been together?'

'Oh, yes, but she was probably there ages before that. The tendency often shows up in childhood. For Andy it wasn't till he was a teenager. Then his mum caught him trying on her dresses and she threw him out.'

'But you didn't throw him out, did you?' Doris's eyes were sharp.

'I didn't. I fell in love with *Andy*, see. The *person*. I met him at work. He was so kind, and so considerate. Nobody's ever been so nice to me. I'm not exactly a great looker, and I was dreadfully shy. He was good to me.'

'So when you found out about Carole . . . ?' Hetty could not formulate her question. It was clear, however, that Mrs McDonald had asked it of herself, and had answered it to her own satisfaction.

'When I first met Carole, I cried and cried. But then Andy showed me he's still the same human being who loved me and married me. And he carried on being the same husband. And, in a way, it doesn't bother me as it used to: I can turn a blind eye. Anyway, by then I was pregnant, so there was no going back.'

'But how do you feel . . . ?' Hetty's voice trailed away. If Stephen . . . it didn't bear thinking about. She doubted if her own reaction could ever have been as measured, or as compassionate.

Mrs McDonald's face was impassive. 'It's up to him. Provided he doesn't get himself into trouble. Or us.'

'Nearly did today,' Doris commented. 'Not supposed to be flouncing about in broad daylight, is he?'

Mrs McDonald shook her head.

Hetty recalled her several sightings of 'Carole' in the neighbourhood. 'At the police station,' she said slowly, 'your husband told us that Carole was taking over. What did he mean?'

'Just that,' answered the woman, 'and it's been getting worse recently. The worry is that Carole will insist on taking over and we won't be able to stop her.'

'And then?'

'Then he'll want to be Carole the whole time.'

There was a silence. Hetty found the solid, unemotional stance of Mrs McDonald almost unbearable. She turned gravely to Doris. 'Are the children supposed to be in on the secret? Is it a secret? Or was I the only one in the block who didn't–?'

'It's an open secret,' Doris elaborated unhelpfully. 'The children haven't been told about it, not properly. But they've caught sight of their dad once or twice. If you don't tell them otherwise, they assume it's normal.'

'For my husband, it is.' Mrs McDonald did not seem flustered.

Hetty could not make up her mind whether the woman was a martyr, a saint or a self-deluding madwoman. Sympathy, even if not entirely whole-hearted, seemed the best response. 'In those circumstances,' Hetty ventured, 'many wives would have shown the man the door, and told him never to come near the children again.'

'But why? He's a wonderful father. He's great in every way – he works hard, brings home every penny he earns, treats us with respect. Doesn't drink, doesn't swear. He loves us, and we love him.'

'Yes. I can see that. You're very lucky, I suppose. But it

must put the marriage under strain, surely?' Hetty was uncertain of her own meaning, then realised she was asking about their sex lives, their right to qualify as a couple, per- haps. Such topics were none of her business or anyone else's.

Mrs McDonald drew herself up with some dignity and gave Hetty a cool stare. 'I have an excellent marriage, Mrs Clarkson.'

Suitably quelled, Hetty munched a biscuit. The bathroom door opened and Mr McDonald emerged in dark slacks and a sweater, the clothes worn but clean. Behind him Hetty spotted the dress, carefully hung up, its torn hem dangling.

'Thank you for your help.' The remark was agonised and evidently sincerely meant, but it was also a dismissal. Doris and Hetty rose, shook hands awkwardly, and left. Behind them came a low murmur of voices: there would be no screaming match, no recriminations in that household.

At the bottom of the stairs Hetty held on to the banister rail to steady herself. 'Doris, what did she mean, she has an excellent marriage? How can that be possible?'

'It takes all sorts,' Doris answered. 'The shop has taught me that, if nothing else. How are we to judge? Your marriage fell apart, hers hasn't. Mine – well, that's another story. But in this block, Hetty, there are two happy couples, and they're one of them.'

'Two?'

'Yeah. The gay men upstairs, Markus and Christian – don't you think of them as a couple? You should. But, com- paring them, I'd say the McDonalds are far more likely to make it till death us do part, et cetera.'

'And how do you figure that?'

'Because they have no illusions, either of them. He's a

cross-dresser – he just *is*. She's a plain dumpy lass that no other man would have, probably, but she's a homemaker. He gave her that chance, that status, and she repays him with total loyalty. And, despite the difficulties, they've promised to care for each other and for the children.'

'My God,' said Hetty, chastened.

Doris prodded her arm. 'Bit of a challenge, hey? A model partnership, Het. A wonderful example to us all.'

'Maybe,' said Hetty, her mind in turmoil, as she trudged slowly up the stairs.

CHAPTER TWENTY-TWO

Glimpses

Hetty stirred her cappuccino, licked her spoon and watched idly as the froth collapsed. 'Shouldn't have done that,' she said out loud.

'What is it?' Clarissa's voice betrayed concern. 'You've not been on form today, Hetty.'

'Doesn't matter,' Hetty answered, and pulled her shoulders back. 'Mustn't slouch.'

'There! I told you,' said Clarissa, in triumph. She rummaged in her voluminous shoulder-bag, found cologne-soaked tissues, and patted her brow. 'You're talking to yourself the whole time, now. This living solo has got to you. I'm sorry, but you seem to have made no progress. In fact, darling, you're going backwards.'

Hetty put her spoon down in the saucer. They were seated under the palm trees in the Bluewater concourse, the vast shopping complex near London that boasted it was the largest in the country, a virtual city. Their packages were piled on spare chairs like First World War trench sandbags, creating a barricade that gave scant protection from swirling Muzak, the whine of four sets of escalators, heavy-metal snatches from a CD shop two floors up and a squalling baby in a pushchair at the next table.

'I'll be crawling out on my knees, if we don't have a quiet half-hour,' Hetty answered ominously. 'Where are we, anyway? How far is the car?'

Clarissa sipped her espresso. 'Back there. We've walked quite a distance.'

Hetty raised her head, her brow puckered. 'The complex is over a mile long, and we're near one of the western exits. So that means one hell of a trek back.'

'All right. My mistake,' Clarissa conceded. 'Back to Harvey Nicks next time. And coffee in Knightsbridge. But if you expect me to traipse round the tube with my Harrods bags, you've got another think coming.'

'What I don't get,' Hetty said, sipping the remaining froth and refusing a tissue, 'is the attraction of these places. It's packed. Entire families have arrived for a day out. The kids hate it, the old ones are confused, the teenagers start nicking, the young mums get exhausted and the fathers despair – that is, when they bother to come.'

'It's shopping,' Clarissa said doggedly. 'And you're supposed to enjoy it.'

With her sore feet rested, Hetty felt more relaxed. 'How's Robin?'

'So-so. As ever.'

'What does that mean?'

'He's having a whale of a time as head of chambers. Dinners every night, lectures, meetings. It'll guarantee him a

position on every committee going plus an income for life –
he's now a confirmed member of the Gee-gees.' Hetty must
have looked blank. 'The Great and the Good. The list of
approved spiritual and temporal leaders, as Robin puts it,
from whom the Public Appointments Unit selects names.
The odds are, he'll spend his retirement chairing one inquiry
after other. He *will* like that.'

'And you won't, I take it?'

'Not much. He's busy, and I'm excluded. If he dines at his
club, the snooty one that won't admit women, I'm relegated
to some chintzy horror on the mezzanine floor to wait for
him. So I stay at home.'

'More women should be put on those bodies,' Hetty suggested.

Clarissa bridled. 'I hope not. It'd mean more women on
his body, that's for sure.'

'All those fact-finding trips abroad?' Hetty smiled.

'Correct. And with the press inquisitive about perks, partners are frowned on. Researchers, on the other hand, are
essential. They travel by the truckload.'

'Your Robin, though. He's not like that,' Hetty explored
carefully.

'They're *all* like that.' Clarissa glowered.

The two women ordered second cups of coffee and
abstemiously shared a slice of strawberry cream gâteau.

'I've applied to an agency,' Hetty said airily. She had been
waiting for the moment to mention it.

'Why? You fed up with your job?'

'No, silly. A dating agency. Soul Mates. Going to find me
a man, they say. I hope so – it's costing over thirty pounds a
month.'

'That's one middling dinner in town, or a ticket in the

back stalls of a hit show,' Clarissa calculated quickly. 'Anything worth while shown up yet?'

Hetty shook her head. 'But I'm determined. Time to abandon my starfish bed, and fill it with basking sharks. I hope.'

'Come again?' Clarissa was briefly mystified. She leaned forward, her voice confidential. 'I bet you could go back. I've heard that your Stephen's been seen moping about at weekends, on his own again.'

'Ah . . .' Hetty pondered. That explained the original letter, and another, similarly worded but shorter, which had arrived the previous week. 'I'm sad to hear that. But it doesn't follow that I'm the antidote to his afflictions, does it?'

'But it could be ideal. Now you've had your bid for freedom, and rediscovered yourself, and taken advantage of . . . what do they call it? . . . having your own space for a while, you two could start afresh on a much stronger footing.' She tapped her nose. 'You could keep in touch with the agency as an insurance policy.'

'The hole in that scenario is that I like my freedom. I like my friends. I like living where I do. It isn't a compromise any more, if it ever was.'

Clarissa's face betrayed bewilderment. 'You sure? Sounds a bit like bravado to me. Surely any sane woman, given what Stephen might be offering, would jump at the chance. That's why girls go to these agencies, for heaven's sake. And he's a handsome man still: Robin and I saw him at a Guildhall dinner the other week. He was alone.'

Hetty kept her peace. Doris would not be impressed if she decamped to Dorset, or set up some imitation of her former life. Father Roger might make supportive comments, but he would also regret the loss of their gentle, platonic evenings out. Markus and Christian would ask anxiously if she were sure that was what she wanted, and if so, she would probably never see them again. Or the McDonalds, and certainly not Carole, who had manifested herself rather less frequently recently. And there was Brian, who had reappeared on his old pitch, careworn and gaunt, but selling the *Big Issue* once more: she longed to take him for another coffee and fill in the gaps. Worst, the job. That would go out of the window. Rosa would not be pleased.

'I suspect you've described accurately what, maybe, the BJs want. But I'm way past that stage,' Hetty said, cagily.

Clarissa prodded her arm. 'The BJs – are these your drinking mates? Hardly the best people to judge, are they? Heavens, Hetty, your lifestyle since you went to live in that hell-hole doesn't bear examination. Talk about sowing wild oats. You, a respectable woman.'

The last person who had called her that had needed rescuing from a police station on a sex charge. Hetty decided not to tell Clarissa about that little adventure. 'I'm okay. Honestly. Probably happier than you, in fact.'

'How do you work that out?' Clarissa was indignant. She began to gather up the bags ready to leave.

'Well, you've just moaned at length about Robin. And when I've seen him, he's not been – the perfect escort, shall we say? Fell over in my brother's kitchen, for example. So why do *you* put up with it? You should get stubborn. Insist he takes your needs into account. And do it soon.'

'*You*'re giving *me* advice?' Clarissa's mouth dropped open.

'Why not? There are worse things to be than a single fiftysomething, Clarissa. In fact, I can assure you –'

The top bag teetered and toppled off the pile. Clarissa jerked out a hand to stop it and knocked over her shoulder-bag. The coffee-cup clattered to the floor. Heads turned, a loud 'tut' came from the woman at the next table.

Hetty went down on her haunches to pick up the broken china and retrieve their belongings. It was then that she saw a slim volume sticking out of Clarissa's bag.

'What's this? You becoming an intellectual all of a sudden?'

'Give that here.' Clarissa snatched the book and stuffed it quickly back into the bag.

'Did I see *Teach Yourself Sociology*?' Hetty's eyes were round.

'Perhaps.'

'But you – are you about to become a student or what?'

'I might.' Clarissa's cheeks were scarlet; she scrabbled about with the carrier-bags until clusters of handles were in her fists, then said stiffly, 'Shall we go?'

Hetty grabbed the remaining shopping and trotted along beside her friend, her tiredness forgotten. 'So, the cosy married life isn't quite as fulfilling as all that?' she teased.

But Clarissa, marching fiercely, eyes straight ahead, would tell her no more.

The following evening Hetty discovered she was the only person of her acquaintance who wished to see the *South Park* movie. Its irreverent send-ups of political correctness, its uproarious two fingers to censorship had her chuckling throughout, even if Kenny died in a particularly gruesome manner. Those politicians who wanted adults to set good examples to children should be aware of the unconventional advice given by the school chef to the eight-year-olds in his care, mainly on seduction techniques. On the other hand, its real target was intolerance, and that appealed to her.

She trudged back across the common. After a moment she

realised that she had taken the wrong path, and was headed away from the corner of Apiary Lane towards the north side. Lost in reverie, she had not noticed where she was.

She halted. Overhead the wind whistled through the branches: rain had been forecast and it was getting dark. This was not the most salubrious sector of the common, with its shrubbery and foliage dense enough to conceal those who did not wish to be observed. Some nights, Hetty knew, it could become quite crowded here; Doris had warned her to avoid this area out of daylight, unless, like those visitors who chose to frequent it, she had pressing reasons to be there.

She was not afraid: she was not seeking drugs, or illicit sex, from the seedy boys who were already lurking near the park bench. They were not all gay, by any means.

She turned and began to walk steadily towards the road. The sun had gone: here, where there were no street-lamps, it was murky and damp. A movement on her left made her jump. Two men had emerged from the shadows, shoulder to shoulder. One was sporting a baseball cap and white jeans – the hallmark, in these parts, of a gay prostitute. He was pocketing what appeared to be money.

Hetty tried not to stare. It was none of her business. If it suited these men to seek love, or whatever they called it, in public with anonymous others, she could only pity them: she would not condemn. Most of all, she should not interfere. But something made her twist half round, to reassure herself they had no interest in her and that she was safe.

The Adam's apple bobbed, the elegant profile swung rapidly away. The golden hair caught the remaining light. Then the tall young man in the green sweater broke into a loping run and was lost in the bushes.

The boy with the baseball cap shrugged, tucked the notes away, found a handkerchief and wiped his hands, then strolled back into the gloom.

Hetty was more than a little shaky as she arrived at her front gate. Was that an illusion? Had she really seen Christian on the common, and if so what had he been up to? Paying for services, or selling them? She had seen the notes in the base-ball boy's hand, though she could not tell whether he was the recipient or the customer. What had got into Christian that he should be so engaged and taking such risks?

The happy couple upstairs were, perhaps, not so happy. It showed how few assumptions could be made about others.

As she stood on the doorstep and fumbled for her keys, Hetty felt deeply upset. Markus and Christian had given no signs of friction, though she recalled Christian joking about the common one Sunday at the Café Pinocchio, about doing it the first time with strangers. Markus had recoiled at the comments but his disapproval had been fleeting and pri-vate. Perhaps the joking had developed further: into a dare? Or did Christian find coupledom in flat six a bit stifling? His earlier experiences, from which he had been rescued by his older lover, suggested a self-destructive streak. Maybe he was heading that way again?

It would help to talk it over with Doris. As she put her key in the lock, however, Hetty heard animated voices coming from Doris's flat: not the usual scolding of Thomas for moulting on the sofa or eating the spare ham, but a male and female in conversation.

Hetty tiptoed into the dark garden. She would not be seen from inside. For a moment she hesitated: she did not normally spy on anyone, let alone her friends. But the film had made her feel mildly unconventional, and she meant no harm.

Doris's kitchen was well lit, the blind up. Inside Doris was at the table, with a thick-set man. She was devoid of pinny or curlers or turban, her lipstick was tidily applied, the excess rouge absent. She was nodding, head on one side, a smile on her lips. The man was about her age, silvery at the temples and bald, in a smart navy suit with a blue shirt and tie. At the far end of the table Thomas was curled up like a ginger cushion, his eyes watchful slits. Between them stood two glasses – Scotch, perhaps.

Doris would not dress up like that for the rent man. It was evidently an expected visit, for the makeup and hair would have required effort. That also explained why she had not been free to go to a movie. The old lady's eyes radiated contentment, even joy. Hetty had never seen her like that before, and suddenly could visualise Doris as a young, sweet-faced girl, exuberant and full of spirit.

And this must be the gentleman friend, Jack, whose wife lived up north, and who owned the sex-shop. Who owned several sex-shops, but had a background as . . . ? Hetty ransacked her memory. On the bus home after the carol service, Doris had mentioned casually that he had been a police officer. In that dark blue outfit he looked the part, as if he might have been a detective. The unstated implication in that conversation, then, was that Jack was _au fait_ with that sleazy trade and would conduct it honourably, so no more questions need be asked. Yet, given Doris' roguishness, her means of earning her living, her familiarity with the law (as demonstrated in the rescue of Carole), Hetty began to wonder. How had they met? Had Doris once been known to the police?

And who, exactly, was Doris, this bustling, cheery woman who had taken on the role of concierge and mother-substitute for the block, and who seemed to know everyone's affairs? Hetty stepped away from the window and slipped back into the shadows. She had every reason to be grateful. Doris had been the soul of kindness during those miserable first days at The Swallows. It was thanks to her that the newcomer had neither frozen nor starved. Hetty had heard tales of single people left to rot in their rooms, studiously ignored by neighbours who scuttled in and out of their own rabbit-holes as if determined to avoid contact. It was depressing enough to find oneself alone, in circumstances not of one's own choosing; but to have been ignored like that, denied human existence, would have been terrible. Instead, succoured by as friendly a biddy as Doris, she had felt almost welcome.

So who was she? Doris had also hinted that she had been married, once – but that, she had said, was another story. Did she have children? And, since she was obviously from a corner of the city some distance away, why had she decided to settle in what must seem, to an East-Ender, the wilderness south of the Thames? Even Christian and Markus reckoned that Doris had secrets. Here was one made manifest, seated a few yards away and cradling a drink, with Doris simpering and luminous before him.

Now was the not the moment to enquire. Hetty's urge to discuss Christian's twilight activities on the common, and her curiosity about Jack, would have to remain under wraps. Meanwhile she laughed ruefully. At least Doris was entertaining a gentleman, and seemed to be on cloud nine about it.

*

More immediate matters awaited in her postbox. A large buff envelope had arrived from Soul Mates. Hetty hung up her coat, disciplined herself to make a cup of tea first, then sat down with the sheaf of papers.

There were six sheets, each with a photograph, passport-size, pinned to a photocopy of the application form. Highlighted on each form in fluorescent green was the home phone number. A covering letter invited Hetty to call the men direct, then to keep the agency informed of her progress.

Bill looked like a criminal. His unsmiling face was podgy, suggesting that his description of himself as of 'average build' was an error. He might have the mildest of dispositions, but Hetty was taking no chances. Andrew was better, quite attractive, but only thirty-five, he said, and lived in Kent. The agency was not as efficient as it pretended, or perhaps the various offices swapped their more promising clients as encouragement. Martin had a London postcode and his photo showed a pleasant enough chap, but his main hobbies were fixing up old cars and jazz. 'Been there, done that,' muttered Hetty darkly, as she drank her tea. And he had a moustache.

Matthew had no interests whatever, as far as she could judge. He had left the section unticked and scrawled 'everything' over it. It could mean that he was the most amazing person, erudite, literate and eclectic in his tastes; but an intelligent man would surely have been a bit more selective. David was a university lecturer, swarthy and with a pony-tail, who had never married; his eyes avoided the camera. Hetty fantasised that he had fathered ten children by four different mothers and did not wish to admit it. Nor did he mention what he taught: that could mean the subject was so dull he dared not boast about it. Engineering, maybe. Or social science – no, that would have produced a proud reference. Forestry, then. Or train-spotting. He was fairly dull himself, or too picky, if in truth no woman had ever won his heart.

That left Norman. His picture passed the test with flying colours, and though he said he was forty-five Hetty, squinting closely, suspected that was an underestimate. Modifying his date of birth was not a disqualification – it might show he was sensitive on the issue, as she was, and felt much younger. He was a widower: his wife had died of cancer two years before, and now, he wrote, 'I feel ready to put my grief behind me, and find new friendships, hopefully long-term.' That sounded intriguing. He had been married, he had loved and lost through no fault of his own, but was not prepared to bid goodbye to the world and wallow in self-pity. A mature man.

The address given was in Hertfordshire. He had his own company in the financial field and liked the theatre, concerts, sport. Hetty finished the tea, held the paper in both hands at arm's length and asked whether she could imagine herself sitting across a dinner table from this person.

She could. She picked up the phone and dialled.

'I called you this evening. You were out. Somewhere nice?'

Hetty giggled. 'Yeah, Sally. Went out for a drink. With a man.'

'Ooh! The agency. They found you somebody.'

'Not sure yet. But yes, the name did come from Soul Mates. And it's Norman.'

'Norman from the agency? Sounds like a character from a Rowan Atkinson film. Or Alan Partridge. What's he like?'

'Don't sneer, dear. He's about fiftyish, fairly well-off – he had a Ralph Lauren blazer, quite smart but casual. Not the leather-jacket type. I think he was originally a chartered accountant, something solid, anyway. Not tall, but slim. Stylish in an understated way. He wore a pink shirt and a cravat – that was how I was to recognise him.'

'Isn't that a bit poncy? And what did you wear?'

'That suit from *Star Style*. I'm beginning to feel quite at home in it.'

'It's nice. So where did you go with Norman from the agency?'

'We met in the bar at his club. Somewhere in Pall Mall. I hadn't been before, but it's swish and the waiter treated him as a regular.'

'Hmm. Don't take anything for granted. What did you chat about?'

Hetty pondered. 'Oh, home, children, the usual subjects,' she said vaguely. 'I let him do most of the talking. He was excellent at that.'

'So he's a charmer. But is he genuine?'

'I think so. How can I tell? But so far, I can't fault him.'

Now it was Sally's turn to think hard before speaking. 'If it helps, I'll come with you next time,' she offered. 'Give him the once-over. But don't reveal your home address until you've checked him out thoroughly. If you like, I can run his details through our computer, see if he's travelled with us, who paid his fare, that sort of thing.'

'Well, first let's find out if it goes anywhere. I'll show you the sheet next time you come round. Anyway–' Hetty giggled again and hiccuped, once.

'What, Mum? Wow, you *have* been drinking.'

''Sright. He bought champagne. It was lovely.'

'Blimey. My mother, gadding about in her old age.'

'Stop it. You're jealous. I *was* going to say, he's keen to see me again. He's asked me out. And that's a recommendation in itself.'

What Hetty could not tell her daughter, for she could still not quite believe it, was that Norman scored remarkably highly on her checklist of manly attributes. And then some.

He was trim, neat and . . . *sexy*. He had pale blue eyes that twinkled merrily and sandy hair cut short: it was obvious he had been freshly barbered. Clean-shaven skin sat without slackness on high cheekbones and a firm jaw with a small cleft in the chin. He kept himself fit, he told her; she could detect not an ounce of spare fat on him, though the wrists under the pink shirt-cuffs and discreet gold cufflinks were wiry and strong. The aftershave was unobtrusive but fragrant. He was rather older than he was admitting on the form – closer to mid-fifties. Not a subject to be broached yet, Hetty reckoned, especially as she had knocked another year off her own age. At this rate she'd be forty before the decade was out: she was in no position to moralise.

The standard opening gambit, Hetty asking him to say more about himself than was on the form, had produced a modest smile and a shrug from Norman. He skated over his occupation as esoteric and of slight interest to a pretty woman at the first meeting. He did give her a card, as clean and tidy as its donor, with a business address in Tring. The lack of flourish or bombast impressed Hetty even more. She tried to assess him as if he were a guest on *Tell Me All*, and concluded that Norman from the agency came across as so manifestly normal, so much at ease that nobody would put him on the show, ever. Yet if he were in a witness-box, whatever story he told would be instantly credible.

His face was open and alert, and he seemed delighted to be in the same room as her, in the buttoned leather arm-chairs, with a bowl of salted nuts before them, the waiter wiping glasses at the far end of the bar and the champagne bottle slowly emptying.

'I ought to ask you for dinner,' he said at last. His voice was light, the accent north London.

'Perhaps not this evening,' Hetty had demurred. 'We are a little late.' They had met at seven; it was nearly nine. The two hours had passed swiftly, not a moment had dragged. Both expressed astonishment at the time.

'We must have been enjoying each other's company, Hetty. This is an enormous pleasure for me, to meet a remarkable, intelligent lady like you,' Norman said, and waved the waiter away. 'Have what's left. No, I insist.' He poured the remains of the bubbly then turned the bottle upside down in its bucket with a tiny sigh of regret.

Hetty felt dazed. The *Star Style* outfit had worked its magic once more. She had steeled herself to expect an encounter more on the lines of that ghastly dinner with James. She should have been silently marking the negative bits, to mull over later when deciding whether to see him again, or to wait for the next envelope. Instead Norman kept coming up smelling of roses – not quite as irresistible as Stephen in his prime, maybe, but much more so than Stephen today. Or James, or Al.

This had started to feel like a lurch in the right direction. Maybe, under the table, she should pinch herself to wake up.

'It makes you wonder,' she ventured, 'why on earth

people like us have to meet via, er, our mutual acquaintance. We're both sociable, warm, solvent, sound in body and mind. Pity we have to resort to – you know. It is so clinical.'

'It's the tragedy of the modern world, Hetty,' he said, and gazed into her eyes. 'Workaholics, we are, the middle classes. We get so engrossed in our professional activities that we realise all of a sudden that our social life is non-existent. Plus, we're British: brought up to be reticent, to put up with it. The opportunities to meet like-minded people are limited – our generation doesn't go out clubbing, like the youngsters. To meet someone like you by chance would be a miracle. So the agencies find us highly profitable. But I don't begrudge them.'

'Agencies? Have you been to any others?'

He looked pained. 'No, but I did get some brochures. Tonight is the first time I've tried this, Hetty. I'm as nervous as you are.'

'I'll drink to that,' said Hetty, and they did so.

'Don't be dazzled,' said the champagne glass. 'He's only a chap. Either he's utterly ordinary and will bore you to tears, or there's something not right.'

'How do you figure that?' Hetty let the effervescence tickle her nose.

'Else why would he have to go to an agency?'

'Same reason I did. Got fed up waiting. Decided to seize the day.'

'That's the alcohol talking. Take care.'

Hetty lifted her head from the glass, to find the new man gazing at her, calm and dignified. 'You and I, Norman, we seem to understand each other,' she murmured.

'I believe we do, Hetty,' he said, quietly. Had he touched her hand at that minute or made any other move towards her, she would have shrunk away. He didn't, but seemed to want to. That was sufficient. 'So maybe we could arrange to have dinner on a future date?'

'Oh! Yes,' she said, trying not to appear too eager. 'I've brought my diary.'

'And I mine. As long, Hetty, as it's soon.'

And he had seen her into a taxi, and handed the cabby a twenty-pound note, as if such excellent manners came naturally to him. As he tapped goodbye on the window, Hetty settled back in her seat, crossed her legs and placed her hand over her beating heart.

CHAPTER TWENTY-THREE

Meat-eater

B ut it was lunch, not dinner, that came next. To Hetty's relief there was no suggestion that Norman hankered after Japanese raw fish laced with chillies. Instead he booked a table at PJ's in Covent Garden. As Hetty approached the yellow-painted frontage with its scrawled blackboard, she realised it was only a step away from Christopher's, the restaurant where Clarissa had started her rescue efforts all those months ago. This was beginning to feel like a familiar stamping ground.

Inside were dark wood, faded mirrors, bar stools and a amiable American manager in a turquoise shirt and wire-rimmed spectacles, who greeted Norman like an old friend.

'Bill, I'd like you to meet Hetty,' Norman said, with elaborate courtesy as their coats were taken. 'Usual table, please.'

They found themselves in a dimly lit alcove, with only two other tables nearby. Norman was smartly dressed in a

City suit and explained that he had two appointments in town that day, but told her no more. The restaurant was filling up with a variety of diners: male and female, both casually attired and smart. Hetty tried unsuccessfully to categorise them.

As if reading her mind, Norman said, 'We're near theatreland. A lot of these people, especially in the evenings, are involved with the performing arts or are on the fringes of show-business. See behind you.'

She twisted about and found that the wall at their table was festooned at waist height with small brass plaques. She recognised the names of Christopher Biggins the actor, and Will Carling the rugby player. 'Goodness,' she whispered, 'd'you think he brought Princess Diana here?'

Norman smiled a curious lop-sided smile, as if he knew more than he would tell. 'I doubt it. She preferred San Lorenzo, the Caprice, places like that.'

Hetty did not quite understand the implications, other than that the other locations were possibly more expensive, or more exclusive, but as the menus arrived, she saw that Norman had given her an entrée into another conversational track. 'You said on your form, Norman, that you liked theatre. Is that a major interest of yours?'

'It is. I've become acquainted with management and certain producers who dine here regularly, so sometimes I get tickets to first nights and previews. *Mamma Mia* for one, *Spend Spend Spend*, that sort of show – brilliant. We're extremely fortunate to have so much live theatre of such high quality in London, don't you think?'

'I do,' said Hetty firmly, and mentioned Christian and Markus, though it was apparent that their work – more elevated, perhaps, than the musicals Norman had touched on –

was known to him only by reputation. It occurred to her that she could name-drop with aplomb these days; moreover, thanks to Father Roger, several hit plays at the National were at her fingertips as topics of discourse, complete with comments on their ethical dilemmas. She no longer felt quite so shy or ignorant in the company of sophisticated strangers like Norman.

'What else do you enjoy doing – when you're not with me, say?' she asked, a mite coyly. 'Concerts, sport? You also ticked those boxes.'

He looked faintly puzzled, as if unsure what he had written. 'That's right,' he said vaguely. 'It depends. If I'm offered tickets for the Proms or Glyndebourne I always go. But I confess that eighty or a hundred pounds a seat at the Royal Opera House does not strike me as good value.'

'No, I can see that,' Hetty sympathised. So he was not about to take her to see Roberto Alagna and his wife in concert. What a pity.

The cuisine at PJ's turned out much more to her taste than the fiery tuna of James's preferred eatery, and kinder to her waistline than the creamy excesses of Clarissa's. She tucked in happily to icy gazpacho, and followed it with seared sea-bass on a bed of spinach: simple, tasty and blessedly recognisable. Norman opted for calf's liver, grilled pink and rare. Hetty peeked over her wine-glass as he speared each thin strip, browned on the outside, squishily soft inside, then delicately wiped up the bloody *jus* with bread. There was something so controlled about him. So carnivorous. It fascinated her.

'What about movies? Do you enjoy them too?' she continued.

'I do. My tastes are quite broad, but I never miss a new

science-fiction or horror film if I can help it. Wherever possible I read the book first, then I can compare.'

'I loved *Star Wars*,' Hetty confessed.

'Which one?' he enquired, his mouth widening in that smile again. It seemed to Hetty, fleetingly, that he was testing her. She was unsure whether he expected her to be impressed or amused. Since the various episodes in the genre tended to get mixed up in her memory, her replies were haphazard. They chatted on about the Lucas films for several minutes until at last Norman said, with a laugh, 'No, no, Hetty. The child becomes Darth Vader, not Luke Skywalker,' at which point it seemed wisest to move on.

'But the special effects were amazing,' she concluded defensively, and suspected she had made a minor fool of herself.

His eyes betrayed nothing as he picked up the menu to select a dessert. 'You are exceedingly good company, Hetty,' he said, as if to console her.

'So are you, Norman,' Hetty answered warmly, and she meant it. There was no need to compare this elegant, charming man with his beautiful manners and open face with her mental ideal. He was remarkably close to any model she might have chosen. His physical presence in that well-cut suit, the discreet cufflinks, the pearly-buttoned shirt, began to stir her imagination. What might he look like without them?

Plucking up her courage, she lowered her eyelashes, once, then gazed at him full in the face. 'Next time, Norman, it's on me.'

One evening soon afterwards Hetty was washing up and pottering round the flat. A few anemones in a vase gave a cheerful air. The knock on the door made her jump.

'Hello, Doris. *And* Thomas.' Hetty eyed the cat with caution. How did he manage to moult the whole time? Doris's apron was covered in his hairs. 'Want to come in?'

'Don't mind if I do,' Doris said. 'You're looking cheerful. How's the love life?'

'It's okay,' Hetty said crisply. 'Ask no questions, Doris, and you'll be told no lies.'

Doris had come officially with information that the water was to be cut off the following day for repairs, but in essence for gossip and tea. As Hetty broke open a packet of biscuits, she wondered if Doris might be in the mood for confidences.

'A couple of weeks ago,' Hetty ventured, 'didn't I see you in your kitchen with a gentleman friend? Was that your Jack?'

Doris dimpled. 'It was. Nice, isn't he? Still got his handsome looks.'

'Not moving in, yet?' Hetty let her voice sound teasing.

'No. Not 'im. He lives in digs in the East End – well, I call 'em digs, but he owns the whole terrace. One of his tenants sees to him.'

'He's done well for a former police officer, hasn't he?' Hetty did not trouble to conceal her curiosity.

Doris's face darkened. 'You might say that.'

Hetty sat back. 'Sorry, I'm being nosy. No reason why a former policeman shouldn't own a row of houses. You've known him ages, haven't you?'

'Must be forty years.' The normally garrulous Doris had acquired a wary expression. Hetty decided to plough on. Her neighbour could always tell her to take a running jump, but had not done so yet.

'Do you have children, Doris?'

'I did. One, a daughter. When I was about nineteen.'

'Where is she now?'

'She . . . she died.'

'Ah.' Hetty found herself examining the old woman closely. Had it been Jack's child? Or the invisible Mr Archibald's? The implication of those lowered eyes was of some tragedy. But, then, losing a child was always a tragedy. Hetty's heart softened. Was this why Doris didn't live where her accent revealed she had grown up – where Jack lived?

Suddenly Doris spoke rapidly in such a low tone so that Hetty could barely hear. 'He was good to me, was Jack. He was the police officer involved. Kept in touch. He's been a decent sort.' She stopped as abruptly as she had begun, then gathered the cat in her arms and rose to go. 'Enough. It's all in the past, thank God.'

At the door, Doris's manner resumed its casual friendliness. 'You're blooming, Hetty. That new figure of yours is very glamorous. Make the most if it.'

'What? Go swimming down the municipal baths, you mean?' Hetty laughed, their amity restored, yet conscious of how little she knew about her widowed neighbour.

'Nah,' said Doris. 'But I bet it's even better in the buff. Not seen you in the shop recently. Anything I could fetch you? Maybe you'd better get a move on, before the podge comes back. No offence, but it does.' She patted her own solid midriff.

'That might be excellent advice, Doris,' Hetty answered, and avoided the dig in the ribs that the old woman was attempting to make. Thomas hissed as if in disapproval. 'So if you hear strange noises from this flat one evening soon, please take no notice.'

With Doris gone, Hetty stood sunk in thought. Dates

with Norman were chaste, but had reached the stage where
his lips at farewell brushed her mouth rather than her cheek,
and lingered. Those tendony wrists had begun to appear in
her mind's eye, resting on a table. *Her* table. And the cufflinks, removed, beside them.

Time for the carrot soup and rosemary lamb routine once
more.

'No, *not* carrot soup,' Hetty said to herself. 'I can't stand
the stuff. I'll make a pâté. Norman is a serious meat-eater.
Now where did I put my recipe book?'

And this time there was no mistake.

The doorbell rang downstairs as Hetty put the finishing
touches to the cornflower blue cloth, the gleaming cutlery,
the china, the linen napkins folded like angels' wings,
wooden candlesticks and a pot of freesias. She opened the
oven door, once, to let the aroma of dinner enter the room as
tantalisingly as possible; checked her appearance in the
mirror (the same low-cut sweater that had thrilled James
and the loose, long skirt), then called down the intercom
and pressed the buzzer.

Norman stood in the hallway, dressed in the Ralph
Lauren jacket, cravat and slacks he had worn on their first
date at his club. A whiff of pleasant aftershave entered the
room before he did, with a smile on his smooth-shaven face
and a very large bunch of scarlet roses, barely opened from
bud, held before him.

'Good Lord,' Hetty said, taken aback. She had the sense
that control of the evening had promptly passed to her male
guest. As she brushed a strand of hair out of her eye, oniony
garlic came from her fingers: hastily, she hid her hands
behind her. Norman was taller than herself and had to bend

to give her a kiss. It was full on the lips, though moderate and brief. It made her own lips tingle mightily, even as she moved aside and let him in.

'Mmm, smells super,' he said appreciatively. 'Lamb? Herbs? Do I detect garlic? Perhaps I should have brought a Côtes du Rhone.' He held out a bottle, which Hetty had accepted before realising it was black label champagne.

'Yes, lamb,' Hetty said uncertainly. Arms full of the rustling roses, she led the way into the living room and with an elbow indicated glasses and an ice bucket. A bag of ice from the off-licence was in the bottom of the freezer, she told him. Norman filled the bucket and expertly, as if to the manner born, sat the wine bottle at a modish angle.

The freesias seemed limp and pathetic beside Norman's magnificent blooms. Hetty fetched her biggest vase and began to trim the stems on the draining-board, chattering lightly through the open kitchen door. He kept appearing and disappearing; she caught glimpses of him walking about, taking books from her shelves, turning over her bits of china and the glass perfume phials, examining the photos and pictures on the walls.

'I'm sorry, I don't have much.' She came back into the room with the filled vase and gestured apologetically. 'That's an Ingres poster, and that print, of course, is Titian. But you'd know that. If I had the wherewithal I'd buy modern paintings. I have a friend who is an art professor and he could advise me. But my savings went into buying this flat, so . . .' She let her voice trail off.

Norman shrugged. 'I'm not after you for your money, you know,' he said coolly. 'I have enough of my own. When my wife died it came to me.'

The roses stood proudly upright on thick stems like

crimson-coated guardsmen. Hetty placed the vase on a low table with some difficulty, for it was now heavy. Norman leaped forward to help. As he did so, water splashed on his jacket. 'Darn,' he said, and dabbed with a handkerchief. Then, 'Ah, well, no damage done.'

Hetty wondered nervously whether to offer to pay for dry-cleaning, then decided against. Anyone able to buy such a spruce garment did not need her hard-earned *sous*. Whether his wealth had come from his late wife's estate or not, he certainly looked exactly as one would expect a comfortably off widower to look.

His children, he had told her previously, were grown-up, a boy and a girl, both working overseas. He had no other ties. Although it had taken a while to get over his bereavement, he felt some obligation to himself to seek new friendships. Whenever he uttered the words 'friend' or 'friendship', he held Hetty's gaze and smiled in a distinctive slow, lop-sided way that kept his teeth hidden. It gave the impression of strength, dignity and self-reliance. It crossed Hetty's mind that the smile had been thoroughly practised in a mirror; but, then, who was she to carp, since that was exactly what she had done herself, ten minutes before his arrival?

The pâté was eaten neatly with many exclamations of praise. Norman's small teeth left uneven semicircles on the spread toast, but they did appear to be his own. Hetty mentally consigned carrot soup for ever to the dustbin. The champagne, chilled and sparkling, set off the crystal glasses liberated from Dorset. Not for the first time, Hetty allowed herself to drink more than Clarissa might have approved of, and felt herself mellowing, willing to listen to Norman's anecdotes without interruption and to laugh without pretence.

Would he be another James? Comparisons were dangerous, of course. But Norman was altogether a tidier, more
orderly person and a cleaner eater. Norman's talk avoided
politics, and he did not whinge about colleagues at work.
Indeed, Norman barely referred to his work, though he
admitted that one advantage of Tring was the ability to get
away for the weekend ahead of the traffic. Better than James,
so far, on every count. But in bed?

'Where do you like to go – what would be your ideal
weekend?' she asked, as he tucked into his meat. He had cut
off every scrap of visible fat and took only a trace of gravy,
bare dabs of mint sauce and redcurrant jelly, the two small-
est potatoes. Hetty envied him his self-discipline.

'It would have to be with a special friend,' he said gravely,
and smiled. 'I do like country-house hotels, don't you? With
a pool, for preference, and wooded grounds to stroll in. A
roaring fire for dark, cold days.'

'And a four-poster bed?' Hetty asked, in a rush, then giggled. Damn the champagne.

'And a four-poster bed,' Norman drawled. 'Of course.'

Hetty swallowed hard. Her heart was beginning to pound,
though whether with the alcohol, the warmth of the room or
that curiously enigmatic smile of Norman's, she could not
tell. She felt herself wilt under his direct examination. 'I'm
afraid I don't have one here,' she continued weakly. 'Wish I
had, but there's no room . . .'

The air between them sang. Hetty stopped breathing.
Norman folded his napkin and pressed it to his mouth. His
plate was almost empty. Then he put the knife and fork par-
allel on the dish.

'So what *do* you have in there, Hetty?' he asked softly, his
eyelashes flickering towards the closed bedroom door.

'Pudding?' she asked desperately, rising in her chair.

'Yes, maybe, but for the moment I'm full. That was a delightful meal, Hetty. Perhaps we could eat our dessert . . . afterwards?'

Hetty wanted to squeal with delight, but it was all she could do to stay on her feet. Her arms, fussing independently, started reaching for used bowls and stacking the plates. Norman rose and came round to her side of the table, took her hands firmly away from the dishes and brought them up to his mouth. He kissed her fingers one by one, wrinkling his nose in pleasure at the cooking smells. 'Mmm! Wonderful. I do enjoy real food, traditional-style, properly served. You are the woman of most men's dreams, Hetty. Who would have thought it?'

'Cooked with love, that's the difference,' Hetty murmured. If she were going to flirt, now was the time. If he wanted to discover whether her intentions were dishonourable, she would send the most accurate message possible. If he wanted bed, *this was it*.

'Ah, love. Yes, I see that. But you mustn't love me, Hetty. It's too soon.'

The rebuke was so considerate, so gentlemanly. Hetty felt her knees buckle. She held his hands tightly and raised her head to look into his eyes. 'Then simply make the most of being with me, Norman. As with the food, I'm here just for you.'

He took her in his arms, then, and kissed her long and romantically on the lips, the tastes of mint sauce and redcurrants mingling as the kisses became stronger. Hetty slid her hands under his jacket. His back was strong and wiry; even as he put his hands up to her face and buried his fingers in her hair, she could feel his tendons move under the taut skin. The sensation excited her more than she could have anticipated. Not a portly James, this one: when Norman claimed to like sport and to keep himself in trim, he was telling no more than the truth.

'I think,' Norman said gravely, 'that I should remove this jacket and hang it on the chair. It has been a nuisance all night and still seems to be getting in the way.'

Hetty stood back and took in the stripe of the shirt, the silky sheen of the cravat. Above the collar he was freshly shaved, the skin smooth as a girl's. No wayward bristle marred his nostrils or ears, no warts, no moles. No distinguishing features. On impulse she touched his hair, stroked it: her palm came away clean, no trace of oil. 'Norman, you're terrific – do you know that?' she told him, half disbelieving it herself.

'I feel we should continue this conversation elsewhere, don't you?' he murmured to her, and led her towards the closed door.

Thank heavens, Hetty said to herself as they entered, that she had not only changed the sheets, but wiped down every surface. This man was so fastidious he would notice the least speck of dust. Here the freesias came into their own: the air smelt sweet and womanly, as the women's magazines said it should. She left the main light off and switched on the bedside lamp. The rosy glow made the bedroom cosily attractive.

Norman began to undo his shirt buttons. Hetty took it as a signal that she should start to undress herself, and wondered if it would hold matters up too much if she offered him a hanger for his trousers. But he glanced about, then draped them without ceremony or comment on the back of a chair. The action was so natural yet so sensible, that Hetty

felt a thrill of anticipation: if Norman could so easily solve a
tricky problem – James had struggled out his trousers and
looked such an idiot – then her confidence was increasing by
the minute that he could deal with *anything*.

In a moment he stood unclothed before her, tall and
rangy, with a splendid, solid penis, partly erect already. It
was not huge, but the skin was dark and it was definitely not
tiny. Hetty covered her mouth with her hands and smiled to
herself at the welcome sight. His upper body was almost
hairless, his legs – the thighs and calves muscular – more so,
and faintly freckled, as his sandy colouring had suggested.
His shoulders and chest were well defined: the glow from
the lamp made him almost statuesque. Not quite
Michelangelo's David, but not far off.

'You are,' Hetty gulped, 'a fine figure of a man, Norman.'

She was standing in front of him in her bra and pants, not
daring to hold him, nor to go any further.

'And you are so special, dearest Hetty,' he said, and took
her in his arms, kissing her and undoing her bra hooks at
the same time, as nimbly and neatly as he had done everything else that evening.

And his performance, Hetty had to admit breathlessly to
herself, was everything that could be desired. He pulled back
the duvet to give a large, clear area on the bed, and pushed
her down on it, giving himself plenty of space to kneel over
her. He kissed her quite thoroughly on the mouth – 'hard'
was not the right description, for there was a soft edge to his
manner, and soft lips, which added considerably to his
appeal.

Then he kissed her nipples, and sucked them, at first so
gently that he had no effect, then more strongly, so that she
arched her back a little, and caressed his head. And

'Adorable,' he whispered, 'you are so pretty,' as he traced his knuckle over her abdomen, as if to get the measure of the firmness of her flesh. In her navel he made a circle, letting her feel the sharpness of his nail, and that made her squirm and giggle, her haunches moving under him, though as yet there was hardly any contact down there, as he carried himself over her like a canopy, blocking out the ceiling.

'May I kiss you?' he asked.

'Of course,' she whispered.

'Only some women don't like it,' he added, as if to himself. Then she realised where he meant to kiss her, and bent her knees up slightly, and spread herself open – not too widely – and at first he simply put his knuckle there, and kneaded the opening, high up, till she pushed his hand quickly the necessary half-inch downwards, till the pressure made her whimper; and then he bent his head, lifted her feet up over his shoulders and crouched down, buried his face in her crotch, and began to nibble.

'Oooh! Norman, oh, Norman,' she wailed, and could not help herself . . .

'Do you like that?' He raised his head briefly, his fingers now busy.

'Oooh! Norman,' was all she could say, feeling herself becoming heated and moist.

'Wait, don't be so impatient,' he laughed, 'I want to make sure you get there.'

And she could feel that fingernail again but this time it was deeper, circling inside her as if to enlarge the opening, while his other hand took hers, and led her to take hold of his penis and squeeze it, four, five times, till it was magnificently upright . . .

But *hard* was the word as it slid inside her, with no more

ado, until she could sense him deeply engaged in her own pulsing tissues; and *hard* was how he started to push into her, *thump, thump,* the bed and her body moving in rhythm with him.

'Ooooh!' yelped Hetty, but tonight she was not pretending. 'Oooh! Fantastic!'

'Aaah . . .' came from Norman's face, buried in a pillow beside her ear. *Thump. Thump.* She could almost hear the sperm begging to be released.

'Now, Norman, oh, Norman,' Hetty begged, and he shifted weight, gave a groan and made one more thrust, and held it, his shoulders arched above her, his face damp, close to her own.

'*Aaaah . . .*'

And he came to climax, not too fast, not too slow, not too aggressively, as if still considerate of her emotions, on this important first occasion . . .

The plop when it came was audible, and reflected the considerable size of the organ responsible. Hetty breathed rapidly, wondering whether to tell Norman that, whatever *his* dreams, he was as close to hers as any chap could be. He rolled over and even tidily adjusted his damp appendages so they should not drip on her bedding. His understated skills, the thoughtfulness they demonstrated, left her in awe. What a truly amazing man.

They lay quietly, their chests rising in gasps, laughing contentedly together. Hetty reached for the duvet and tugged it over their damp bodies. Norman's arm was round her shoulders; he kissed her once more on the mouth before lying back. 'Not bad for an old one, eh, Hetty?' he said roguishly. 'Those youngsters think they know it all, but they don't. We can still enjoy ourselves. Can't we?'

'We can,' Hetty agreed happily. Then she raised her head, her tousled hair collapsing over her forehead. 'Though on your agency application, Norman, you said you were forty-five. That's still young.'

'And your form, if I recall, said the same.' On his forehead, beads of sweat shone dimly in the light.

With a jolt Hetty recalled that he was correct. She giggled. 'Oh, well, so what? You're as young as you feel.'

He was smiling indulgently, as if both had uncovered a secret; as, indeed, they had. A shared secret, but not a dangerous one. 'And right now, dear Hetty, I feel about twenty-one. You are a great lady. Thank you: thank you *so* much.'

This seemed a remarkably elegant speech for a man who had just made love to her, Hetty reflected. Almost as if he had said it before – as if he had braced himself to remember, in a rather stilted way, to say thank you. *Yum, yum*, would have been more like it, she reckoned. But he did not seem a man who would indulge in baby-talk. James, on the other hand . . .

She stopped herself quickly. Norman was not to know that she was in the habit of bringing strange men to her bed. He, on the other hand, had been without a wife for two years; his remarks had implied, though not explicitly, that he had been celibate even before his wife's death, as her illness had progressed beyond intimacy. Her soul filled with pity and affection towards him.

In a while, when he was rested, she would reach down and see if that splendid member could be encouraged to perform once more. Afterwards, she might enquire if he would like to relax over a slice of apple cake, with cream, in bed. They could spoon morsels into each other's mouths. If some were spilled, it wouldn't matter: a blob of cream on Norman's torso could easily be dealt with . . . naughty, but *nice*. Then it might be time to brush their teeth – a new, spare toothbrush sat in its wrapper in the bathroom – and maybe slip off to sleep together.

'Oh, Norman,' Hetty said, with feeling, 'I'm so glad I joined that agency. You're exactly what I was hoping for – couldn't be better, not even in my wildest imaginings.'

He hugged her to him. 'And you, Hetty, and you.'

CHAPTER TWENTY-FOUR

Corny as Kansas

The recording for the day was coming to a satisfactory end. None of the guests had come to blows, the audience had been of a respectable size, wide awake and relatively enthusiastic, and the subject – breast implants – just within the boundaries of family viewing. Rosa had drawn the line at implants in other parts of the anatomy, despite one male guest offering to demonstrate his for free. *Tell Me All* was recommissioned for a third series; for its crew, the show had settled into a steady routine.

'Thank heavens that's done. Another useful contribution to parish funds. And since they have decided to thrust a young curate on me, we'll need every penny.' Father Roger ran a finger round inside his clerical collar: the studio was hot.

'When's he coming?' Hetty asked, recalling his disapproval.

'Next month. Not appointed yet. He could be a she – lots

of women ordinands are job-seeking at present. I can't imagine anything worse.'

'Don't be such a rotten old misogynist. She could be gorgeous. You might fall in love, Roger.'

'Not if I can help it.' The priest shook his head. 'Talking of which, Hetty, dear girl, tell me what's going on. You are positively glowing.'

'Am I?' Hetty tried to appear nonchalant.

'Yes. Whenever you think no one's watching, your face settles into a faraway little smile. That has not always been the case in our acquaintance. There have been moments when you have appeared very down. No longer.' He waited.

'Life has certainly taken on a rosier tinge,' Hetty admitted carefully. She pretended to riffle through the production sheets on her clipboard to avoid his gaze.

'Aha! At last. *You're* the one in love.'

'Don't tease. Anyway, what if I am?'

'You've met someone.'

'Maybe.'

'Name?'

'His name, if it bothers you so much, is Norman. He is a widower, he has his own business, he's charming and respectable. Anything else?'

Father Roger picked up Hetty's hand, raised it to his lips and kissed it dramatically. 'Your eyes say everything, my dear. I'm so pleased for you. And will you be booking nuptials? I can recommend St Veronica's . . .'

Hetty pulled her hand away. 'No! Anyway, you couldn't marry people like us in church – I'm divorced.'

Father Roger pressed a finger to the side of his nose. 'It can be arranged. But only for those entwinings of which I approve. The necessaries are dispatched at the register office, then you stroll through the park, trailing rose petals from your bouquet as you go, straight to the altar where I indulge you both with the *lushest* of blessings.' He warmed to his theme. 'Many second-time-rounders say they adore walking up the aisle together: it feels as if they are entering matrimony hand-in-hand, instead of the unequal partnership implicit in the traditional service . . .'

'I do not need the spiel, Roger.' Hetty tried to retain her dignity. 'I met Norman only a few weeks ago. He is – *nice*, and we are enjoying each other's company. Talk of marriage is seriously premature.'

'But not impossible?' Roger winked.

'I don't know,' said Hetty, more sombrely. 'Once bitten, twice shy, perhaps. Or maybe the established way – couple-dom – isn't for me any more. I do like my current arrangements, that's not pretence.'

'But this Norman might do the trick. You have hope written all over your face, dear girl. That's splendid. And do I take it that this is a full, mature relationship?'

'Roger!' Hetty giggled.

'The days when a girl was a virgin for her wedding night vanished years ago. Doesn't apply to you, anyhow. But you do need to winkle out any strange habits he may have, Hetty. Not much use discovering them later. Suppose you find he likes to chain his women to the bed?'

Hetty gave the priest a playful dig. 'I think I might get quite excited, Roger. Some of us positively like sex. Now, push off and let me be. If there are any significant developments – *if*, I say – you'll be the first to know. Will that do?'

Did it show that much? Roger was the shrewdest person on the set and accustomed to extracting revelations from the merest shred of body language. He could be trusted to be discreet. Hetty had always felt that, if she had a problem, he would be easy to turn to, and committed by his calling and vows to secrecy. Rosa was another matter. Had Hetty dropped any hints, the information would have been broadcast in no time, probably by the producer announcing it gaily at the next staff meeting.

In fact she ached to tell everyone. It was as much as she could do to maintain a calm exterior, to go about her daily activities as if nothing new had occurred. Concentrating on other people's conversation had become difficult. It was easier to withdraw a bit, to spend more time by herself, not least to indulge in repeated bouts of daydreaming.

Was it entirely a fantasy? Was she simply a lonely woman, desperate for undivided attention, with the unsatisfactory episodes of Al and James behind her, creating out of thin air the relationship that would make her life complete? She forced herself to reflect, yet could come up with no negatives. He was, so far, everything he had declared himself to be: with the one exception that his age was higher than he had claimed on the form. That peccadillo she regarded with affection. Every other detail was spot on. Indeed, he was far better than she could have conjured up by herself.

It was early days yet: her common sense had not left her entirely. Time enough, if and when he made a declaration of love, to match it with one as heartfelt of her own.

Meanwhile, the refrains that ran through her brain seemed to be taking over.

'I'm as corny as Kansas in August . . .' It was a Friday afternoon. Hetty was clearing out kitchen cupboards, J-cloth in hand, humming as tins and half-empty packets gathered behind her in untidy ziggurats. 'High as a flag on the fourth of July . . .'

The bell rang. Hetty got up off her knees and went to the door.

'Oh, God, Hetty, have you any milk?'

'Hello, Annabel. Milk? I think so. You make it sound like a matter of life and death.'

'It is. My parents are about to descend and the first thing they'll want is a cup of tea.'

Hetty motioned the young woman inside and headed for the fridge. 'You're welcome, but what's wrong with the min-imarket at the garage?'

'No time! They'll be arriving any second. If they ring the bell and I'm not there, they'll go spare. Thanks, Hetty, you're a pal.'

Annabel was dressed, as unflatteringly as ever, in a black cropped T-shirt that showed her midriff, and leggings that cut into her calves. The diet had either been abandoned or had not sufficed, though Hetty had seen her still trudging across the common. But agonies about her size no longer seemed to trouble the girl. Perhaps Annabel had become resigned to a larger than average fate.

At Hetty's door Annabel hesitated. 'Het, would you like to come in? They're not too bad. And I never know what to say to them.'

'You sure that's okay?'

'Course. Why not? Leave it about twenty minutes or so. Then we'll have gone through whether I'm eating my greens or sleeping properly and changing my sheets. I've never grown up as far as my mother is concerned. My dad says nothing but just sits there.'

Hetty chuckled. 'You'll always be a child to your parents.'

Annabel shifted the carton of milk from one hand to the other. 'Is it true the other way round? I s'pose it is. They'll always be parents to me. Old and sexless and interfering. Not real people, if you see what I mean. But I do love them. Or I try.'

Hetty recalled Sally's initial wariness of her mother's altered state, and how her son Peter had slid away from the family circle and never enquired about her welfare, as if it could be taken for granted. 'Families were ever thus,' she said. 'I'll come.'

It would be a useful distraction. Not merely from the chores, which were not pressing, though they seemed to answer a resurgent nest-building instinct; but from those jumbled crazy noises inside her head, the floating pictures of smooth-shaven cheeks and a slight, closed smile, and of twinkling male eyes that seemed to be laughing both at and with her at the same moment.

With Roger she had dissembled, but could not deny that something significant was under way. She had tried to conceal her own bewilderment; it was important to appear cool about the whole thing. But as she had uttered his name, her voice had trembled. She could not conceal how precious that name was becoming to her.

Norman. Norman with his Turnbull and Asser shirt, that neat pinstripe. Norman with his cravat, or tie, of silk in a Paisley swirl. Norman eating, the irregular pattern made by his teeth in a piece of toast, to be memorised and marvelled over. Norman's hands, the narrow wrists with the veins outstanding, taut and elegant. Norman with his shirt off, the light from the bedside lamp slanting across his freckled shoulders. Norman –

Norman . . .

In her mind, crowding out everything else, an invasion was taking place. Norman walking down a street beside her, talking, glancing at her and nodding when she made some comment as if it were the most intelligent remark in the whole universe . . . his sloping handwriting on a card, thanking her for another dinner 'and a wonderful few hours', as if manners must not be forgotten amid the joy and passion . . . the cadence of his voice, the thrill of his fingers . . . Norman's presence when she awoke in darkness, not wanting to return to sleep for fear of losing each detail of him at her side, breathing slowly, his warmth filling the bed . . . the indentation of his head on the pillow, the lingering aftershave in the bathroom . . . the single curly hair in the corner of the shower, picked up and treasured and hidden away . . .

'If this is love, then it's amazing,' Hetty sang to herself blithely as she quickly bundled rice, flour and tinned tomatoes back on to their respective shelves. A packet of Jaffa cakes just within their sell-by date would do for Annabel's. 'Second spring. Better? What was it like before? Can I remember?'

Not the same. With Stephen it had been a delicious whirl, naturally, but against an entirely different backdrop. Hetty had then seen herself as, and had been, a woman of her time. In her twenties she had hoped to meet a marvellous chap, fall headlong, marry, have babies, run a home and live happily every after. All but the last bit had happened, more or less successfully. Her preoccupations, in those days, had been the ponderous questions – is this a reliable person? Will he make a good father? Will he be sensible with money? Do we have enough in common to carry us through an entire lifetime? She had forced herself to be objective, however cynical it might have felt. To her mother she had put a solemn assessment the day of the engagement: that Stephen, tall, handsome, and such fun to be with, was also a worthy man whose values were much the same as her own, who would be, all things considered, an ideal husband.

With Norman – or, indeed, with any new male friend – other criteria applied, far more superficial. She was not seeking a father to her children: if a new date hated children, that would be a black mark (since it implied a selfish or immature nature), but in a theatre escort it didn't *matter*. She was not yearning for a home or an income; these she could provide alone. Nor, more subtly, was she in search of an identity. In the difficult months since leaving Dorset, she had established one for herself, more emphatically than ever during her marriage. Indeed, if a man, whoever he was, asked her to abandon her single status, her flat, her independence, to rely upon him for everything as before, as a wife or a virtual wife, her reaction would have been unclear.

But Roger had put his finger on it. Suppose the name in the frame were Norman's?

Except that no such possibility had escaped Norman's lips. He was the soul of discretion, of controlled, manly dignity, as if he sensed that she should not be pushed too far, too fast. Moreover he was witty, charming and considerate: his every word, every movement were to be cherished. And he was *excellent* in bed, though she did not intend to pander to Roger or anyone else with the delicious evidence.

'I'm in love, I'm in love, I'm in love with a wonderful guy . . .' she hummed, as she washed and dried her hands and rubbed Nivea into the skin. Chapped fingers and cracked cuticles were not the stuff of middle-aged romance.

Then, Jaffa Cakes in hand, she crossed the landing.

*

The atmosphere in flat four, as Annabel had foretold, was stilted, baffled even, but not hostile.

The parents, as Hetty could not help labelling them, were seated in the two armchairs. Spread out, rather, for both were overweight: Annabel's struggles evidently stemmed from her genes. On the coffee table were a lidless pot of tea, three mugs, an open box of sugar cubes, a single spoon and Hetty's milk, still in its carton. Both parents were shorter than their daughter, the father in a navy suit, the mother in grey tweed. From previous mentions Hetty had gleaned that they were in trade somewhere on the Essex coast. Annabel had once spoken with blunt loathing of Billericay.

Annabel sat on the sofa, right in the middle, as if the space each side conferred some protection. Her hands were pressed nervously together between the fat, black-legginged thighs. As Hetty knocked and pushed open the unlatched door, she jumped up with every sign of relief. 'Hetty, my neighbour,' she said. Hands were shaken.

'Good Lord!' Annabel's father said. 'You're quite old!'

Hetty's mouth dropped open. She shut it quickly. 'Pardon?'

'Harry!' Mrs Leighton was flustered. She prodded her husband. 'She's not old. She's – she's the same age as us. Aren't you?'

'I've no idea,' Hetty murmured, trying not to laugh. Annabel's face was aghast.

'I meant,' Mr Leighton hissed to his wife, 'I guessed Annabel's friend would be – you know, about thirty. This one isn't.'

'That is undeniable,' Hetty answered, as she handed over the biscuits. She perched on the arm of the sofa. 'But why should you have thought otherwise?'

'But how can you be *friends*?' It was Mrs Leighton's turn. The curl of disapproval in her voice made Hetty wince. 'You surely can't like their music. Or their clothes. Or approve of what they get up to. Do you even understand what they *say*?'

'I get it,' Mr Leighton hissed behind his hand. 'She's an ageing hippie.' He pulled back his shoulders and challenged Hetty, but his manner was not cold. Indeed, he was examining her with much more interest. 'That's right, isn't it? Flower-power and such. Beads and caftans. It's coming back. Is that why you're here?'

'No, no.' Hetty waved a hand politely. This couple conceivably intended no offence, so she would take none. 'Tea, I think you said, Annabel? Please. A mug is fine.'

'I gave her china cups and saucers when she moved in, but where they are now?' Mrs Leighton complained.

'Things get broken,' Hetty said soothingly, aware that one surviving cup was in the bathroom cupboard as storage for condoms. The saucers served mainly as ashtrays.

'Flower-power,' Mr Leighton insisted. His eyes were shining. 'Free love. Beatles and stuff. Was that in your youth?'

'Just about,' Hetty smiled, 'but I was never a hippie. I didn't believe in it. Conventional, me, then. Not any more, that's true.'

'But you can't possibly *like* living here?' Mrs Leighton pushed away her tea with a grimace.

'Yes,' Hetty said firmly. 'I have everything I want. Including the friendship of your daughter and her flatmates, who are splendid young women.'

'Well, I suppose if you've no one else . . .' Mrs Leighton commented, dubious.

'Oh, but I have.' The refrain of the song cut through her

brain. 'I have my own family, and a job I'm lucky to have, and a wonderful guy. Life's great. Believe me.'

Mrs Leighton sniffed. Mr Leighton was watching her with renewed intensity.

'And one great advantage, I should add,' Hetty continued, 'is that I've got to know these young people, and it's made me young again. Given me a fresh outlook. Brought me closer to my own daughter, too. It's too easy to regard the next generation as useless simply because they dance to different music, say, or wear outlandish clothes.'

'It's not as if she hasn't the money,' Mrs Leighton grumbled. 'We give her an allowance on top of what she earns. She could dress beautifully if she wanted.'

Hetty patted Annabel's shoulder. 'She *is* beautiful. You should be proud of her.'

This produced astonished silence from both parents, and an audible sigh from Annabel, who pulled Hetty close and whispered in her ear, 'That's what Nick says. Nicholas – the writer.'

Annabel was blushing furiously, her face turned away from her parents. 'You remember, Het. From your programme. Don't let on.'

The conversation continued, endlessly repeating the pattern. One parent or the other would make a disparaging remark, to be countered by a sincere compliment from Hetty. Meanwhile Mr Leighton was smiling at her a mite too obviously, that cheesy smile she had seen on studio guests who had something to sell: themselves. It came to Hetty that he had her address. She wondered what he might do with it.

Eventually she tired of the game, rose to leave and shook hands formally. Annabel followed her to the landing.

'Thanks, Het, you're a darling. They won't go on calling this a den of sin and prostitution now they've met you.'

'Glad to help,' Hetty replied. She decided not to mention the father's odd behaviour, nor to be inquisitive about Nicholas. 'I don't get it – why shouldn't an older person make genuine friends across the generations? Up as well as down, come to that. Is there a law against it?'

'It just isn't done. My parents do their socialising with people exactly like themselves. Same age, same class. Anybody else, they're suspicious of and avoid like the plague.'

'Daft, I call it,' said Hetty robustly. 'There's a big gap between feeling comfortable with people your own status and generation and being terrified of anyone else. But I can see your dilemma. Don't take too much notice of them, Annabel. You're doing fine. And I bet Nicholas – Nick – says so too.' And with that she gave the girl a supportive hug, and returned to her own flat.

Her routine interrupted by the tea party, Hetty felt restless. Norman was away at a conference till Monday so was unavailable. Sally was rostered to the New York flights and would be sleeping between shifts near 43rd Street, with or without Erik, to whom she had not referred for ages. Her mother was at a Rotary Charter night with the Colonel, another opportunity to dress up. Rosa and the crew would have dispersed for the weekend. Hetty had made no plans other than finishing off the cupboards and watching some television. It was a bit late to arrange anything more substantial.

After some thought she decided to walk down to Swallow House, the old people's home. She had taken to dropping in to see the Professor, or sometimes Phyllis or Moira if he were not free, and would leave goodwill messages for Clarissa's aunt.

But the assistant matron informed her that the residents she wanted were away on an outing and were not expected back for another hour yet.

'The Professor too?' Hetty was surprised. He was usually contemptuous of such events.

'They've gone to a stately home near Aylesbury. Waddesdon Manor, it's called. He was quite keen – it belonged to the Rothschilds and has tapestries and paintings and such. So he got himself carried on board the coach. We do take the disabled ones as well, if they want to come.' She shrugged. 'He'll probably make them late. The others'll have to sit in the tearoom while he's badgering the curator.'

'Good for him,' said Hetty. 'I won't wait.' She scribbled a note for his pigeonhole, and one for Millie, Clarissa's aunt, fastened her coat and went outside once more.

The restlessness continued. She was in the fresh autumn air, and did not need to return home. Alone this evening in the flat, she sensed she might become a little gloomy, and miss Norman more than was wise. Then it came to her. 'I fancy a movie. Something silly.' She returned to the lodge of the home, borrowed an evening paper, checked the listings and made a choice.

Soon she was on the dirty, clacking tube, then pushing through West End crowds towards the Leicester Square Odeon and the latest special effects sci-fi blockbuster. It was the sort Norman liked, so she could pretend he was with her, at least.

The square was alive and buzzing. Her spirits lifted. Along Cranbourne Street the restaurants and cafés were noisy and full, their tables spilling out into the street. The pizza stand on the corner was half hidden by a gaggle of tourists trying to eat the slippery triangles, mobile in their paper napkins. The smell of the food wafted through the air, tangy and tempting, and made her feel hungry. The carillon at the Swiss Centre was clanging off-key as the hour struck, observed by a flock of tiny Japanese women who twittered like exotic finches. A row of portrait artists and caricaturists touted for customers. Hetty paused to watch as a plain girl was transformed into a pin-up, to the obvious delight of her boyfriend. The background music of pan-pipes, played by a blanketed group of Peruvian musicians, their black hats pulled well down over their ears, added a haunting, international air. They could all have been anywhere, in a dozen cities in the world: Bogotá or Budapest or Bangkok. But this was London, on a Friday night in September. The garish flashing lights above their heads announcing the latest entertainments were like magnets attracting young and old.

Pity Norman wasn't here. He would be impressed, when she told him about it next week, that she had chosen his kind of film. Hetty realised with a jolt that her tastes were changing quite substantially, becoming much more adventurous. That made her feel even more intrepid, and cheered that she was using her free time well.

She was early, so could wait in the queue, purse in hand; if this house was full, she would buy a ticket for the next and eat a pizza or a bowl of spaghetti in the meantime.

The queue was about six deep. Immediately in front of her were two towering youths in overlarge black jackets. Hetty, cursing her lack of height, craned at the window. The set of a man's shoulders further up struck her as familiar. Who was that? A tallish man, his coat collar partly turned

up, obscuring his colouring. A woman hung on his right
arm; they were talking animatedly. The man held up his
other hand to point at the booth and pulled off a leather
glove. A gold wedding band glinted on the third finger.

How splendid that was, to see a man out with his wife. A
married couple, who did not have to debate who to go with,
who did not have to pick up the phone book or trawl hopefully through messages from friends. A pang touched her.
Though she and Stephen had never been to this particular
cinema themselves, they had occasionally gone to a film.
Infrequently, when there was nothing on TV, or when no
one was coming for dinner, when the children were away.
Just to relax. The two of them. It was Stephen who decided
what they saw: westerns, or heist movies, mostly straight-
forward Hollywood. He disdained her then preference for
what he dubbed 'women's films'. He would be astonished if
he could see her here on her own.

The man ahead turned slightly, as if to check how many
others were waiting behind. The pair were at the window
now. The neon lights round the booths caught the edge of
his nose, flickered on the whites of his eyes and made them
greenish.

Hetty gave a stifled little cry and ducked down behind the
two youths. She had recognised the loving husband, the
man with the wedding ring. And she desperately did not
want him to recognise her, or to know that she had seen
him.

For it was a face she knew too well, and had not expected
to see within a hundred miles. And not with such a companion as the woman on his arm.

It was Norman.

CHAPTER TWENTY-FIVE

Incantation

Rosa, Sally, Doris and Hetty filled their glasses with Oddbins Californian Syrah and raised them in unison.

'To men!' Rosa ground out. 'May they rot in hell.'

'To men!' The quartet downed their glasses in a gulp.

'Bastards,' growled Sally. 'I can't believe he did that to you, Mum. What a *cunt*.'

'There's another bottle. Don't stint yourselves, girls.' Hetty pointed limply towards the kitchen. 'And some sandwiches. Smoked salmon. You are so sweet to come.'

The curtains were drawn, the main lights dimmed. A fat wax candle emitted a perfumed flame; on top of the television set, thin smoke snaked from three joss-sticks in a brass pot, brought by Rosa. Sally, Rosa and Hetty were dressed in midnight shades, though there had been no collaboration beforehand. Doris wore a vividly coloured silk housecoat and a purple turban. The effect, which had not gone unnoticed, was of a coven of witches in session.

'You sounded so miserable on the phone,' Sally commiserated.

'And you were mooning about on the set, and no one could get any sense out of you,' Rosa added.

'And I saw you coming in. Crushed, you were.' Doris rose in a flurry of vibrant silk, fetched the sandwiches, nibbles, plates and napkins and set them down on the small tables. 'Post-mortem time. First – you certain it was him?'

Hetty snuffled. 'It was him. I've never met the lady, but they were obviously close. If they weren't a happily married couple, they were giving a realistic imitation of one.'

'Bastard,' said Sally again, with feeling. The others raised their glasses in agreement.

'They *aren't* a happily married couple, or he wouldn't have been seeing *you*,' Rosa pointed out. 'He wouldn't have been anywhere near the agency. Heavens, he could be seeing a new squeeze every week.' She caught Hetty's stricken face. 'Sorry, Het.'

'It's the wife you have to feel sorry for, too,' Doris said. 'He's philandering around, deceiving decent women, while she's in blithe ignorance.'

'Maybe she knows?' Sally wondered.

'Wives never know,' Hetty said sadly. 'At least, I didn't, when your father was – out and about. Never had a clue. The curse of the credulous married.'

'Cursing's too good for him,' Rosa asserted. 'It'd serve him right if he got a dose of his own medicine.' She raised her voice and glass. 'May he be cuckolded by his wife with the village idiot. No, with the entire rugby club. In public. May his thingy drop off. May it sprout evil-smelling protuberances –'

'It *is* an evil-smelling protuberance,' said Hetty, laughing despite herself. 'Stop it, Rosa. I don't wish him any harm. I just wish our paths had never crossed.'

'Have you confronted him?' Doris asked. 'I mean, you could be mistaken. It might have been his sister, p'raps.'

'He was wearing a wedding ring,' Hetty reminded her. 'I haven't seen that before. Plus he had his arm round her waist. And, no, I haven't had the chance to speak to him yet. *He*'s supposed to be calling *me*. I'm not sure what I'll say.'

'You could ring him. Seize the high ground. Play hell.'

'I could have phoned his office, but what's the point? Home must be in Tring, or nearby. It wouldn't be difficult to find his private number, I suppose, but what if his wife answered? Oh dear.' Hetty picked up a sandwich and took melancholy bites.

'It isn't your fault,' Rosa said, kindly. '*You*'re smashing, Het. You're the tops.' She raised her glass in salute.

'You're the tops – you're the Coliseum,' Sally began to sing.

Doris and Rosa took up the refrain, three female voices in crackling discord like cats on a moonlit rooftop, till suddenly Rosa cried, 'I remember the naughty version – rhymes with Dr Seuss, I think. Wait . . . wait – "You're the tops – you're the breasts of Venus, you're King Kong's penis, you're self-abuse!"'

Hetty squealed with laughter. 'God, where did you hear that?'

'Oh, a chap I used to sleep with. Worked in musicals. Told us the great maestro had such a dirty mind,' Rosa explained airily.

'King Kong's penis I'm *not* after,' Hetty added. Then, with a hiccup, 'Heavens, did I really say that?'

'"Sigh no more, ladies, sigh no more. Men were deceivers

ever".' Rosa's cheeks were flushed. She had been to the pub and had started drinking earlier than the others.

'They're *not* all the same. I don't believe it – I won't believe it,' said Hetty. 'There must be loads of honourable, respectable, sexy men out there. Nearly half of marriages end in failure, so that's millions of free blokes, isn't it? They can't *all* be bastards.'

'Men think differently.' Doris's turban was tilted to a rakish angle. The earrings were silver and amber and flashed in the candles' flicker. She had brought a bottle of Scotch, 'for later'. 'They see themselves as the hunters. We women, we're the quarry. We're expected to run, of course, and not let ourselves get caught too easily. But they get a taste for the chase, and can't stop.'

'Americans write books on those themes. *Men Are From Mars, Women Are From Venus*, can you credit it? Very non-PC, but they sell by the bucketload.' Rosa twirled a cheese stick. 'Men like it the other way round as well. They adore being chased. Getting caught is another matter.'

'In my generation, it's the females who do the chasing,' Sally joined in. 'Girls are expected to be forward – the blokes have to pretend to be shy. It can be a pain – you can never tell if they're interested, or not.'

'Look at their trousers,' suggested Rosa wickedly.

'*Staying* caught is today's problem,' said Doris. 'Nobody wants to stick with it any more, see. Come the rows, and they're off, squealing that it's not working. In the old days they tried harder, I reckon.'

'Those women had no choice,' Rosa reminded her. 'No child-care, no money. Nowhere to go if the husband was violent – no refuges. The police wouldn't interfere in domestic disputes. I mean, where would you go then, if your

husband started knocking you about? I've made programmes about *that*.'

Doris seemed about to say more, then coughed and
glanced away. The second bottle was empty, the plates
denuded but for a few crumbs. The air was fuggy and
sweetly scented. Rosa pulled out a tobacco tin and, with a
glance at her hostess, rolled a joint which she offered
around. Sally and Doris accepted; Hetty refused politely.

'You could say we four are the representatives of the new
order,' Hetty mused. 'Four women, single. Earning our own
living, living alone. Two never married, one widowed, one
divorced. Reasonably content, most of the while, aren't we?
We like men. Preferably men who are capable in bed, and
lively talkers, and genuine. We're not hostile to them, in
any way: I don't regard myself as some militant anti-male
feminist. We live in hope. But where are they?'

As if in response, the phone rang. The four women sat
transfixed. Sally nudged her mother. 'Go on, answer it.'

It rang four times before Hetty, clutching her wine-glass,
picked it up. 'Hello?'

'Hello, Hetty. How are you this evening? I missed you this
weekend.'

Hetty pushed the speakerphone button and Norman's
voice floated out into the room.

'Oh, hi, Norman. Did the conference go well?'

'I loathe those events. Too much to drink, terrible company, and the speakers are overrated or tell dirty jokes. I'd
much rather have been with you, Hetty.'

'Ye-e-es. Well, I kept myself busy. I went to a movie in
town.'

'Really? I'm delighted. What did you see?'

'I went to see *The Mummy*, Norman. And so did you.'

'Er . . . what do you mean? I was in Manchester.'

'I think not. You were a short step ahead of me in the queue, Norman. And you had your wife with you. I saw you both.'

Behind her the women began to cat-call angrily.

He began to bluster, his voice rising and sharp. 'Who's that you've got with you, Hetty?'

'Friends,' she said. 'Better friends than you've proved to be, Norman. Why did you do it?'

'Because he's a bastard,' said Rosa, loudly enough for her voice to carry.

'*Bastard!*' they shouted.

The line went dead.

Hetty stood dolefully, her eyes filling with tears, until Sally came and helped her back to her seat. Doris uncapped the whisky and poured measures for those whose glasses were empty. Rosa set about rolling a second joint.

'Face it, most men our age are closer to the grave than to the altar.' Rosa the pundit blew a wobbly smoke ring. 'You can't blame them for wanting to play the field.'

'But I *do*.' Hetty was stubborn. 'Why should their behaviour deteriorate like that?' She pointed to the mute phone. 'Age is no excuse. Am I truly to be driven to the conclusion that, leaving aside those guys who are gay or too decrepit to consider or already hitched, nobody worthwhile is left? I don't believe it. I *won't*.'

'It makes chasing men a hiding to nothing,' Sally continued gloomily. She toked on the joint and handed it to Doris. 'What will you do, Mum?'

'Play hell with the agency,' said Hetty savagely. 'Ask for some more names – and this time, do some checking of my own before I jump in deep. It's been a salutary lesson.'

The phone rang again, shrilly. Four faces turned to it in surprise. Was it Norman, ringing back to cajole, or to apologise? Hetty hesitated as if loath to suffer another confrontation, then shrugged and picked it up.

'Hello? Is that Hetty Clarkson?'

'Yes . . .'

'Splendid. Then I've got the right number. I had to try you through directory enquiries.' The voice was gravelly and sounded boisterous but nervous, as if its owner was used to giving orders but found himself in unfamiliar circumstances. Hetty turned her back on her guests and tried to concentrate.

'Who is this, please?'

'Ah. Yes. Do you remember, we met?'

Hetty removed the phone from her ear and gazed at it, as if it might carry an image of the caller. 'We met? I'm sorry, I'm being stupid tonight. Where was that?'

There was a roguish giggle. 'Across the corridor. In flat four. You came to tea. This is Harry Leighton.'

Hetty did not reply.

'Hetty? Harry Leighton. Annabel's father.'

'Yes, I'm with you now. How can I help you, Mr Leighton? As far as I know, Annabel's fine.'

'Ah, it wasn't Annabel I wanted to talk about, Hetty. It was you. I was very impressed with you when we met. Very impressed . . .'

Hetty waited, a frown creasing her brows, her lips pursed.

'. . . and I was wondering – would you like to meet for a drink sometime? Next week, perhaps? Of course, you wouldn't have to mention it to Annabel, so how about it?'

Hetty forced herself to speak. 'Thank you. That's very kind. But . . .'

'You're such an attractive woman. I haven't been able to stop thinking about you. Only a drink, heh?'

'No,' Hetty said briskly. And she put the phone down quickly.

'Someone else you want cursed?' asked Doris, eyes bright.

Hetty shook her head. 'Another bastard. At the moment, they outnumber the good guys.' She picked up the whisky glass. 'A toast, girls. To us. And sod the bastards.'

'To us!'

The discussion rolled on, with Hetty revealing the identity of the second caller and swearing her companions to secrecy. Minicabs were summoned for Rosa and Sally: as they waited for their arrival they reassured her that the strange invitation had a positive tinge.

'How long did you spend with Annabel's family?' Rosa asked.

'About half an hour. No more.'

'You made a big impact, that's clear. You must have looked nice.'

Hetty laughed. Her head was woozy, but with Rosa, Sally and Doris she felt utterly secure. 'I'd been cleaning out cupboards. No makeup. I was a fright.'

'No, you can't have been. You're fit and well, you look ten years younger than you used to.' Sally's speech was slurred.

'Father Roger said I glowed. That's because I was in love. Or thought I was.' Hetty was rueful.

'You should celebrate your lucky escape,' Doris advised briskly. 'You could have got badly stung. Suppose he'd started borrowing money from you? Or whatever. Fate worse than death.' She hauled her squat body from the depths of the armchair. 'Celebrate. Your freedom. There are worse things than a bad marriage, believe me.' Her face was suddenly sad, as it had been earlier in the evening, but she said no more.

'How'm I to celebrate, Doris? Or advertise my availability? Should I put a poster in the window – "Men Wanted"?'

'Dorothy Parker used to keep a "Gentlemen" sign she'd lifted from a public loo,' Rosa said. 'Whenever she was feeling horny, she'd hang it on the outside of her door.'

'Have a party,' said Sally decisively. 'Yes, that's it. It's almost a year since you moved in here. You've lots of pals now, Mum. People you'd never have met before. Far more interesting than Dad's lot. You had a house-warming and I was a bit snide about it. I'm sorry now. Time for another.'

'Hmm. I might do that. Would you all come?'

'Yes!' they chorused, as the doorbell shrilled for the taxis. And so it was settled.

Girl-power was fine as far as it went, but Hetty's mood, albeit defiant, did not lift in the next few days. So much had been planned around Norman and his habits that her diary was immediately a collection of blank spaces. She had not been to the theatre with Markus and Christian for months and had no idea what they might be up to. Companionable invitations from the crew to join them in the pub had been declined till they were no longer made. Father Roger she saw on the set and nowhere else, despite his appeals to attend the many special services he dreamed up to attract worshippers. Her bike-riding was entirely solitary and involved no socialising. She had no further need to attend the slimming class. Even the continued presence of Brian, the *Big Issue* seller, at the tube station, had had no impact; instead of buying him coffee, she had hurried past and barely acknowledged him.

'I was sliding back into being a wife,' she told the mirror in her bedroom, as she towelled her hair dry one morning. 'Reverting to type. I am so furious with myself.'

'Amazing how fast it can occur,' the mirror sympathised.

'Becoming narrow and self-satisfied again,' commented the mousse dispenser.

'Once more the living shadow of a male, no longer yourself,' hummed the hair-dryer.

'And yet . . .' Hetty paused, dryer in hand. 'It was great while it lasted. Haven't felt as light-hearted in years.'

'You're not *absolutely* devastated, are you?' The mirror had a mocking tone.

'I was, when I saw the two of them together.' Hetty took several breaths and let the air out of her nose in a slow snort. 'Felt a complete dope for being taken in so easily. That can only have been because I *wanted* to be taken in.'

'"You used to be so wise . . ."' the hairbrush was singing gently.

'I did not have stars in my eyes. Stop giving me that old Broadway hooey,' Hetty chided. 'But I did start off after the divorce with a pile of resolutions I've forgotten. Like valuing people for what they are, not as sex objects. Like not wishing to be regarded myself as a sex object. That didn't last, did it? Like not treating the world as a collection of men on the one hand and women on the other, but as individuals . . .'

'Like not chasing men, because it was undignified.' The mirror again. It appeared to be the leader of this talkative troupe.

'Stand up straight, Hetty,' urged the wardrobe, as it handed over her woollen skirt and a new sweater, a gift from Sally. 'Face the outside world with confidence.'

'At least they're chasing me now.' Hetty flicked back her

hair and applied some lipstick. 'An improvement on being unchaseable. There, how's that?'

'Tasty,' complimented the mirror, and shivered in emphasis. 'Very tasty. You'll do.'

The Professor, she was informed, had not been well in the couple of weeks since her last visit. Unusually, he was not in his wheelchair in the lounge, or in the quiet corner that passed for a library. Given his determination to live in as civilised a manner as possible, it was early for him to have retired to bed. Hetty began to be alarmed.

'I think you'll find him changed, Mrs Clarkson,' said the assistant matron, when she enquired. 'He is over eighty, you know, though he won't admit it. Getting frail. We think he's had another stroke. Affected his speech, mostly.'

'Shouldn't he be in hospital?'

'He was for a couple of days, but wanted to come out. Stroke patients get distressed in unfamiliar surroundings, especially an open ward. And there's not much can be done for them. They'll have more little episodes, each one more disabling, till when the end comes, it's a blessing . . . Anyway, he's made it clear he'd rather not be moved. Doesn't want to be parted from his precious pictures.'

'Can I go up and see him?'

'Of course. I'm sure he'd like that. He's had his tea served. Don't tire him, will you?'

Hetty felt anxious as she went up in the lift. She had brought the catalogue of the exhibition of Rembrandt self-portraits at the National Gallery and had intended to enthuse and seek his opinion. Instead she feared he might be morose or depressed. Her heart sank as the floor number appeared and the lift doors swished open. She found his room, tapped on the door and cautiously let herself in.

'Herro, Hetty,' he said. *Hello*.

He was in bed, dozing, his upper body propped up on pillows. The scrawny neck emerged from pyjamas of magenta silk, louche and incongruous, a tuft of white fuzz at the neck. His long silvery hair was sticking up and needed brushing. Whoever had shaved him that morning had done it perfunctorily, and left bristles under his nose.

In his left hand rested the remote control for the mini-console; Glenn Gould was playing the Goldberg Variations. With a struggle he pressed the button to reduce the volume, though Hetty indicated no objection. His right hand trembled, lifted an inch but no more. The fingers that had painted with such verve were white and useless.

'Carn hear you,' he said, and attempted to smile. *Can't hear you, with that music on*. He was choosing his words with economy.

The room was not quite in darkness: a light over the bed made a halo round his head. More than ever it resembled an Aladdin's cave of vivid imagery. On each wall the prints and paintings made a jumbled and magical display, crowding each other out – were there more, perhaps, than before? Maybe he had had a few more hung, or she had not taken them in on previous visits. A still-life appeared to float in suspended animation, the landscapes were windows to a distant, beckoning horizon. The little bronze dancer on her pedestal seemed about to pirouette. Most striking, the many nudes were so real she could almost hear them breathing: it was as if the women were in the room, eyes lowered modestly or wide in challenge, flesh gleaming and ghostly, in reverent attendance, with Hetty, at the bedside of the man who had adored them.

On the bed-top table sat the tray with the remains of tea. Hetty removed it, put it on the floor outside the room for collection and returned to sit with him, leaving her coat on a chair.

She opened the catalogue on the bed where the Professor could examine it. 'I thought you'd like this. You've made me examine art with such curiosity. The exhibition was amazing. Rembrandt started off a cocky youth, posturing and eager, and ended up, quite plainly, dreadfully battered and much wiser. The paintings of himself as an old man are almost unbearable. Wonderful stuff.' She turned the pages.

'Ay am . . . mee.' *Same as me.*

'Same as us all.' Hetty was quiet. 'Professor, do we get wiser as we get older? Or do we only learn the lessons when it's too late? When we've gone past the point where we could apply them?'

His eyes slid towards her. 'Wassup, Hetty? You sad . . .'

She slumped in her chair. 'A bit. I thought my boat had come in. Then I found it ahead of me in a queue. And I knew it had been holed.' She told him the story of Norman from the agency, dwelling on her emotions before and after, particularly her euphoria followed by her sense of having been played for a fool.

'He has taste. Pretty woman like you.'

'Oh, stuff, Professor. I hoped he might see me as an intelligent person he wanted to spend time with. Not just as a physical being, a plaything.'

'You *are* intelligent. And kind.' Beads of sweat broke out on the Professor's brow with the titanic battle to talk. Hetty fetched a flannel, dampened it under the tap and patted his thin face. She found a hairbrush and brushed the silvery strands of hair that he had worn Bohemian-style, in defiance of the short-back-and-sides tradition of his time. His eyes went to the water jug. She poured a glass, helping him to hold it and sip.

'Thank you. Hate being ill,' he mumbled at last. 'Can't do anything.' Then he tried again, as if he had decided to devote his remaining strength to this dialogue. 'You *are* a physical being. You're beautiful, Hetty. That matters too.'

The faces on the walls seemed to sigh and nod in agreement. Hetty glanced over her shoulder as if half expecting them to join in. She placed a hand on his, on the dead hand with the relentless tremor. 'You've said that before,' she answered. 'I wish I'd known you earlier. At your fiery best. Maybe I could have posed for you. I think it must have been tremendous fun, being painted by you.'

He chuckled at the notion, gagged, spluttered. The spasm lasted a minute while his face contorted and Hetty held him. Then he lay quietly, his chest heaving, and chuckled to himself again. The CD changed, more robust music filled the room: Ravel's *Bolero*. The Professor's gaze strayed to the paintings opposite the bed, those he had made himself, particularly those of the lovely woman who had been his wife.

'Exquisite,' he murmured. He raised himself a little. 'What I miss most, Hetty, is women. Seeing women, as they should be.' He stopped, as if unable or unwilling to elaborate, jaw thrust forward in the pugnacious manner he adopted when arguing the toss with the ladies of the book club.

The music was getting louder, insistent in its pacing and rhythm. Without understanding why she did so, Hetty left the bedside and began to move round the room in time to it, her body swaying, much as she had seen skaters do on the ice, in imitation of the little bronze dancer. The old man raised his left hand and haltingly adjusted the overhead lamp so that it fell on her like a spotlight. He tilted his head, a smile on his lips, his index finger conducting her as if she were an entire orchestra.

'*Beautiful . . .*' he croaked hoarsely. '*Don't stop . . .*'

The curtains had been drawn, probably when the tea was delivered. They would not be disturbed. If a tray was placed outside in the corridor, as in a hotel, staff understood that the occupant wished to rest. Even when they knew that the resident could do nothing whatever for himself. Still, it made sense to lock the door.

His brow darkened in the dim light. Hetty twirled in slow motion as if in a dream, her arms like fronds above her head, letting him control her, judging from those hooded, limpid eyes, what he wanted her to do: whatever she could give him, a last gift, she would lay freely before him.

They were alone, with the music coming to a steady crescendo, in the warm room, surrounded by striking images of feminine grace. The pictures' subjects seemed to form a chorus: it was almost as if they were murmuring descants to the music. The Professor beat time awkwardly, directed her, his head up, mouth half open. He increased the volume slightly, not so loud as to bring complaints, but sufficient to make his intentions absolutely clear.

And Hetty danced for him, for the gaunt figure in the bed, for the dying spirit, in homage to the undimmed adoration this man felt for all women, but especially those before him, in the portraits on the wall from his earlier years, and for the living woman who was now slipping out of her clothes, and letting them lie where they fell.

The skirt came first, then the sweater and the unbuttoned blouse; she kicked them out of the way. The undergarments followed swiftly, as if they were a constraint. There was nothing unduly sexual about the small heap of white lace on the edge of the rug. The male artist needed to observe, without adornments: the female model needed to be admired, uncovered, unashamed . . .

The light fell on her body, on her hips and her thighs, on her belly and her shoulders and breasts, as Hetty danced for him. Round and round, arms in the air, eyes closed, on tiptoe, running her fingers down her flanks, letting the surging harmonies take over: like a lone priestess dancing in the depths of the oracle before her god, a soul in ecstasy, acquiring new truths and ancient knowledge, offering herself in supplication and thanks . . .

'Oh, Hetty . . .'

. . . dancing, dancing, a woman for a man who could see, and could ask for no more . . .

Then it was over. The music came to its sudden full stop. The Professor pressed a button and the silence lingered. She stood calmly, her fingers entwined in her hair, then let her arms fall, and picked up her clothes to put them on.

The Professor was clapping, slowly, one hand coming down on the palm of the other, his uplifted face wreathed in joy.

'And now I have to go,' said Hetty, in as matter-of-fact a voice as she could muster. She fastened her skirt, swung it round, slipped her feet back into her shoes. For a moment she fumbled with her coat, then recovered her composure. 'You take care. I'll call and see you again soon, maybe at the book club.' She kissed the desiccated cheek and brushed the withered hand.

As she unlocked the door and glanced back, the Professor was still applauding.

CHAPTER TWENTY-SIX

Revelations

H etty sipped the infusion of raspberry tea and gave a grateful if wan smile to Markus, its originator. Weary after the day's recording, she had decided against a movie; it might be a while before she joined a cinema queue again. A mild headache, beans on toast and a slothful night in front of the television had been her agenda, until a knock had brought the craggy features of her upstairs neighbour into view.

'Haven't seen you for ages,' Markus had said, reproachfully. 'Not on Sundays at the café, not at the theatre, not in and out of our living room like earlier this year. Then by chance I spot you putting out the rubbish and you're bent over with misery. Here am I, trying to read a bad script and bored to tears. Come and cry on my shoulder.'

Soon she was settled on the tan leather sofa, her feet on the silk carpet, fingers fiddling with the fig tree in its minimalist pot. A Japanese print had been hung in an alcove with a squat jade Buddha, the whole tastefully illuminated by an exactly placed spotlight. The décor with its understated elegance could not fail to calm Hetty's jangled nerves.

'So, what's the matter?' Markus poured tea and pushed a cookie jar towards her.

'I'm sorry. I've been busy. Bit preoccupied, I'm afraid.'

'Work?'

She shook her head.

'Family?'

'No, nothing like that. All well.'

'Aha. Love?'

Hetty snorted. 'How did you guess? Or at least I thought I'd found it at last. Instead I was subject to the oldest cliché in the world.'

Once she started talking, to Markus's sympathetic nods, it came out: not in a rush, but composed, self-critical and rueful. She recounted the tale of Norman from the agency and the queue for *The Mummy*. Then, for good measure, she added James the trainspotter, Al the jazz player, and Stephen the ex. She kept to herself the call from Annabel's father; its brevity and lack of outcome meant it didn't count. And then she described, briefly, her distress at the Professor's illness and its appalling effect on him. The dance had been buried in the innermost recesses of her heart, and would never be alluded to. 'Hence, I'm off men,' she concluded.

Markus sipped the fragrant tea. 'I'm not surprised, after a string of misadventures like that. But temporarily, please. They can't all be bad.'

'That's what I say. The Professor isn't. But one gets discouraged. And I ask myself, Why do I feel such an idiot? Because I was letting myself down, that's why. For the first time ever, I know who I am. Made real progress in the last year. If some chap seriously tried to persuade me to get hitched again, I'd hesitate. I hope.'

Markus waited, but Hetty did not elaborate. 'You said that your ex has been dropping heavy hints?' he asked.

'Mmm. I've had four letters. A card for my birthday – he didn't forget. A dreadfully sloppy card for the date of our anniversary, which *I'd* tried to forget. He hasn't actually come out with it, but I could go back. What I haven't figured out is whether he believes he's being kind to a poor lost soul, or whether the lost soul is him.'

'Maybe both. Have you spoken to each other?'

'No. I wouldn't want to,' said Hetty sadly. 'Got quite enough on my plate without further complications. He'd make me feel small again, and insecure, like I did before, and guilty for not rushing to his side, if he needed me. Too much muddle altogether.'

Markus checked the pot and poured in hot water. 'You didn't run away from that life willingly, Hetty.'

'True. I was suited to it then, but now? For example, I adore working these days, and can't imagine how I'd spend my time otherwise.' The image of Clarissa laden with shopping surfaced and she shuddered. 'The pressures in the village on wives *not* to take outside work were enormous, but I couldn't see how unfair it was. If I'd got a job, become a commuter like my husband, the gossips would have had a field day. I'd have been accused of neglecting my home and setting a bad example. Then when my marriage broke up it would, naturally, have been regarded as *my* fault. Not his.'

'Sounds like double standards to me,' Markus grunted.

'By the bucketload. Oh, if I had got a job, of course something would have gone to the wall. The garden, probably. I must have been mad: I was devoted to that sodding garden, and now I don't have one I couldn't care less.' She giggled and held up the cup. 'Here's to gardeners. May they never learn how futile their passion is.'

'You don't mean that. You enjoy the common,' Markus rebuked her gently.

'I don't have to mow it, or weed it. That helps.'

Markus laughed. 'Dear Hetty. Almost cynical. But many people would have envied you. Isn't it supposed to be most women's dream – a big house, a half-acre garden, two cars, children? And if you could have that back again, wouldn't you be tempted?'

Hetty sighed. 'Not with the accompanying social strait-jacket. The squeals of censure if you don't do what the old biddies say you should. The bleak looks if you miss church or refuse the rota for meals-on-wheels. The whispers at the post office. You should be thankful, Markus, that you and Christian never have to put up with any of that.'

'I was expected to serve on the committee of Gay Pride, and drew the line,' said Markus tartly. 'Too much bickering and in-fighting. If it's old biddies you despise, Hetty, the gay community has more than its share. It was their way of trying to make me come out publicly, and I was not about to satisfy them.'

Hetty's voice lifted in frustration. 'Why does everyone want us to conform? Why can't they leave us be? If we're different, we're not doing any harm.'

'Quite.'

'I hadn't thought of it before,' Hetty said. 'But gay or straight, a couple is a couple. If you're still devoted, and still have lots in common, it's fabulous. If one partner's hankering after something illicit, there's a problem.'

Markus's face darkened. 'Straight couples have children.

That can keep some marriages alive, can't it? The children are what they have in common. Many gay men find it hard to form long-term relationships. They flit from conquest to conquest, and only feel the buzz in the opening stages. It's a man thing, I suppose.'

Hetty was startled. 'But you and Christian?' Into her mind came the fleeing figure on the common. She spoke more slowly, 'You're the most durable pairing I know at the moment. With the possible exception of the McDonalds.' She gazed up anxiously from her tea. 'There's nothing wrong, is there, Markus?'

The older man shifted in his tubular steel chair. The furniture of their apartment had probably been chosen more for style than for comfort; behind Hetty's knees a numbness was spreading. She shifted also, as if in sympathy.

'I am getting older,' Markus said quietly. 'I keep myself in shape. But Christian – when we met, he was very young, very troubled. Today he's the talk of the arts magazines, his name pops up everywhere. If he strayed, it wouldn't be surprising . . .'

'But you'd be devastated.'

'Absolutely. Perhaps it matters more just because we don't have children. Or a dog, or even a budgie. We have only each other.'

A silence fell, brooding and sombre. Then Hetty stirred. 'What about the other way round? My husband didn't set out to fall for somebody else. It started off as a fling, I'm pretty sure. Might it happen to you? Could you imagine yourself straying?'

Markus treated the question solemnly. 'Not under present circumstances. But suppose Christian became a fat old man with a paunch and unpleasant personal habits. Would I try

to find a younger version, maybe? I don't know the answer
to that. Some gay men are repeatedly attracted to lovers of
the same age and appearance. Except that the age gap
widens till it's quite grotesque.'

'Not just gays. Straight men often fall for retreads. My
Stephen, for one.'

'A man thing, like I said.'

'In which case, I'm awfully glad I'm a woman. I can't start
having a second family. That at least, Markus, is a great
relief.'

Instinct had warned Hetty not to raise, however obliquely,
the mystery of Christian's outings on the common. One
glance between the two at the café months before had shown
that the young actor regarded such activities with a levity
not shared by his partner. Maybe Christian was restless, or
frustrated, or simply flighty; or maybe a joke had twisted
itself into a dare, then had slid into a habit. Maybe, as
Markus had hinted, Christian preferred casual relations, and
the older man turned a blind eye, desperate to keep him. She
cared too much about both to wish to cause them any grief.

Meanwhile her gloomy feelings persisted, though she
threw herself into the research for *Tell Me All* and drummed
up enough new guests for half the next series. Soul Mates,
the agency, sent fresh sheets of names but Hetty could not
bring herself to give them more than a perfunctory shuffle.
Some brightness had been extinguished in her, and made
her melancholy.

Doris rode to her rescue over a warming tot of Scotch in
her kitchen one evening. The turban was pink cotton, the
pinny fixedly in place, the tarot cards unboxed. The effect
was oddly incongruous, as of a wizard caught doing his

chores. 'Tell Doris, dear,' the old woman urged. In her hands the overlarge cards slithered and flicked over, as if by their own volition.

'I can't shake off this sense of failure. All the men I've dallied with so far have been a disaster. What do I do next?'

'Try a younger bloke?' Doris suggested. She turned over a card: a knight in armour appeared, as if by a miracle.

'God forbid,' Hetty muttered. Then, 'Markus says that's quite normal amongst gays. That tastes don't change even if one gets older. And we can think of loads of straight men like that. Rod Stewart, for example. Or Donald Trump, that millionaire.'

'When they're asked why they do it, they answer, "Because I can,"' said Doris grimly. 'They're saying, if they can still pull the dolly-birds, why shouldn't they?' The next card was of a buxom maid with a wayward eye.

'But I can drum up loads of reasons why not.' Hetty was definite. 'Who wants a pretty bimbo with no brain?'

'*They* do.' Doris was equally definite. 'Usually 'cause the last thing that matters to them in a partner is a brain. A girl with something between the ears'd see through them in two shakes of a lamb's tail. Even the bimbos do, eventually. Then they start again.'

'It does clarify one's values.' Hetty accepted a second small Scotch. She had no intention of getting drunk but the liquor helped her delve into subjects that would once have left her tongue-tied. 'Markus was speculating how he might react if Christian got old and fat. I don't know – does personality get more important, as we get older?'

Doris did not reply, but pushed the next card towards Hetty. It showed a still-life, a basket of fruit. Neither commented. Hetty continued, 'For me, if a bloke popped up tomorrow who was unattractive but nice, I can imagine a chummy platonic friendship, but not sex. Bed still means that spark has to be there.'

The memory of Norman suddenly seized her and she almost started to cry. 'Sorry, Doris, but Norman was – excellent in that department. I do miss him. *It*.'

'Buy new batteries for that gadget I gave you,' Doris advised stoutly, as she gathered up the cards. 'It'll keep you going. Something better will come along.'

Hetty smiled through her misery. 'You are a pal, Doris. And quite right. I shan't give in. I'm not about to hang up my boots and spurs yet.'

Doris sat up. 'Boots and spurs? Oooh! You didn't say you were into S and M. Got some terrific new stuff in the shop. You must come . . .'

Clarissa was in a rush and had only a moment to talk on the phone. 'Another party? We missed the last one. I'll check with Robin but the date sounds okay. Is it bring a bottle?'

'Bring whatever you like. I was wondering if your aunt would like an invitation.'

'Millie? Good Lord, one doesn't think of the aged as suitable invitees. It's up to you. I dashed in there yesterday – the whole caboodle's as ghastly as ever, but she's on good form. Your friend the Professor is no more, of course.'

'The Professor?' Hetty went cold.

'Died. Buried yesterday morning, in fact – he was Jewish, or his family were, and they can't hang about, have to do it within twenty-four hours. He'd had a stroke.'

'Yes, I knew about the stroke.' Hetty's voice dropped till Clarissa told her to speak up. 'I saw him about a week ago. He was a bit poorly, I had meant to pop in again.'

'No need now,' said Clarissa airily. 'But rumour has it he's left you something in his will. His family mentioned it to the matron. He'd taken quite a shine to you, Hetty.'

'I loved him,' said Hetty softly. 'I never told him, but I'm sure he was aware.'

'Loved him? Surely not. He was *old*, Hetty.'

'He was wise, and kind, and funny, and . . .' She wanted to add *sexy*, but stopped.

'Ugh!' said Clarissa. 'I can't bear it. Those scrawny bodies. The mad eyes. I've told Robin, the moment I start to disintegrate, he's to take his shotgun and bump me off.'

'I was going to invite him,' Hetty continued wistfully, 'to the party. It's a kind of celebration of my freedom, and he was part of that. We'd have got him here somehow, even if I'd had to push the wheelchair myself.'

'You're a basket-case. Let me know about the will, won't you? I'm dying of curiosity,' said Clarissa. ''Bye.' The handset clicked.

Slowly Hetty put the phone down. Where had she been yesterday? At the studio, but it would not have been impossible to take the morning off for the funeral, had anybody bothered to tell her. She felt an agonising choke of remorse. If she had been a daily visitor or had checked more regularly on his welfare, staff would have informed her in time. It had not happened, and was probably nobody's fault. As she was not family, and had never met them, the relatives had not thought to include her. Since she had felt faintly embarrassed in retrospect about the dance in the dark, and worried that he might ask for a repeat performance, she had put off calling. And now it was too late.

The Professor was gone. Even at this minute, his room was probably being cleared and disinfected, his clothes packed in suitcases and bags, the pictures stacked higgledy-piggledy, with little consideration for their intrinsic or artistic value or what they had meant to the dead man. The flamboyant silk pyjamas would be destined for an Oxfam shop along with the bottle-green velvet jacket. The little dancer would be pawed over at auction. His wife would have lost her significance and be yet another fleshy nude in an obscure gallery, if that. Maybe the paintings would languish in an archive or basement somewhere: most would never again see the light of day. Hetty wondered if the home would keep quiet about the many works belonging to him on the walls, or whether the beneficiaries would allow them to remain. At least at Swallow House they had been displayed and gave pleasure, as the Professor had insisted they should.

'I loved him, and I grieve for him,' Hetty whispered. 'Oh, poor man.'

She abandoned the minor tasks she had been doing and cast around for a way to honour his memory, but none came easily. Then she decided to take a long walk across the common towards St Veronica's. If Father Roger were available and free she might explain, a little, about her extraordinary friend. If not, then she would say a prayer for the Professor and maybe light a candle, then return on the bus. The ritual would have meaning and would soothe her battered spirit, if nothing else.

It was a Thursday evening; the service was a Sung Eucharist. Here, too, to her disappointment, her low mood obstinately lingered. The ceremony seemed meaningless, the liturgy irrelevant. Her flagging interest was aroused, however, by the new arrival: the curate. A female, as Roger had feared, thin and ungainly with a nervous manner and buck teeth, who had previously been a teacher in a northern town.

'Call me Alice,' she said, with a toothy grin, as Hetty introduced herself. *Alisss*.

'I hope you'll be very happy here. What did you teach?' Hetty enquired politely.

Alice rolled her eyes. She wore a dove-grey, full-length garment and a dog-collar. Her hair was brown, drawn back from the plain face. 'Classics.' *Classsicks*.

'Really? Roger will be pleased. He buries himself in the great philosophers.'

'Ooh, yes, he told me. We've been arguing already. I'm into Marcus Aurelius myself.'

This left Hetty at a distinct loss. It came to her that she was marginally jealous. Should Roger ever decide that humankind merited as much attention as a shelf of books, the lady curate would be in pole position, with Marcus-whoever in tow. The woman had an eagerness about her that Roger would find either an irritation – or endearing. Hetty tried to speak to him, but he was busy with parishioners wanting banns called. He kept glancing over his shoulder with a frown at his new assistant, who scurried about like a little grey mouse and seemed to be everywhere.

Hetty was half-way out of the door before she remembered the origin of her errand. She went back inside, purchased the biggest candle in the box, and lit it in front of a side altar. Then she knelt for a moment, and prayed that the Professor, somewhere, had been reunited with his love.

Sunk in reflection, Hetty descended from the bus on her way back from the church. It was dark and had been raining; the street-lights cast pools of harsh yellow on the wet pavements. The whole episode had served to intensify her sense of pain and loss.

With head bowed and damp tissue in hand, she looked
about for Brian to buy a *Big Issue*, but he was missing. His
absence felt like a further blow, some other partial responsibility she had wilfully ignored. Chiding herself as she came
to The Swallows, she pulled off her gloves and started to
unlock the street door.

A noise came behind her, a loping pace up the path. Wary
that some unauthorised person might try to push inside,
she swiftly removed the key and let the door close.

'Oh, don't do that, Hetty. I've forgotten my keys.'

It was Christian, in his black tracksuit, a rollneck sweater
hiding the Adam's apple. His head was up, the blond hair
unruly, a flush high on the cheekbones. A fleck of spittle
marked the side of his mouth. He appeared agitated; his
eyes would not meet hers.

Hetty's hand began to shake. Jerkily she held up the key
to the lock a second time and began to turn it. Then she
removed it once more, with the door still shut.

'Where have you been, Christian?' she asked him coolly.

'What? Out for a run, that's all. None of your business,
Hetty.'

The rudeness of the reply confirmed her suspicions. She
was blocking the entrance, her hands held out as if the
locked door were not enough to bar the way. In the corner
of her eye through the lighted window she could see Doris
moving about in her kitchen. The old woman waved briefly.
Hetty responded with a weak smile, then focused her entire
attention on Christian.

'It *is* my business, because I make it so. I'll let you in if
you'll come to my flat for a minute. I want a word with you.'

She was not entirely sure why she did it, any more than
she could have explained her secret dance for the

Professor, except that it was exactly the right action for the moment. She waited, fiddling with the antique perfume phials on the mantelpiece, switching on the side-light then switching it off again. As Christian, who seemed to be panting slightly and fidgeting, edged into her room and circled her, she put down her bag and gloves and turned to face him.

'I know what you've been up to, Christian. You've been on the common, and you've been with some other man. For money.'

The fidgeting stopped. 'Rubbish. You shouldn't make accusations like that.'

'It isn't rubbish. I've seen you heading over the road more than once. And I saw you in action, by the bushes. I wasn't spying, but you were with a boy in a baseball cap and white jeans. Money changed hands. Don't deny it, Christian. What were you up to?'

'You seem to know already, Miss Public Morals,' Christian sneered, with a guttural edge she had never heard before. He wiped the back of his hand across his mouth.

'Christian. For heaven's sake. Why do you want to mess about like that?'

'It's not messing about. It's sex. Rough trade. Terrific.' The sneering tone was still present, but was wavering. Christian's eyes were unnaturally wide and darting about as if searching for escape. Their colour, dark and unfathomable, was the same murky blue-green as the antique glass on the mantelpiece behind him.

'But Markus adores you. Doesn't that count for anything? What happened to loyalty? You shouldn't hurt him, Christian, you can't. You're part of a couple, not just a single man. You can't ignore that bond. If he knew what you've been up to he'd be destroyed: you must realise that. If you're having any difficulties in – in that direction, sex, I mean, you should sit down together and talk about it.'

'Oh, yeah? Like you did with your husband, I suppose, Hetty.'

She saw red. The air screamed at her, and burst in vivid starry showers about her head. Fury welled up inside, and bitter righteousness, and an overweening need to punish, and to underline the grossness of what had taken place. She did what she should have done years ago, with the man she had married, who had betrayed her as thoroughly as this boy was betraying his lover . . . His casual cruelty was about to shatter what was most precious and elusive in human life, the love of another person . . .

Hetty raised her hand and with every ounce of force she could muster, slapped him hard across the cheek.

'Oh!' He held his face as if she had taken a knife to it, and staggered back. Behind him one of the glass bottles fell, and smashed to tiny pieces in the hearth.

Now it was Hetty's turn to breathe heavily. 'You fool,' she hissed. 'You unremitting miserable bastard, Christian. You have the love of someone who's worth ten of you. Wants to spend his life alongside you. If you lose him, you'll never get anyone as fine, or as suited. For God's sake, stop it. Or you'll regret it for ever.'

Suddenly the anger drained from her as quickly as it had come, and she pointed to the hallway. 'Go on, get out. And mind what I say.'

He stumbled away, still holding his cheek, his eyes fearful and clouded.

Hetty slammed the door after him, shook her stinging fingers and collapsed into the nearest armchair, still in her coat. The dull twinkle of the broken glass merged with her own tears, until the room swam with her misery.

Christian did not hear the words she addressed to his vanished form as he trudged haltingly up the stairs. Even as she heard him hesitate then tap on his own door and enter, she had admitted to herself what had been true all along.

'You're right, Christian. I should have seen the holes in my marriage years ago. And instead of pretending everything was rosy, tried to put matters straight. But I didn't. Bloody complacent: it'd sort itself out without any intervention on my part. How could my adored husband want someone else? Why should anything ever change?'

She raised her still throbbing hand in the air, swept it proprietorially around the tiny flat, at the prints on the walls, the shabby furniture and the ill-fitting curtains, the pathetic china and shards of glass, the cheap television set: mute witnesses to her fate.

'And look where *that* got me.'

CHAPTER TWENTY-SEVEN

Hetty's Party

Hetty was soon in agonies over her party and wishing she had never decided to hold it. Since nearly everyone greeted her invitations with enthusiasm, she began to worry as to how the numbers – possibly as many as forty – would fit inside the flat.

Partners were to be included. Sally answered promptly that she would be alone. Doris promised to ask Jack. Her mother would be on the arm of the Colonel, and if not him, then of someone else. The couples – Larry and Davinia, Clarissa and Robin, the McDonalds – had accepted, the former still as if doing her a favour. The men in number six had not responded, and she had not seen them since her furious confrontation with Christian, but neither had she noticed any more nocturnal wanderings. The BJs would attend, with current boyfriends; Father Roger asked, gruffly, if the new curate might come; Rosa, Kate, Bob and the entire television crew would be there, along with assorted other halves, adding another dozen.

After some discussion, Swallow House had agreed to bring Moira, Phyllis and Millie to the party for the first hour, as representatives of the book club. The assistant matron would drive the minibus and take them home. 'An hour's enough,' was the advice. 'And please don't give them too much to drink: they're enough of a handful as it is.'

'No problem, Hetty,' said Annabel, when the danger of crushing was confided. 'You can use our place as well. D'you need anyone to sleep over? Our sofa's a Put-U-up . . .'

Party day came: Rosa had scheduled it as a non-shooting date. In the morning Hetty fitted in the hairdresser and a manicure, then fretted about each stray hair as she furiously cooked, dusted and tidied. The *Star Style* suit was waiting on its hanger with a fuchsia blouse. The flat was soon pristine, with new cushions on the sofa, spring flowers in every vase, glasses from Oddbins ranged alongside crates of wine, sale or return. The Lladro statue had a green ribbon, to match the surviving perfume phials. A CD player had been borrowed from the BJs with suitable music.

In the late afternoon Sally and Doris arrived and busied themselves with the food. Rather than peanuts and dim sum, Hetty had decided to draw on experience; hot *bœuf bourguignon*, wild rice, baked potatoes, coronation chicken, salads, an assortment of ripe cheeses and fresh breads would be the fare. The meaty smells would emanate from the kitchen and tantalise her guests, as in the seduction scenes she had twice set up. Not that she was planning an orgy, but what had entranced both a rum cove like James and a sophisticate like Norman should satisfy the entire social spectrum. Neither man was on the list, though she had left a vague message on Al's answerphone.

'Almost done, Het.' Doris wiped her hands on a tea-towel.

The turban concealed a forest of rollers and pincurls. 'You're short of plates, so I'll bring up some of mine.'

Around six came an interlude. Hetty and Sally sipped sherry and watched the news.

'No Erik?' Hetty decided to be direct.

'Finished,' Sally said.

'Oh?'

'It was going nowhere, Mum. I clung to it simply because I was afraid of not having a man – you know, when people ask, you like to say that you've got a boyfriend? But I've seen you on your own and you're fine. And now, so am I.'

'Thanks. But it's not the ideal state.'

'Maybe nothing is.'

Hetty laughed ruefully. 'When you're in a couple you're fighting, or lying, or taking each other for granted. But when you're single, you have no one to be possessive about, no one to care exclusively about you. And a reduced role in society, less respect, more – pity. And self-pity. Then you daydream of coupledom once more.'

'Do you?' Sally was curious.

'Not in my *head*. But my actions belie my words – why else would I go to an agency? I count my blessings, but work and friends are not quite enough.'

'If some decent chap turned up tonight and asked you to share his life, would you be thrilled?' Sally asked slowly.

'I'd be amazed.' Hetty laughed again. 'No one's in the offing. The liaisons I've had so far have been highly unsatisfactory. Sharing with a wife is *not* my idea of fun.'

Her daughter collected the glasses and washed them without further comment; but when her mother went into the bedroom to change, Sally tiptoed to the phone.

*

'Hetty! Mwah, mwah!'

Davinia was getting plumper, but Larry seemed delighted. As they removed their coats and peered nosily around, he pinched Davinia's rump playfully. 'She's becoming domesticated at last,' he boasted. 'We're trying for another baby. We have two boys – I'd like a girl.'

'I'm having hormone treatment,' Davinia whispered. 'That's why I'm fat. Had trouble producing enough eggs.'

'Great,' Hetty enthused. 'It's so lovely to see you so settled.' It occurred to her that Davinia, too, might have lied about her age. If she were forty rather than in her mid-thirties, the fertility treatment could be explained. On the other hand, in their circle it did not do to get pregnant easily: a tale of woe and torment was desirable.

Clarissa and Robin came next. He was portlier and more full of himself than ever, and was propelled by a harassed Clarissa, dressed in a satin suit and a cream fur jacket. 'Auntie Millie says she's coming! Heavens, Hetty, what possessed you? Now I'll have to talk to her.'

'No, you won't,' said Hetty firmly. 'Unless you'd like to, of course.'

Clarissa screwed up her eyes. 'Where shall I hang this jacket, Hetty? Robin insists I wear it – he's been defending mink farmers in court. It *is* mink. I don't want it nicked.'

'Hmm. On the bed? Or maybe *under* the bed would be best. I doubt if anybody here would be drawn to it, but it is beautiful.'

Clarissa hugged the jacket to her bosom, and went to find a drink.

The McDonalds appeared with Doris, as if by prior arrangement. The couple slipped into the room and stood, backs to the wall, with glasses of wine, and murmured to each other, tapping their fingers to the Madonna beat. Whenever Hetty checked they said cordially that they were content. Evidently they needed no more than to be left undisturbed.

And behind Doris, with a bashful grin, came Jack. He shook hands formally with Hetty. Cradled in the crook of his arm was a litre bottle of whisky, its neck label marked 'For Export Only'. Fallen off the back of a lorry, his hostess concluded, but she accepted it without remark.

The living room was becoming cramped; the decibel level had risen to the point where the music could no longer be heard. Not even Bruce Springsteen could compete. The front doorbell rang every few minutes and another face, wreathed in smiles, showed itself, more hugs were exchanged, another bottle was pressed on her until the gifts were ranged on the bookcase slightly out of line like tipsy sentinels, along with caskets of chocolates and an Italian sponge cake from Davinia. The air was redolent of scent and aftershave, the aromas of food, wine, cigarettes and Robin's cheroots. Her mother swanned in with the Colonel, waxed moustaches a-bristle, and spoke gaily of their latest Saga holiday. When the *Tell Me All* crew and researchers, who had met beforehand, strolled in arm-in-arm and merry, the party began to take off.

'Good Lord, Hetty, I had no idea you knew so many people.' Larry was at her side, his eyes darting and inquisitive. The throng was starting to spill out into the corridor.

'Not everyone's come yet. The girls from across the hall are missing, and the old ladies from the home. Father Roger, and Rosa. That'll be about it, though. Fortunately.'

'It feels like half the neighbourhood is here.'

'Why not? Why shouldn't I know a lot of people? You sound astonished, Larry.'

'I am, sis. Gob-smacked. We were expecting to help make up the numbers. You don't think of your divorced, middle-aged sister as the heart and soul of the party.'

'Maybe you should,' said Hetty, but she tried to keep the tartness out of her voice. Then, relenting, she pressed her brother's hand. 'I'm so glad you both came.'

Larry seemed genuinely confused. 'Maybe we should get together a bit more, huh?'

Hetty could not answer, but a lump came to her throat. She moved away, and found Clarissa at her elbow.

'Het, I have to tell someone. But you'll keep it to yourself, won't you?'

Clarissa seemed excited and edgy. Hetty wondered with a sinking heart whether it was a new lover or a new shopping centre her schoolmate was about to extol.

'I'm going to take a leaf out of your book.'

'You are?' A lover, then. Poor Robin: he would not manage well without Clarissa.

'Yes. I was convinced you were going to fall flat on your face, and you haven't. Sodding marvellous, I call it. So I told myself, "Old girl, maximise your resources."'

'You're talking in riddles, Clarissa.'

'Listen. I'm going to do something I should have done years ago. Get an education,' said Clarissa, chin up. 'You saw that textbook? I'm going to be a BA with honours. Or, at least, in about four years' time,' she added hastily.

'*You* are going to *university*?'

'Yes,' Clarissa answered huffily. 'Don't be so shocked, Hetty. Some of us have a brain, you know.'

Hetty squeezed her arm wordlessly, unsure how to reply. She was by the door when the bell rang again. It opened to reveal Christian on the threshold, with Markus behind.

Christian's height filled the door frame. He stood awkwardly, his expression taut and serious, lips pressed into a line, but as he bent his head and entered the packed room, he held both her hands tightly for a long while. Then he kissed her on both cheeks. 'Oh, Hetty,' was all he could say. Markus pushed him further into the room with jocular force and handed over two bottles of champagne trailing gold ribbons, and uttered more accolades of affection than Hetty could take in.

A commotion arose from the street below. Hetty craned from the window then ran downstairs, calling Markus to accompany her. The Swallow House minibus was at the kerb, parked askew. On the sidewalk clustered the three elderly residents accompanied by a stocky woman in a nurse's uniform, who toted a carrier-bag packed with necessaries for the outing. They were remonstrating with a tramp.

'You've got the wrong house!' If stout Phyllis had had an umbrella she would doubtless have set about hitting the man over the head.

'Go away!' shrieked Moira in support. 'Leave us alone! We haven't any money.'

Hetty noticed that Millie had her head down and her hands buried in the depths of her coat pockets. The wealthy old lady liked to show off her riches on fingers and wrists. 'Markus, maybe you could help the ladies inside.' Hetty was crisp.

As he did so and trundled them up the path, the assistant matron in tow, carrier-bag close to her chest, Hetty turned fiercely to the tramp. He was dressed in a relatively clean tweed coat and had shaved that day, but had a wary set to his shoulders. 'Brian, were you begging from my guests?'

'I only asked them if they had any change,' he whined.

'You've scared them witless. And what is this? I thought you'd stopped begging.'

'Old habits die hard.' He cringed under her disapproval. 'You having a party?'

The racket from the lighted flat was unmissable; denial would have been pointless. Hetty sniffed, but the only odour she could detect on him was soap.

'I been to the refuge. The deli owner said you was having a gang in. Had a bath, new clothes. See.' He unfastened the tweed coat. Underneath was an ancient tuxedo jacket with a white dress shirt, but no tie. Teamed with baggy black jeans, the effect was comic but gallant. His eyes betrayed a yearning Hetty had not witnessed before.

'Goodness, Brian,' she giggled, 'you're a sight for sore eyes.' She hesitated still. Then, 'I must be insane, but if you want to come up for a quick – ah, orange juice, you're welcome. First, you'll apologise to the ladies. And the moment you misbehave, I'll have you thrown out of the window. Savvy?'

Back up the path they went, with Brian following in a rapid shuffle like a grateful dog. At the entrance he plucked at her sleeve. 'Is it yer birthday? I haven't brought nuffin.'

'Your presence is enough, Brian,' she answered gently, and wondered what other surprises might be in store.

The buffet meal was dished up to cries of approval and further reflections from Larry as to her incredible progress. Hetty drank two glasses of wine and chewed a bread chunk with a slick of Brie, but was too keyed up to be hungry. The elderly ladies, whom Hetty increasingly thought of as 'the old BJs', were ensconced side by side on the sofa with trays on their laps, served by an attentive Doris and a reluctant

Clarissa. The assistant matron stood, feet planted apart, plate in one hand, fork in the other, and chatted to Christian, who still looked rather pale. Markus had discovered that he had filmed with Bob, Gerry and Phil from the crew; they were embroiled in reminiscence. Brian had apologised as instructed and been brushed away; his dress shirt brilliant and incongruous in the light, orange juice in hand, he was squinting up at Robin, who seemed unfazed by this unconventional audience. Hetty recalled the hint Brian had dropped, once, that he had been a businessman, a millionaire. It was not impossible.

Hetty stood on tiptoe and checked around for her own family. As she watched, her mother moved seamlessly from one side of the room to the other, over to Larry and Davinia, with the Colonel, glasses in hand, behind. Soon the two couples were conversing animatedly, especially the women. Hetty felt a sudden pang. The links between the various branches of her family might well become stronger as a result of the party tonight. But it would feel strange, after such coolness, to develop close relations with such as her brother once more. Maybe more parenthood would mellow them; this new baby might wreak not havoc but improvement.

Sally was no longer alone, either. She was leaning against the door jamb in conversation with Kate, the bespectacled researcher. She caught her mother's eye and gave a merry wave, but carried on talking. Hetty was puzzled. Though Kate was highly intelligent, after a few drinks the main focus of her thinking would swing to sex. Kate would not waste time pursuing a liaison with no future. Yet Sally seemed fascinated. Both young women were slim, dressed in linen trouser suits with a mannish cut; both had a direct way of looking – *in your face* – that was a challenge. As Hetty watched, Kate put a hand on Sally's shoulder. Her daughter did not flinch, but smiled warmly.

Another latecomer arrived. Rosa slid up to her from behind and almost crushed Hetty's ribs with a bear-hug; the man accompanying her was Richard, as pleased with himself as were most of the other men present. 'We've been together nearly a year,' said Rosa with pride. 'That's a lifetime for me.'

'Thanks to you, Hetty.' Richard's smile was almost sincere. Hetty gestured hazily at the rapidly emptying dishes and flitted away.

Into the mêlée came Father Roger, alone, still in his cassock and dog-collar, with many regrets for his lateness: confession that evening had taken hours and been gruelling. 'That pesky choir,' he muttered as he swung off his cape. 'At it again. Why can't they keep their sticky paws on the hymn sheets and off each other? And why, in heaven's name, do they come and tell me?'

'Because you're their priest,' Hetty chuckled.

'Not for much longer,' he said darkly.

'Oh? What's up?'

'You'll see. I've had it, with so many crass idiots seeking the road to enlightenment and the true path through Bible readings and Sunday worship. They don't repent, Hetty. They want absolution, but they don't repent.'

She was nonplussed. 'D'you mean you're going to leave the Church?'

'That is in God's hands,' he answered, deepening the mystery.

Her attention was distracted by the arrival, almost as the food was finished, of the girls from number four. All three were already equipped with a full glass. As they poked their bright heads round the door, Hetty realised why they might have chosen to delay their appearance. For each was on the arm of a man.

Flo bounced in, braids flying. 'I believe you've met Jonathan,' she said coyly.

'Hello,' said the languid presenter graciously, as if he were greeting Hetty for the first time. He held out limp fingers to be shaken. 'Oh, yes, now I remember you – from the studio. Thanks *so* much for the invite.'

'You two been an item long?' Hetty was mischievous.

'Let me see, about a month.' The presenter turned limpid eyes on Flo. 'I'm besotted.'

And Annabel sidled in with Nicholas, who promptly swept Hetty off her feet and planted a hefty kiss on her mouth. 'I've got a contract! I'm to write two novels, and they're going to pay me. The advance came yesterday. I can't believe it – and just because I was on your programme, Hetty. *And* I've got Annabel, the most darling girl in the universe. Pinch me – it's not real!'

Annabel stood bashfully at his side, still attired in black, but in an ankle-length dress with a breathtakingly low neck that showed off her remarkable cleavage to advantage.

'Champagne's inside,' Hetty told them. 'And, Nicholas – so is my sister-in-law, Davinia. She's trying to get pregnant, she says.'

'So are we,' said Nicholas happily, and clasped Annabel's hand. 'Thanks for the warning. But that's in the past.' The pair headed for the kitchen.

Shelagh was with an older man Hetty did not recognise, but whose carrotty hair and freckled skin gave away his identity even before she introduced him. 'My father, Jim

O'Brennan,' said Shelagh. 'The famous sausage manufac-
turer,' as if answering an unspoken query.

'Pleased to meet you,' said Hetty. 'Would you like a
drink?' She was carrying a bottle of Chardonnay still relatively chilled, and topped up their glasses.

'I'm glad we could make it,' said Mr O'Brennan. 'You see,
Shelagh's coming home next week. For good.'

The girl nodded, her wild hair falling over her shoulders.
'I'm going to get involved with the family firm,' she said.
'Personnel director of a subsidiary, to start with. *Director*,
note – I shall be on the main board.'

'Do you know a lot about personnel?' Hetty could not
help asking.

'No, but I'll learn.' The voice bubbled with confidence.

'And what happened,' Hetty asked slyly, 'to those notions
of a big family – eight kids you wanted, wasn't it?'

Shelagh shrugged. 'Plenty of grand fellows on that side of
the Irish Sea,' she replied airily. 'And they're *much* keener on
getting married than over here.'

'Ireland's changing, Mrs Clarkson,' said Mr O'Brennan
expansively. He had to raise his voice to be heard above the
hubbub. 'Young people are coming back. After centuries of
emigration. Place is booming. Can't get the staff. Any time
you want a job, you contact me.' And he pressed a card into
Hetty's hand.

Dazed and hot, Hetty slipped into the corridor for a
breath of air. She was pursued by the assistant matron carrying a package wrapped in brown paper and string, who
had evidently been waiting for this opportunity. 'I am sorry
we didn't let you know about Professor Bernstein's funeral,
Mrs Clarkson,' the woman said formally. 'It was such a rush,
religious reasons and so on. And in north London. Wasn't

till afterwards the ladies said you might have liked to attend. I can only say it didn't occur to us.' Her chin jutted, as if expecting criticism.

'No, that's all right,' said Hetty sadly. 'I was very fond of him.'

'Yes, you do get attached,' said the woman, in a common-sense tone. 'We go to funerals every week, and you tell yourself you shouldn't get sentimental, but you can't avoid it sometimes. Though the Professor wasn't a favourite with the staff.'

Hetty smiled despite herself. 'Why was that?'

'He kept making sexual remarks. About their buttocks and so on. They didn't like it.'

'Yes, I can imagine,' Hetty said. 'But he wasn't really a dirty old man. He just worshipped beauty. They should have taken it as a compliment.'

The woman looked at her askance, and sniffed. 'Be that as it may. The executors have got one hell of a job on, what with those dozens of paintings. But he's left some small bequests and, wherever possible, I've been told to hand them over. So here's yours.'

She plonked the package in Hetty's arms. It was solid and cold, and quite heavy. Fearful of dropping it, Hetty gingerly unwrapped a corner, till the object was exposed.

It was the little bronze dancer.

'It's got a plinth too – d'you want that?'

Hetty, her throat constricted, nodded silently.

'You can collect that from the lodge. And I'm supposed to tell you to get it insured, though I don't expect it's worth much,' said the woman. 'They'll be writing to you.'

Hetty pulled away a scrap of paper at the base of the stat-uette and traced her fingernail over the scrawled signature etched into the metal. *Degas*, it read. 'I shan't be selling it,' she managed at last. 'It'll be a memento – of a wonderful man.'

Her task complete, the assistant matron set about collecting her charges. Hetty hid the statue behind the sofa, where Millie was fast asleep, head back, mouth open. Moira and Phyllis demanded to use the bathroom before venturing a step into the cold night. After many protestations about headaches and stiff limbs, the three donned their outer garments, wrapped scarves round their necks and, with the help of Markus and Clarissa, creakily made their way downstairs.

'Splendid party,' said Phyllis, with the suspicion of a burp, as they regrouped on the pavement. 'Haven't enjoyed myself so much in years.'

'Love you, Hetty,' said Moira sleepily, and put up her lips to be kissed.

'I'm going to change my will –' Millie began to say, but Hetty interrupted.

'No, you are not. You are going to read the set book in time for the club's next session.'

'I am?' asked Millie in astonishment, as the assistant matron, Clarissa and Hetty eased her into her seat. The door was slammed shut, and the vehicle drove off into the night.

'Nine thirty. Time to clear away the tables and try a little dancing, Hetty?' Markus said, as they went back up the stairs.

'Provided I don't pass out this time.'

'Oh, you'll be safe in our hands. Anyway, there are a few words to be said first.'

'No speeches. No.' Hetty stopped dead.

'Thank-yous, a few minutes, that's all.'

At the top of the second flight they halted. Before them at eye-level, teetering carefully up each step on high heels, was a pair of fishnet tights covering muscular calves. Above floated a gauzy concoction in midnight blue lace, nipped in at the waist. A powerful waft of freshly applied perfume lingered. The hair was shoulder-length, the tilt of the shoulders unmistakable . . .

'Carole?' Hetty lifted her voice.

The figure stopped. Then half turned, keeping its face averted. 'Hetty – do you mind?'

'Let me see you properly. Is your lipstick tidy?' Hetty commanded. The apparition came full face, the mouth trembling. Hetty came close and pretended to check. 'Carole, that's excellent. Go on in. Have a drink.' She caught Markus's eye. 'He'll be safe in our hands too,' she hissed. 'Be nice to him. Her. Whatever.'

'And to your tuxedo johnny, and to everyone else? You do have odd friends, Hetty.' But Markus's manner was one of amused tolerance.

'When I bought this flat I was told I'd have odd neighbours. That includes you,' she teased. He grinned at her, and carried on upstairs, mimicking Carole's ungainly gait as he did so.

The plates and glasses were cleared; despite Hetty's protestations, Doris, Sally and Kate set to and made short shrift of the disorder. Tables and chairs were pushed back. Markus took ostentatious charge of the CD control: Abba filled the room. At a suitable point he switched it off, called for silence and took centre stage.

'I trust everyone has a full glass?'

'Yes! No!' greeted him, and bottles were passed round.

'Now we've had a marvellous evening, and it's not over yet. We have a tremendous thank-you to say to our hostess. So raise your glasses, and here's our toast: to Hetty!'

'To Hetty!' came the cry.

'And we want to give you – this!!'

Christian came forward, gawky and handsome, his blond hair falling over his brow, cradling an enormous bouquet. It must have been hidden in their flat. The lilies gave off their scent, the roses were just opening, fronds of eucalyptus and fern waved gracefully, the crinkly Cellophane was contained in a huge purple bow. The concoction was almost as big as Hetty herself. He presented it with an embrace, and a half-smile, and a whispered message of his own, that only Hetty could hear.

Behind the vast sheaf Hetty suddenly felt small and insignificant. This was not for her, surely. She did not deserve it. All she had done was invite a few friends round for a drink. Her main anxiety was that they shouldn't run out of alcohol, and that the food was attractive enough, smart enough, for this extraordinarily disparate bunch. But the emptied dishes told their own tale, as did the flushed happy faces ranged in a semicircle around the worn carpet.

Markus clapped his hands. 'Before we continue, one or two other matters. I have an announcement.'

Groans and cat-calls. Hetty had been right: nobody liked speeches.

'I have never said this before.' Markus raised his voice. 'But I'm proud to do so now. I am gay. There! I've come out with it at last.' There was a ripple of sardonic applause, though Hetty saw out of the corner of her eye that Larry and

Davinia were shrinking back. 'Not only that, but I have found my life's companion. Christian here.'

He beckoned: Christian moved, stumbling, into the circle.

'And we are going to be married.' There was a moment's stunned silence. 'Unfortunately, we can't do it in this country – *yet*. So it'll have to be in Amsterdam. And, Hetty, we'd like you to come. Will you?'

'Oh, yes . . .' she said, and felt herself smiling broadly.

'*I'll* marry you.'

Father Roger stepped into the middle. 'Or, at least, I'll give you a blessing. Can't do it in St Veronica's but I'm sure we could find somewhere suitable.'

Behind him hovered Alice, the curate, who had slipped in without Hetty noticing. Like Roger she was wearing her clerical collar, with an ill-fitting black jacket and skirt. Bony wrists poked out of the sleeves, the thin fingers were clasped together.

'Because it's time for me to take my fate in my hands, too,' Roger said, slowly. The room went quiet again: those present were hanging on every syllable. 'I believed I could manage with God alone, with no human being getting in the way. I was above *that*. Then dear Alice came along and altered my perspectives. We have prayed together. She has changed everything . . .'

Alice's expression was shining and ecstatic; she came forward, as shyly as Christian had done, and stood by Roger, her hands twitching. The church mouse had proved a doughty and speedy operator, Hetty reflected ruefully. The priest's shoulders sagged, as if abandoning a terrible burden. Then he beamed at Hetty, and at Doris and Markus.

'Well, I still think the Golden Tulip Hotel in Amsterdam

is the place to do it,' said Markus calmly, pressing the control button. As the Abba songs resumed, the engaged couple and the clericals slid away, and were soon comparing diaries.

'Bloody hell!' It was Rosa, at Hetty's side. 'Gorgeous flowers, Het. But Roger's taking a big step, if he means to preside at a gay wedding.'

'What'll happen?' Hetty buried her face in the blooms. The forlorn reminder of Norman's flowers flooded back and was quickly banished. Nobody in the room tonight was likely to announce that he was marrying *her*.

'St Veronica's is High Anglican. If he and whassername – Alice – start publicly undermining the church's teaching, the parishioners won't take it. He might have to leave. Who knows? That was a brave act. He must know the risks he's running.'

'He seems to have decided he's leaving, anyway. He could earn a living in so many other ways: as a teacher or college lecturer, perhaps. Or as a media guru. Could he still be on the programme?'

'Oh, yes, he's the best there is. In fact, we could drum up an idea for a series revolving around him. Father Roger's view of modern *mores*.' Rosa was looking pensive.

'Like Sister Wendy's view on old master paintings?'

'Yeah, but altogether less dotty . . . Fancy being assistant producer?'

Hetty carried the bouquet into the kitchen. Every vase was full, so she deposited the blooms in the sink next to the dirty glasses. A quick count showed that around thirty guests remained, though Shelagh and her father had slipped away and those crew members on early duty had also made their farewells.

'A change would do you good,' Sheryl Crow trilled, in a tune Hetty had not heard before.

As the music swelled, couples formed and danced. Annabel with Nicholas, locked in a close embrace; Rosa and Richard, writhing at each other with unabashed sensuality; Flo and Jonathan, smoochily; then Markus with her mother, the Colonel with Mrs McDonald – and Sally, unabashed, with Kate. Even Brian was twirling solo, orange juice doggedly in hand, swivelling his hips in a passable imitation of hip-hop.

Hetty paused at the entrance to the kitchen and watched, wistfully.

'You okay, Hetty?' Doris was stacking dishes.

'Mmm. None of this would have occurred in my previous incarnation. I've gained so much from my odd neighbours, and my friends . . .' She let her voice trail off.

'Your odd neighbours?'

'Yes . . . When I bought this flat, the agent was a bit off-hand. Said you were all *odd*. He may've been correct, but I'm comfortable here.' She pointed. 'The BJs. I wouldn't have given them the time of day: young sillies, forever partying, irresponsible and drunk. But they're great kids. The McDonalds, the lads upstairs. Won't that wedding be terrific? And my daughter, and Brian, our resident down-and-out, here, in my flat and smelling of shaving-soap. I'd have run a mile if anyone'd suggested – *well*. Even you, in that creepy sex-shop. Yet you're all so darned *normal*.'

'You don't know the half of it,' said Doris quietly. 'I don't go in for public confessions. There was a time I didn't need to. My picture was on every front page.'

Hetty did not entirely register what Doris was saying, but half turned in sheer politeness. 'Why was that?'

'Because I killed someone. That's how I met Jack.'

Eyes wide, Hetty gave Doris her entire attention. 'Who?'

'My husband. Oh, yes, I'm a widow. That much is true. I was nineteen, with a baby, and he was a brute. No self-defence in those days, was there? Women were supposed to take what punishment came to them. I was nearly hanged. I'll tell you the details some day, if you're interested. Long time ago, now.'

Hetty struggled with fragments of memory. 'You had a child who died?'

'Yeah.' Doris's voice was soft. 'When I saw what I'd done, I didn't want to live. I smothered the baby and cut my wrists. But we was found.' She held up her arms, fists curled inwards and Hetty saw the faint scars. 'Like I say, a long time ago.'

The conversation was finished. Hetty swallowed hard. Doris patted her on the shoulder, and moved back into the main room.

'Mum, do you have a minute?'

It was Sally, with Kate hanging about nearby. It was nearly ten o'clock.

'Sure. You've been getting very pally with Kate,' Hetty murmured, preparing herself.

'Would you disapprove, Mum?'

Hetty pondered. 'If you were happy . . . God, I dunno. Another facet I barely knew existed before. Take it gently, I suppose.'

'Right. We will. But that wasn't actually what I wanted you for.' Sally was jumpy.

Hetty peered past her, and understood at once.

'Hello, Hetty.'

It was Stephen.

He was as tall as anyone in the lounge, dressed in an open-necked shirt and brown slacks and the beige sweater she had bought him for Christmas three years before. Now he appeared haggard, with heavy circles under the eyes. He stood awkwardly, ignored by everyone present; those who might have recognised him, such as the family, were occupied elsewhere.

'God in heaven.' Hetty clutched at the door-handle for support.

'Sally phoned and said you were having a few people round, and that possibly you wouldn't immediately throw me out if I showed up too,' Stephen mumbled, glancing at his daughter for aid. Sally nodded, then let herself be dragged away by Kate.

'Er – yes.' Hetty tried to pull herself together. 'Er – would you like some wine? There's a clean glass . . .'

'Not at the moment.' Stephen's voice was rougher than she recalled, but it had been a while since they had spoken. His presence filled the tiny kitchen.

'Hetty, I've come with one purpose. I've been hanging around outside for hours, trying to summon up the courage. I saw you out there with the old ladies, but I couldn't do it. Look, I see now that I've been a complete and crass fool. And I'm here to ask – will you forgive me?'

Hetty felt her mouth drop open, and tried to shut it again. She could barely breathe.

'Come back, Hetty. Come back to Dorset. The house is empty without you. Nobody else could possibly fill your shoes. I'm living on takeaways. The garden's a wilderness. I'm lost – I miss you terribly. Please . . . ?'

Hetty lifted her head and gazed over his shoulder at her

gyrating companions, barely a few feet away: at Doris, now entwined with Jack, who caught her eye and winked, at lip-sticked Carole and Mrs McDonald, holding hands, as were Roger and Alice, clumsily, as if neither was accustomed to physical contact. Her mother was glancing towards the kitchen with raised eyebrows; she had been alerted by Sally. Davinia was staring openly, as was Clarissa, although Robin was engrossed in persuading Larry and Brian to try his che-roots. The room was full, and clamorous; and every single person had come because she, Hetty, had organised it, had asked them.

And Stephen knew nothing of her journey in the last year, was utterly untouched by her misfortunes and suc-cesses. He had not ridden the bike with her through the fresh grass of spring, nor shared the struggle to get into shape, or survived the visit to the dating agency and its dismal outcome. He did not know about the pink plastic dildo in the box under her bed, or her skill in the seduction of strangers, or her diversity of friends. Unlike Larry, he probably hadn't noticed or drawn any conclusions from the lively group in her lounge; hell-bent on his own personal mission, he had started from the same position he had occupied when she left, and was totally ignorant of the mile-stones since along her path.

'*A change would do you good . . .*'

The change had already occurred. What Stephen referred to – keeping house, catering, gardening, ministering to the comforts of one man in cosy, slippered matrimony – were parts of an old life that had vanished round a distant bend in the road. That she had never expected to find again, and that she had contrived not to miss.

And yet, and yet . . .

She could dance with any man in the room, and yet was not dancing, not tonight. For every man there, with the sole exception of Brian, was spoken for, the chosen partner of another present. There was nobody just for her. Her attempts to fill the gap had been fruitless; no Norman, no James. There was no guarantee that next week, next season, would bring an improvement. Even Al had proved as unreliable as ever, and she could not recall why on earth she had left a message for him. Perhaps because it would have been fabulous to have *one man* . . .

Stephen was gabbling. He could not follow her trains of thought. 'Come back. I can get you out of all this – it'll be terrific, you'll see.'

He did not understand. Any of it. She reached out a hand to steady herself and was met by the glasses on the draining-board and the nodding lilies and roses, the gifts of those who cared about her.

Hetty bent her head and answered, 'Oh, Stephen . . . I can't go back. It's not as simple as that . . .'

She made to push past him but then, as his shoulders sagged and his face crumpled, she relented, and handed him a tea towel.

'What am I supposed to do with this?' he asked, in astonishment.

Hetty merely smiled, and left the kitchen to rejoin her friends.

An extract from Edwina Currie's latest book, THIS HONOURABLE HOUSE, *published in June 2001 in hardback by Little, Brown and Company, price £14.99:*

'I wish,' said Frank Bridges venomously, 'that somebody would sort out the bloody cow once and for all.'

He picked up the chunky pint glass and downed the remains of his beer in a gulp. There were clucks of sympathy around him. To many of the thick-set, grizzled men seated at his table and nearby, Frank was the local hero. His successes were theirs, his worries grafted seamlessly on to their own. If Frank was upset, so were they.

The Right Honourable Frank Bridges, fifty years old, overweight, red-faced, crumple-suited and aggressive, should not have been upset. Indeed, he had considerable reason to be hugely pleased with his own situation, and with life in general. Newly elevated to the seat in the Cabinet he could once only have dreamed of, he was trusted by the public, envied by colleagues, and regarded with ragged affection by his constituents, who included the scruffy occupants of the Admiral Benbow, a run-down pub in a Bootle side-street near the now derelict docks.

Vic, Scouser, Bill the Fixer, Mad Max and others had truanted with him from the inner-city school where expectations were destroyed with the cane and sarcasm. As boys, they had scattered down alleys behind his stocky form, their pockets stuffed with illicit loot. But Frank had kept running, beyond the despair and hopelessness. None of the others had followed where he led. He had not gone to the dogs like them but had made something of himself. He had risen to the top, or close to it. Of Frank Bridges they were inordinately proud.

For Frank was a salt-of-the-earth type, the press generally

agreed. A police sergeant had once challenged him to make a man of himself. Shamed, he had applied, with the sergeant's gruff help, to join Liverpool police cadets; to his surprise and the ribbing of his mates he had been accepted. He had worked his way up through the byzantine networks of the force to national prominence, particularly during the bitter dock strike of 1982. In that prolonged struggle, he had contrived to become a solidly admired figure. While speaking in the same strong Merseyside accent as the militant strikers and displaying an understated, dignified disdain for the government of Margaret Thatcher, he had contrived to prevent conflict and bloodshed even as the nation's trade was brought to a standstill. His erstwhile comrade Arthur Scargill had asked him how he had managed such a feat. Frank had begun to confess that he did not know, that chance had played its part. Then he had thought better of it and suggested vaguely that working with the system was better than trying to destroy it, that politics might achieve more than the picket line. Scargill's derision convinced him. Soon afterwards Frank offered himself as a parliamentary candidate. He had represented the Dockside division of the seaport ever since.

'It's a bummer, it is,' came a voice, as more pints were splashed down on the sticky table top. The air hung thick and acrid with smoke. 'Salt and vinegar okay?'

Frank nodded glumly and ripped open the packet of crisps, eating them two or three at a time. He brushed crumbs from his midriff, tugged impatiently at his tie and unfastened the top two buttons of his shirt. He was sweating, a damp line visible on the inside of his collar. 'Mustn't eat too many of these,' he mumbled, indicating the crisps. He waved away a cigarette. 'Look gross on the telly. Gotta keep a new young wife happy. An' that's another story.'

'She's a peach, your new lady,' said Scouser respectfully. His accent was so strong that even Frank sometimes asked him to repeat himself. 'Hazel, innit? You're a lucky dog, you.' An elbow was dug into Frank's ribs.

'I know, I know.' Frank sighed. 'But I could murder Gail. Really murder her. And that slob Melvyn. Spin doctor. The sanitation squad, he's called. I'd like to sanitise *him*. Did you hear what happened? I could slaughter them both. Maybe I should arrange with some of me old mates to tie the pair of 'em together with a lump of concrete and chuck 'em in the Mersey one dark and stormy night. They deserve it.'

'You should've told Melvyn where to go,' said Vic. He wiped a roughened fist across his mouth and flexed his biceps. Vic had tried his hand at boxing in his youth; his convictions were all for GBH. Not a man to argue with.

'Nah, couldn't do that.' Frank brooded. His listeners settled happily in anticipation. They were not to be disappointed.

'There we were,' Frank started, 'all packed and ready to go on holiday, in the VIP lounge at Heathrow. The luggage was checked in. Gail was excited, kept prancing around and ordering more coffee just for the sake of it. God, does she love being important! I thought to myself even then, If you'd taken more interest on the way – not moaned so much about "Where are you going, Frank, you off out again, Frank, another meeting is it, Frank?" – then I wouldn't have minded. But she never used to lift a finger. Now she's Lady Muck and adores every minute.'

He took a prolonged swallow of his beer. His audience sat quietly. Once Frank was embarked on a tale, he needed no prompting.

'So the phone goes. The mobile. I'd forgotten to switch it off – you know how keen the Boss is that we keep in touch. "Oh Frank," she says,' he mimicked a woman's high-pitched voice, "oh, Frank, not again. Surely not. We're going on holiday. To the *Seychelles*."' He raised his voice to show that Gail was determined everyone in earshot should hear. '"First class. Couldn't you have left it at home for once?" Only what she didn't know was that it was that bastard Melvyn. An' he's on the line to say the *News of the World*'s gotta story on me and Hazel. Pictures of her coming out of my flat in Westminster. And what do I want to do?'

'How did they get them pictures? Was it a set-up?' Vic asked.

'Nah. Not really. She comes to my place regularly in her car, see, and parks it on a meter. So I go out in the morning when my driver comes, and I feed the meter. And there's a journalist hanging about, and instead of pushing off when I leave, he's curious. He knows Gail's in Cheshire. So why'm I feeding a meter? Who's there? And when Hazel shows and jumps in her car, his nose tells him he's gotta scoop. After that he hovers with a photographer till it happens again, and out they pop and confront her. Bob's your uncle.'

Heads were shaken at the brazen callousness of the gutter press. 'They don't care,' said Mad Max, and cracked his knuckles.

'Bastards,' added Vic, with menace.

'So then we have Mr Melvyn O'Connor, spin doctor number two – number one, Mr Alistair McDonald being on duty elsewhere – Mr Melvyn O'Connor, who's never done a proper day's grafting ever, calling me to say the Boss is asking which way I'll jump. Who's going to be on the guest list in future? Is it the wife, or the girlfriend? He'll back my decision either way and doesn't want to push me, but they need an answer so they can put out a statement. Would I mind deciding? Honest, right in the middle of the VIP departure lounge, with me cursing like a trooper and Gail telling me to mind my language. God.'